ANOTHER CHANCE

A Novel

Best wishes!
Candie Checketts

Candie Che

Covenant Communications, Inc.

Covenant.

Published by Covenant Communications, Inc.
American Fork, Utah

Printed in Canada
First Printing: February 2003

10 09 08 07 06 05 04 03   10 9 8 7 6 5 4 3 2 1

ISBN 1-59156-181-7

Library of Congress Cataloging-in-Publication Data

Checketts, Candie, 1971-
     Another Chance: a novel/ Candie Checketts
        p.   cm.
     ISBN 1-59156-181-7 (alk. paper)
     1. Mormon women--Fiction. 2. Single women--Fiction I. Another Chance.

PS3603.H435 A56 2003
813'.6--dc21
                                        2002041202

For those who have hope,
for those who seek it,
and for all those who have believed in me and touched my life.

Chapter 1

I was running down a dark tunnel. Far ahead in the distance I could see a bright white light. I ran toward it with all my might, terrified of the darkness that enveloped me. Cold gray swirls of mist lapped at my heels and I struggled to get away from them. Icy fingers wrapped around my arms, sending shooting pains through my bones. They began to pull me back.

"No!" I felt the scream catch in my throat. I strained against the force that held me and I could hear a voice calling to me from where I had been. *No,* I thought desperately. *No. Please let me go.* I felt myself being pulled back, back into the churning dismal sea that I'd briefly escaped. The voice grew increasingly louder. With one final yank, the light disappeared and I returned.

"Mom-*my!*" My head was throbbing. My arms still ached. Reality began to sink in. "Mommy, I'm *hungry!*" My head hurt so badly it felt like it might explode if I spoke. Trevor shook my shoulders, which made it even worse.

"No, Trev, no. Please. Mommy has a headache." I felt the sun burning my eyes behind closed lids. Moaning, I rolled over and pulled a pillow over my head.

Trevor leaned over me and insisted, "But, Mommy, I want breakfast."

"Okay, honey, I'll be there in a minute."

"I'll go get my spoon!" he said excitedly, and ran down the hall toward the kitchen.

The memories of the night before floated painfully back. Ted had come home late again—and drunk.

I had gone to bed around midnight, tossing and turning until he finally pulled into the garage at one-thirty. It was just like always. First I had felt relieved when he didn't come home on time—a few more peaceful moments. Then as I got the children into bed, with no help, I began to feel angry. *I wonder what his excuse will be this time?* I fumed to myself. *New project? Late meeting? Had to take some clients to dinner? I know where he is—at some seedy bar, drinking himself under the table.*

The anger grew slowly inside of me, like an inflating balloon, until I went to bed filled with it. I lay there alone in the dark, the long minutes ticking away. Some of the anger began to seep out as worry crept in. What if something had happened to him? What if he was in a car accident? What if he had been arrested? Or worse—what if he was dead? It was always like this. My mind would go crazy worrying and imagining terrible things until I heard the garage door open. Then I would feel overwhelmed with a combination of relief, terror, and fury.

I heard him toss his car keys on the kitchen counter and come down the hall. As he tried to sneak across the room, he tripped and fell. He swore, then started to laugh. *Oh, yeah,* I thought despairingly, *he's drunk.*

It took him a few moments to get up and sit down heavily on the edge of the bed. I could see his silhouette against the window as he took off his shoes. Then he crawled up near me and leaned over me. He reeked of alcohol.

"Hi there, honeybun," he slurred.

I feigned sleep and silently prayed for strength to hold my tongue. *Please let him give up and fall asleep quickly,* I pleaded.

"Don't you have a kiss for me, baby?" he chortled, kissing my neck.

"Not now, Ted," I answered sleepily as I waved him away. I felt sick. I couldn't stand him like this.

He kissed me again and teased, "Just one little kiss, darlin'?"

"Ted, I said no." I pushed him away. He leaned toward me again. I realized that praying for him to go to sleep was futile. I jumped up and said firmly, "Ted, you're drunk. Stay away from me!"

I was surprised at how quickly he pulled himself to his feet. I could see his face in the moonlight. Sparks flew from his eyes. He flipped the light switch as his goofy grin turned into a sneer. His sandy hair fell over his forehead and he tossed it back angrily. His shirt hung wrinkled and dirty, and he looked like he hadn't shaved that day, though I knew he had. The alcohol distorted his ruggedly handsome features so much I hardly recognized him . . . or perhaps I couldn't recognize the real Ted anymore. It had been too long.

"I . . . am . . . not . . . drunk," he said slowly, as he enunciated each word.

"Then where have you been, Ted?" I demanded.

"Out, Maren." He paused as if in thought. "I've been *out.*" He wasn't very creative when he was drunk.

"Out with whom?"

"*Whom?* Spare me your high-and-mighty attitude, okay?" Then he hissed close to my face, "If I wanted to live with my mother, Maren, I wouldn't have bothered to marry *you.*"

I fought back tears as I said, "I am *not* your mother, Ted. I am your wife, and I think I have a right to know where you've been until two o'clock in the morning."

"And I think that *I* have the right to go where I want to, when I want to, and with *who* I want to, and it's none of your business," he said coldly. "You've been running my life for far too long, and I'm not putting up with it anymore. You got it?"

"I don't run your life, Ted!" I shouted. "You run mine! I'm chained here! I'm in prison! I'm alone all the time with the kids. I get no help or support. I never know where you are or what you're doing. You won't talk to me. You don't do anything around here. You're never here for me or for our children!" I watched him lean against the wall to keep from wobbling, and wondered if he would even remember this conversation in the morning. Even if he did, I knew he wouldn't acknowledge it. I'd tried countless times to have a real conversation with him, but he was never willing to talk.

"I do plenty for you, Maren," he said cockily.

"Like what!" I yelled at him. It wasn't a question. How could he possibly think he did anything for me—anything at all?

He grabbed onto my upper arms and pulled me closer to his face. The alcohol on his breath made me nauseous. I knew he was over the edge again and wished that I could take back what I'd just said. *Why can't I control myself?* I thought.

"I work myself to death for you . . . to support you and those kids," he snarled at me. "And if I ever take a little well-deserved time for myself once in a while, I come home to this!" I could feel his ice-cold fingers searing into my arms like liquid nitrogen, a chill oozing through my blood and into my bones.

"Okay, Ted. Please, you're hurting me."

"You belong to me, Maren. I'll do what I want with you." He kissed me hard on the mouth. It stung.

Please, God, I prayed silently, *Please make him stop. Take him away. Oh, Lord, I wish he had died on the way home.* I felt the horror of my thoughts. *How could I even think something like that? What is wrong with me? I must deserve this.*

"Please stop, Ted," I pleaded softly in a desperate attempt to calm the storm I knew was coming. "I'm so tired."

His eyes burned with hate. "Look at you, Maren. You're a mess."

"What?" I tried to think, to pinpoint what was wrong with me. I'd taken a bath that night, washed my hair that morning. My nails were done, my hair was curled. I'd taken my makeup off before going to bed. Was that it—no makeup?

"You're a fat slob, a lazy Mormon housewife. It's your fault, all of it. You drive me away. You should be grateful to have me at all. You disgust me," he slobbered. "I don't even want to look at you." He pushed me away with such force that I slammed into the wall and hit my head on the dresser as I fell down. I felt a burning sensation near my temple. I wanted to curl up on the floor and hide, but I couldn't do that anymore. He might go down the hall to Rebecca and Trevor. I had to get up and protect them.

My head was throbbing as I pulled myself up. "Ted, I want you to leave!"

He laughed. "I don't think so. This is my house. I pay for it with my sweat and blood. I'm not leaving. You want out? You leave!" He grabbed the alarm clock from the nightstand and hurled it at me. I ducked, but it ricocheted off the wall and fell, hitting me on the head. I saw stars for a minute, but I shook them away. I prayed that the children would stay asleep.

I started to sob. "Please leave, Ted. Leave!"

"No way, baby."

"Ted, you can't just smash up our house! Stop it!"

His eyes were on fire and he slammed a fist through the wall, leaving a jagged hole that was all too familiar. "*Are you telling me what to do?*" he shouted. "This is *my* house! I will do *whatever* I want to in it!"

He reached for an object on a shelf above the bed. "No, Ted, please, not that." It was the figurine from the top of our wedding cake. Somehow it had survived through all the tumultuous years.

An evil grin turned up the corners of his mouth and he threw it so hard that I had to jump sideways to avoid being hit head-on. It exploded against the dresser. I didn't even feel the porcelain shards biting into me as I knelt down and ran my fingers over the destruction. Looking at the now-shattered memory of how this had all started and what it had become made something finally snap in me.

In the pit of my stomach I felt the rage that had been building for years. It swelled up to my heart and surged through my veins. "I hate you!" I screamed. "For ten years you've been ruining my life! I am finished! Get out! *Get out!*" I rushed at him and began pounding on his chest with all the fury that was in me. "I hate you! I *hate* you!" I felt full of hate, and the adrenaline coursing through me gave me strength.

Ted looked shocked that I would stand up to him so fiercely. For a brief moment, I saw the flicker of a wounded child in his eyes, and I pitied him. "Fine," he said coldly, and turned to go.

I felt my heart lurch. I wanted to grab him, tell him I was sorry, protect that little boy inside him. I clenched my fists and swallowed my heart back down. *No*, I thought. *Not this time.* I would not call him back. I was through. When I heard the door slam, I sank to the floor and sobbed. I cried for Ted, for myself, and for my children. I wept for the broken dreams, the broken lives, and the young girl—full of hope—that had died in me ten years ago. It was the end of the only life we had known for over a decade . . .

Chapter 2

Remembering Trevor, I slowly pulled myself up, trying not to moan. I went into the bathroom to get some aspirin from the medicine cabinet and cringed at my reflection in the mirror. I just had a tiny cut near my left temple, but my whole face was red and puffy. Dark shadows lurked under my eyes. I splashed some cold water on my face and headed for the kitchen. Trevor was sitting up to the counter on a barstool, holding his spoon and grinning. "Hi, Mommy! I want Cheerios, please!"

I couldn't help but smile at his angelic little face, his hazel eyes and wavy, sandy hair. I thought Ted must have looked like this thirty years ago. What had gone wrong? Was it his parents? Just his agency? Or was it what I feared most—something I had done, or not done? I shook the thoughts from my mind as I got Trevor's cereal and milk. I leaned across the counter to look into my three-year-old's eyes. "I love you, Trev-Trev," I said as I tousled his hair.

"I love you, Mommy." He smiled with milk dribbling down his chin. I was truly blessed to have my children.

"Mommy?" Trevor asked.

"What?

"Why do Cheerios stay on top of the milk, but oatmeal doesn't?"

"Because Cheerios are lighter than milk, and oatmeal is heavier."

"Oh. How come milk is white?"

"It just comes out of the cows that way, Trev. You've watched Grandpa milking cows before. You know that."

"Grandpa's cows are white *and* black. Is some milk black?"

"No, buddy. Eat your breakfast."

"Okay, Mommy."

I smiled at him as I flopped down in a yellow overstuffed chair in the great room and stared out the French doors at the deck. The trees in the backyard were almost budding. How ironic, I thought, that everything around me was just coming to life, when inside I was dying. A cold brown autumn morning would have fit my mood better than the bright sunshine of early spring. I had met Ted in the spring. It was April, my freshman year at BYU . . .

* * *

Ted moved into my ward just before the semester ended. He had recently returned from his mission and had come to Provo to get settled before summer term began. He took over a vacancy in the apartment assigned to our home evening group. Ted was good-looking and friendly, funny and spiritual. He talked like his mission to England had been a great success when he brought pictures to show us one Monday evening. I'd seen my share of missionary pictures that year, but Ted was so entertaining that he actually captured my interest. After the guys left that night, my roommate Jana said, "Wow. I think I just might stay with you for summer semester, Maren, and see if I can get my hooks into Ted."

I laughed and said, "Why don't you do that?" Much to my surprise, she did. Our other four roommates left at the end of the month to spend the summer at their respective homes across the country. Ted and Seth were the only two guys from our home evening group who stayed. During the two-week break between semesters, before new roommates arrived for any of us, they came over.

"Hi, Sister Griffin." Ted beamed when I answered the door.

"Hi." I smiled. "Come in." Ted and Seth came in to sit on the couch.

I called down the hall, "Company, Jan!" She purposely took her time before floating into the room.

"Oh, hello, brothers!" she joked. "How nice to see you." Jana was very pretty. She had long thick chestnut hair and gray eyes. She dated a lot. I didn't think she'd have too much trouble "hooking" Ted if she really wanted to.

"So, girls, we've been thinking," Ted began. "Since it's just the four of us, we thought maybe we could do something a little more exciting for family home evening this week."

"Exciting?" I asked skeptically. "What do you have in mind?"

Ted shrugged. "Oh, I don't know. We were thinking it might be fun to do something on Friday, for a change. We could go out to dinner, and then maybe bowling or something."

"That sounds suspiciously like a date, Ted," Jana observed slyly, but I knew she was secretly delighted. I didn't think she noticed the adoration in Seth's eyes as he watched her. She was too busy flirting with Ted. Seth was an Idaho farm boy with reddish blond hair and freckles, not really her type.

A grin broke out on Ted's face as he said, "Call it whatever you like."

"So, who's paying?" Jana teased.

Seth was quick to answer her. "We are."

"How about if we just all pay our own way?" I offered. I could see where this was headed. Jana was going to end up with Ted all night, leaving a disappointed Seth with me. I didn't want to feel guilty about him spending money on me when he knew I had a boyfriend.

"That wouldn't be very gentlemanly of us to invite you girls out and then expect you to pay, now would it?" Ted smiled at me.

I couldn't resist smiling back. "Look," I explained, "I don't mind hanging out with my family home evening group, but I am dating someone seriously."

"Yeah, we knew that." Seth nodded his head.

Ted looked over at him and asked, "Did we?" I wasn't sure if he was serious or joking.

Seth shrugged like it was no big deal. "I thought I told you. She's been going out with him all year."

"You're not engaged or anything are you?" Ted asked me.

"No."

"Well, then there's no problem!" he announced as if it were obvious. "Besides, it's only one evening with your harmless home evening brothers. I'm sure your boyfriend wouldn't object to that, would he?"

I couldn't help thinking that his crooked grin was a little charming. "No, I suppose he wouldn't really mind," I said.

There was a knock at the door. "Well, there he is now!" Jana said brightly. "Let's ask him."

I gave her an annoyed look as I got up to answer the door.

"Hi, Mar." As always, Jake's smile melted my heart.

"Hi."

"Are you ready?"

I wanted to just escape with him, but I knew it would be rude. "Just about. Why don't you come in?" I was always in awe at Jake's presence. People just seemed drawn to him—he never went unnoticed. The funny thing was, he seemed so oblivious to it all. That particular day he was wearing a light blue shirt with jeans—both perfectly ironed of course—and brown loafers. His wavy jet-black hair was parted on the side and combed back neatly, and his eyes met mine with sapphire intensity as he stepped easily into the room.

"Hi, Jana," he said warmly.

"Hi, Jake," she answered curtly. I shot her a look. I never did figure out why she didn't like him. He was never anything but nice to her. Maybe that was it. Maybe his genuine goodness baffled her. *Or maybe she was jealous.* I brushed the thought and my own silly pride away.

"You know Seth, don't you, Jake?" I asked.

"Yes, how are you?" Jake extended a hand and Seth answered with a friendly, "Good to see you."

Then I turned to Ted. "Ted is our new home evening brother, as of three weeks ago. Ted, this is Jake."

They exchanged greetings, and I asked Jake to sit down while I went to get my purse. I glanced in the bathroom mirror before heading back to the living room. I stopped to put on fresh pink lipstick and fluff my longish blond hair that hung in carefully curled waves. I wore jeans and a pink sweater. My blue eyes were pretty, I admitted to myself, but they weren't the deep, piercing blue that Jake's reflected. We were an attractive couple, and I knew it. "You know we'd have beautiful blue-eyed children, Maren," Jake often joked.

As I returned to our cozy living room—my first real attempt at decorating—Jana was explaining in her singsong voice, "So anyway, Jake, seeing as how our poor brothers are all alone for a couple of weeks, I didn't think you'd mind if we stole Maren for just one night."

I gave him an apologetic look as I sat down next to him on the couch. Jake leaned back and put his arm around me. Then he smiled at Jana. "Maren's a big girl, Jana. She makes her own decisions."

Jana gave me a bright smile and said, "Well, there you go, big girl. It's your decision."

I looked at Jake. I knew he wouldn't object. If our relationship had anything, it was complete trust. I couldn't help feeling a subtle uneasiness though.

Ted cut into my thoughts by saying, "Why don't you call us when you've had a chance to think it over? We don't want to put any pressure on you. We just thought it might be fun to do something. Let us know before Friday."

"Thanks, Ted," I said, feeling relieved. I ignored the pouty look Jana was giving me.

Jake grabbed my hand and smiled, flashing straight white teeth at me. "Are you ready then?"

"Yes."

As we walked across the parking lot to Jake's shiny green sedan, I said, "I'm really sorry if you felt uncomfortable with Jana putting you on the spot like that."

"It seems more like she was putting you on the spot," he laughed. "You know, Maren, you don't have to go if you don't want to."

"I know. It's just that Jana has her eye on Ted and . . ." I thought about Ted for a minute and then impulsively asked, "What if I did want to go, Jake?"

"What do you mean?" he asked sincerely, as he continued to hold my hand and lead me across the parking lot.

I took a moment to consider my motives and get my thoughts together before I said, "What if I did want to go on a date with someone else?"

Jake raised an eyebrow at me and his jaw muscle twitched, but he asked calmly, "Is there someone you're interested in?"

"No . . ."

"Are you trying to tell me that you want to see other people?" He looked puzzled.

"I don't know . . . Maybe."

Jake was quiet for a minute until we reached his parking spot. He dropped my hand to run his fingers through his hair. Then he leaned against the car and folded his arms on his chest. "It sounds like we need to talk, Mar," he said quietly.

"I guess we do," I conceded.

He watched me expectantly. When I didn't say anything, he prodded, "Why don't you tell me what you're thinking?"

"I'm not sure . . . Maybe I'm just confused."

"All right," he said softly. "Why don't you tell me how you're feeling then?"

I looked into his sweet, sincere face. I didn't feel confused; that wasn't it. I'd been dating him for seven months, and I knew exactly how I felt about him. I loved him, pure and simple. He had been a brand-new convert when I met him in the fall. Our friendship had come quickly and easily, and somewhere along the way we had grown to love each other. We had been discussing marriage recently, but we both thought it would be best to wait the few more months until he could go to the temple after his one full year as a member of the Church.

I felt pretty strongly that Jake was the one for me. We were so much alike. It was almost like we could read each other's minds. It wasn't hard to imagine that I'd known him before, simply by the way our souls seemed connected from the beginning. He treated me so well. I always felt beautiful and wonderful and uplifted when I was with him. He was a perfect gentleman. I admired the way he could be so assertive and stand up for his beliefs, and yet still be so gentle and calm. We had never really argued through all our months of dating, and I had rarely felt anything but happiness with him.

"I guess I just feel a little . . . overwhelmed, Jake," I finally admitted.

"Why, Mar?"

My thoughts spilled out and ran together. "Well, it's just that . . . we've been dating all year, and we've been dating each other pretty exclusively for the past few months, and we're talking about getting married. But if we do get married, we want it to be in the temple . . ."

Jake nodded in agreement as he continued to listen quietly.

"And you can't go until September, because you have to be a member of the Church for a year. You'll be twenty-four by then, but I won't even be twenty until November. We can't really think seriously of marriage for five more months, and that's a long time to date someone exclusively, Jake, especially when it's been so long already. We have some deep feelings going here, and I'm starting to wonder if continuing as we are is a good idea.

"And then when I think about actually getting married, and the gravity of such a decision, five months doesn't seem like nearly enough time. This is my first year away from home, and I don't know if I'm ready to get married. I do love you, Jake, but I'm not completely sure if you're the right one for me yet, and how can I decide that when I don't date anyone else, and I have nothing to compare it to? I'm sorry. I just feel . . . Well, like I said—overwhelmed." I felt tears threatening as a result of too many emotions, and I tried to blink them away.

Jake reached out to pull me to him, and I looked up at his six-foot-two frame. He was eight inches taller than me, the perfect height. "I didn't realize you were struggling so much with this," he said gently. "I'm sorry." I closed my eyes and leaned against him. He just held me. His words of understanding, and his strong arms around me helped to calm my racing thoughts and fears. In that moment, he was my anchor. I relaxed in the security of his embrace, and breathed in his familiar scent, cool and clean and soothing.

Jake finally pulled back to look at me, but he kept his arms around me as he spoke. "It sounds like you need a little bit of time and space, Mar. I can give you that. Five months is a long time, I know—or not very long, depending on how you look at it." He smiled, and I smiled back, just watching him for a few moments. I could see that this was difficult for him.

Jake's look turned more serious as he said, "But I do hope to marry you then, when I can take you to the temple. You know that. The last thing I want, though, is to have you feeling doubts later on, or resenting me for robbing you of your youth. I don't want you to ever wonder whether you made the right decision. If you do marry me, Maren, I want it to be because you want to, because you love me. I want you to feel as sure of your decision as I do."

I couldn't hold back the tears that spilled down my face. Jake brushed them away, but I could see the moisture in his own eyes. "So . . ." he began with resolve, "you go out with your home evening brothers on Friday, Mar. And if you want to date other people, go ahead. If you want me to back off, I will."

I shook my head. "No. I still want to see you, Jake. I *need* to see you."

He seemed relieved as he said, "I'll respect your decisions, and I'll give you as much freedom as you want. The only thing I ask is that you be honest with me."

"I will, Jake. And if you want to date other people too, you can. It's only fair."

He gave a painful chuckle and stroked my cheek. "That, my dear, would just be a study in disappointment for me. Like you said, I'm older than you. I've had more time. I know what's out there . . . and I know what isn't. I've already found what I'm looking for." He studied me for a minute, as though wondering if it was still all right, before he bent to kiss me. I put my arms around his neck and melted in his arms. Nothing felt as good as Jake kissing me. When he pulled away, he looked into my eyes and said, "I love you, Maren. No matter what happens, I'll always love you."

"I love you too," I told him firmly.

Early evening, on the following Friday, Jake called. "Hi, beautiful," he said.

"Hi, handsome."

"So . . . I heard this vicious rumor that you're going out with another man tonight."

I pretended to suck in my breath as if I were shocked. "What? Me?"

"Then it's not true?"

"Well . . ."

"Maren, tell me it isn't true!"

"Actually, Jake, I'm afraid it is. I can't lie to you."

He gasped. "But what's he got that I don't have?"

"Well . . . You are awfully good-looking, Jake, and smart and funny, and you're the perfect height, and oh, let's see . . . you're rich!"

"Yes, yes, go on."

"And spiritual, and talented, and kind, and wonderful . . ."

"That's right, I am. This guy can't possibly be as wonderful as I am."

"Truthfully, he's not. You see, I had this revelation . . ."

"Oh, no!" he groaned.

We both started laughing. After a minute, Jake said seriously, "Have fun tonight, Mar."

"Thank you, Jake. I will. And we're still going on a picnic tomorrow, right?"

"Absolutely. I'll see you then."

"Bye."

"Bye, Mar." I listened to the hum of the dead phone for a moment, not wanting to let go of his presence. A while later I heard the doorbell and went to join my roommate.

Apparently, there was a misunderstanding. When Ted and Seth escorted us out of our apartment, Ted took my arm and left Jana gaping after us. I turned around to give her a helpless look as she reluctantly took the arm Seth offered her.

All through dinner we listened to Ted's animated stories of his mission, and laughed at his jokes. He was so entertaining. I tried to steer him toward Jana, asking her questions about her life, and pointing out her interesting qualities.

"Jana's from Denver. It gets even colder there than it does here, doesn't it, Jan?" I waited for her to nod and then asked, "Have you ever been to Denver, Ted?"

"Nope, can't say that I have."

"Do you ski? Jana's a great skier."

"Actually, I never got into that. Too expensive."

I kept trying all night. "Hey, Ted, did you know that Jana toured with the Young Ambassadors last year?"

"Really? That's great!" he finally said to her. "So, did I hear someone say you're a dancer, Maren?"

"Well, yes, I am."

"Why did you stay for summer semester?" he asked me impulsively.

"Oh, I'd just like to get through school as quickly as I can." I didn't add that it was because I was thinking about getting married soon. It seemed inappropriate under the circumstances. "Also, because I wanted to be near Jake."

"So, tell us about this Jake. What does he do?" Ted asked.

"He's premed. He's almost finished."

"Impressive. How's he working his way through school?"

I felt an uneasiness tug at me. "Well, uh . . . actually, his parents are helping him through school."

Ted laughed out loud. "Boy, that must be nice!"

"What do you do, Ted?" I asked, suddenly curious.

"Accounting—mostly taxes and things. I'm working on getting some bookkeeping business from some of the smaller companies around town."

"What company do you work for?"

"I just kind of do it on my own. I like working for myself. I'm hoping I can build up enough business to keep me going through the school year, so I can set my own hours with classes. I'm majoring in business."

"Wow," I said, feeling genuinely impressed. "It must be nice to be so self-sufficient." The night went on and Jana barely got a word in.

The following Thursday night I was working on a calculus assignment when the phone rang.

"Hi. Maren?"

"Yes?"

"It's Ted. How are you?"

"Fine, and you?"

"Just great. So, you're not with Jake tonight?"

"No. He's helping with an elders quorum project in his ward."

"Oh, great! Well, I just started thinking it might be fun to go dancing. Would you like to come?"

"Tonight?"

"Sure, why not?"

I thought about it for a minute. Ted was a lot of fun, but what would Jake think about me going on a second date with him? I knew that he'd told me to date other people, and that he wouldn't really care if I had fun while he was busy, but I still felt a little hesitant. I hadn't been dancing since the winter formal. Jake dutifully took me to it, but admitted he wasn't much of a dancer. I looked distastefully at my unfinished math assignment.

"I have a math assignment to finish . . . but dancing does sound like fun," I finally said.

"Good. I'll be right over." He hung up before I had time to reconsider.

I closed my math book and changed into a red skirt and white blouse. I brushed my hair and sprayed it, and managed to apply red lipstick before he arrived. "Wow! You look great!" Ted said when he saw me.

"Thank you." I tried not to blush at his exuberance.

We had a blast. I loved to dance, and Ted certainly had the energy to keep up with me. When a slow song came on, I was a little uncomfortable. Ted pulled me into him as we moved together to the music. He was an inch or two shorter than Jake, but a good height to dance with. I felt myself getting tingly as I followed his lead. I started to feel tired as I came down from all the fast dancing, and was tempted to put my head on his shoulder, but resisted. Ted looked into my eyes. A lock of sandy blond hair hung over his forehead. His eyes were so different from Jake's. They were grayish with green flecks. His eyelashes were long. "You have nice eyes," I said without thinking.

"Thanks." He smiled. "You know, Maren, you're a lot of fun to be with."

"Thank you. So are you." I started to feel a hint of confusion. There was so much energy between us. Things with Jake were always so calm, sometimes almost too calm.

After dancing, Ted took me to get an ice-cream cone at the Wilkinson Center. I found myself very interested as he told me about his life. He had grown up the second of four boys in American Fork. He'd been born and raised in the Church, like me. He seemed very driven and motivated, with clear goals and a plan for his future. He talked with firm conviction about his beliefs and his desire to make a good life for himself and for his future family. I admired his courage and ambition.

* * *

That Sunday, I went to church with Jake. A recently returned missionary spoke in sacrament meeting. He bore his testimony at the end, becoming tearful when he said, "I'm so grateful to my parents for the example they set for me. Being brought up in the Church has given me a firm testimony. I wanted to serve a mission when I was a little boy because of the stories my father told about his mission."

My heart began to pound. Jake had not been brought up in the Church. He couldn't help it, of course. But if I married him, would it make a difference to our children? Our sons would never hear about his mission. I glanced up at him uneasily. He squeezed my hand and smiled.

After church we sat on the tabernacle lawn reading the Book of Mormon. My thoughts drifted elsewhere as Jake's steady voice read from Alma. He stopped abruptly and moved to sit cross-legged in front of me, taking both my hands in his. "Something's bothering you, Maren. What is it?"

"It's nothing." I smiled as I snapped back to the present.

"Maren," he said gently, "please don't shut me out. Talk to me."

I sighed. "I'm not sure what's bothering me. I guess I've just been thinking lately, and some little things are nagging at me that never bothered me before. It's no big deal."

"If it's bothering you, it's a big deal. Tell me." I was always amazed at the adoration I saw in his eyes. They held such tenderness and love for me. It seemed like he could look right into my soul and see what I was feeling deep in my heart. "You're concerned about something with me . . . right?"

"How can you read my mind like that?" I asked.

He just shrugged and smiled.

"Jake, I don't want this to seem hurtful to you, but I have some questions."

"All right," he said quietly.

Tears welled up in my eyes. He was so kind and good to me, so Christlike. "Jake, you weren't raised in the Church. I know your parents are good Christian people, but you didn't grow up with those specific values and beliefs instilled in you. I guess I'm concerned about raising children. If we got married, would you be able to teach our children how important the gospel is, even though you grew up without it?"

"Maren," he answered gently, "even more so. I know what it's like to live without the gospel, and the difference it has made in my life. My testimony continues to grow. In fact, I think I appreciate it even more than I would have if I'd been raised with it, because I had to gain it myself. I love the gospel. I will do all that I can to instill that love in our children."

"Since I'm on a roll, speaking of 'gaining it yourself,' does it bother you that your parents are still supporting you even though you're twenty-three years old?"

He looked hurt. "You know I believe firmly in self-sufficiency, Maren. My parents have plenty of money, and want to put me through school. If I can put everything I have into it, I can get done more quickly. I'm thinking of my future, of trying to get through school as fast as I can."

"But, Jake, there is no way that I could feel comfortable having your parents continue to support us if we were married."

He laughed softly. "Of course they wouldn't, Mar. I'll get a job before then, and I would support our family. Don't worry."

"Do you ever think that you might be a little too materialistic?" I asked him bluntly.

"What do you mean, exactly?" he asked, narrowing his eyes.

"Well, you're in college, but you drive a nice car and wear nice clothes, and take me out to eat at nice restaurants. I don't want to take money from your parents if we get married, and I worry that you won't want to live without it. Have you ever had to live without anything?"

He sighed and looked away before muttering, "Not that I can think of."

"That concerns me, Jake."

He looked back at me and ran his long fingers through his thick dark hair. "Yes, I like nice things, Maren. I'm not going to lie to you. But I believe I've noticed that you do too."

I felt a twinge of guilt hearing him call me on that. If I was truly honest with myself, it was important to me to look good and to be comfortable. However, I was willing to struggle through the early years of marriage on love until we could make our own money.

Jake looked at me seriously and said, "I'm working very hard to get through school so I can have a job that I like, and make enough money to keep my family comfortable. No, I don't intend to live off of my parents forever. I know it won't be easy, Mar, but I could handle it. I could live without things. Could you?"

"Yes, Jake."

"Good." He studied me for a moment before he said, "Why are you asking me all of this now, Maren, after all these months? Why do you suddenly have so little faith in me?" There was an urgency in his eyes as he took my hands in his own again.

"I don't know," I mumbled. "I just . . . never really thought about some of these things until now."

"Is it because of Ted?" he asked. I'd briefly told him about our most recent date.

I looked into his eyes and answered honestly, "Maybe. I'm not sure."

He watched me soberly for a long moment before asking, "Is there anything else?"

I gazed up at the tabernacle. "Have you ever thought of going on a mission, Jake?"

His mouth dropped open. "*What?* Maren, I'm twenty-three years old! Most guys my age have already been back for two years!" He just stared at me. "You know by the time I could even think of going—after I've been through the temple—I'll be twenty-four. I wouldn't be home until I was twenty-six, and that would mean almost three more years before we could marry—" He stopped short and stared at me. "You can't be serious, Mar."

I looked away. He dropped my hands to rest his face on his palms. As he looked up, I could see tears glisten in his eyes. He looked so handsome, and yet so vulnerable. I was tempted to take it back, tell him I didn't mean it, but I didn't.

"Maren," he said with urgency, "I love this gospel. I love the Lord. I love you. I want to marry you in the temple someday and be sealed to you forever. I don't want to wait three years for that. I know you need some time, Mar, but if we do get married, do you really want to wait three years?"

"No."

"Have your feelings changed?" he asked me.

I shook my head and gave him a firm, "No."

"Don't you want the same thing I do?" he questioned earnestly.

I watched him carefully for a minute before I said, "I guess I want to marry a man who's served a mission." I regretted it as soon as I saw the pain etched in his handsome face, but it was too late. "How do I look at my sons, Jake, and tell them to go on missions, when their own father didn't go?"

He gazed at me in disbelief. "After all these months, Maren, when we are this close—you would do this to me? Why didn't you tell me this before?"

"I don't know, Jake. I guess I just didn't think about it. There's so much good in you that it didn't seem to matter. But now that I'm thinking seriously about things, about raising a family, it suddenly seems more important."

"I don't know what to say," he muttered.

"Say you'll pray about it," I urged. "I will too."

I could see the agony in his eyes. It was painful to hurt him. I loved him more than anything else on earth. I knew he would never do anything to hurt me so badly.

He sighed and pulled me to him. "If that's what you want, Maren, I'll pray about it. You mean everything to me."

"I'm sorry, Jake. I know this is hard, but thank you." I hugged him tightly. What had I done? What if he felt that he should go? Could I bear it?

"Jake?" I whispered.

"Yes?"

"Will you take me dancing?"

He pulled away to look at me quizzically. "You know I'm not very good at it, but I'll take you if you want me to."

"You're not good at it, or you don't want to be good at it?" The words slipped off my tongue before I could stop them.

"What do you mean by that?" Jake asked a bit defensively. I could tell my barrage of questions may not have been timed very well.

"I don't know, Jake. I'm sorry. It's just a big part of my life, and I wish we could enjoy it together."

"I don't mind dancing, Mar. I just don't love it like you do. It's not my greatest talent."

"I know, Jake. I know," I replied, a little deflated.

We were both quiet for a minute before Jake hinted, "You know . . . I would like to serve a mission with my wife one day, Maren."

I caught the amusement in his eyes, and realized that he was trying to smooth things over. I knew he meant what he'd just said and that his intentions to live the gospel were sincere. I smiled and said, "I bet she'd like that."

Jake did take me dancing, and for all his commanding presence and athletic agility he kept tripping on his own feet. He was quick to laugh at himself and keep trying for my sake, but I could tell he was uncomfortable. He shrugged and said jokingly, "I guess I'm hopeless." We left early, and I missed the energy I had felt dancing with Ted.

A few days later, after fasting and praying, Jake told me that he'd decided a mission wasn't the right thing. I felt relieved, but still uneasy.

As the days passed my mind started to spin and I found myself in a veil of confusion. Ted began asking me out more often, and I continued to accept. True to my word, I was honest with Jake. We sat on his couch one night, alone, except for one of his roommates studying in the back bedroom. He knew that I'd been seeing Ted more frequently. I explained to him that I was beginning to have feelings for Ted, and that I was very confused. Jake simply listened, his eyes intent on my face. "Is this because I didn't feel right about a mission right now, Mar?" he asked.

"No," I said. Then, "I don't know. I don't think so, Jake. I just feel so confused."

I expected him to be furious, but he didn't show it if he was. He looked as if he was thinking things through, then faced me calmly, with the quiet love and adoration I had grown accustomed to seeing in his eyes. "Maren, I love you more than anything else on this earth. I can't imagine not spending the rest of my life and eternity with you. We would be happy, Mar, I promise. I can't tell you what's in your heart. You have to make your decision. If you need some time, I can wait for you to sort through your feelings. Please just talk to me whenever you need to, and remember that I love you." His face was calm, but I could see the controlled frustration in his eyes.

He pulled me close to him. I rested my head on his chest and cried. I wondered what I had done to deserve such a blessing as Jake Jantzen in my life. I felt the truth of his words. He did love me. We would be happy. We were at peace together, and comfortable. He held me far into the night until I fell asleep in his arms. He gently shook me awake much later that night. "Maren? I think I'd better take you home now. As much as I would love to hold you all night, I don't think I can take much more of this and still remain honorable."

I smiled and brushed my lips across his. "I love you," I whispered, and meant it.

A week went by, and although my feelings for Jake ran deep, I continued to feel drawn to Ted. I just didn't want to stop seeing him. As Jake had pointed out, I didn't want to wonder or have regrets later on. That week turned into several and the summer flew by quickly as my thoughts became more tangled and my vision less clear. One hot August morning Ted called and asked to take me on a hike. I again felt the exhilaration and energy in his presence that I was becoming accustomed to. He always kept me laughing. After three hours we reached the summit. The view of the Provo valley was breathtaking. Ted held my hand in his and I felt sparks shooting up my arm. As we looked down at our surroundings, he said, "So, have you decided to marry me yet?"

"What?" I sucked in my breath.

"You know I love you, Maren, and I'll be a good husband."

"I love you too, Ted." I realized as I spoke the words that they were true. It was different, though. How could I love two men at once? Was I crazy? "It's just that . . ."

"That what?"

"I just feel torn. I've been dating Jake for almost a year now—"

He cut me off. "Look, Maren, I'm tired of these games." There was fire in his eyes and for some reason it thrilled me. I had never seen Jake speak with such passion. "You've got to quit playing around. You know I'm the man for you, and I won't take this anymore. All summer you've been having your cake and eating it too. You need to make a decision, and make it fast. I don't even know what you see in that Jake guy. Didn't he just get baptized?"

"It's been almost a year now," I told him. "He can go to the temple next month."

"Then he hasn't been on a mission," Ted pointed out.

"No . . ." I felt a subtle unease.

"So, when's he going?" Ted asked.

"What?" I gave him a puzzled look. "He's not going—"

Ted lifted his eyebrows in surprise and interrupted with, "He's not going on a mission?"

"No. He's almost twenty-four years old, Ted. He considered going, but it just wasn't right for him. He's trying to get through medical school . . ." I let my voice trail off as I realized that it sounded worse that I had to defend Jake.

Ted let the silence sink in before he challenged, "Huh. I thought the Lord asked all worthy priesthood holders to serve."

I jumped to the defensive again. "Jake is a good person, Ted. He can't help the fact that he didn't have the gospel in his life until now."

"I'm not suggesting that Jake isn't a good person, Maren . . . but is he good enough for you?"

I didn't say anything. Ted was asking me what I'd been asking myself for months now. Was Jake himself good enough for me? He was probably the best man I'd ever known. But I did want to marry a returned missionary. I wanted my husband to be absolutely committed to the gospel. If I married Jake, would I be settling for something less? I still didn't have an answer.

Ted continued, "He lives off his parents, right?" He didn't wait for my response. "Doesn't that say something about self-sufficiency? I have always worked to support myself through school, and I will support my family. I've proven myself. I can promise you, Maren, that no one will ever work as hard to make you happy as I will!" He slammed a fist into his palm as he said it. Then he came toward me, and I felt like the world was spinning. I turned away from him and sat down fast.

"Look," Ted said after a moment's hesitation, "you need to make a decision soon. It's time to decide what you want and move on, Maren. Have you just put your life on hold for a year, waiting for this guy? You deserve better." He stood above me, looking at the canyon below while I thought about what he'd said. I had to admit that I felt alive with him. I loved his strength, his power, his willingness to fight for me. Jake just seemed to sit by and hope everything would work out, instead of fighting for what he wanted. I knew that I would never get bored with Ted. He was a good man, a strong man, a returned missionary. I knew he would work hard and be a firm leader and a good provider. He'd never had anything handed to him. He was handsome too, though in a different way than Jake. He had a burning testimony and firm convictions. I held my face in my hands and shook my head, wondering what I should do.

After a few moments in silent contemplation, Ted sat down beside me and asked, "So, how many kids do you want, Maren?"

I looked at up at him and smiled. "Four, and you?"

"Oh, at least four, maybe five or six." He grinned.

Ted and I talked for a long time up on that mountain about our hopes and dreams, our goals, and what we wanted out of life. Everything seemed congruent. We seemed to match. He agreed with everything I said. He told me everything I wanted to hear.

It occurred to me that in all our months of dating, Jake and I had never talked about some of these things. I had just assumed that we felt the same way. When I got home late that afternoon, I called and asked him to come over so we could talk. There were many things we agreed on, but to my dismay, I found some that we did not.

"Maren, I just assumed we'd go back to New York. That's where my family is. I love it there. I want to take you there. You would love it there too."

"I would not love it, Jake!" I insisted. "My family is in Idaho. I love the country. I don't want to live in some big dirty city where my kids can't go out and play!"

"We can talk about it, of course. Don't get upset," he said calmly.

I felt angry. Why didn't he ever get angry? "When, Jake? When will we talk about it? Why didn't you tell me this before?"

"I guess I didn't think it would matter. . . as long as we were together," he answered quietly.

"Do not assume for me! It matters to me, Jacob!"

He winced at his full name. I knew he hated it. "I can see that," he said simply.

"Get mad, Jake! Why don't you ever get mad? Don't you care enough about me to be infuriated sometimes?"

He chuckled softly and pulled me to him to kiss me. "I think you're mad enough for both of us, Mar."

I sighed and collapsed on the couch. "You're exasperating, Mr. Jantzen," I told him. Then I asked, "How many children do you want?"

He raised his eyebrow at me and answered, "Not very many. One or two."

"That's it?" I asked in shock.

"Yes, why? How many do you want?"

"At least four."

Jake's eyes nearly bugged out of his head. "What?"

"Four, Jake. I want to have four children, and I would probably take more if I felt like God wanted me to."

Jake sat down next to me, leaned forward with his elbows on his knees, and said earnestly, "Maren, I have to be honest with you. I know it's important to have children, but I really don't want a big family. There was just my sister and me growing up, and it was perfect. My parents were able to provide for us, and spend time with us, and still have energy left to put into their marriage. I'm going to be a doctor, Maren. That's a stressful job with a trying schedule. Having a large family would be difficult. Truthfully, I don't think I'm very good with children anyway."

I just stared at him. "Why would you think that?"

He shrugged. "I've just never been around them a whole lot."

"But you have a younger sister," I pointed out.

"Yes, but she's only four years younger than me. She's older than you, in fact. I watched out for her, but it's not like I was old enough to take care of her. Look, I think I could probably handle two kids, Maren—"

"Jake!"

He held up his hands in self-defense and conceded, "If you feel that strongly about it, Mar, you might possibly be able to talk me into three, but I'd have to think about it."

I stared at him in disbelief, not knowing what to say. He was being honest with me. Wanting to break the tension, I finally smiled slyly and said, "Oh, yeah? Well, I think I could talk you into four."

His eyes went wide with surprise at my coyness, and I felt a little embarrassed. He grabbed me and started to tickle me. We ended up on the floor with me rolling all over, screaming and trying to get away. Finally, he stopped, and I gazed up into his handsome face. I felt breathless as he leaned over to kiss me. His kisses were so tender and full of love, but not the sparks and fire that I felt with Ted. I held him to me. I wanted that moment to last forever. I loved him so much. How could I possibly feel torn? Finally, Jake pulled himself away and stood up. "Whoa," he breathed as he ran his fingers through his hair. He extended his hand to help me up. "No more tickle sessions. That's more than I can handle."

"Sorry," I mumbled. "I didn't mean to do that."

"It wasn't you, Maren, it was me. One more month and I can go to the temple. Then I'll finally be able to ask you to marry me."

At his tender words, I began to cry. I was still overwhelmed with confusion.

"What is it, love? What did I say?" He took me in his arms and I clung to him.

"I talked to Ted for a long time today, Jake."

I felt him tense a little, but he still held me. "And?" he asked.

"He told me to choose between you and him, and to do it soon," I admitted.

Jake's eyes went wide. "What did you tell him?"

"What could I tell him? He wants to move on with his life, and I have to respect that."

He searched my face and then tightened his hold on me. "How are you feeling, Maren?" he asked gently.

It occurred to me that I could talk to Jake about anything, even Ted, with no fear of criticism. I couldn't even mention Jake around Ted though. He either said something negative or totally cut me off anytime I tried. It made me uncomfortable and uneasy sometimes.

"I feel so confused, Jake. I love you, I do. There's a part of me that loves Ted, too though. And you and I . . . we have some significant differences of opinion that I wasn't aware of."

Jake only nodded.

I suddenly blurted out, "Aren't you going to say anything? Don't you care enough to fight for me?"

"I've told you how I feel, Maren. What more do you want me to say?" he asked genuinely. But he seemed momentarily impatient.

I sighed and shook my head. I was being stupid. It just wasn't in his nature. "Nothing," I said softly.

He watched me quietly for a minute, as if in thought. "What are you going to do?" he finally asked. He always left it up to me. He never told me what to do.

"I'm going to fast and pray like I never have."

"Then I will too."

I smiled up at him. "Thank you, Jake. That would mean a lot to me."

He took my hands in his. "Maren, I want you to know how much I love you. I trust you completely. I know that you will make the right decision, whatever that decision may be."

"You must be the best man on earth," I said.

"Let's hope so, for my sake." I didn't miss the urgency in his eyes.

That night I knelt in prayer and begged the Lord for guidance. "Please help me make the right decision, Heavenly Father, please."

For almost a month I prayed. I pored over the scriptures seeking guidance. I read my patriarchal blessing. The only reference it made to my eternal companion was that, "Having chosen" him, we could be sealed in the temple. For some reason the answer would not come. I just kept feeling something telling me that the choice was mine. Was it inspiration, or confusion? Why, when I most needed the guidance of the Lord, was I not receiving it? . . . Or was I?

Ted came over toward the end of that time to talk to me. "I called last night and you were gone."

"Yes, I was."

"Where were you, Maren—with Jake?"

I wondered why I would feel so guilty around him when he knew full well what was going on. "Yes, with Jake."

He whirled around to leave, but then turned back and demanded, "How could you go and see him behind my back like that? You know I love you! How can you lead me on like you do, and then go see another guy?" His jealousy upset me, but at the same time it made me wonder if he did love me more. Why didn't Jake get jealous? I was pretty sure I'd feel jealous under the same circumstances.

I felt the tears threatening as I said, "I'm sorry. I don't know. I just feel so confused, Ted."

"We are *meant* to be together, Maren!" he insisted. "I am sure of it."

Could that be true? I wondered. *Are we meant to be together? How can he be sure of that? And if that is truly the case, why aren't I feeling it too?* I could only shake my head and say, "Well, I'm *not* sure of it, Ted—not yet."

He looked upset, but his voice was smooth. "It's been almost a month, Maren. I'm ready to move on with my life. I need an answer soon, or I'm gone." He turned and left.

I felt terrified, though I wasn't sure why.

That night I lay in my bed staring at the ceiling, a thousand thoughts running through my mind. Why wouldn't Jake fight for me? Did he not really love me? Why wouldn't he slam his fist down and say, "Darn it, Maren, I love you! I need you!" Why did he stay so calm? Would he be so sedate in our marriage? I wanted a man who loved me enough to fight for me. I slipped out of bed to my knees.

"Heavenly Father, I think I'm going to choose Ted. I never felt that before, but suddenly, I do. I need his passion and his zest for life. He was raised in the Church and will be a good example to our children.

He's a returned missionary. Please tell me if it's right." I went back to bed, still feeling nothing; and no confirmation came.

Two days later, Ted took me on a drive up the canyon. The late September chill was beginning to turn the leaves brilliant colors. He parked and led me up a short path to a quiet clearing. *Oh, no,* I thought. I could feel it coming. I wasn't prepared. I thought of Jake at home praying and fasting and getting ready to go through the temple the next morning. *Please, Lord,* I prayed silently, *Please help me to know if I've made the right decision. I've been praying for an answer for weeks.* Still nothing.

Ted took my hand and led me to sit on a large rock with him. The trees stood around us, watching. It was beautiful. I was not prepared. I needed more time. "I love you, Maren," Ted said. "Will you marry me?"

My head was spinning, my heart was lurching. I knew this was it. If I told him no, even told him I needed more time to think, he would be gone forever. The thought terrified me. *Please tell me, God, what should I do? If I don't hear anything, I'm going to say yes.*

"Maren," Ted said, "This is it. You have to decide."

When I still heard no heavenly counsel, I decided the Lord had left the decision to me. I knew Ted would raise our children firmly in the gospel. I knew he would keep life interesting and fun. I loved the excitement I felt when I was with him. I loved him. I looked into his eyes, and plunged in. "Yes, Ted, I will."

He placed a ring on my finger and kissed me. I felt happy, and relieved to have finally made a decision . . . I only hoped it was the right one.

Despite my lack of sleep, I woke early the next morning. I looked at the ring on my finger and smiled. Then I thought of Jake. I glanced over at my alarm clock—seven o'clock. He would be leaving for the temple. I was glad that he could go in peace, not knowing my decision yet. I knew I had to talk to him that day, before he found out another way. I thought it would be the hardest thing I'd ever have to do.

I fell to my knees before going to take a shower. "Heavenly Father, please let me feel peace in my decision. Let me know that this is right. I need Your guidance." I waited several moments, but nothing came. I pulled out my patriarchal blessing again and searched once more for the confirmation I needed. I had been told that I

would have many difficult decisions to make throughout my life—
you could say that again, I thought—and that I would also have many
opportunities for growth. My blessing admonished me to seek for
guidance through prayer. The words only frustrated me. I'd sought for
guidance for weeks. Maybe this was simply a decision that the Lord
had left to me. I sighed and got up, still admittedly confused.

I dressed carefully. I knew it might be the last time Jake would see me,
and I wanted to look beautiful, though I didn't know why exactly. I was
going to break his heart. I wore a taupe floral skirt that flowed around my
ankles. My white blouse was carefully ironed and tied in the back to
accentuate my waist. I curled my hair all over and let it hang loosely down
my back. I spent twenty minutes getting my makeup just right. Silver
earrings and necklace glistened against my tanned skin. My light pink nail
polish still looked good, and I looked into my clear blue eyes in the mirror.
"Hello, Mrs. Saunders," I said to myself. I smiled at my reflection, but
then saw a twinge of guilt and sadness on my face. I didn't know how I
was going to tell Jake, a man I had loved and dated for nearly a year, that I
was going to marry Ted—who I'd only known for a few short months.

I prayed again before I dialed the phone. "Please, God, let me
know what to say to Jake. Let him know that this is right, and please
let him be happy. I want so much for him to be happy. He's the best
man I've ever known, and he deserves that."

Jake answered the phone in a contemplative tone. "Hello?"

"Hi, Jake."

"Hi," he said softly.

"How was the temple?"

"Oh, Maren, it was so beautiful and wonderful and peaceful. I
can't wait for you to go." Then, after a brief pause, he asked, "Can I
see you? I want to share this feeling with you, love."

Tears welled up in my eyes and splattered on my blouse as I gazed
at my ring. Had I made the right choice? "Yes, Jake," I answered.
"Where?"

"Why don't you meet me on the temple grounds? I really want to
hold onto that feeling a little longer."

Oh, perfect, I thought. *I'll go break his heart on the temple grounds.*

"Sure. Now?" I asked.

"Yes. See you soon."

I drove to the temple, praying all the time for guidance to speak to him. I wanted him to know how much I loved him, and to understand that this would be best for all of us. I didn't know if I was sure of that myself though. I gazed up at the golden spire of the Provo Temple and bit my lip to keep from crying. I glanced at my reflection in the rearview mirror before grabbing the door handle. Looking down, I saw my diamond flash in the sunlight. I couldn't have him find out first thing by seeing my ring. I pulled it off and put it carefully in the glove box.

I looked up the hill to the temple and saw Jake standing there. He wore a loose white shirt and black slacks. The jet-black of his thick hair contrasted boldly against his shirt. He stood tall and lean, one hand in his pocket, one clasped in a tight fist at his side. He grinned broadly as he watched me from afar. It broke my heart to realize how happy he was to see me.

With the temple close to him, he seemed to glow. I stared up at him and saw light all around him. I could feel his eyes piercing my heart, even though I couldn't see them closely. I could see the peace about him, and the love that emanated from him as he gazed at me. A sob caught in my throat, and I whispered out loud, "I will love you forever, Jacob Adam Jantzen." It was too late. My choice was made.

As I climbed the hill to him, a light autumn breeze came up and whipped my skirt around my legs. It ruffled Jake's hair and shirt too, but he stood firmly. It was odd that he didn't come to meet me. He just waited for me to come to him. I thought that I would remember the way he looked right then forever.

I could see the joy of the temple in his eyes when I reached him. "I've never seen you look so beautiful, Maren," he said.

"You paint quite a picture yourself, standing there against the sky like that."

He smiled, but the usual music of his laughter didn't come. He looked into my eyes and I forced myself to look back, praying that he wouldn't read it all in my face. There was a barely perceptible change in his expression, as he slowly slid his closed fist into his pocket. He bit his bottom lip and clasped my hand in his free one to lead me to a tree. We sat beneath it on the grass. Jake toyed with my fingers and then looked into my eyes. "I've missed you these last few weeks, Maren. We haven't been together as much as we were before. Thank you for coming today."

"Of course I would come, Jake," I replied, trying to hide the emotion in my voice. He looked toward the temple. I studied his profile, wanting to remember every detail. I loved him with everything in me, and yet I loved Ted too. I had to choose sometime. I couldn't have them both. I tried to memorize the curve of his jaw, and the laugh lines near his deep eyes and smooth lips. He sat straight and tall, his shoulders broad. A wisp of black hair peeked above his shirt at his throat.

"Tell me about the temple, Jake," I pleaded, wanting to know.

"It's so peaceful there, Maren. You know that no matter what happens out here, things will always be right in there. I know God lives and loves us and wants our happiness. I know the gospel is true. I long to go back inside and take you with me. I thought I would feel such joy at this moment. I do feel happiness, and a peace . . . but it's not what I want to feel." He turned to face me and brush a tear from my cheek. I saw the moisture in his eyes as he said, "You've come to tell me something, haven't you?"

I stared at him and said nothing.

"Something I don't want to hear, perhaps?"

"How do you do it, Jake? How do you read my mind, my heart, so clearly?"

He gave a melancholy shrug. "Let's have it, Mar. What do you want to say?"

Tears ran freely down my cheeks. There was no way I could stop them. "I don't know how to say this, Jake. For so long I thought it could only be you. I've been so confused lately," I said, then added bitterly, "as you know. I've prayed and fasted and read my patriarchal blessing over and over again, trying to know what to do."

Jake held both my hands as silent tears fell down his cheeks and past the square of his jaw.

"Jake, I love you, but . . . I've decided to marry Ted. I love him too." A sob escaped me as I said it and Jake nodded. "You are the best man on earth, and I will always love you. I will pray every day for your happiness. You will always have a place in my heart."

He sat tall, with his shoulders squared and answered me firmly, "You know that I trust you, Maren. If you believe this is the best decision for you, then it must be. I will miss you so much—" His voice cracked. "But all I want in the world is for you to be happy. Promise me that you'll be happy."

I smiled and said, "I promise." I leaned forward to hug him and he held me tight. I pushed my fingers into his hair and held him to me and sobbed. Part of me wished desperately that he would beg me to stay, tell me that he knew we should be together, that I was making a mistake, or that he would just stand up and fight for me. The fact that he did none of those things gave me some assurance that I was doing the right thing.

I didn't ever want to let him go, but I had to. "I'd better go," I sniffled. I looked at him. His white shirt was smudged with makeup and tears. "Oh, Jake, I'm so sorry about your shirt." We looked at each other and laughed. It seemed so trivial to be worried about a shirt, when two hearts and all of eternity were at stake. We both saw the irony in it.

"My shirt will be fine . . ." he said and after a pause, "and so will I."

We stood and I kissed his cheek before turning to go.

"Maren?" he called out.

My head shot around as I turned back. Was he going to call me back? Put up a fight? I hoped he would, but he simply said, "I'll love you forever. Be happy."

I smiled through the tears. "I will. You too."

As I walked away I thought I heard him whisper, "Good-bye, love."

Before I drove away, I took one last look at him there on the hill with his rumpled shirt and tear-streaked face. I watched him study his closed fist intently before he looked back up to meet my gaze. "Dear God, if you do nothing else for me, please help Jake to be happy," I prayed. Then I added, "Thank you."

I stayed in my apartment and cried most of the day. Jana finally came into my room and sat on my bed. "Maren, maybe I'm being nosy here, but aren't you supposed to be floating on a cloud or something the day after you get engaged?" It wasn't like her, but then she added softly, "You know I've had doubts about Jake, and well . . . you know how I feel about Ted, so this is hard for me to say, but . . . are you sure you're making the right decision here?"

"I appreciate your concern, Jan, but the decision's made."

"Did you ever get a chance to talk this over with your parents?" she asked. "I know you haven't seen them all summer."

"Summer's the busy season on a farm," I explained. "They couldn't get away, and I guess I just never felt like I had the time to drive clear up to Idaho Falls this summer. It's been crazy. I've talked to them on the phone a few times though. I talked to them today, in fact."

"So, what did they say?" She wouldn't let up.

I sighed. "They're not very objective, Jana. They love Jake. You know we went up there a couple of times during the winter, and they came down a few times during the regular school year. They've spent a fair amount of time with him, but they've never even met Ted. They just got used to the idea of me marrying Jake, I guess, and it was a little hard for them when I made a different decision."

"Do they think you made a mistake, then?" she pried.

I felt irritated. "No. They advised me several weeks ago to take my time and make my decision carefully. They told me that they knew I would make the right choice. They said they'd be praying for me, and that they would support me in whatever I decided."

"What did they say when you talked to them today?" she asked. "When you told them you were engaged to Ted?"

I wanted to tell her that it was none of her business, but I knew there wasn't much point. "They said, 'Congratulations. We're happy for you. We can't wait to meet him.'"

"Is that all?"

"Jana, why do you keep pushing this?" I asked her.

"I'm just concerned for your welfare. I just want to know. What else happened when you called them?"

I sighed loudly and finally admitted, "My dad said, 'Are you sure you've given Jake a fair chance, honey? He's a good man.' And I told him yes I was, and that Ted's a good man too. He said that he's sure he is."

"And your mom?"

"My mom said she loves me and she's happy for me. Then she asked me if Jake was all right, and . . ."

"And what?"

"I'm not sure . . . but it sounded like she was crying," I admitted. "But it's just because they haven't met Ted yet. Jake's easy to love, but they'll learn to love Ted too."

"Yeah . . . I guess so," she said. But there was still some tension in the air as she asked, "Did you talk to the bishop?" I was getting annoyed now.

"Jana, he can't tell me who to marry!"

"I know, but maybe he could have given you some advice or a blessing or—" My scowl cut her off.

"I'm a big girl, Jana. Remember?" I added the last word to break the tension; after all, it had hurt her that I'd dated Ted at all, and it showed unselfishness on her part to even care.

"Well, I'm happy for you then, Maren." She wasn't exactly annoyed when she said it, but she did seem sad somehow. I couldn't understand what was bothering her though, and I didn't ask.

That night Ted came to take me out, and when I saw his smile, I knew everything would be fine.

We were married in December over Christmas break. In the temple, I finally found the peace that I had been looking for as I looked into his eyes. I knew that Ted was a worthy priesthood holder, and that we were both committed to the gospel. We loved each other, and I was sure that we had a wonderful life to look forward to.

The first two weeks were a little rough, but I figured maybe marriage took a little more getting used to than I had thought. At the beginning of winter semester, I ran into Jake on campus. "Maren!" he said, and hugged me. I felt a mixture of emotion. I wanted to hug him too, but I held back. I was married after all.

"Jake, how are you?" I asked sincerely.

"Fine, and you?"

"Fine."

"Is marriage treating you well?" he asked. I saw pain behind his eyes that I didn't want to see. I almost felt ashamed for being married to Ted, guilty of some sin—because it meant hurting Jake.

"Yes," I answered, feeling less than honest. It hadn't been long enough to tell, I told myself. Everything would be fine. "You didn't come to the reception."

He looked at me pointedly. "No, I didn't." Then he picked up my left hand and studied my ring. He shook his head as if in disbelief, "So, you're really married."

I pulled my hand away. "Yes, Jake, I am." I felt a twinge of anger. *How dare he come and behave this way now that I belong to another man?* I fumed to myself. *If he wanted me, why didn't he fight for me when he had the chance?* He seemed to sense my irritation, so he changed the subject.

"I have something to tell you." He grinned.

"What?" I asked. My heart pounded. Had he found someone else already? I hoped he had, but then my heart ached . . . Oh, why was I being so ridiculous? I wanted him to be happy.

"I'm going on a mission," he announced proudly.

"You are?" I hugged him that time. "Oh, Jake, that's wonderful! When?"

He laughed. "I thought you'd be happy. It was you who inspired me, you know." He gave me a gentle smile and then said, "I'm going to Spain; I leave in two weeks."

"Two weeks?"

"Yes. I stayed to work through the holidays, and thought an extra week wouldn't hurt. So, I'm going home on Saturday to pack up and then come back to the MTC."

So many thoughts ran through my mind. "Stayed to work? You got a job?"

He smiled shyly. "I thought it was about time I started paying my own way. I've been working since October, saving money for my mission."

I shook my head. "I can't believe it. Jake, it's all so wonderful!"

"Thank you. I owe a lot to you, Maren. I've made some good changes, thanks to you."

"There wasn't a lot that needed to be changed, Jake," I said honestly.

After too long a pause he said, "Well, good luck to you, Maren, and thank you for everything." There was an earnestness in his eyes.

I smiled. "I wish you all the best on your mission, and . . . with everything, Jake." We parted, but as I started to leave, he grabbed my arm.

"Maren?" I knew he was looking into my soul.

"Yes?"

"Are you happy?" he asked.

I swallowed and then smiled, thinking of the dreams I had that I was sure would come true with Ted. "Yes," I answered him.

He smiled and waved good-bye. It was the last time I saw him.

Chapter 3

My mind was suddenly jerked back to the present by the flash of a little blond head, and Rebecca climbing into my lap. I felt warm tears still on my cheeks from the memories. "Good morning, Becca Bug." I hugged her.

She looked up and touched my face. "Are you okay, Mommy?"

I smiled down at her. "Yes, I'm fine, sweetie."

She looked uncomfortable for a minute, and then said, "I heard you and Daddy fighting last night."

"You did?" I wondered how much she had heard. My poor children had been through more than their fair share of fights, that was certain. "I'm sorry, Rebecca."

"Did Daddy leave?" she asked.

I choked back the tears that were threatening to start again. "Yes, honey, he did."

"Is he coming back?" she asked with five-year-old concern.

I paused for a minute. We'd had fights before. He always ended up coming back. Either he sobered up and came to half-heartedly apologize, or I felt lost without him and called to ask him to come home. I knew it would be incredibly difficult for me, but I had to mean it that time. I couldn't let Ted come back. Not ever. The reality was heartbreaking.

"No, Becca," I finally said, "Daddy's not going to live here anymore. But don't worry, you'll still get to see him."

She hugged me and said nothing. I wondered what was going on in her young mind, but didn't know if I had the strength to deal with it. I couldn't even handle what was going on in my own head.

Trevor slid down from the barstool and came to hug me too. I looked into their innocent faces. I had to tell them. "Hey you two, we need to talk."

They watched me expectantly.

"You know that Daddy and I have had some problems getting along." I hesitated, wondering how much I should tell them. Even though they were young, I didn't want them to think people just dissolved a marriage because they couldn't agree. "There are some other things, too. Daddy has made some choices that are really hard for me to live with. They're hurtful to me. I've tried to help him change his mind and make better choices, but he doesn't want to right now."

"Is Daddy bad?" Trevor asked me.

My heart lurched. There was a lot of anger inside me, and part of me wanted to scream, "Yes! I wish I'd never met him!" But when I contemplated it, I realized it wasn't true.

"No, Trevor, Daddy isn't bad. He's made some poor choices, but he's a good person. We've both made mistakes. I don't think that Daddy and I can live together anymore . . . but I want you to know that we both love you very, very much. Nothing will ever change that. No matter what happens, you will both always have a mom and a dad who love you more than anything else in this world." I hugged them to me. I couldn't say any more.

"Mommy, do you love Daddy?" Rebecca asked cautiously. She seemed to dread hearing the answer.

I had to think for a minute. Did I? In some ways I just felt devoid of any feeling—empty, indifferent. But if I didn't love him, would I have stayed there for ten long years? Would I hurt as much as I did? "Yes, honey. I will always love Daddy, and I hope he will be happy someday." She seemed relieved and content with my answer.

"I don't love him!" Trevor stated defiantly. "He's mean and he yells all the time and he won't play with me anymore." I winced at his young perception of how things had worsened in recent months.

"Don't say that, Trevor. It's okay to feel angry with Daddy, or sad, or disappointed, but you do love him. And he loves you. He's just confused right now."

"Confused about what?" Rebecca questioned.

I sighed and wondered how I should answer all their young inquiries. "Just about what he wants to do with his life, Rebecca. It's hard to explain it all to you. I'm a little confused about things myself right now. I'm not sure exactly what we're going to do or what will happen, but I promise we'll talk about it, okay? And I want you to know that you can talk to me about anything you want to. It's important to talk about your feelings."

"Okay, Mom," Rebecca answered.

"Okay, Mommy," Trevor echoed.

"I love you both so much, and I'm so glad you're mine." I smiled at them.

"Mommy?" Trevor said.

"What, honey?"

"I'm sad that Daddy's gone."

"Me too, baby."

The day was difficult to get through. Being Saturday, I didn't have as much of a normal routine to cling to. I started with regular housework, and then ended up scrubbing everything from top to bottom. I thought about how much I loved our house. We'd been in it for two years. We were going to build, but found a brand-new model home with a contractor anxious to sell it. We lived in a wonderful neighborhood with lots of children. I'd earned my interior design degree, and although I'd never worked professionally, I practiced a lot on my own home. I had decorated our house with such love and hope.

I stopped working intermittently to check on Trevor and Rebecca playing outside. I was glad to see them laughing and having fun. We had put a fence up the previous summer, and they loved the backyard. I thought of our finances and wondered how I would pay for the house, but then I pushed the thought to the back of my mind. There was no way I was leaving our home. I would find a way for us to stay there. A bittersweet memory flashed through my mind of the hope I had felt when Ted and I first moved there with the children. We were so excited to finally have a house, and I had felt like things would improve at last.

I made it through the day, but the real difficulty came later that night after the children were in bed. I read to them, tucked them in, and kissed them. They didn't mention anything more about Ted. I worried that maybe they needed to talk about it, but I didn't know if I could do it. Then I realized that perhaps things didn't seem so different to them. Ted was rarely home when the children went to bed anyway. Still, there was a more permanent change in the making.

I didn't want to give myself time to think, so I tried to find something to watch on television. After the news there was simply nothing else on that I could stand to watch. I turned off the TV and sat staring at the front door. I began to feel the familiar lonely ache, and I longed for Ted to come home, take me in his arms, and tell me he was sorry. I wanted to go to bed and sleep close to him, knowing he was there. Why hadn't he called yet? I fought the urge to call his parents' house, looking for him. I felt a hollow ache in the pit of my stomach.

I got on my knees and poured my heart out in prayer. "What should I do, Father? Should I call Ted and forgive him and try again, or should I stand firm?" I closed my eyes and just listened for several minutes.

I thought back over the last ten years. Ted had started drinking only a few months into our marriage. I still didn't completely understand why. I knew something wasn't right, but he managed to cover it up for a while. By the time I found out, we'd been married over a year, and I had no idea what to do for him. That simply wasn't something I'd ever planned on having to confront in my marriage. He kept promising to stop, but then he didn't. I hadn't wanted anyone to discover the embarrassing secret, but over the months it became increasingly harder to hide.

It was during my first pregnancy that Ted began to get violent along with the drinking. I was filled with foreboding. I began to be afraid that Ted didn't have control over his drinking like he claimed to, that it was becoming an addiction. I wanted to do what was right, but I didn't want to live with a man who willingly put himself in danger.

The thought of divorce began to whisper in the back of my mind. I had a child to think of, a child that I did not want to raise in a home where there was drunkenness and violence. The thought of leaving my baby to go to work was not desirable either. I struggled with the weight of a hard decision for several weeks. I didn't take my temple covenants lightly, and I was terrified of going against God's will. I needed His presence in my life.

When my baby daughter was born and then died the same day, I was too brokenhearted to even think about leaving my husband anymore. I was also seized with a new terror: the fear that if I left Ted, I wouldn't have the chance to raise my baby in the next life. I couldn't take the risk. I felt that I had no choice. I resigned myself to doing everything I could to fix my marriage and help Ted. I hoped that putting all my energy into my marriage might alleviate some of the unbearable pain of losing my baby. It was all in vain. After another year of anguish and frustration, I directed the anger at God and quit going to church.

In subsequent years, I had matured enough to realize that it wasn't God's fault, and blaming Him had been a grave mistake. All that I had done was deprive myself of the comfort and blessings that I could have been receiving. I didn't believe that God had wanted me to suffer. He had simply allowed me my agency, and He'd done the same for those around me. Maybe the Lord had wanted me to grow. I'd certainly done plenty of that. Or perhaps Ted had needed me. I didn't know. Either way, God hadn't left me; I had left Him. When I humbled myself enough to be obedient, I became aware of just how much God did bless me, despite the difficulty of my circumstances.

I also realized that the Lord hadn't taken my baby to punish me. For whatever reason, Ashlyn had been meant to return to Him after only a brief stay on earth. I knew that I still had the promise of being with her someday if I earned that blessing. When I repented of my foolishness, the bitterness left me. It was such a relief to let go of that. But I still had the grief. Every hour of every day I felt the emptiness around me. I wondered what Ashlyn would have looked like, what milestones she would have reached. I longed to hear her baby coos, see her learn to crawl, and help her take her first steps. Worst of all, I felt alone in my mourning. Ted seemed virtually unaffected by the whole thing, except that he started to drink more.

I began going to church again and found some comfort there, though it was extremely difficult to watch the children. I was always comparing them to how old Ashlyn would have been. I observed frustrated parents hauling screaming toddlers out of the chapel, and ached for such a delightful burden. I visited Ashlyn's tiny grave often, but it wasn't enough. I worked to earn the privilege of attending the temple again, hoping that I might somehow feel closer to her there.

When Rebecca was born, I was overjoyed to at last have a baby in my arms, but I almost wished that she had been a boy. It would have been easier. So many well-meaning friends and family members said things like, "Isn't it wonderful that you have a little daughter now?" as though this baby could replace the first one. I loved Rebecca with all my heart, and she did help fill the void somewhat, but I still longed to place her in the arms of her three-year-old sister. I ached to watch them grow up together. As Rebecca grew, I wondered if she looked like Ashlyn would have, if their personalities would have been similar or very different. Gradually, my heart seemed to bleed a few less drops every day, but I didn't think the wound would ever heal completely.

As my mind drifted back to the present, the pain was still tangible. I tried to push Ashlyn from my mind as I thought about the situation at hand. I pleaded with God, "Should I call Ted to come home, or should I stand firm?"

I wanted him to change so badly, but I knew in my heart that it wasn't likely to happen. How many times had he left before? How many times had I tried again? More than I could possibly count. There might be a few hopeful days, but then Ted always got drunk again. We always fought again. I always cried again. It was a never-ending cycle. In fact, it was worse than that. It was a downward spiral, spinning lower and lower. I realized that it was impossible. This was the bottom for me. I had to get off. Nothing was going to change unless I did something differently. I was not willing to sacrifice another ten years of my life for a hopeless cause.

I prayed again then. "Please help me find the strength to stand firm on this and not call him to come back . . . I miss him, Father. I miss him. Please be with him and guide him. Please help him. There is nothing more that I can do."

I had not talked to the bishop in my present ward about my circumstances. I supposed that I had wanted to keep up the façade of a normal life after we moved into our new home and made a fresh start. I realized now, however, that I needed to talk to him and that I needed some guidance.

I tossed and turned all night, feeling the empty space beside me. The next morning I read from the Book of Mormon and prayed again before calling Bishop Rowley. He said that he could see me half an hour before church started.

I called my best friend, who lived across the street, to see if she would watch Rebecca and Trevor for me while I met with the bishop.

"I know it's kind of a pain on Sunday morning, Ann . . ." I said brokenly, hoping that she wouldn't notice. I should have known better.

"All right, Maren, what's up? Did Ted leave *again?*"

"Oh, you hush. You don't know what it's like."

"No, I don't, and I never will. When are you going to get rid of him? Haven't you had enough yet?"

"Actually, I think I have," I answered quietly.

"Really, Maren?" Ann asked me. "Because you know I've offered my legal services to you free of charge at any time. All you have to do is ask."

"I'm not asking quite yet," I told her. "But I'm close."

She sighed loudly. "Okay. I'll keep praying for you. Bring the kids over whenever you want. Tyler and I are both ready for church. We'll meet you over there with Rebecca and Trevor."

"Bless you," I said to her, as I often did.

"Yeah, well, who else's kids am I going to take to church?" she said good-naturedly, but I knew there was pain behind her comment. Ann and Tyler had been married nearly as long as Ted and I had, but so far they hadn't been able to have children. I knew it was a terrible source of grief for both of them.

Bishop Rowley was a kind man, gracefully graying in his early fifties. He was always friendly, but seemed to accomplish it by forcing himself out of a shell of shyness. He shook my hand warmly. "Good morning, Maren."

I smiled tentatively. Once I was seated across the desk from him, I felt nervous and discouraged. I didn't want to tell my story to another bishop. I had so hoped that I wouldn't have to do this again.

Bishop Rowley seemed to sense my concern. "Before you begin, Maren, let me say some things. I'm here to help you, and I have no desire to see you suffer. As your bishop, anything you tell me will be held in the strictest confidence."

"Thank you," I said. I told him that Ted and I had married worthily in the temple, but I explained the series of poor choices that had brought on increasingly painful results. I told him about the fights, the despair, the hope, the drinking, my own period of bitter inactivity in the Church, my decision to come back to church and to the temple, my personal struggles, my hopes for Ted, and my confusion about what to do. I expressed my concern about divorce, but told him of my fear of raising my children in a home where alcohol and violence were becoming more frequent. Tears ran down my face as I finished, despite my efforts to disguise my emotion.

Bishop Rowley leaned forward for a moment with his forehead on his hands, saying nothing. I wondered if he was praying. Then he looked up at me, and I saw genuine compassion and concern in his eyes. "Maren, the Lord loves you. He does not intend for His daughters to go through such suffering. I personally admire your courage and your strength. I am sure the Lord is aware of your struggle, and that He will help you through this."

I felt relief flood through me. "Bishop Rowley, am I . . . I feel like I've done everything I can, but I don't want to make a grave mistake . . . Am I justified in divorcing Ted?"

I was surprised to see the bishop's eyes grow misty as he said quietly, "Maren, I feel for Ted. I know that alcohol addiction is a powerful thing. I would certainly be happy to talk with him and see if there's anything I can do to help if he's willing. However, there is no excuse for violence. I do not believe that God would require any wife to stay in circumstances such as yours. Divorce is a grave thing, but sadly it's sometimes the best option. It's not my place to tell you what to do though. You have to make your own decision, but you're certainly entitled to receive guidance and inspiration from the Lord if you seek it. Would you like a blessing?"

"Yes . . ." My voice broke. "That would be helpful. Thank you."

I felt a degree of peace as I heard the gentle words of my bishop. He told me that the Lord loved me and wanted me to be happy. He advised me to trust my own judgment and to stay close to the Lord through prayer as I sought for guidance. He promised me that a way would be provided for me to meet the needs of my children if I acted in faith. I was told that these difficulties would act for my good as I grew in knowledge and understanding, and that, by faith, great blessings often come at the end of our trials. He blessed me with peace and hope, and a desire to do good and follow the Lord's commandments. I was admonished to trust in the Lord with all my heart and to lean not unto my own understanding. Finally, I was told that all things would be made clear to me in due time.

Chapter 4

I unlocked the kitchen door late Monday afternoon to let Ann in. "What took you so long?" I teased.

"Some of us have to work for a living," she retorted as she kicked off her pumps and dropped onto a kitchen chair. She obviously hadn't even taken the time to change clothes.

"You don't have to work for a living. You only do it because you love practicing law. Admit it."

"All right. I admit it." She grinned. "Where are the kids?"

"It's actually warm enough for them to play outside. Isn't that wonderful? I'm praying it doesn't snow again this year."

"Dream on," she said. "It's not even April yet." She paused and looked around. "So, is he still gone?"

"Who?" I asked innocently.

She gave an exasperated sigh, pushing her chicly styled sleek brown hair behind her ears. "You know who, Maren. Your charming husband. Is he back or not?"

I threw the dishcloth in the sink and sat down across from her. "No," I said sadly. "He's not back."

"What did he do this time?" she asked distastefully. "Same old thing?"

I nodded. "He came home drunk again."

"Did he hit you again?" she demanded.

"He doesn't hit me, Ann."

She rolled her eyes and crossed her shapely, stocking-clad legs. "Hitting, pushing, throwing things . . . what's the difference?"

"There's a big difference," I insisted.

She leaned back in her chair and crossed her arms over her stomach. An expensive gold bracelet dangled from her wrist. If I didn't know Ann so well, I could easily have felt intimidated by her. She looked at me with caramel-colored eyes for a moment before asking, "Do you ever stop and listen to yourself?"

"What do you mean?"

"If you spent half as much time standing up for yourself as you spend standing up for Ted, I'd wager you'd be a much happier person."

"You're supposed to put your family first, Ann."

"Haven't you ever heard the old adage, 'Love thy neighbor as thyself'? Who was it that said that . . . ?" she mused.

"Very funny."

"How can you learn to love another person completely if you don't love yourself?"

"I'm not that easy to love," I remarked dryly.

"I'm your selfish, snobby best friend, and even I love you. You can't be that bad."

I laughed and answered sarcastically, "Oh yeah. You're just about the most selfish person I've ever met, Annie girl."

"How can you call me that? That is so undignified. What kind of attorney goes by the name 'Annie girl'?"

"I just like to ruffle your feathers once in a while. It keeps you humble."

She smiled and turned in her seat to tap perfectly manicured nails on the tabletop while she considered me. She finally said, "Dare I ask whether you want to file for divorce yet?"

I rested my face in my hands and sighed before looking up to answer her. "Do I *want* to? No. But I'm afraid I may have to. It tears me apart to think about something so awful, Ann. I don't know how I can make him stay away . . . but I feel like that's the right thing to do, unless we get some counseling and he gets some help. Part of me just hates him, you know? But there's a part of me that loves him too."

"You make it sound like you're the one divided into two parts, Maren. Look, I know you love him, but you hate his behavior. Who wouldn't?"

I nodded thoughtfully. "Yes, you're right. That's a pretty good description."

Ann leaned closer to me across the table and said quietly, "I've told you this before, Maren, but I see things like this a lot practicing family law. People who are unwilling to get counseling or seek help just don't change. It's sad, but they don't. Being the one to sue for divorce first does give you some advantages you know."

I just watched her, wishing that I wasn't having this conversation, that this wasn't the reality of my life.

"Maren, he's been like this your whole marriage. You've told me that."

When I still made no reply, she asked, "Do you honestly believe he'll change?"

"I believe he can," I said firmly.

"But do you believe he will?"

I closed my eyes and swallowed hard. "Not if we stay married, no."

Ann's eyes were sad. "Maren, your self-esteem is so low right now that you think you don't deserve anything, but you do. You deserve to be treated well. You deserve to be happy. You're the only one who can change your life. It sounds terrible to end a marriage, but it also sounds terrible to stay in a miserable one forever."

I felt a spark of anger. "You don't know what it's like, Ann. You can't possibly understand. You and Tyler have a perfect marriage."

Her eyes flew open wide. "You don't think Tyler and I have any problems?"

"Do you?" I asked bluntly, almost laughing.

"You know we do! I'm your best friend. We have plenty of disagreements—"

I interrupted her. "Oh, disagreements, sure. But you don't have any big problems."

"Except that we can't have children," she said quietly.

I felt sick. "Ann, you know I didn't mean *that!* I'm sorry. I can't imagine what that pain is like."

"I know you didn't mean that," she said. "And you're right, I don't know how it feels to be in your situation. We all have our trials I suppose."

I nodded.

"But, Maren, you could get out of yours," she insisted.

"I could divorce Ted, yes. But then I'd just be trading one set of trials for another. I'd be a single mom. I'd have to go to work. It's not like Ted would ever be completely out of my life. We have two children." Three, really. But Ted didn't acknowledge that. I paused before voicing my worst fear, "And I'd be alone forever."

"You won't be alone forever. You could get married again someday."

"Yeah, right," I laughed.

"Maren, you could."

"I'm not sure I'd ever want to try this again, Ann, even if that was an option," I admitted.

"Well, maybe after you had some time to heal, you'd change your mind. And why wouldn't it be an option?"

"I'm not eighteen anymore," I pointed out the obvious. "I got fat. Everything's drooping."

"You're not fat, Maren."

"Stress does wonders for your figure, I guess. Maybe I'm not fat anymore, but I'm not thin."

"You were never fat. You are thin. Have you looked in the mirror lately?"

I laughed. "Only when I have to."

"Yeah, well look closer. You might find yourself."

I raised my eyebrows at her.

"Really, Maren. You're very pretty."

"Now I know why you're my best friend," I joked.

"No one's paid me off, I promise. I do have some integrity you know." She grinned.

"You can afford to. Look at you." I waved a hand at her. "No wonder I feel insecure. Next to you, I'm just an old frumpy housewife."

Ann laughed out loud. "That will be the day!" She stood up and grabbed my arm, dragging me down the hall to my bedroom mirror. "Look at yourself," she ordered. I looked, trying not to cringe. "Your hair is that perfect flaxen blond color, the color most women can only dream about. You're not too tall and not too short. You have those fascinating pale blue eyes, high cheek bones, perfectly shaped lips, those long dancer's legs . . . and look at your figure, girl! Look at that waist! In what world are you fat?"

"Oh, Ann, stop it!" I said in disgust. "You're completely exaggerating."

She shook her head and insisted, "Maren, you need to get some confidence back. Maybe you'd feel better if you got your haircut updated, or bought some new clothes. Or both, what the heck? Why don't you come to the gym with me in the mornings? I keep trying to convince you that it makes me feel a lot better."

"Where would I find a babysitter at seven o'clock in the morning?" I asked seriously.

"They have daycare at the gym, silly. It's pretty cheap, I think. I know some of the moms volunteer there to get reduced membership. They just have this giant playroom for the kids. It looks like a lot of fun."

I felt something stir inside me. I thought it was about time that I did do something for myself. It couldn't hurt. "All right. You present a convincing case, counsel. I'll try it."

"Good," she laughed. "We'll start right away."

* * *

I had some money tucked away that Ted didn't know about. My great aunt had left it to me when she passed away. She'd never had children or grandchildren of her own, and I had been closer to her than anyone else. I'd only told Ted about half of it. We used that part for the down payment to get into our house. I felt bad about being less than honest with him, but my parents knew we had some problems by then, so they convinced me to put the other half in an investment account in case I needed it later.

Truthfully, I was afraid that I would need it someday. I always worried about Ted losing his job. It had happened before. He managed to stay more on top of things at work than I would have expected him to, but some times were worse than others. He'd go for months without problems, but then there would be bouts of too many late nights and too many hungover mornings that would eventually catch up with him and get him into trouble. Occasionally, I even worried that Ted might just take off one night and not come home. I decided that his behavior justified not telling him about the money, and even necessitated me saving it for the sake of my children.

It now looked like I might need the money to live on for a while, but I decided it was worth it to dip into the funds if it would help me feel better about myself. I got a babysitter on Saturday and went with Ann to go shopping, and to her stylist. I bought just a few things—

newer styles and classics that would go with what I already had. At the end of the day I looked in the mirror and couldn't believe what I saw. I actually saw a glimmer of my old self. My long blond hair was cut clear up to my shoulders, but it looked healthier and thicker that way. The new makeup I'd bought in more subtle tones made me look more natural. And it was such a relief to get out of the T-shirts and jeans that I'd taken to wearing lately and into some nicer clothes again. I pulled myself up to my full five and a half feet and looked into my clear blue eyes in the mirror. I looked so much better! I felt so much better. "Bless you," I said to Ann as I hugged her. I used those words so often with her that I wondered if they might wear out one day.

"My pleasure." She smiled back. "See? I knew you were in there somewhere."

We both laughed, although something in me wanted to cry. Where had I been? I wasn't even sure if I knew who I was anymore.

I couldn't help thinking of Ted again that night after the kids went to bed. He'd been gone a whole week and he hadn't even called. He'd never stayed away so long before. I had to admit that things were more peaceful without him around, but I still missed him. I wondered if he was using the time away from his family to think about things, or just to drink himself into oblivion. I hoped with everything in me that it was the former. I thought maybe if he saw my new look he'd want to make things work. "Oh, right, Maren," I said out loud to myself. "Or maybe he'd yell at you for spending money on yourself."

I heard Ann's voice in my head, playing back what she'd said earlier, "No one else will respect you until you respect yourself, Maren."

Ann called at six forty-five on Monday morning. "Ugh," I said when I answered the phone. I had barely managed to drag myself out of bed and get everyone dressed by then. Becca and Trevor were sitting at the counter sluggishly eating cereal, too tired even to complain.

"Don't worry. You'll get used to it," she said. "I'll meet you at the gym in ten minutes." She had to go straight to work, so we'd agreed to go in separate cars.

"Hurry up, Trev-Trev," I prodded. "We need to go." I hoped Ann was right, that I would get used to it.

After the first week it did get easier to get up. I even managed to get Rebecca's hair done most days before we left. The working out part was another story though. I watched Ann pumping weights with envy. "How do you do that?" I asked in awe.

"I just built up to it. You will too. Don't pay attention to what I'm doing. If you start watching everyone else, you'll give up before you even get started. Just do what you can and be thrilled with it. When you start to build up to heavier weights you'll feel great." I took her word for it as I huffed and puffed. After weights we walked on the treadmill. More accurately, I walked and she ran. I didn't think I'd ever get up to that. I thought no one would ever guess that I'd once spent hours a day in dance classes.

I kept going to the gym with Ann over the next few weeks and found that it did help my self-esteem. By April I'd lost ten pounds, and it felt wonderful.

I was getting used to the days without Ted by then, too. I filled them up with Rebecca and Trevor, working in the yard, keeping the house clean, and if there was ever any free time left, I usually filled it with a book.

Nighttime was the worst though. I felt the emptiness beside me creeping into my soul. My nightmare came back again and again. I was forever running in that dark tunnel, and no matter how hard I ran, the light at the end seemed to get farther and farther away. The dream sounded silly. I never would have told anyone about it during the day, but at night when that gray fog consumed me, it was terrifying. Some nights I tried to stay awake just to avoid it. The nightmare was so real for me, in fact, that when Ted finally called in the middle of the night, I almost let him come home just so I wouldn't be alone.

Ted agreed to keep paying the bills and giving me money for groceries, which was a big surprise as well as a relief. The money I had in savings wasn't enough to live on for more than a few months, and I didn't want to use it unless I absolutely had to. Ted said it would be better for the kids if I was with them, especially during the summer before Rebecca started kindergarten. It must have been the work of the Lord, because Ted had always resented my staying home. I told him I didn't want him to come home until he had a plan for overcoming his addiction, and some concrete evidence that he was working on it. I still thought we needed to go to marriage counseling together, but he said, "No way."

Still unwilling to admit that he even had a problem, he quit staying at his parents' house in American Fork and moved into an apartment closer to his job and to our house. He seemed to think that I would eventually get lonely and lost enough to back down. He was so close to right. I prayed constantly for strength to hold firm to what I believed was the right course of action. I loved Ted, and I wanted so much to see him get better and be the man I thought I'd married, but I could not go back to living with violence and alcoholism. I couldn't let myself do it.

The thought occurred to me that I could go to counseling by myself, even if Ted wouldn't go with me. I thought it might help me figure out how I'd gotten myself into this mess in the first place, and how to get out of it still intact. I asked Ann if she knew of a good counselor through her practice, and made an appointment.

Also in April, Ted told me that he wanted to take the children two weekends a month. I reluctantly agreed, wanting to handle things peacefully, but insisted that he not drink on those weekends. "Please take care of them, Ted."

"Of course I'll take care of them, Maren. They're my kids."

The first weekend with their father, Trevor and Rebecca were a little reluctant to go. It was difficult for me to send them, but they actually enjoyed themselves. I felt immensely relieved.

Chapter 5

The executive secretary called me and said the bishop would like to meet with me on a Tuesday night. When I sat down across from him, Bishop Rowley smiled and said, "Maren, we would like to call you to the position of Laurel advisor in the Young Women organization."

"Oh, no!" I blurted out. "I mean . . . I just don't know, Bishop."

"Do you need some time to think it over?"

"It's not that. It's just . . . Oh, all right, I'll just have to say it like it is. Bishop Rowley, I tried so hard to do everything the Lord asked me to do when I was a teenager. I went to church, read my scriptures, tried to uplift others. I never smoked or drank or ran with wild crowds. I certainly made my share of mistakes, but I did my best to follow the commandments and the counsel of the Church. I married a returned missionary in the temple, and here I am—married to an alcoholic, on the brink of divorce. I might as well have done whatever I wanted to when I was younger. Things couldn't be worse.

"I think all the time about those Young Women leaders that I had, who kept telling me how wonderful their marriages and their lives were. They said that if I did what was right, even if we had problems, we'd overcome them together if I just got married in the temple. They never told me that I could still end up as a single mom, alone. I can't fill those girls full of false hope. The illusion has been completely shattered for me."

Bishop Rowley nodded. "As far as false hope is concerned, I don't believe in preaching it. Maybe you can actually offer a different perspective. For instance, about not following the gospel, do you really believe that? Do you think you would be happier, or even that you couldn't be more miserable, if you were making choices not consistent with what God asks of us?"

I thought carefully about my life, my children. Even my marriage had not been all bad. There had been good times. I had to admit that I had been very blessed for my obedience, both before my marriage and after. If Ted had not chosen to start drinking, or even if he was willing to get help, maybe we would be working on things together. "No. I guess things would just be worse," I admitted. "Much worse."

"You know, Maren, Ted has his agency, and so do you. God won't change that. That's what this whole life is based on."

I nodded.

"As for this calling, it has been prayerfully considered by the Young Women presidency, and by myself. We feel strongly that this is where the Lord wants you. If you feel you can't do it, though, I understand. You have a lot on your plate right now."

"I'll do it," I decided. "I need all the blessings I can get."

He laughed. "You know you're going to be all right, don't you?" There was a firmness in his tone that made me almost believe him.

"I'm hoping."

The bishop told me that they were planning a river run for the young men and young women in July, and hoped there was some way that I could go. However, he said not to worry if I couldn't. I didn't know how I possibly could.

My first week teaching the sixteen- and seventeen-year-old girls went more smoothly than I had expected. They were actually quite friendly and welcoming. I decided that maybe by sixteen the girls were a little more secure with who they were. It seemed like the years between twelve and fourteen were harder. They had been for me anyway.

Christine Allen seemed to be the kind of unspoken leader of the group. I'd known her since we moved in, though not well. She was clean-cut, kind, and knew all the right answers. The only girl of the eight I taught that really worried me was Abby Gillis. Just looking at her concerned me. She wore thick black eyeliner that drowned her pretty gray eyes. Her dark brown hair had harsh bleached streaks all through it, and her deep purple lipstick made her young skin look even more pale. She didn't really give me any trouble, though her posture reeked of attitude. She asked a lot of questions, but didn't answer any. I thought she probably just asked them to see if she could catch me off guard.

From the first week I taught them the girls were already talking excitedly about the river run. They couldn't wait. I decided I'd better let them know right off that I wouldn't be going with them. "What?" Lindsey exclaimed. "You have to go! You're our leader!"

"Why would you want to miss it?" asked Karli.

"Look, you guys, she has little kids. She probably has her hands full," Christine defended me.

Abby looked me straight in the eye and said, "Yeah, obviously."

For some reason she hit a nerve. I had accepted this calling. These girls were my responsibility. So, Ted wasn't around. Maybe there was something else I could do. I vowed silently to try and work things out so that I could go. I suddenly wanted very much to earn the trust of these young women.

I left my children with Ann one evening later in the week to go to my first counseling appointment. The counselor was very friendly and non-threatening, much different than what I'd expected. He told me that people who stay with addicts in abusive relationships often lose themselves in the other person. Their whole life centers around that person and their behavior, sometimes to the point where they actually become "addicted" to the addict. The result, he told me, is that the addict has total control of the situation. They never have to deal with any consequences of their actions because the other person walks on eggshells around them, accepts blame, or buffers them from the logical effects of their behavior. It often turns into a very unhealthy cycle, he said. I could attest to that.

"So, what do I do?" I asked him.

He smiled and said, "Exactly what you're doing. You break out of the cycle. You get away from the addict if they won't get help, and leave them to deal with the consequences of their actions by themselves. Sometimes that's enough to shock them into seeking help, and sometimes it's not. But that's out of your control. You take care of what is within your control, yourself and your children. You start to do things you like to do again, find yourself, remember who you were before you got married. You stand up for yourself. You go to counseling if you need to for support, and to gain insight into yourself. You get healthy so you can model healthy adult behavior for your children, and be the stable person in their lives. And you do it one step at a time. It's a process."

"Actually, that all makes a lot of sense," I told him. "I think I can do that."

"I think you can too." He smiled.

* * *

When Ted came to get the children in the middle of April he said, "It's been a month. We need to decide what we're going to do."

"I need some more time, Ted," I admitted quietly, but my stomach began to churn.

"Look, Maren, I'm not going to keep staying away from my family, paying rent, and paying a house payment too. This is completely unfair to me. I'm tired of playing your little game."

"It's not a game, Ted." I wished that I could have dismissed the whole thing so trivially.

"Are you going to let me come home or not?" he demanded.

I remembered to stand up for myself, to hold firmly to what I'd said. "Are you getting any help yet?" I asked quietly.

"Help for what?" he said. "Are you getting any help?"

I sighed. "Actually, Ted, I am, and I don't think this is going to work anymore." I felt hollow. I wanted to cry, but I was just too numb.

As I said it, Ted directed the children toward the car, then surprised me with, "Then I'm moving on. I'm done paying you. You can take care of yourself."

"Ted, I have the kids! You know there's no way I can keep the house even if I work full time, and I'll have to leave them all day—"

"Bummer, baby." He smiled and shut the door in my face. I ran out after him, not wanting to make a scene in front of Rebecca and Trevor, but feeling frantic.

"Ted, wait!" I grabbed his jacket sleeve. "Please. They're your children, too. They need a house. If we lose this house, I'll never get another one."

"Yeah, well, you seem to think you can replace me. Maybe you can find a new man to get you a house."

"Ted, this is not fair! If you would just stop drinking—"

He blew up. "No one could live with you and *not* drink, Maren! *No one!*" He squealed out of the driveway and I felt terrified that he had the children.

Why did I have to make him mad before he took them? I thought. *Why?* I called his apartment and left a message, "Ted, I'm sorry. I know you're mad. Please just don't take it out on the kids. If you can't handle it this weekend, I'll come and get them. You know you can't take care of them if you drink. Please."

He didn't call back. I tried to call a few more times, but there was no answer. Finally at ten o'clock, Rebecca answered the phone. "Hello?" she whispered.

"Hi, baby, it's Mommy. Is everything all right?" I asked, trying not to sound as worried as I was. I knew all too well how Ted reacted to stress.

"Mommy, I'm scared," she admitted. "Daddy's acting that funny way again."

"Let me talk to him," I said firmly.

"No, he'll get mad. He told me I couldn't answer the phone."

"Okay, Becca Bug. You just take care of Trevor for a few minutes, and I'll get there as fast as I can."

"Okay," she said softly. I could tell she was trying not to cry.

I drove as fast as I could to Ted's apartment and banged on the door. He threw it open. "What do you think you're doing here?" he slurred.

"Ted, you're drunk. I can't leave the kids with you when you're like this."

"The kids are asleep." He held his arm across the doorway to keep me from going in.

I yelled inside to them, "Rebecca! Trevor! Come out here!"

They both came running, calling, "Mommy!" I could tell they were scared. I'd tried to keep them from ever seeing Ted like that. When he'd come home drunk it was usually late and they were in bed. The few times they had seen him, they had been confused and afraid.

"It is *my* weekend, and you are not taking *my* kids!" Ted barked at me.

They both started to cry. "Please, Daddy. Please let us go," Rebecca pleaded with him.

"I don't want to stay with you when you're mean!" Trevor said.

"You'd try to turn my own kids against me?" he spat at me.

"Please, Ted, let them go. You can take them when you can stay sober long enough to take care of them."

He looked down at their crying faces, but then turned fiery eyes on me. "You can't just come over here and take them away," he hissed.

I couldn't believe that I wanted to cry and beg him. The whole thing was ridiculous. I told myself to model healthy adult behavior. I had to be strong. I could not, I *would* not leave my children there under such circumstances.

I reached under his arm and grabbed both of them. "Go get in the car," I instructed. Rebecca took Trevor's hand and they ran fast for the car. Then I turned to Ted and pulled myself up to face him. "Ted, I am taking the children home with me. They do not have to put up with this, and neither do I. You terrify them, can't you see that?"

"That's your fault. You teach them to hate me," he said bitterly.

"No, Ted, I do not. You are their father." Then I softened a little. He looked so pathetic. "Can't you see that they love you? We all love you, Ted. You're the one who doesn't love yourself. This is what I cannot live with." I waved my arm at his whole drunken self. "This is what your children cannot be exposed to. If you want to ruin your own life on your own time, you go ahead. But if you want to see your children, you *cannot* drink when you have them."

He opened his mouth, but the alcohol oozing through his brain blocked his words so that he couldn't grasp them in time. I walked away quickly.

When we were safely at home with the doors locked and bolted, I decided I had to tell my little children the truth. "Daddy is addicted to alcohol," I said simply. "That means his mind and his body want to drink things that are bad for him, and that make him behave differently than he normally would."

"You mean like beer?" Rebecca asked. We'd talked a little bit about the Word of Wisdom and things that are bad for your body before.

"Yes," I said.

"And that's why Daddy acts scary sometimes?" Trevor wondered aloud.

"Yes. I love Daddy and I want him to get some help for his problem, but he doesn't want to. That's why he can't live with us right now."

"Is he ever coming back?" Trevor asked.

"Honey, Daddy and I are going to get a divorce," I admitted the inevitable truth to them and to myself. "He will still be your dad, and he still loves you. He wants to spend time with you, but I won't let him take you when he's drunk."

"You mean when he drinks beer?"

"Yes, Rebecca."

"That scares me," she confessed.

I answered her, "Me too. That's why I won't let you be around it. I'll take care of you, I promise."

"Mommy?" Rebecca asked.

"What, honey?"

"How come Daddy says it's all your fault whenever you guys fight? Is it all your fault?"

"Do you think all of our problems are my fault, Becca?"

She thought about it for a minute and then said, "No. Daddy's a lot meaner than you are, and he always makes you cry."

"I've made many mistakes, you two. I'm not telling you that everything is Daddy's fault. But it is *not* my fault that he started drinking alcohol, or that he keeps drinking it. It's not my fault that he gets so mean and scary sometimes. And it's not my fault that he doesn't get help for his problems. He decides what he's going to do, not me. I'm not completely sure why he blames me for everything. I guess it's because he knows he's doing something wrong, but he doesn't want to change it. I think he doesn't want to take responsibility for the mistakes he's made, so he blames them on me instead. It's hard to admit when you've done something wrong, especially if what you've done has hurt other people. But that's the right thing to do. You take responsibility for your own choices, and do your best to fix your mistakes, or at least to learn from them. You both need to know that none of this is your fault either. Do you know that?"

They both looked at me and nodded slowly, but I felt a need to reaffirm what I'd just told them. "It's very important that you understand that, Rebecca and Trevor. None of this has anything to do with you. It's not your fault that Daddy drinks. It's not your fault that we fight, or that I cry. It's not your fault that we're getting divorced. The two of you are the most wonderful thing that ever happened to

Daddy or me. Don't ever forget that."

"Okay, Mom," Rebecca answered.

Trevor echoed, "Okay."

I kissed them both and said, "Now let's get you two in bed, and we can talk some more in the morning if you want to." They were so exhausted that they fell asleep almost immediately.

Chapter 6

On Saturday morning I called Ann. "What do I have to do to file for divorce?"

"I'll be right over," she said. I sent the kids downstairs to play and we sat down at the kitchen table.

"There's no legal way to keep him from drinking, even around the kids." She shook her head after she'd heard about the previous night. "You could try to get a restraining order against him to keep him away from both you and the children, but you'd have to convince a judge that he's a threat."

"I can't do that." I rubbed my temples with my fingers, trying to stop the throbbing.

"Are you sure, Maren?" she asked. "He sounds like a threat to me."

"I'm sure."

"Well then, let's write up what we propose as far as division of property and finances go. Then we'll put down visitation as you've both already agreed to it, but I'll make it known to his attorney what action we'll take if he endangers the children by getting drunk when he has them."

"He's never done it before," I said. "I made him mad."

"You *made* him mad? Give me a break, Maren. You are not responsible for his behavior, but you are responsible for your own. You have to stand up for yourself and take care of these kids."

I nodded. "You're right."

She smiled a soft smile and her eyes were moist. "I'm so sorry you have to go through this, but I think you're doing the best thing for you and your children by filing."

Her empathy choked me up. I couldn't say anything. I just prayed that she was right.

It didn't take long to fill out the forms. Ted and I didn't have much to divide up. We proposed that I would keep my car, the house, and its contents. He would pay child support and minimal alimony. He would still take the children two weekends a month, and we'd alternate holidays. He would keep his car, his tools, his stereo, and all his personal things. We tried to make it as reasonable as possible so he would accept it without a fight.

"Even if he goes for this, I'm not sure if I can make it financially," I said. I could probably scrape by on the bills and groceries, but there would be nothing extra for things like clothes, birthdays, car repairs, doctor bills, and any number of things that could come up. I had my savings, but if I started using it regularly, that money would quickly disappear.

"Don't you have a degree?" Ann asked.

"Yes, in interior design, but I never worked after college. I've always stayed home. I guess I could go back to work, but I don't want to leave my children with everything else they're going through right now."

"I don't blame you," she said. "Don't worry, Maren. We'll figure something out. Tyler and I can help you if you need it."

"That's very generous of you." I smiled at her. "But that wouldn't be right. I need to find a way to do this on my own."

"All the same, I mean it. I don't want to see you going hungry or anything."

"Thank you so much for all you've done for me already," I said sincerely. "You're the best friend in the world. Someday maybe I'll be able to repay you somehow."

"You already do," she smiled. "You're my best friend too, you know. Let me borrow your kids a few nights while you do something for yourself, and we'll consider your debt paid."

"You're doing your math backwards again, Ann. I have to pay the babysitter, not the other way around. That would put me impossibly further in your debt."

Her answer was serious. "There is nothing more wonderful than the sound of little voices and tiny feet in my house, Maren. Borrowing your children is as close as I can get to motherhood right now. I consider it a great blessing that you're willing to share your children with me, and so does Tyler."

I laughed. "I'll bet he does."

She laughed too. "Oh, he loves it and he knows it. He just complains to get attention."

I called my family later in the day to tell them that I had filed for divorce. "Come home, honey," my mom told me. "Let us help you with the children so you won't have to work."

"Thank you . . . but I don't have to work right now," I said. "And I want to stay here in our home. I don't want Trevor and Becca having to make any more big changes right now. This is where we belong."

They told me they were sorry, but relieved that I was finally getting out of a bad situation. They said they'd be praying for me and asked if I needed anything. I told them about my new calling and the upcoming river run. They said they'd be happy to have the children come and stay with them while I went. It was the perfect solution. Rebecca and Trevor would love spending a few days with their grand-parents, and I could fulfill my obligation to my Laurels.

* * *

When I came home from the grocery store later in the week, Ted's car was in the driveway. I left again and took the children to the library, but when we got back, his car was still there. "Hey, do you two want to go visit Ann and Tyler for a while?" I asked Trevor and Rebecca.

"Yeah!" they said in unison. I parked in front of Ann's house and we rang the doorbell.

When she answered, they smiled up at her and I said brightly, "Would you mind if the kids stayed here for a few minutes?" I jerked my head toward my driveway, indicating my dilemma. I didn't want the kids to know that Ted was there, and they thankfully hadn't noticed his car.

"Of course not!" Ann said. "Tyler's in the kitchen. Why don't you guys go ask him for a cookie?"

They scampered into the kitchen and Ann whispered to me, "What do you think he wants?"

"I don't know. Do you think he got the divorce papers?"

"No," she said. "It's too soon. Why don't you just stay here until he leaves?"

"I already left and came back once. I don't think he plans on leaving. I'm going to have to talk to him."

"Let me come with you then," she offered.

"No, I'll be fine."

"Do you want me to send Tyler over instead?"

I shook my head. "If he thinks I'm afraid, he'll only get worse. I'll be back in a few minutes."

"Okay. Be careful." She looked worried.

"Ann, it's not that big of a deal. I'm just going to tell him he has to leave again, that's all. Don't worry."

"Yeah, right. If you're not back in ten minutes, I'm sending Tyler over."

"Give me an hour. It might take that long. Maybe he just wants to talk. He's fine when he's not drunk, you know. It's not like he's some kind of monster."

"Whatever you say, Maren," she answered sarcastically.

I gave her a dirty look and walked across the street in the fading dusk. Ted was in the great room. "It's about time," he said.

"Time for what?" I asked. I couldn't tell if he was drunk or not. The room was dark and Ted was sitting down.

"Time you showed up. Where have you been?"

I sighed, wishing that I could just disappear. "I've been at the grocery store and the library."

"For three hours?"

I felt unnerved that he'd been waiting there that long. "It takes a while when you have two kids with you, Ted."

"Where are the kids?" he demanded.

I wondered whether or not I should tell him. "I left them with Ann and Tyler," I finally said.

"Why?" I heard the slight slur in his words at the same moment that I noticed the empty liquor bottle next to his chair. My heart sank. He'd never brought the stuff into our home before.

"Because I didn't think they needed to see this. It will only confuse them to see you here and then have you leave again."

"I'm not leaving," he said calmly.

"Ted, this is just not going to work. Please don't make it any harder than it has to be."

"You're the one making it hard, Maren. You're the one telling me I can't even come home to my own house. Why don't *you* leave?"

"You know why, Ted. If it was just me, I'd leave right now, but it's not. I have the kids. They need a house. They need some security."

"How secure can they feel when their own mother won't let their father see them?"

"You can see them if you can stay sober." I tried to make myself stay calm. Getting emotional in front of Ted when he was drunk was like bleeding in shark-infested waters.

Ted sprang out of the chair and grabbed hold of my arms. "Who do you think you are, Maren?" he yelled. "You can't tell me when I can see my kids. You can't tell me what I can drink. You can't tell me what to do. You can't tell me *anything.*" His words were slow and laced with venom. He pushed his face into mine and shook me. "You got it, baby?" He grinned his evil grin at me.

"Ted, please just go," I pleaded. "Please."

He threw me against the wall and I tried not to moan at the pain that shot through my shoulder. "Make me!" he hollered. That demonic green fire shot from his eyes and I wished that he was dead. Then I chastised myself for thinking something so awful again. I felt suddenly sure that I'd done the right thing in filing for divorce, but I was terrified of what he would do when he found out about that.

I stood up and said firmly, "Ted, I'm warning you. Leave me alone."

"Warning me?" He laughed out loud and then came to put his face only inches from mine. "Oh, Maren, that is precious." He grinned and then his lips curled into a snarl as he leaned down to look me straight in the eye. "I don't think you're in a position to *warn* me about anything."

"You can't push me around, Ted." I attempted to swallow my fear. "I'll call the police." I tried to move, but he blocked me. He didn't touch me, but he kept his body only inches from mine.

"And what are you going to tell them?" he hissed. "That I'm breaking the Word of Wisdom? I'm not even touching you, Maren . . ." He curled his hand into a fist and held it up to my face. "But I could, if you want me to."

"Go ahead!" I screamed, losing all the composure I'd fought to hold onto. "Go ahead and punch me out, Ted! Would that make you feel manly enough—decking your wife?"

He jerked his fist and I flinched, making him laugh again. "Wouldn't you just love that?" he said. "Then you could bawl over your black eye and file your little police report to hold over my head."

I stared at him, praying that he would leave, praying for help. I didn't know why it struck me with such fresh horror every time, but with every confrontation I felt shocked. I could not believe that this was Ted, that this was my life.

Ted twirled a piece of my hair around his finger and hissed in my ear, "Do you think I'm *stupid*, Maren?" He pulled back just enough to look me in the eye, obviously expecting an answer.

I shook my head. "No, of course not, Ted." My mind was racing. How could I possibly stand up for myself in this situation? He could kill me if he wanted to, and when he was like this, I was afraid that he might.

"You're so pathetic, Maren," he said. "Such a worthless . . . I don't know why I even concern myself with you."

"Neither do I. Maybe you shouldn't," I answered.

He took a step back and watched me with amusement, as though triumphing in my loss of self. I finally said, "All right, Ted. You stay. I'll leave."

"Oh, nice try, Maren. Sorry, but I can't do that now. You had your chance. You blew it." I watched him move to the doorway and fold his arms across his chest. I thought of trying to get out the back door, or through the kitchen, but I knew I'd never make it. He'd catch me. It would only make things worse.

Ted picked up a flower arrangement from the foyer table. "How much did this cost me?" he sneered. He tossed it on the ground and stepped on it, crushing the dried flowers into the carpet. Then he moved toward me. He stopped at the coffee table, looking down at an arrangement of square candles nesting in a pebble-strewn tray. "Oh, I *love* what you've done with *this,*" he said in a mocking tone. With a sweep of his arm, he knocked candles, pebbles, and magazines to the floor. Then he picked up the table and threw it at the ground with surprising force. It smashed and splintered into a terrible mess.

I watched in horror as Ted went on a rampage, throwing bar stools and couch cushions, tipping over tables, and smashing anything he could get his hands on. "Ted, stop it!" I finally yelled at him, fearing he'd destroy the entire house.

He lunged toward me and hollered in my face, "I paid for *everything* in this house, Maren! It's *mine*—all of it. And you think *you* have the right to tell *me* I can't live here? I am *tired* of breaking my back ten hours a day so you can lounge around here and enjoy *my* house!" He shoved me away and moved to block the front door again.

I was gripped with terror. We hadn't had such a terrible confrontation in several months. I thought of apologizing. If I told him how sorry I was and cried and begged long enough, he sometimes softened. I couldn't bring myself to do it, though. I hated what I'd let myself become. I'd let Ted suck out my self-esteem like some kind of blood-thirsty leech, thinking that someday he'd decide that it was enough. Someday, I kept hoping, he would come to realize that I'd sacrificed my entire self for our marriage—for him—and then he would appreciate it. I had hoped that maybe it would even make him change. I thought about what the counselor had told me about becoming so absorbed in Ted that I'd lost myself, that I had unintentionally made it easier for him to be an alcoholic and not face the consequences of his behavior.

I looked at the man I'd married, blocking the doorway with a frame I could never compete with physically. He had the same sandy hair he'd always had, but it hung in a disheveled mess, casting shadows over his face. The gray-green eyes that had once seemed so full of life and determination sparked with hatred. The bright mind I'd so admired—all that drive and vision—was slowly rotting away, drowning in dose after dose of alcohol. For ten years I'd been waiting for him to find himself again, hoping that he'd tap back into that inner light and be who he was meant to be. But I could see who he was then, who he kept choosing to be, and it sickened me. I had to face it. The man in front of me wasn't the man I'd married at all. The man I'd married was lost deep in a sea of bad choices. To me, he was irretrievable. It would take a hand much more powerful than mine to pull him from the path he'd chosen, and he was going to have to turn around and reach for it himself.

I began to realize that the more I had let Ted take from me, the more he had continued to demand. As I slowly lost my own identity, I seemed to have blurred into an object for him. He no longer saw me as an individual, a human being; certainly not as a person of worth. The more I hated myself, the more he hated me. Perhaps Ted would continue to hate me, but I was tired of hating myself. I'd been waiting all this time for him to change. I decided it was time I changed myself. Ted took a step back, teetering on his heels. He grabbed the doorknob to steady himself. I took the opportunity to run around the bar and grab the kitchen phone. I dialed 911 as quickly as I could.

"Put the phone down, Maren," Ted warned. When I didn't comply, he came toward me and said, "Put it down, or you'll be sorry." He yanked it from my grasp just as the dispatcher answered. Ted's face was filled with fury. He knew from past experience that if I hung up once they'd answered, the police would show up. I'd called them only a handful of times, and I'd always regretted it later. That time was going to be different though. He was leaving, and he wasn't coming home.

Ted covered the receiver with one hand and ordered, "Tell them everything's fine, that it was a mistake. Tell them one of the kids dialed."

He held out the phone and I took it with shaking hands. "Hello?" the voice on the other end said again.

"Hello . . ." I stammered. I struggled with what to say. I was terrified of Ted. I wanted him out of there. But I knew that he could do a lot of damage in the time it took for the police to arrive. I was grateful, at least, that the children were safe at Ann's house.

"Is there a problem, ma'am?" the feminine voice asked.

"Um . . ." Ted slid icy fingers around my upper arm and squeezed. He squeezed so hard that I wanted to cry out in pain, but I bit my lip instead. "No," I finally managed to say. "One of the children dialed . . . Sorry for the inconvenience."

"Are you in trouble, ma'am?" the woman asked again.

"Yes, that's right," I answered, hoping that Ted couldn't hear her.

"I'll send someone out right away."

"All right."

"Can you stay on the phone with me until the officers arrive?"

"No, but thank you." I hung up quickly.

Ted narrowed suspicious eyes at me. "Did they believe you?"

I nodded slowly.

He shook me and said close to my face, "You'd better not be trying to pull something over on me." I nearly swooned from the horrible stench of alcohol on his breath. He dragged me down the hall and shoved me down on our bed. "Stay there," he ordered. Then he wobbled out of the room.

I heard the knock on the door a few minutes later. Ted cursed loudly from the kitchen and the knock came again. I heard Ted open the door, probably realizing that he had no choice. Refusing to answer would likely only have made things worse for him. I forced myself to stand on shaky legs and move down the hall.

I could see the two police officers standing on the front porch before they saw me. "We got a call from this residence. Is there a problem, sir?" The heavyset officer with the blond mustache spoke.

Ted chuckled easily and answered, "No, I'm afraid there's been a mistake. It was just the kids playing on the phone. Thanks for stopping by though." I was amazed at how smoothly he could speak, how calm he could appear, even when he was drunk.

The second officer was taller and more muscular than the first. He leaned close to Ted and asked, "Have you been drinking, sir?"

"Yeah, I had a few beers."

The officer looked inside and saw me a few feet away. "Are you all right, ma'am?"

Ted shot me a warning look. I nodded at the policeman.

He looked toward Ted and said, "Why don't you step outside with me, sir? I'd like to have a word with you."

"About what?" Ted asked nonchalantly. "I wasn't driving or anything." I knew that was a lie too. He'd driven to our house.

"Just step outside with me please."

Ted reluctantly followed. The other officer came inside to talk to me. He let out a long breath that whistled through the gap in his front teeth when he saw the state of disarray that the room was in. "Did he do all this?" he asked me.

I hesitated, but then nodded. He picked up the empty liquor bottle and looked at the label before he put me through the old familiar drill: Name, date of birth, age. How long had we been married? Were there children in the home? What happened? How long had all this been going on? How often did Ted drink? Was he always like this when he drank? How was he when he was sober? They were aware of Ted's previous domestic violence reports . . . et cetera, et cetera. The whole thing was degrading, humiliating. I prayed that the neighbors wouldn't see the police car.

When the officer finished his report he said quietly, "You know, lady, you don't need this."

I could only look at him numbly and think that I certainly didn't.

They told me they had to take Ted in because he was drunk. They thought that I could be in possible danger if he stayed around that way, and they couldn't make him drive home while he was intoxicated. They said they'd keep him overnight and let him sober up. I felt sick at the thought of Ted going to jail. That had never happened before. I asked them not to take him, but they said they had no choice. I felt terrified and relieved and guilty all at once.

Ted cussed a blue streak at me as they handcuffed him and led him to the police car. I wondered what would come of the whole ordeal. The blond officer walked back to talk to me before they left. "You ever think about filin' for divorce, ma'am?"

"I already have," I admitted quietly.

"Good for you," he answered gruffly. "That takes a lot of guts." He nodded and moved to go, but then turned back and said, "You might want to think about changin' your locks, too."

I nodded and watched them drive away. I called Ann to fill her in and then found a locksmith willing to come that night for an outrageous fee. I cleaned up the disaster Ted had made while he changed the locks. Then I wrote him a check and made a mental note to transfer money from my savings account the next morning.

I had trouble sleeping for days, and I was constantly looking over my shoulder, but amazingly Ted never came back to give me grief. Ann changed the divorce paperwork to say that I wanted full custody with no visitation rights.

"He'll fight it," I told her.

She grinned broadly. "Won't that be fun?"

Despite the anguish of my situation, I couldn't help smiling at her. "You're awful," I said.

"No, I'm not. I'm a lawyer. This is what I live for. It's a rush—you'll see."

"Ann, I don't think this is going to be a rush for me," I said seriously. "I have no desire to see Ted hurting any more than he already is. I would love to settle this peacefully. But I have to think about Rebecca and Trevor." . . . *And Ashlyn*, the words always echoed in my mind. At least she was safe.

Ann's look turned sorrowful. "I know it won't, Maren. I know this whole thing is devastating and awful. It's not funny at all. You know me. I'd rather scoff at painful things than acknowledge them."

"I know."

Later on I went to another counseling appointment and talked about my feelings of grief and loss, and how to deal with them. We also discussed how I could help my children through those feelings. I realized that it felt good to stand up for myself, even though the circumstances were painful and downright frightening at times.

Ted finally called, after he'd seen the divorce paperwork. I braced myself, but his voice sounded relatively calm. "Maren, what are you doing?"

"Trying to take care of myself and my children."

"Come on, Maren. You don't want to do this." I was surprised that he was trying to sound so sweet. I had expected a lot of yelling and a long list of threats.

I sighed. "I feel like it's the only option under the circumstances, Ted. I'm sorry." I was sorry, very sorry. I wished that it could be different.

"You know there's no way I'm agreeing to this," he said.

"Why not?"

"I'm not giving up my kids."

"Then find someone to supervise your visitation, Ted. I can't let them go with you alone."

He surprised me again by switching topics instead of arguing about the kids. "Why should I give you the house?"

I was so tired of playing his games. "Look, Ted, I'm trying to settle this peacefully so we can get through it quickly and get on with our lives. I don't want to spend thousands of dollars fighting in court, and I don't want to drag the kids through a long battle. I think it's a reasonable proposal."

"How will you stay in the house if you agree to this payment schedule anyway?" he asked. "Where are you going to work?"

"That's my concern, Ted. I'm done arguing. I hope you get your life together. I honestly do. Sign it or don't. You think about it." I hung up.

Chapter 7

"What am I going to do, Ann?" I was picking up toys off the great room floor when she came over on Saturday morning. "Rebecca! Trevor!" I called down the hall. "Will you two get out here and help clean up? I've asked you three times!" Then I continued to plead my case to Ann. "I have to figure out some way to make money without leaving my kids all day. I went over my budget, and there's just no way I can make it without doing something."

Ann started wiping off my kitchen counter, cleaning up the breakfast mess. "Will you cut it out?" I said. "You make me feel like I can't keep up with everything."

"I know you can. You always do. But I'm just standing here talking to you. I might as well be doing something."

I raised my eyebrows at her. "Did you clean up the breakfast mess at your house before you came over here?"

She grinned at me. "You know me too well."

"What are you doing cleaning my house then?" I asked.

She shrugged. "It doesn't bother me if my house isn't perfectly tidy. You're the one who's nutso that way. You'll never sit down and relax until this is done, so I might as well move the process along."

I shook my head in disgust and she added, "Besides, the mess doesn't multiply at my house. If *you* don't keep moving, you'll never recover with those two around here." She nodded her head toward the hall where my children had finally appeared.

"Hi, Ann!" Rebecca greeted.

"Good morning, sweetie. How are you?"

"Fine." Her smile melted into a pout. "Except that Mom keeps making me clean up Trevor's messes."

"Nuh-uh!" Trevor protested, smacking her on the arm. "They're *your* messes!"

Ann smiled at them. "Hey, you guys. I have gum in my purse. If you hurry and clean up, I'll give you a piece."

"Oh, good," I said. "Bribe them. That'll teach them to be responsible."

"Hey, I can get away with it. I'm not the mom."

"Yeah, you're a lot nicer than 'the mom'!" Becca giggled.

"You'd better watch it, sweetie," I told her. "I'll send you to live with her."

"Yay!" she said.

"What a surprise," I remarked to Ann. "Speaking of giving you my kids, could you watch them next Thursday night for an hour or so? I have a meeting for the Young Men's and Young Women's leaders."

"I'd love to."

"Thank you." I lowered my voice. "I don't quite dare to leave them home with a teenager yet, just in case Ted comes around."

"I know." She smiled sympathetically. She doled out the promised treat and then sat down on the couch when Rebecca and Trevor went outside to play. I watched them wistfully through the French doors, wondering what Ashlyn would have looked like that day. I always pictured her with long blond hair, like Rebecca's. Maybe she would have had blue eyes like mine. She would have been eight years old by then, almost eight and a half . . .

"So, what have you thought about doing?" Ann's voice brought me back to the room.

"What?" I asked her.

"You said earlier that you were trying to think of a way to earn money without leaving the kids."

"Oh. So far I haven't come up with anything."

"Maybe I could help with them if you got a job at night," she offered.

"Thank you," I said sincerely. "But that wouldn't be much of a life for any of us."

"How about doing that scrapbook party thing? You like that."

I shook my head. "That's too unreliable. Besides, I like working on my children's scrapbooks, but I don't think I'd like trying to sell things to other people."

We both sat quietly thinking.

"Hey, what about babysitting?" she suggested. "If you did daycare, you wouldn't have to leave Becca and Trevor at all."

"Who would I babysit? Most of the moms in our ward stay home . . . don't they?" I figured she would know. She was the Relief Society secretary. She knew everything.

"Actually, someone asked me if anyone in the ward did daycare just a couple of days ago. That's what made me think about it. Some guy called me who just moved in."

"Some guy?"

"Yeah. He's divorced. He has the kids I guess. That's a little strange, isn't it?" She suddenly gave me a mischievous grin and said, "I haven't met him, but I hear he's drop-dead gorgeous."

"So, what if he is?"

"So . . . you're getting divorced . . ."

I felt a spark of anger. "But I'm not divorced yet."

"I know!" she said defensively. "Calm down, Maren. I wasn't telling you to go running after him today, but you do have a future to think about at some point."

"A future alone," I snapped. Then I pointed a finger at her and said, "Don't go getting any matchmaking ideas that involve me in any way, even after I *am* divorced. I have children to take care of, and . . . stuff to do."

"What stuff?" She was trying not to laugh.

I slugged her on the arm, but the anger diffused. I admitted the truth, "I love Ted, Ann. I can't live with him, but I love him. I have a whole lot of grief to deal with here, and then . . . well, I don't need a bunch of nonsense fairy tales clouding my brain. It wouldn't do anyone any good, especially me. I don't believe in that stuff anymore. Besides, there are a lot more important things than looks. If this guy's that attractive, he's probably a conceited creep."

"He can't be too big a creep if he has the kids," she pointed out.

"Maybe. Either way, it's irrelevant."

"But you told me yourself that you were afraid of being alone forever."

"And that's a fear I'll have to face, I guess. I don't need a man to make me happy. I've got to figure out how to find happiness by myself."

"Wow. Now that's the most sense you've made in a long time." She smiled. "So what about the babysitting thing?"

"I'll have to think about it. What's this guy's name?"

"I don't know. Brother . . . something."

I laughed. "You are one on-top-of-it secretary, aren't you?" I teased.

She held her hands up. "Give me a second. It'll come to me. Brother . . . It starts with a *J*. Johnson? No . . . Jensen, I think. Brother Jensen. Yeah, that sounds right."

"How old are his kids?"

"I don't know. Sorry. I didn't ask."

"You can give him my number, I guess. I could meet them. I can always say no."

She grinned broadly. "Are you sure about that? I know how good you are at saying 'no.' Didn't you win the 'people pleaser of the year' award recently?"

"Oh, shut up!" I snapped. "I'm a new woman. It will be good practice for me. I'd love to tell someone no, just to see how it feels."

She laughed.

* * *

"Have you guys seen the phone?" I asked my children who were planted in front of the television set.

"Nope," they muttered in unison.

I sighed. I'd been looking for it all morning, but to no avail. By the time I found it, I figured the battery would be dead and I'd have to charge it all over again anyway. I was looking under the couch for the third time when I heard it ringing and found it stuffed between the cushions. I pushed the button and said, "Hello?" The battery wasn't dead yet, but it was close. The static was terrible.

"Sister Saunders?" The masculine voice sounded raspy over the phone line.

"Yes, this is Maren."

"This is . . ." There was so much interference I couldn't tell what he was saying.

I put a hand over my free ear, trying to drown out the noise of the television. "What? I'm sorry. I can't hear you very well."

"This is . . ." I struggled to make out what he was saying. Did he say Jensen? Somebody Jensen?

"Oh!" I remembered where I'd heard that recently. "You need a babysitter, right?"

"Yes, that's right."

I asked him if he'd like to bring his children over to meet me and we could see what we thought after that. The voice was still unbearably gravelly. I wondered if I sounded that awful to him. I gave him my address and said, "Could you come around five o'clock?"

"That would be fine."

"What day is good for you?"

"How about the sixteenth?" he asked, just as the phone let out a long beep.

"I'm sorry, but my phone's going to die. The sixteenth would be great. See you—" The signal went dead before I could finish my sentence. "Stupid invention, cordless phones," I muttered as I hung it up. I wrote down Friday at five o'clock on the calendar, so I wouldn't forget.

"So, did Brother what's-his-name call you?" Ann asked me that afternoon.

"Yes. He's coming over on Friday."

"Good luck. Maybe his children will be charming and it will work out beautifully."

"Wouldn't that be nice?" I laughed at the remoteness of the possibility.

"At least he can afford to pay you well. He's a doctor." She wiggled her finely-arched brows at me.

"Really?"

"Really."

"Lawyers . . . doctors . . ." I muttered, shaking my head. "What is this neighborhood coming to? Why don't you rich people move back uptown where you belong and stay out of our humble subdivision?"

"We happen to live in a very nice subdivision," Ann argued. "It's great here. He lives over in the newer section anyway, where the bigger houses are."

"Are you still planning on watching Rebecca and Trevor on Thursday night?" I asked her.

"I can't wait!" she said.

"You are a wonderful friend, Ann. I don't really want you to move. Not ever."

"I know. I won't."

Thursday turned out to be a hectic nightmare. I took Rebecca to a kindergarten orientation in the morning, and then had errands to run all afternoon. When we finally got home, I piled the groceries I'd just bought all over the table. The counter was still covered with the breakfast mess. Rebecca and Trevor threw their jackets on the couch and dumped the library books we'd just checked out on the floor. I started macaroni and cheese for dinner, and looked around to decide where to start. I had a lot to do before my meeting. I decided I'd better get the groceries put away first.

Trevor pulled Rebecca's hair, and she screamed. I told him to leave her alone as I pulled the half-empty gallon of milk out of the refrigerator to put the new container behind it. I didn't realize that the lid was loose until Rebecca chased Trevor into the kitchen and he slammed into me. The lid flew off the plastic jug and milk splashed all over me, all over Trevor, and all over the floor. That was the last straw. "Darn it, you two!" I yelled. "Get out of here!"

To add to my frustration, the doorbell rang. I threw a couple of towels over the mess on the kitchen floor and wiped off my arms with another one. I scrubbed hopelessly at my clothes, and wished that I hadn't dressed in nice slacks and a shirt that day. The doorbell rang again, and Rebecca and Trevor ran to the door, fighting over who would get to answer it. I wanted to scream. I walked out to join my children at the door, and saw a little boy that I didn't recognize. I tried to place him. He looked close to Rebecca's age, but she didn't seem to know him either.

"Can I help you?" I asked him. When I got closer, he looked vaguely familiar, but I still couldn't recall who he was.

"My dad had to go answer his phone and Lizzy went with him 'cause she was scared. He'll be back in a minute."

"Your dad?" I asked, confused.

"Yeah." He grinned at me. He had large dark eyes, and darker wavy hair. Something about the cut of his little jaw was so familiar . . .

"Who are you, sweetheart?" I asked him.

"I'm Jeff," he announced proudly.

"Do you know Rebecca or Trevor?" I asked him, pointing to my children.

"No."

I crouched down to look him in the eye. *I know this child,* I thought. I had to. Who was he? It was driving me crazy that I couldn't think of who his parents were. I could almost remember who he looked like, but not quite. I was sure that he must have the wrong house though. "I think you're at the wrong house, honey," I said.

"No, my dad said this is the right house."

"And where is your dad?"

"He had to go back to the car to get something for somebody on the phone 'cause they're at the hospital I think."

I looked toward the driveway, but I couldn't see anyone. The garage stuck out too far beyond the porch, blocking my view. "Who's at the hospital?" I felt increasingly confused, wondering if someone was hurt.

He shrugged. "I dunno. The hospital calls him all the time."

I furrowed my brows at him. "Who are you looking for, Jeff?"

"Karen. Are you Karen?"

"No, I'm Maren."

"Oh. Maybe my dad said 'Maren.'"

"And why are you here?" I asked again as I stepped outside. I had just decided to go investigate when Jeff said, "We're supposed to meet you to see if you're going to babysit us."

"Oh, no." I pressed a palm against my forehead. On top of everything else, they had to come on the wrong day. I started mopping hopelessly at my clothes with the wet dish towel again, wondering exactly how bad I looked. I didn't have to wonder about the house. I knew how bad it looked. Of all the wrong days they could have picked to show up, it had to be that day.

I looked back down at the small boy and my heart softened when I saw the look on his face. He suddenly appeared worried and upset. I crouched down to meet his gaze again and tried to soothe him. "Don't worry, Jeff. I just thought you were coming tomorrow instead of today, that's all. I'm Maren, and I'm happy to meet you."

His face broke back into a grin and I couldn't help but smile at him. "Hey, your shoe's untied," I noticed before I stood up. "Would you like me to tie it for you?" He nodded. I knelt to tie his shoe as I heard a deep masculine voice coming around the corner of the garage.

"Jeffrey, did you hear me—Oh, I'm sorry. I didn't know he rang the doorbell. I had to go back to my car to—"

The voice drew my eyes up and I froze. All I could see was blue. Deep, riveting blue. I wondered if I'd hit my head. The apparition could not be real. It would have been too much of a coincidence. I couldn't find my voice. It was lost somewhere in the neurotransmitter breakdown inside my brain. I finally managed to will myself to stand, but I still just stood in awe, waiting for the hallucination to fade.

The figure in front of me seemed to have been caught in the same paralyzing freeze that had come over me. Only the electrical currents in his eyes still moved. After a handful of eternal seconds, his lips parted to form a word, but it took too long for the sound to reach me. "Maren."

The warmth in his voice washed over me, but with the thaw came the awful awareness of what my house looked like, what I looked like. I touched a hand to my hair, thinking that I hadn't combed it since that morning. I knew that my makeup had likely faded through the day, too . . . and the milk. My clothes were covered in milk. To top it off, he'd probably heard me yelling at my children before Jeff rang the doorbell. The whole thing was just too much. I started to laugh. I leaned back against the door frame and laughed myself almost to tears, but then I had to put a hand over my mouth to make myself stop before the tears actually came. "You would have to pick the worst day of my life to show up at my door, Jake," I finally said.

"Are you . . . ? Am I at the right house? Is this a bad time?" he asked, looking plenty confused himself.

"Yes, yes, and yes. But it's all right. It's good to see you." I smiled.

His face relaxed into a smile so familiar that I could have forgotten it had been over a decade since I'd seen it. He still stood tall and lean in a white shirt and navy slacks. He had the same neatly-combed wavy black hair, the same gentle yet commanding presence, the same sweet dimple in his right cheek. I impulsively stepped forward to hug him. It just seemed the natural thing to do. He hugged me too, then stepped back to look at me. "You look wonderful, Maren," he said.

I laughed again. "I look awful, Jake. And my house looks even worse. I just spilled milk all over me, and I . . . well, it's just been a crazy day. I'm sorry. I thought you were coming tomorrow. I didn't know it was you . . ."

"I didn't know it was you, either. The Relief Society president just told me 'Sister Saunders,' and I didn't think about it. I couldn't hear you very well on the phone. I thought you said your name was 'Karen.'"

"And I thought you were 'somebody Jensen.' I couldn't hear you either."

He laughed. Then he raised an eyebrow and asked, "Is this really the worst day of your life? Do you want us to come back tomorrow?"

"No. Truthfully, I've had much worse. But on normal days I've combed my hair sometime in the past eight hours, and the house is reasonably uncluttered—enough to find the couch anyway."

"I won't look," he promised.

"Come in," I offered, holding the door. Jeffrey pranced right in, and only then did I notice the little girl clinging to Jake's leg.

He bent to pick her up and kiss her head. "It's all right, sweetie," he said. "This is Maren. Do you know that Maren and I were friends a long, long time ago? You'll like her, I promise."

"You must be Lizzy." I smiled up at her in Jake's arms. "It's nice to meet you."

She stared at me with the same large dark eyes that Jeff had, but the similarities ended there. I decided that she must look like her mother. The thought made me wonder about her mother. I never would have imagined that Jake would get divorced. But then, I never imagined myself getting divorced either.

I scooped up the library books and set them on an end table. Then I scooted my children's jackets to the end of the couch and invited Jake and his children to sit down. I self-consciously tried to straighten a few things until Jake finally said, "Maren, I don't care what your house looks like."

"I'll bet yours is spotless, isn't it?" I asked, as I reluctantly sat down on the love seat.

"Actually, no." He grinned. "There are boxes everywhere, and I can't find a thing."

Trevor and Rebecca came to sit on either side of me, looking curiously at the strangers in our home. "These are my children," I said. "Rebecca and Trevor."

"It's nice to meet you." Jake smiled at them. "You guys look close to the same ages as Jeffrey and Elizabeth."

"I'm three," Trevor offered.

"Are you?" Jake smiled at him and then seemed to be thinking out loud as he remarked, "You certainly do look like your dad, don't you?"

Trevor wrinkled up his nose and said, "You know my dad?"

"Sort of," Jake answered. "I knew your mom a long time ago."

Trevor looked up at me and I explained, "Jake and I were friends before I married Daddy."

"I'm three too," Lizzy announced, speaking for the first time.

I smiled at her. "I thought you looked about three."

"Are you five, by any chance, Rebecca?" Jake asked her.

She nodded.

"Then you are the same ages. Isn't that funny?"

Jake glanced around quickly before asking, "Do you only have two children?"

I tried to ignore the stab of pain in my chest and answer smoothly. "I had another daughter, three years older than Rebecca. She only lived a few hours."

"Oh, Maren, I'm so sorry."

"It's been difficult," I admitted. "But time does heal things to a certain extent, I guess."

"So, how's Ted?" he asked, apparently eager to change the subject.

I bit my lip, trying to keep the tears from rushing into my eyes. "We're um . . . separated," I answered quietly, not wanting to bring up the fact that I'd filed for divorce right then.

He looked stunned for a moment, but didn't ask any more questions. I was grateful.

"So, do you think you'd trust me with your children?" I asked, looking at Jeffrey and Elizabeth, and then back at Jake again. "I promise to clean up the house before they come over."

He smiled. "You might forget you did it a few minutes after they arrive."

I laughed.

"Are you sure you want to do this, Maren?" he asked me. "Do you want to take some time to think about it?"

"No. Do you? I won't be offended."

He shook his head. "To be perfectly honest, I'm so grateful it's you that I . . ." He stopped to clear his throat. "Well, it's pretty difficult to leave them, that's all. Knowing they're with you will make it easier."

I blinked back the moisture that came into my eyes at the sight of his emotion. "That must be hard. I'm sorry."

"Well, it's not fun, is it? I guess you're facing some of that, too."

"I'm afraid so."

We talked about the hours and how much he would pay me. "It will only be four days a week," he told me. "I have Wednesdays off."

Trevor interrupted to say, "Mom, can we go downstairs and play?"

"Yes, for a minute. Why don't you invite Jeff and Lizzy to go with you?"

Lizzy hesitated, but Rebecca offered, "I'll show you my kitchen." That convinced her.

We watched the children go and then I turned back to Jake. "So, you *are* a doctor now, right?"

He ran a hand through his hair. "Yes, I actually made it . . . Did you think I wouldn't?"

"No, I knew you'd make it." I smiled.

"I just finished my residency in New York before we moved here."

"I thought you'd stay there," I commented, remembering how he'd planned on that.

"No. That's no place to raise a family. This is the place." He grinned.

"I'm glad you finally saw the light," I quipped. "So, did you go into cardiology like you were thinking about? Are you up at the university or what?"

He smiled somewhat sheepishly. "You'll never guess what I went into, Maren."

"Don't tell me you're a veterinarian!" I joked.

"No," he chuckled. "Actually, I'm a pediatrician."

"Very funny."

"No, really, I am. I'm licensed to do surgery, but I just joined up with some other doctors at a regular office. Private practice won't take as much time away from the kids."

"You can't be serious."

"I'm serious, Mar. Having children of my own changed my perspective a lot. I didn't think they'd be so wonderful."

"So, what other drastic changes did you make?" I smiled. He didn't look much different than he had in college, I noticed, except that there was a weariness in his eyes that hadn't been there before.

He looked deeply at me for a long moment before answering, "Maybe I'll tell you about that sometime."

I saw the pain in his expression and wondered if it showed that obviously in my own countenance. The whole situation was just so . . . ironic.

"How long have you lived here?" he asked me suddenly.

"Two years. It's a great neighborhood, a great ward. You'll like it."

"I think I will. We've only been here two weeks, but people have been very friendly. I'm surprised I didn't see you at church."

"Have you been to church already? That is surprising. Actually, maybe it's not. My kids keep me so busy that I hardly notice anyone else at church."

"You have a point." He smiled.

"How was your mission, Jake?" I asked, suddenly wanting to know.

"It was great, Maren. I'm so glad I went. Thank you, by the way."

We sat looking at each other for a moment until Jake pulled his eyes away to look at his watch. "Oh, my gosh. I have to go. I have a meeting at the church. I'm sorry I took so much of your time. I didn't realize we'd been here this long."

"It's fine, Jake. It's good to talk to you," I said genuinely. "I have a meeting too, though, so I'd better get moving. Hey, what's your meeting for?"

"Oh, I'm the new priests quorum advisor," he answered as he stood up.

"You are? How'd you get a calling so fast?"

He shrugged and smiled again. "Just lucky, I guess."

"I'm the new Laurel advisor," I told him. "So, I guess I'll see you over there."

"Really? What a coincidence."

"This whole thing is actually a rather bizarre coincidence," I observed.

"It certainly is. I can't believe I moved into your neighborhood, and . . ." His voice trailed off and he furrowed his brows as if pondering something. "Anyway," he finally said. "I'm grateful. Thank you for agreeing to watch my children, Maren."

"Thanks for letting me. You'll be helping me to stay home, you know. I didn't want to leave Rebecca and Trevor to go to work."

"Things are that bad, huh?"

I nodded and looked down.

"Then maybe this is a blessing for both of us," he said quietly.

I looked back up to smile at him. "Yes, I think so."

* * *

I had to go to the gym a little earlier on Monday morning to make it home in time to meet Jake. When he stepped inside with the children, he laughed and said, "You had time to clean up, I see."

I smiled. "I'm glad you noticed. This is what my house really looks like."

"Did you finish your interior design degree?" he asked.

"Yes."

"Good," he said firmly. "You have a gift."

"Thank you."

Jeffrey was only too happy to run down the hall with Trevor, but Lizzy cried and clung to her father's neck. "I don't wanna stay, Daddy," she whimpered.

He hugged her tightly and said, "Elizabeth, I have to go to work. You'll have fun with Maren, and I'll be back to get you just as soon as I can."

He blinked back tears and pried her little arms from around his neck to hand her to me. I was surprised at how difficult it seemed to be for Jake to leave his daughter. I didn't know why I was; it certainly seemed consistent with the loving, caring man that I'd known. I supposed that I was thinking of the conversation we'd had about children. He'd said he only wanted one or two, and even that had been with obvious hesitation.

"It will be all right, Elizabeth," I told her, taking her from Jake. "Would you like me to read you a story?"

She nodded.

"Don't worry," I told Jake. "I'll take good care of them."

"I know you will, Maren."

After he left, I read a story to Elizabeth and then told her that I had to finish getting ready. "Would you like to come with me, or go play with the kids?" I asked her.

"Come with you," she answered timidly.

"All right." I smiled and she followed me into the bathroom. She watched intently as I finished putting on makeup. Rebecca enjoyed watching the ritual sometimes, but I couldn't remember ever seeing her look as fascinated with it as Elizabeth did. I wondered if it was because she'd never watched her own mother getting ready.

"Would you like some?" I asked, holding a makeup brush out to her. A look of awed delight came over her face as she nodded. She stood on a little stool and watched in the mirror as I brushed a tiny bit of pink blush onto her cheeks. Then I handed her some lip gloss and she stared at it as though it were some foreign treasure. "You put it on your lips like this," I explained. "It makes them shiny."

She dabbed the lip gloss on and wiggled her little mouth in the mirror, laughing. She warmed right up after that, and ran to show Rebecca how pretty she looked. She watched while I did Rebecca's hair, and I was surprised when she got up the courage to ask if I would curl her hair too. Jake just put barrettes in her shoulder-length auburn hair, but it was so thick and glossy that he didn't really need to do anything with it. I curled Lizzy's hair anyway, and she was thrilled.

The day went quite smoothly. Our children got along well, and I was thankful. Elizabeth asked me several times if her lip gloss was gone, and if she could go put on more. I made a mental note to buy her some little girl's lip gloss the next time I went to the store.

"How did it go?" Jake asked me when he came to pick up Jeff and Lizzy.

"You know, it went very well, Jake. Our children seem to really like each other. I think this is going to be a good thing."

"I'm glad." He smiled.

"I'll get the kids for you," I offered. "They're downstairs playing. Have a seat if you want."

Jeffrey and Elizabeth went running up the stairs ahead of me to greet their father, and Rebecca and Trevor followed. "Did you have a good day?" he asked, stooping to hug them.

"Yeah, it was fun!" Jeffrey told him. "Maren's nice." I was glad someone thought so.

Jake smiled at me. "Yes, she is."

Elizabeth jumped into his arms and puckered up her little mouth for him. "Look at my lip gloss, Daddy! Maren let me put some on, and she curled my hair like Rebecca's. Do you think I'm pretty?"

He laughed and kissed her cheek. "I think you're beautiful, honey, just like always." He looked from her to the other three children standing there together and shook his head. "Would you look at that?" he observed in wonder. "Not a blue eye in the bunch."

Ann tapped on the front door and let herself in just as Jake was leaving. She nearly ran into him, saying, "I can't believe you left the door unlocked, Mar—Oh! Excuse me."

"This is my best friend, Ann," I introduced her to Jake. "She lives across the street and has a tendency to make herself at home here," I teased her.

"Well, I try anyway," she answered. "If Miss Paranoia here would leave her doors unlocked once in a while . . ."

"This is Jake Jantzen," I told her.

She glanced at him and then gave me a questioning look.

"You know," I filled her in. "Brother what's-his-name."

"Oh! *Jantzen.* That's it!"

Jake gave me a confused look then, so I explained to him, "Ann's the Relief Society secretary. I think you called her before the president gave you my number. She couldn't remember your name."

"I see." He smiled. "It's a pleasure to meet you, Ann." He extended his hand and she shook it.

"Yes, you too, Jake. Welcome to the neighborhood."

"Thank you."

"This is Jeffrey and this is Elizabeth," I told Ann.

She smiled at them. "What beautiful children."

"We were just leaving," Jake said. "So, I guess we'll see you later."

Ann stepped aside and I told Jake's children good-bye.

Jake smiled at me before he pulled the door shut behind him. "Thanks, Mar. See you tomorrow."

"Bye."

"Mar?" Ann turned to me when he'd gone and Rebecca and Trevor had thundered back down the stairs. "You two sure got comfortable in a hurry."

I laughed. "Not really."

"Not really? You've seen him what, twice now? He's already got you nicknamed? And you certainly seemed comfortable enough."

"Did I? I guess that would be because I've known him for eleven and a half years."

"I think I missed something," she said as she flopped down on the couch. "Maybe you'd better fill me in."

I sat down too, preparing myself for cross-examination. "I knew him in college."

"You did?" Her eyes went wide.

I nodded.

Her eyes narrowed. "How well?"

"Quite well, actually. We were very close once."

"How close?" she demanded.

"I told you—very."

"Oh, for heaven's sake, Maren! Give me the details!"

I considered her for a moment, not really wanting to expound on things. But I knew she'd never let it die until I did. "I dated him for a year," I finally admitted.

"A *year?* You dated him for an entire year? What happened? Did he turn out to be a 'conceited creep' or something after all that time?" She smiled as she quoted the conclusion I'd drawn before realizing who "Brother what's-his-name" was.

"No." I smiled back. "Quite the contrary, actually."

She threw her hands in the air. "So, what happened?"

I sighed, knowing she was going to let me have it as soon as I told her the truth. "I married Ted, that's what happened."

"What?!" she shrieked. "You broke up with *him* to marry *Ted?"*

"Something like that."

She blew her bangs off her forehead and just stared at me.

"Don't give me any guff, okay?" I warned. "I don't need it."

"Well, the rumors are certainly true, aren't they?" she finally remarked.

"What rumors?"

"He's definitely drop-dead gorgeous. And you say he's actually a nice guy, too?"

"Amazing, isn't it?"

"Well, not *that* amazing, not for me anyway. I've been trying to tell you there are decent men out there. I was lucky enough to find one of them." She raised her eyebrows at me. "It looks like maybe you were too."

"Oh, stop it!" I snapped. "I knew you'd start into this. Look, that was over a decade ago. I'm not even the same person anymore, Ann. Besides, I'm still married."

"You've filed for divorce, Maren."

"Yes, I have. But that doesn't mean I suddenly stopped loving my husband. Anyway, I'm not divorced yet. And besides, Jake's obviously been through the wringer himself. Whatever we had once is long gone. We're friends, that's all."

"Whatever you say, Maren. Someday your divorce is going to be final though, and maybe then you'll realize that it's all right to think about building a life for yourself."

"I am building a life for myself. I'm going to be fine."

She smiled. "I know you are."

Chapter 8

The combined Young Men and Young Women activity in May was a service project. We were going to help with yard work for some of the elderly people in the ward, and a few others who were in need.

We met at the church on a Saturday morning. Since all the ward babysitters were in on the service project, I brought Rebecca and Trevor with me. We went over addresses and passed out tools at the church. Jake came toward me and gave hand spades to Rebecca and Trevor. "Hi, guys," he said, smiling.

"Hi, Jake!" Rebecca greeted him.

"Where are Jeff and Lizzy?" Trevor wanted to know.

"They went to visit their grandma."

"Oh." Trevor sounded disappointed.

"Grandma?" I asked Jake.

He nodded. "My ex-wife's mother lives here. She's tried to keep up a relationship with the kids in spite of the circumstances. She's thrilled that we moved back to Utah, where she'll be close to them."

"That's good," I answered.

"It's helpful today, anyway." He smiled. Then he crouched down to talk to Rebecca and Trevor again. "So, are you guys ready to get to work?"

"Yeah!" Trevor answered him enthusiastically.

"Why don't you two go get in the car?" I suggested.

Jake stood up and folded his arms on his chest. "I guess I'll see you over there."

"Come on, Mommy!" Rebecca called.

"She looks a lot like you," he noted. "Except that her eyes are green."

"Astute observations, Doctor," I laughed. "I'm glad to see you didn't spend eight years in medical school for nothing. Have you also noticed how closely your son resembles you?"

He flashed his straight white smile and said, "Did I ever tell you that you're the most intelligent woman I've ever met?"

"Stuff it, Dr. Jantzen." I gave him a playful shove and went to get in the car. "Come on, girls!" I called. By the time they all managed to squash into my car, the boys had left in Jake's van.

With as many girls as I could pack into my car, I pulled up in front of Sister Lever's house to see Jake following the elderly lady around her yard, listening patiently to her instructions. He made a list as she pointed things out.

We trimmed shrubs, cleaned out rain gutters, weeded flower beds, swept out the garage, and did a myriad of other small tasks for her. I didn't talk to Jake much, except to look at his list of things to be done. I heard Lindsey and Karli giggling later in the morning as they stuffed weeds into the garbage can.

"He is so cute!"

"Did you see the dimple he has in his right cheek?"

"Who's the lucky young man you girls are giggling over?" I teased as I came up to deposit an armload of trash.

They looked at each other and giggled again. Lindsey rolled her eyes and said, "Really, Maren. The guys in our ward are geeks. We were talking about Brother Jantzen."

I was a bit taken aback and didn't hide it well enough. "Come on, Maren," Karli prodded. "You have to admit he's very cute."

I glanced at him quickly and laughed. "He's also *very* much too old for you. You'd better look for a guy a little closer to your generation."

"He's not that old," Lindsey protested.

"He's a lot closer to your father's age than he is to yours, sweetie." I grinned at her.

"No way! My dad's almost forty!"

I laughed again, remembering that forty had once sounded ancient to me too. "I rest my case," I answered.

Karli cut in, "He can't be over twenty-five."

"He has to be older than that, dummy," Lindsey pointed out. "He has a five-year-old kid."

"All right, twenty-six then. Maybe twenty-seven."

Lindsey nodded in agreement.

"Girls, girls," I sighed, brushing my hands off on my jeans. "He's a little older than twenty-six. He's even older than twenty-seven—which is also way too old for you, by the way. I don't know that he'd want to look that young even if he could." Personally, I was glad that he didn't.

"How old is he, Maren?" Karli asked.

"Thirty-four," I answered automatically.

They both gaped at me. Lindsey challenged, "How would you know that?"

So much for trying to bond with teenage girls, I thought. I hadn't meant to let that slip, but since I had, I decided I might as well have a little fun with it. "Isn't it obvious?" I said seriously. "Look at him. Why don't you ask him what he uses to cover his gray hair?" They gave me horrified looks, and I ordered, "Let's get back to work."

"Hey, Bro Jantzen!" Karli called to Jake, who was on a ladder cleaning out rain gutters.

He turned to see who was talking to him. I got very busy pulling weeds out of the flower beds with Rebecca and Trevor, trying not to laugh.

"Yes?" he answered Karli.

"How old are you?" she asked.

I glanced up discreetly to see him wiping sweat from his brow with a gloved hand as he gave the girls an amused look. "How old do you think I am?" he asked, coming down the ladder with a bag full of leaves.

"We think you're twenty-six. I guess you could possibly be twenty-seven, but our fearless leader over there thinks you're thirty-four."

I turned to see her flipping a careless hand in my direction.

"Does she?" Jake gave me a friendly grin, and I shrugged my shoulders.

"I was just guessing," I lied, knowing he wasn't fooled.

"So, are you going to answer us?" Lindsey asked.

Oh, to be a bold and brazen teenager again! I thought

Jake laughed and said, "I'm afraid your 'fearless leader' is right on."

"What? Maren was right?" Karli stared at him.

He shoved his bag down deep into the garbage can and jerked his head toward me, saying slyly to Lindsey and Karli, "I wonder if she could guess when my birthday is, too?"

They looked suspiciously at me. "February twenty-ninth," I shot back dryly. "If you count all the birthdays he should have had, he's really one hundred and thirty-six."

The girls gave me strange looks, but Jake threw his head back and laughed, making me smile. He leaned over as he walked by and whispered, "I'm glad to see you haven't changed, Mar."

I turned away from him and muttered with a hint of bitterness, "I'm glad to see you're so easily fooled, Dr. Jantzen. I've changed so much I'm barely recognizable."

I was surprised when he turned back to crouch down beside me and say quietly, "It's rough, I know, Mar. But you're still you. Don't let him take that away from you." I looked up to meet his sincere gaze and wished desperately that I could believe him. Trevor jumped on my back just then and spared me from having to answer. Jake smiled and went back up the ladder.

The girls sauntered over from the garbage can. "How did you know that, Maren?" Karli demanded of me, putting her hands on her hips.

"Lucky guess," I answered. "You girls are headed in the right direction, you know. Marry a guy who's like Brother Jantzen." I smiled and added, "Only a little less ancient."

They both stared at me. I looked them both straight in the eye and grinned broadly before turning back to the flower bed. They evidently couldn't think of a comeback, so they walked back around to the side of the house.

I turned to see Trevor scampering up the ladder after Jake. "Hey, Jake!" he called to him. "What are you doing?"

"Trevor, get down here!" I reached up to grab him but he pushed past Jake to escape me, nearly knocking him off the ladder.

"Whoa there, buddy!" Jake steadied himself and reached down to catch Trevor's arm. "You can stand up here and help me, but you have to hold still, okay?"

"Okay!" Trevor said enthusiastically.

"Jake, you don't have to let him stay up there," I said.

"He's fine, Mar." I watched him hold Trevor's hand and help him climb up the ladder to stand in front of him. "I'm cleaning leaves out of the rain gutter," he explained.

"What's a rain gutter?" Trevor asked.

I went back to weeding the flower beds, laughing to myself. I didn't think Jake knew what he was getting himself into. The child was insatiably curious and demanded an explanation for everything under the sun; how it worked, and where, and why. He wondered about things I'd never even considered, and often baffled me with his inquiries. I listened to Jake patiently answering Trevor's endless questions as I worked. He wanted to know why houses have rain gutters, what would happen if they didn't, what they're made out of, where the rain goes after it runs out, whether a bug could get out of the rain gutter if it fell in, why some bugs have wings and some don't, where the leaves came from, why some were brown and some were green, what made them crunchy, and on and on. Many times Jake just said, "I don't know, what do you think?" I decided I liked that answer.

I looked up once in a while to see him holding onto Trevor with one arm, and scooping leaves into the bag my little son held with the other. Every time he came down to move the ladder, Trevor followed him back up. It was hard to believe that Jake had once thought he wasn't good with children.

After Sister Lever's place, we helped with one other yard. Taking my children along proved to be much easier than I'd anticipated—for me anyway. Trevor attached himself firmly to Jake for the day, and Rebecca followed my Laurels around, trying to appear helpful and grown-up. The girls kept commenting on how cute and funny she was, and seemed to enjoy having her tag along with them.

When we finally left for home, Jake ruffled Trevor's hair and said, "Thanks for all your help, buddy. You're a hard worker."

"Yeah," Trevor agreed. "And I'm tired!"

"I'll bet you are," Jake laughed.

"Does your brain hurt?" I asked him with amusement.

He grinned. "It's killing me. I'm going to have to reread all my medical books, just so I'll have something to talk to him about next time. Are you raising him to be a rocket scientist, or does he come by it naturally?"

I smiled. "The child just has a zest for life. He's been that way since birth." I paused thoughtfully before adding, "I think Ted must have been like him when he was little . . ."

Jake raised an eyebrow at me and then looked at Trevor running circles around us on the grass. "I do envy his energy," he said.

"Amen to that. I get tired just watching him."

Trevor grabbed Jake's leg and said, "See if you can catch me, Jake!"

"I think he likes you," I laughed.

"Come on, Mom!" Rebecca called from the car. "Let's go!"

Jake chased Trevor a few feet before catching him and throwing him over his shoulder. Trevor screamed and giggled as Jake carried him to the car. "Can you come home with us, Jake?" he asked.

"I think he's had enough, bud," I said. "He probably needs to go home and take a nap. Get in the car, please."

Trevor reluctantly obeyed. After I helped him buckle his car seat and had closed the door I said to Jake, "Thank you for letting him follow you around all day. Ted hasn't paid a whole lot of attention to him lately, but Trevor misses him anyway."

"He's a good kid, Mar. You're doing a good job."

"So are you." I smiled.

Chapter 9

"What are you going to do with Rebecca and Trevor when you go on the river run?" Jake asked me one evening when he came to pick up his children.

"I'm taking them to stay with my parents."

"In Idaho?" He seemed surprised.

"Yes, in *Idaho,*" I answered with mock horror. "Clear up there on the edge of the world."

He laughed. "I'm just surprised you're taking them that far, that's all."

"It's really my only option for that many days," I answered. "Ann would take them, but I can't ask her to miss two days of work for that."

"No, I guess you can't."

"Are you going to go?" I asked him.

"You'd better believe it!" He grinned. "I'm not missing that."

"You sound like one of those mischievous teenage boys you teach." I smiled.

"That's because I *am* one of them."

I laughed. "So you're taking time off work?"

"Yes. Three days."

"What are you going to do with Jeff and Lizzy? Are they going to stay with their grandmother?"

"No. Actually, I have a cousin down at BYU. He and his wife are going to come and stay with them. It's during their summer break, so it works out well."

"Oh, that's good. I'm glad."

"Me too. The kids are excited about it."

"As excited as you are?" I teased.

"Almost."

* * *

We went to court in June. The judge agreed to allow Ted's parents to supervise his visits with Rebecca and Trevor at their home. He gave Ted two weekends a month. I felt a little nervous about the whole situation, but there was nothing I could do about it. I knew that the Saunders did love their grandchildren, and that they would enjoy spending time together. I didn't approve of how they denied Ted's actions, but I did believe that they would make certain my children were safe. They were warned that they could not leave the children alone with Ted. That brought me some relief.

The first time they took them, Ted's parents picked Rebecca and Trevor up just before Jake arrived to get Jeff and Lizzy. I tried to wipe the worry from my expression when he got there.

"What's wrong, Maren?" he asked. I was grateful that Elizabeth and Jeffrey were still outside playing in the backyard.

"I filed for divorce a few weeks ago," I admitted. "The judge gave Ted supervised visitation. This is the first weekend that his parents came to get Rebecca and Trevor."

"Oh, that must be hard," he said sympathetically. "Are you all right?"

I nodded, trying to swallow the lump in my throat.

"You filed for divorce?" he asked.

"Yes," I managed.

"Wow," he muttered. "Life just doesn't give you any guarantees, does it?"

"I guess not. But you survived it, didn't you?" I tried to comfort myself.

"I'm still breathing, if that's what you mean." I heard the bitterness in his voice and closed my eyes, realizing that I had a long road ahead of me.

It was very difficult to send my children away twice a month. I tried to act cheerful about the whole thing for their sakes, but I did a lot of worrying and praying while they were gone. Trevor and Rebecca seemed to enjoy the visits with Ted's family. They always came home happy, with stories of the fun they'd had. I said a prayer of thanks every time they arrived home content and safe.

As for myself, I kept going to counseling appointments once a month. That was all I could afford, but they did seem to help. I was learning a lot about myself, and about how to handle things and be a support to my children.

Ann was an angel of mercy to me, especially on my long lonely weekends. She frequently appeared to take me to lunch or ask me to go shopping with her. She sensed the void and tried to help me breeze by it. I appreciated her more than she could ever have known. I knew she was sacrificing precious time away from her husband to comfort me. I was grateful to Tyler too, for being so willing to let her go.

Toward the end of June she told me that my divorce would be finalized soon. She'd managed to push it through in a hurry. "This will all be over, Maren, and you can get on with your life," she said. "I hear it's kind of a shock sometimes, when that letter comes, so be prepared. I guess people are a little bit numb when they're going through this."

"I'm not sure I'll ever be prepared for it," I answered honestly. "Part of me just wants to have Ted out of my life forever so I don't have to worry about this anymore. Truthfully, though, I have to admit that something in me still wants to run after him and beg him to come home, even after all this."

She tilted her head and looked at me. "I can't understand you, Maren. Why would you want to stay in that?"

"I've told you, it's not all bad. Ted has good points. He used to be so fun, Ann, when we were dating . . . Once in a while he's still like that. He's just so . . . confusing, you know? Part of him is this confident, outgoing man with so many intriguing ideas. That's what I was attracted to, his sense of humor and his determination. But then sometimes he acts like a child, like a lost little boy that I feel obligated to protect. That's the part of him that gets to me the most, I think, the part that makes me feel guilty and responsible for him. And, of course, there's the raging alcoholic, the nightmare. If he could just pull himself together. If he could just quit drinking . . ."

"He won't until he gets help, Maren. You know that. Maybe this is what he needs, too. You told me you felt this was the right decision."

"You're right. I do, but it's still hard. He was my main worry and concern for over ten years, you know . . . I guess I just want this whole nightmare to be over."

She patted my arm sympathetically. "I know. It almost is."

"You've done so much for me, Ann. Thank you for being with me through this whole mess. I'm so grateful for you."

She smiled. "It's nothing."

* * *

The second week of July, I made the five-hour drive to my parents' home on Tuesday and then stayed overnight. My younger sister Natalie had returned from a mission a few months earlier and was living at BYU—Idaho. It was only half an hour away, so she came home to see me after classes. She banged the front door shut, just like she had when she was little, and burst into the kitchen with the same childish exuberance. "Maren!" She ran toward me with her arms outstretched. After she hugged me she pulled back to look at me. "You've lost weight!" she observed.

I didn't tell her it was only due to stress. I smiled at her instead. Her brown eyes sparkled. I had always envied her olive skin and thick brown hair that grew faster than the hay in the surrounding fields. "Yes," I answered. "And you're beautiful as always, Nat."

"Where are the kids?" she asked.

"They went out to feed the calves with Dad. They're in heaven."

She laughed and sat down at the kitchen table with me. Her cheeks were flushed and she rambled on about summer school, what the neighbors and her old high school friends were doing, how hot it was, and how she still missed Mom's cooking when she was at school, even though she'd spent a year and a half away.

Finally, as Mom opened the oven to poke the potatoes, she said to Natalie, "Well, are you going to tell her, or not?"

"Tell me what?" I asked.

"Oh, Maren, it's so wonderful! I was going to tell you on the phone last weekend, but then I decided to wait and tell you in person."

"Tell me what?" I repeated with an inexplicable feeling of dread.

She and my mother exchanged gleeful looks before she gushed out, "I'm engaged!"

I didn't know why, but the words stung like a slap in the face. If I was surprised, I shouldn't have been. With her intelligence, good looks, and sunny personality, the amazing thing was that my little sister had stayed single long enough to actually serve the mission she'd planned on her whole life. Always the oblivious optimist, Natalie waved her hand in front of my face. Her diamond's reflection sparkled painfully in my eyes. I didn't know how I'd missed seeing it before. "Maren! I *said* I'm getting married!"

I tried to pull words I didn't feel out of the air. "That's wonderful, Nat. Really. Congratulations."

She puffed her bottom lip out in an almost imperceptible pout. "Maren! Be excited for me!"

I smiled at her angelic face and remembered my own dreams when I had been in her place. The pure joy and exuberance she emanated were foreign to me though. I had never felt that way. But then, I never was as vivacious as Natalie. "I am happy for you, Nat. So tell me about the incredible man who's finally captured your heart."

That seemed to satisfy her, and she went on and on about "Douglas" and all his endearing qualities. I watched her with fascination, hoping that Douglas didn't brandish a secret weapon that would burst her bubble in years to come.

She told me they were getting married on December fifteenth, and I laughed at her. "You'll move it up. I'll see you in September. October, maybe."

Natalie laughed back and said, "No I won't, Maren. That's when it is. I'm not fickle like you are."

"What do you mean?" I asked, narrowing my eyes at her.

She shrugged her shoulders and said matter-of-factly, "I remember your wedding. What was I . . . eleven or twelve? I wasn't completely old enough to know what was going on, but I was old enough to pick up on the fact that you were unsure of things. You weren't as happy as you should have been."

"What?" I was shocked.

"I remember thinking it was strange, even then, that you would take such a big step if you weren't completely sure of it."

I thought back over the years, and wondered how my uncertainty could have been so obvious to a preteen girl, even if she was my sister.

But I'd been so torn between Ted and Jake that I didn't know how I ever could have gotten to a point of complete faith in my decision either way.

"It just didn't seem like you," Natalie went on. "When you came up for the wedding Ted was always bossing you around, and you let him. It made me mad."

"Really?" I asked in astonishment. "You remember it being like that?" I didn't even remember it being that way.

She nodded and said, "I watched you closely. I always looked up to you. I didn't say anything because I figured no one would listen to me anyway. But I did decide that I would never let any guy boss me around . . . You know, I'm sorry you have to go through a divorce, but I think this might be the best thing that ever happened to you."

"Natalie!" I protested. I wanted to let her have it, but I reminded myself that she was young. It was easy to think that marriage could be perfect or that divorce wasn't so bad if you'd never experienced those things. She'd have a better perspective after a few years of marriage, I was sure.

"I mean it, Maren," she insisted, pushing her freckled nose close to my face. "Filing for divorce is the healthiest thing you've done in a long time. Maybe having to get up the guts to finally leave Ted has made you tougher. Maybe you'll remember how strong you used to be now. You always stood up for yourself when you lived at home you know. I remember all the guys you dated who came around in high school. You never had a problem speaking your mind with them, or politely dismissing them if they didn't respect you. Remember when that Wilkins guy brought you home from the prom and told you that you owed him a kiss? You did a fine job of telling him off. I felt so sorry for the guy. I wondered if he'd left in tears." She grinned at me.

"How did you know that?" I asked her, though I did recall the incident.

"Duh, Maren. How do you think? I used to watch out my window and then sit on the stairs to listen when you came home from all your dates."

"You did?" I asked in surprise.

She laughed and said, "Of course I did! I wanted to learn from the pro."

I pictured her curled up on the stairs in her pajamas, listening in wide-eyed amazement to all my teenage escapades and I laughed too. "It's a wonder you aren't completely screwed up," I teased her, "if I was your model for life."

She smiled and said, "I think you actually set a pretty good example. You were almost always kind, but you stood up for yourself. You were strong . . . I think you've forgotten your own strength, big sis."

Mom came to join us at the table, a mature version of Natalie, and agreed, "She's right, Maren. Your father and I have mentioned this to you before, but I think you have forgotten your own strength to a certain extent. You seem to be regaining some of it, though, and I'm glad to see that."

"Thanks," I mumbled. I looked at both of them for a minute before asking, "Did you see all that too, Mom? Before I married Ted?"

She considered me thoughtfully. "It's easy to look back and say that we should have seen it, dear, or even to think that we did. But, honestly, if your father or I had seen something that concerned us, we would have said something to you. We wouldn't have watched you walk into what we thought was a bad situation without saying anything. I can see how Natalie thought you let Ted boss you around for the day or so that you were here before the wedding, but I just thought you were trying to be agreeable, to make him feel comfortable here. I didn't see any red flags of warning any more than you did. Ted is a good person, Maren, he's just made some bad choices."

Natalie nodded and said, "You're probably right, Mom. I probably didn't know everything that was going on. But I did feel angry with Ted for taking you away, Maren. I was a little bit sad that you were getting married, even though you'd already been away at college. I knew you'd never be coming home to stay again. And I liked Jake. He was so nice to me whenever you guys came up here, or when we went down there. I'd gotten used to the idea of you marrying him . . . but then you didn't."

Mom agreed, "Yes, that was an adjustment for all of us, I think. We all loved Jake. But you were an adult, Maren, and we trusted you to make your own decisions. We grew to love Ted too, you know. He has many redeeming qualities. He's not all bad, Natalie."

"I know," she admitted reluctantly.

"Anyway, you can't go back," Mom told me. "All you can do is move forward. It's sad for us too, but I do think you're making the right decision. I wish Ted would get some help, but we can't force him. The point is that we're your family, and we love you, and we're here to support you in whatever way we can."

Natalie nodded in agreement. "Me too, Maren. I wasn't trying to make you feel awful or anything. I'm sorry. I just want you to remember how . . . vibrant you used to be. I remember. I know you've been through a lot of pain, but I think you're resilient enough to pull through it."

"So," Mom said, "What can we do to help you through this, Maren?"

I smiled at both of them. "You already do plenty, Mom. You guys call and check on me all the time, you're watching the kids for me so I can fulfill my church responsibilities, you're honest, even when I wish you wouldn't be." I stopped to smile. "Most of all, I know you all love me. And I love you. I'm grateful for all of you."

"I wish we lived closer to you," Mom admitted sadly, "and that we could help more with the children, or money."

"I wish you lived closer too." I smiled. "But you're wonderful with the kids when we do get to see you. It's the highlight of their lives. And I'll be all right financially, too. I know I could move up here with you if I had to. I just feel like we belong down there."

I reflected for a few moments before observing, "I did used to be strong, didn't I? I wanted a strong man too. I remember thinking that. Ted stood up to me . . . but then I let him defeat me . . . Maybe I wasn't looking for the right kind of strength."

Mom and Natalie both watched me quietly, nodding in agreement.

After another lengthy pause, my mother changed subjects by asking brightly, "And how are things working out with watching Jake's children?" I'd told her about that on the phone several weeks earlier.

"Yeah . . ." Natalie's eyes sparkled with mischief. "Is he still as sweet as he used to be?"

"Yes." I smiled. "He's a good friend."

"And is he still as adorable as he used to be?" Natalie continued.

I smiled and shook my head. "Yes, Nat. And you can drop it now. I need to work on finding my strength right now, remember? Not chasing fairy tales."

She smiled back and said, "Good plan."

I left on Wednesday morning, kissing Becca and Trevor before I went home to pack for the river trip. "Have fun, and be good for Grandma and Grandpa," I instructed.

"We'll see you at home on Sunday night, then," Dad said as he hugged me good-bye.

Trevor and Rebecca stood waving after me and calling, "Bye, Mommy!"

I kept thinking of Natalie's upcoming wedding. I envied her youthful optimism. The drive home was long and I had lots of time to feel a longing ache settle in. The awful awareness that a divorce loomed in front of me became more real with every mile. I felt like one of the lost, lone fence posts I had seen in the deserted Idaho fields, the barbed wire connecting it to other posts long since torn away. The rails that had stood near it once were gone; any trace of it's once-worthy purpose hidden by overgrown sagebrush and prairie grass.

Unfortunately, I arrived home early enough on Wednesday afternoon to be there for the mail delivery. I tore open the certified letter with trembling hands to read: Final Decree Of Divorce. So, that was it. Ten and a half years of my life had just been wiped out. Ted was gone. I was alone. I felt some relief that it was all over, but it was mostly overshadowed by an overwhelming sense of loss.

I sank to the floor in numb, dark silence and stared at the paper in my hand. I didn't know how to react or what to feel. I was grateful that the children weren't there. I couldn't will myself to move from that spot on the floor where time stood frozen and black. I didn't know how long I sat there before hate crept in to devour the emptiness. I was suddenly filled with it. I hated Ted for doing that to me, for leaving me alone. I questioned God for allowing me to end up on such a terrible road. Most of all, I hated myself for making the choices I'd made and for staying so long in the hope that it would work out somehow, only to have it end after a ten-year struggle.

I stood up in a blind fury and grabbed the closest thing to me, the family picture I had kept sitting on the foyer table for some reason. I threw it at the front door and watched it smash on the tile floor. The anger dissipated as I stared at the shattered glass. Realizing my foolishness I knelt to pick up the mess. I brushed pieces of glass off of everything, trying to recover the photograph. Clear slivers clung to it and it was terribly scratched. I tried to put the metal frame back together, but it was bent and scratched too. What had I done?

I carried the picture to the kitchen and wiped it off with a paper towel. I looked at Ted's scratched, smiling face and laid the last remnant of my family on the kitchen counter. Then I returned to the foyer with a broom and dustpan to clean up the mess I'd made. I didn't even notice the blood on my hands until I went to wash them in the sink. I let the warm water run over them until the wounds were clean and ready to heal. I went to bed alone, in my empty house, and stared into the unknown.

When I finally slept the dream came back. The mist was pure black this time, and it threatened to suffocate me. Instead of getting closer to the light, I was being pulled even farther away from it. Black smoke filled my lungs until I couldn't even scream. My heart was still racing when I woke up to dress for the trip.

Chapter 10

We met at the church at six o'clock on Thursday morning. Peggy Williams had told me that my class and I would fit in her Suburban, so I didn't need to drive. I was relieved that I wouldn't have to spend money on gas. I'd already had to pay for the trip and for gas to drop the children off in Idaho.

Jake saw me in the chaos of getting everyone loaded up. "Hi, Mar," he said brightly.

"Hi," I managed to say.

"Are you all right?" he asked.

I nodded. He gave me a searching look, but didn't press it. Instead he went to herd teenage boys into his van. "See you down there!" he called.

"See ya."

The girls chattered during the whole three-hour drive, for which I was grateful. It didn't leave much room for my thoughts.

I had to admit that the first day on the river was great. I even ended up laughing. Abby seemed to be having fun. I hoped the trip would be a positive experience for her. That night after dinner we had a devotional. Bishop Rowley talked for a few minutes and then turned the time over to the bearing of testimonies. I could feel a strong spirit there, as though we were somehow closer to God in the mountains. Reminders of Him were everywhere—the trees, the river, the stars, even the beautiful teenage faces touched by the experience.

Christine bore her testimony first, and several of the other young people followed. Abby just listened. I knew I should make myself get up for my girls, but I couldn't will myself to do it. Jake did a better job of leading his class. His testimony was short and simple and pure.

After the devotional I made sure that my Laurels were as settled in their tent as they were going to get that late at night. Then I went for a walk. I wandered up a little dirt path, gazing up at the stars and the pine trees. The place was amazing. I felt awe at God's power and majesty. I knew my spirit had been lifted by the devotional, and by hearing the testimonies of others, but my mortal side felt overwhelmed with loneliness. I thought of Rebecca and Trevor at my parents' house. I knew they were having a ball. They probably didn't even miss me. I was alone. I might be alone forever. I was going to have to face it.

I went down a little hill to the edge of the river. It flowed calm and wide there. I gazed out at the moonlight on the water. It was so beautiful. I wanted to stay there forever and just feel the peace and solitude, and never return home to my troubles. My thoughts wandered to Ted. I wondered where he was right then. Did he know the divorce was final yet? Did he feel as lonely as I did? Then I felt angry. If he did feel lonely, he had brought it on himself. I had felt alone for most of the past ten years. How could I love him, and yet hate him so much at the same time? I decided to say a silent prayer for him. "Father, please bless Ted. Help him to get on the right path, and bless him with a desire to change. Please be with him."

I thought of the teenagers who were there on the river trip. They were so happy, so full of life and hope. It seemed like a million years since I'd felt that way. The contrast was unbearable. The numbness fled as the truth of my situation descended on me. I was divorced. The life I'd known for more than ten years was over. I had failed in my marriage. My children were going to grow up in a broken home. I was consumed with grief. Emotion finally broke through and I sat down to cry. I rested my forehead on my knees and curled my arms around my legs, trying to disappear, to trickle away with the tears.

After an indiscernible amount of time, my head shot up suddenly at the sound of my name being spoken in a deep gentle voice. "Maren."

Jake sat down beside me and touched my arm. His face was full of concern and I felt humiliation in addition to my other emotions. I turned away from him and wiped frantically at my face. I hadn't even heard him approach.

"What's wrong, Mar?" he asked tenderly.

"Nothing. I'm fine."

"You're obviously not fine, Maren." He reached over to turn my face toward him. I wiped at the unrelenting tears. "You've never been a very good liar," he insisted. "Tell me."

"I don't need to unload my burdens on you, Jake," I sobbed. "I just can't help it. I feel so . . . awful."

"Do you ever unload your burdens on anyone, Mar?" he asked quietly. "Or do you just try to carry them all yourself?"

I just watched him for a minute, surprised at his insight into my heart, even after so many years.

"You know I'm not going to just walk away," he told me. "So . . . why do you feel awful?"

I knew from past experience that he wouldn't give up until he'd pried it out of me. I took a breath and said, "I'm divorced. It's final. I got the notice yesterday."

He squeezed his eyes shut. "Oh, Maren," he whispered. "I'm so sorry."

His empathy reminded me of what it was like to have someone care. I tried to hold back the emotion from realizing such a lack in my life, but to no avail.

"Come here, Mar." Jake pulled me into his arms, and I leaned against him and wept. Ten years of anguish and longing and excruciating loneliness came pouring out of me until there was nothing left to let go of. "It hurts, Jake. It hurts so much."

"I know it does. I know."

"He's gone. I'm all alone. I'll be alone forever."

"Shh. No you won't, Maren. You're going to be fine." His soothing voice and familiar embrace were surprisingly comforting. I suddenly wished that I could stay there forever. "Are you fine, Jake?" I asked quietly, as the tears subsided.

"What do you mean?"

"Your divorce. You told me it's been a year. Are you fine now?" I pulled back to look into his eyes and saw the pain. "You're not fine, are you," I stated flatly. It wasn't a question.

"Not yet," he admitted. "But I will be."

"How has it been for you?" I wondered. "This past year? The past ten years? How has it been?"

He looked down and I touched his face, bringing his gaze back up to meet mine. A few stray tears escaped down his cheeks and I brushed them away, feeling suddenly as close to him as I had eleven years ago. "Awful, Maren," he whispered. "It's been awful."

"We're quite a pair, aren't we?" I shook my head.

He chuckled softly. "Maybe we can help each other survive this, huh?" I smiled.

"I'm so grateful to have found you again, Maren," he said softly, brushing tears from my face with his thumbs. "You're probably one of the best friends I've ever had."

"The feeling is mutual," I answered. He kissed my forehead and pulled me to him again. I leaned against his chest and we sat looking out at the water together, saying nothing, for a long, long time.

I watched the soothing, cleansing current meandering by as thoughts of moving on drifted into my mind. I felt a calm acceptance settle in my soul. I knew I still loved Ted. That would never go away. I felt sad that my marriage was over, but I knew it was the best thing for me, and for all of us. Looking back over the previous decade, I became aware of how much I had grown. I realized that God had been mindful of me all along, and that the whole thing had not all been just a big mistake. I thought back to when I had decided to marry Ted. There was no way I could have foreseen that he would become an alcoholic. I had married him worthily in the temple. I had tried everything that I could think of to be a good wife. I had stayed long enough to give him every opportunity to change. Although I had certainly made mistakes and had admittedly contributed to some of the problems in our marriage, the divorce was not my fault. I felt the burdens of regret and guilt that I'd been carrying for so many years being gently lifted from my heart.

Eventually I succumbed to exhaustion and let the melody of the river lull me to sleep. I didn't know how long it had been when Jake squeezed me and whispered my name. "I'm betting that you didn't get much sleep last night," he chuckled.

"No . . . I'm sorry."

He stood up and offered me his hand. "For the sake of propriety,

I think I'd better walk you back to camp before everyone's up. I wouldn't want all these teenagers we're in charge of to get any ideas."

I let him pull me up and smiled. "No, I guess that wouldn't be very smart." I shivered in the breeze that swept over me from the river as we started back down the trail.

"Cold?" Jake asked me.

"Just a little."

He put a warm arm around me as we walked. "You know, Jake," I said. "I feel a lot better."

He smiled down at me, revealing that sweet dimple in his right cheek. "I'm glad, love. So do I."

"Did you suddenly remember my nickname?" I asked, stopping.

"What?"

"You just called me 'love' again. Did you just remember it, or do you call everyone that?"

"Well, not *everyone*," he mused as we resumed walking. "I've never used it on . . . a checker at the grocery store, for instance, or . . . the plumber . . . I don't believe I've ever called my dad that, but I'm not sure . . ."

I elbowed him in the ribs. "Very funny."

He laughed before he answered me. "No, Maren. That name is just yours." I felt my heart flutter just a little bit, but I dismissed it as quickly as it had come. Jake was only a friend this time around.

Chapter 11

I was really looking forward to the second day on the river. I felt more lighthearted than I had in a long time. After breakfast we packed up camp, donned our life jackets, and set off in the rafts once again. All morning long I listened to the lively banter between the young men and young women. Inwardly I thanked God for allowing me to be there at that moment in my life. I was suddenly glad that I'd found out about my divorce before the trip, while my children were tucked away safely at my parents' home. I was grateful to be in such cheerful company for three days, to give my spirits a chance to lift before I went back to get my children. Just before noon our guide looked ahead on the river and said enthusiastically, "Who's up for a little white water before lunch?"

A cheer went up from our raft, and the two others nearby. I saw Jake waving excitedly with the young people in his raft. He looked up and smiled at me, as if to reassure me that everything would be all right. I didn't hear our guide suddenly yelling, "Watch out!" until I saw a worried look pass over Jake's face. There was a huge smash as we hit something, and then a ripping sound. "Jump!" the guide yelled. I looked desperately around to account for all the teenagers I was in charge of as I went under.

I waited for a second, expecting my life jacket to pull me above the water, but my head kept hitting an impenetrable rubber wall. I started to panic. I fought to get to the surface, but I kept getting pulled back under the raft. I tried to think, and realized that my life jacket must be caught on something. I struggled to get it off. My lungs began to burn and I instinctively opened my mouth, trying to get air. Instead, I inhaled cold dirty water. I fought for the surface again in vain. Black fog closed in around me. I started to lose consciousness. I felt a strong arm grab hold of me just before I blacked out.

There was nothing but blackness for a few moments, and then I was in my dream. There were swirls of gray mist and a light, but it wasn't scary. The place felt peaceful somehow. I saw two figures in the distance—two children, a boy and a girl. I couldn't be sure, but there was something about that little boy's eyes . . .

The children disappeared in the mist as words that seemed familiar ran through my mind, *The whole point is growth, Maren. You might not get all the answers you seek. You're going to feel alone sometimes, you're going to lose people you love, you're going to hurt. It all goes along with free agency. Your only guarantee is that you will have opportunities for refinement, and you will be able to choose how you handle them. Try to keep your perspective, and remember it's a gift . . .*

I heard a voice pulling me out of the dream again. I didn't recognize it at first, though I knew it was familiar . . . Jake. It was Jake's voice. I tried to resist, but the urgency of his words overpowered me. "Don't leave me, Maren! Don't you leave me!" he was shouting.

I was suddenly awake, coughing and spitting out water. I felt achy and exhausted, but there was a lingering peace.

Jake held me to his wet bare chest. "Oh, thank goodness. Thank you, Lord," he whispered. Then he looked at me. "I thought I lost you, Maren. I thought you were gone. I've never been so scared." I felt overwhelmingly confused.

I looked around and realized that all the young men and young women, the bishop, and the rest of the leaders were standing close by. Many of them had tears on their cheeks. The accident had been traumatic, I was sure. Suddenly I felt very concerned for them. "Is everyone okay?" I managed to ask Jake. He nodded, and I could only mumble, "Thank goodness," before I started coughing again.

"All right, kids," Bishop Rowley announced, "Now that we know Sister Saunders is going to make it, why don't you all go get your lunch."

Peggy took over with directions, "Come on everyone! Sandwiches on that big rock over there!"

As they turned to go, Bishop Rowley came up to kneel beside me. "What do you think, Jake?" he asked, concerned.

"I think we'd better get her to a hospital to be looked at. Even if everything else is okay, I'm a little concerned about hypothermia or pneumonia settling in within a few hours."

"My jeep isn't far. I think I could drive it in fairly close to here. It's parked just a little way down, where we were supposed to stop for lunch," the bishop said. "But I don't think we should both leave. One of us ought to stay here with the kids."

"I think you should stay, Bishop. I'll drive her into town and find the nearest hospital, if you don't mind us taking your car."

"No, I don't mind. I'm very grateful we had a doctor with us, Jake," the bishop said seriously.

"So am I." He smiled back.

When Bishop Rowley pulled his car off the road, as close to us as he could get, Jake bent to pick me up.

"Jake, this is silly," I said. "I can walk."

I tried to get up, but felt incredibly dizzy, and fell back down. He caught me. "I'm the doctor. I'll be the judge of that, Mar. I'm carrying you." Reluctantly I let him, hoping that I wouldn't break his back. He seemed to lift me like it was nothing.

Bishop Rowley opened the passenger door, and Jake carefully set me down on the seat. I realized that I was shivering.

"I think I might have a blanket in the trunk," the bishop said. He rummaged in the trunk and returned with a soft, warm quilt. Jake tucked it in around me and fastened the seat belt over me. I fell asleep on the way to the hospital.

I drifted in and out of awareness, hearing voices here and there. When I finally woke up after what seemed like hours, everything in my room was dark except for a tiny light on the nightstand. Jake was asleep in a chair by the window, his head leaning against the wall. He still didn't have a shirt on. I realized that he'd been in his swimming trunks the whole time. I knew he must be cold and uncomfortable. I smiled gratefully. He had been a dear friend for a long time. I sat up and switched on the lamp by the bed.

Jake sat up suddenly and blinked. "Maren!" he whispered, rubbing sleep from his eyes. "How are you?"

"Fine. How are you?" I laughed at his rumpled hair and bare chest. "Comfortable?"

He smiled. "I'm glad you haven't lost your sense of humor."

"Do they have a gift shop here?" I asked. "Why don't you go down and buy yourself a T-shirt or something—my treat." I offered. "It's the least I can do for making you sit in a hospital all night."

He laughed and scooted his chair closer to the bed. "I already tried that. I'm afraid we're lucky they even had a bed to put you in. I think we're somewhere in the middle of nowhere."

"And by that you mean the population is under two million here?" I joked.

He smiled. "All right, country girl. We're definitely not in New York. I saw cows. The place isn't completely uncivilized though. I think there's a Wal-Mart down the road, but they're not open yet."

"Bummer."

"It's not that bad. At least I didn't wake up with shaving cream all over me again."

I laughed at the thought. "Did they really do that? Those charming young men must not be as innocent as they appear."

"Not even close."

I suddenly had a vision of what I must look like. I tried to comb my hair back with my fingers. "I must be a mess," I muttered self-consciously.

Jake smiled at me. "You're fine, Maren."

"Yeah, right," I laughed.

"You are, Mar. You're beautiful."

"You're just saying that because I nearly drowned," I said teasingly, but regretted it when I saw the shadow of concern that fell over his face.

He squeezed my hand and said, "I'm so glad you're all right."

The fervor in his words and look in his eyes prompted me to ask, "Jake? What happened exactly?"

He hesitated before answering me. "Your heart stopped. I thought you were gone. I did CPR and prayed and prayed, and finally I felt you breathe again."

I gasped. "It was that bad?"

He only nodded.

I stared at him in wonder. "You mean . . . you saved my life?"

He shook his head. "It wasn't me."

"But you were the instrument . . ." I studied his handsome face. "Weren't you?"

He watched me silently for a long time before answering, "I guess you could say that." Then he stood up and added, "I'm going to let you get some rest. I'll check on you later. Do you need anything?"

I shook my head and watched him leave. Then I said a silent prayer of gratitude for my life, for my children, for the peace I felt, and for Jake's friendship.

Chapter 12

In the morning a nurse came into my room. "Good morning!" she said brightly. "I just need to take your blood pressure and temperature. If everything looks okay, we'll let you go. You're very fortunate."

I still felt confused. It hadn't seemed like that big of a deal, really. I did feel tired though, and my chest ached.

"You're doing well," the nurse told me. "Dr. Jantzen's waiting to see you. Shall I send him in?"

I knew I was a mess, but I guessed he'd seen me look worse in the last few hours. "Sure," I said.

Jake peered around the door and smiled. "How are you feeling?" he asked.

"Great!" I said, only half meaning it. "Should we get back to camp?"

He laughed. "I wish we could, Mar, but I'm afraid that by the time we made it back they'd just be getting ready to leave anyway. I talked to Bishop Rowley on his cell phone this morning. Since he and Carol met us at the river later, no one rode down with them. They're going to take my van back with the boys and I'm going to drive you home in their jeep."

"Jake, you don't have to do that. Let's just go back and meet them, and you can get your car—"

"Maren, you need to rest. Those girls of yours are a lot of fun, but not exactly conducive to relaxation." He grinned. "Anyway, it's not a big deal. Everything will work out fine."

"But, Jake—"

"It's already been decided, Mar. You might as well save your breath. Your lungs have been strained enough," he joked.

I sighed and gave in. "All right."

"Here," he said. "I bought you a present." He tossed a pair of gray sweatpants on the bed. I noticed he was wearing the sweatshirt that went with them. "They're a bit big for you, I know. At least you won't have to run around in your swimming suit though." He winked at me.

"Thanks."

"They said you're free to go as soon as you're ready, so I'll wait for you outside. Take your time."

I watched him walk out the door, and got up to take a shower. I did feel a little weak. I wished that I had my curling iron with me, but I hadn't planned on plugging it into any nearby trees. And my backpack with my makeup and everything in it was back with the river party. I tried to do the best I could with soap and water and a comb, but the results were not astounding. I didn't have anything to take with me, so I pulled on the sweatpants over my swimsuit, rolling the waistband down twice to keep them from falling off.

"Ready?" Jake asked when I opened the door.

"No." I smiled. "But I guess I'll have to do. Everything I had with me is back at camp."

"A dilemma I sympathize with completely," he quipped.

We had three hours to converse on the way home, uninterrupted by children. It was strange. After some lighthearted talk, and a few silent moments, Jake finally asked, "So tell me, Maren, what happened?"

"What do you mean?"

"Why did you get divorced?" he asked as he glanced over his shoulder to change lanes.

I wondered why he hadn't asked me earlier, but then I supposed it was because we always had children with us when we were together. I tried to speak without emotion. "Ted has a drinking problem. He's just not the same person when he drinks. It started out difficult, and it just kept getting worse. He got violent when he drank, abusive really. He acted as though the children and I just cramped his style. We were an annoyance, a burden. He treated me like . . . nothing, like I wasn't even there. He quit going to church. I kept hoping, kept praying, but nothing worked. I lost all my self-esteem . . . Then I finally got angry enough to tell him to leave. The only things that seemed to matter to him were alcohol and power."

"That's what your life has been like for the past ten years?" Jake asked.

"Yes. There were some good times, but not enough to make up for the pain."

He sighed loudly and shook his head. "I'm sorry, Maren."

"I made plenty of mistakes too, Jake. I started to shut him out because the pain was too much. I got angry. I quit going to church for a while myself. I quit caring, quit trying to help him. I became indifferent. We just kind of coexisted for a long time, and then one day I snapped. I couldn't take anymore. I told him to leave. It's been very hard, but I know it was the right decision for me."

When Jake didn't say anything, I prompted, "And what about you?"

He gripped the steering wheel tightly and stared straight ahead. "I met Tess right after I got home from my mission. We got married six months later. I jumped into it way too soon. I was afraid that if it was the right thing and I didn't hold onto her . . . well, anyway, she just wasn't prepared for how difficult medical school was going to be, and I didn't know her like I should have.

"She got a great job when we moved to New York to start my residency. She loved it. Things were a little better for a while. I wanted her to stay home after we had Jeffrey though. It would have been tight, but we could have made it. She wouldn't do it. I never thought that would upset me so much. I didn't know that I would feel so . . . I just didn't understand what it meant to be a parent, Maren. I couldn't stand leaving the kids in daycare, not when there was another option.

"After we had Lizzy, Tess told me she was going crazy. All she wanted to do after work was go shopping with her friends, go to dinner, to the theater . . . anything but go home to her children. Sometimes I'd come home late at night from the hospital and find a babysitter still there. She ran up some big credit card bills and wanted me to take money from my parents to pay them off, but I wouldn't. When I cut them all up, that was the last straw for her. She told me that if I wouldn't take my family's money to keep her happy until I had my own, then there wasn't anything there for her."

"Ouch," I said. I couldn't help remembering the conversation we'd had so many years ago when I'd told him that I *didn't* want him to take money from his parents.

"That wasn't the worst of it," he muttered grimly.

"Really?" I asked hesitantly, wondering if I wanted to know what was.

"She moved right from our apartment into her boss's penthouse. He was a high-powered business executive who could give her what she wanted . . . and apparently had been doing just that for some time before she left."

"Your wife had an affair?" I couldn't believe it.

"Is that any worse than abuse?" he challenged.

I shook my head. "I don't know. It's all terrible."

"It certainly is. But even after all that, I tried to get her to come home. I wanted to work things out. I didn't want to see her go any further off the deep end."

"You could have lived with that?" I asked.

"I'm not sure. I never thought I could have before, but I would have tried. When you're actually faced with something you never thought you'd have to face, it's not as cut-and-dried as you thought it would be. She was my wife, the mother of my children."

"I guess I can understand that."

"Besides," he said, "I felt like I was partly to blame."

"Why?" I wondered.

"Because I was gone so much. I had no choice, really. Getting through a residency is a nightmare. I knew the people at the hospital better than I knew my own family. I didn't know how much work it would be to have children . . . and I didn't even begin to comprehend how I would feel about them. I'll never forget the night Jeffrey was born . . ." He smiled at the thought.

"They handed me this little squalling pink bundle and I couldn't believe what I felt. I didn't think it was possible to feel that way. It was instant love. I was filled with it, then and there. Right from that very first moment I would have done anything to protect him or help him or make him happy."

Tears came streaming down my face at his sweet recollection.

"I looked at that baby," Jake went on, "and thought of everything I knew about the biology and the genetics, all the medical science of how he came into being. It didn't come close to explaining the miracle I was holding. I thought of the whole plan of salvation and all that we are blessed to know. I wondered how anyone who's ever held a baby could doubt that there's a God.

"But Tess was just tired. She only wanted to sleep. I stayed up all night though, and held my son. I was in awe. I thought of how tiny and fragile he was. I thought of how profound it would be to help children who had their whole lives ahead of them, to impact their futures for the better. I realized that was where the opportunity to truly change the world was, with children. That was when I decided to specialize in pediatrics."

Jake turned to see my tears and asked suddenly, "What did I say, Mar? I didn't mean to upset you."

"I'm sorry." I grabbed a tissue from a box on the floor and wiped at the tears again. "I just can't hear about a baby without thinking of Ashlyn. Losing her was so hard . . . It's still hard. I can't even tell you what it would have meant to me if Ted had felt the way you just said you did. He didn't even seem to care. He left me in the hospital, mourning alone, and then acted as if she'd never been born."

Jake reached over to squeeze my hand. "I'm sorry, love. I can't imagine the agony of losing a child."

I took a breath and dried my eyes. "So, finish your story," I encouraged.

"That's pretty much all there is," he said. "I spent a lot of time chastising myself for not helping Tess more. I should have been there more, been a better support. Maybe I even should have taken money from my parents. Ironically, my grandfather passed away just a few months after we divorced. He left me a sizeable trust fund . . ." Jake's voice trailed off and he stared out the front window for several moments before adding thoughtfully, "Maybe it was a blessing that she was already gone then. She could have blown all that money in a hurry and not done anything worthwhile with it . . . Maybe the way she spent money was my fault too, though. Maybe she was just trying to fill the emptiness. I obviously didn't make her feel loved enough—"

"Jake," I cut him off. "Do you really think you could have done anything that would have made a difference?"

He looked at me for a moment with sad eyes. "No," he finally admitted. "I just wasn't what she wanted. A family wasn't what she wanted."

"Didn't she want to take the children?" I asked.

He shook his head. "She walked away and never looked back. She asked to see them once every few months, but that was it."

"I can't imagine being a mother and feeling that way."

"Neither can I, but in some ways I'm grateful. I don't think I could handle it if I only saw them every other weekend. Elizabeth doesn't even remember her mother, and Jeffrey rarely asks about her anymore. I wanted to come back here after I finished my residency. I called and told Tess that we were moving. She said, 'good luck.' That's it. I told her that I was taking her children, who she'd only seen two or three times in a year and a half, clear across the United States, and she just said, 'good luck.' I had to get away from her, away from that huge city. My family didn't want us to go. They were close enough to visit often there, and they were a big support, but I wanted Jeff and Lizzy to grow up here. I felt like this was where we belonged."

"It is." I smiled.

He turned to smile back. "Thanks, Mar."

"How is your family?" I asked him. I'd met his parents and his younger sister when we were dating. They'd flown out just to meet me in fact. They were good people.

"They're fine. My sister's married now, but she doesn't have any children. They miss Jeff and Lizzy terribly. I do feel bad about that."

"I'm sure they miss all of you very much," I said quietly, thinking that it must have taken a lot of courage for him to move so far away from them, even if he did feel like it was a better place to raise his children.

After a few moments in silent contemplation, I felt compelled to say, "It's not your fault, Jake. Everyone makes mistakes. Every couple has problems. That doesn't mean they run off with other people and leave their spouses and their children behind."

"And it doesn't mean they have to resort to drinking and violence," he put in. "It's not your fault either."

"I know," I said.

"I know too," he answered. "But it certainly feels good to have someone *tell* me that it's not my fault."

"How do you feel now?" I asked him.

"There's still a lot of grief, Mar. I'm not trusting like I used to be. The thought of ever getting close to someone again terrifies me. After that and . . ."

"And what?" I asked.

He looked deeply at me for a moment before saying, "Nothing . . . I've just had enough pain. Honestly, Maren, it's a relief that she's gone. It's profoundly sad for me, but it's a relief."

I nodded. "I think I know what you mean."

"Yes, I think you do."

Chapter 13

Just before we got home Jake said, "Can you get into your house?"

"Yes. I keep a spare key in the front flower pot, just in case."

"You trust me with that information?" He grinned.

"If anything turns up missing now, I'll know where to look."

We both laughed, but it faded when we pulled into my driveway and Ted's car was there. I sucked in some air and tried to slow my heartbeat. "What's wrong?" Jake asked.

"That's Ted's car," I told him.

"What's he doing here?" he asked.

"I'm guessing he got the notice about our divorce being final too."

"Is that good or bad?"

"I'm not sure."

"Do you want me to come in with you?" Jake asked.

I shook my head. "No, I can handle it. I had the locks changed. He doesn't even have a key. Unless he found my spare . . ." I couldn't imagine that Ted would think to look in the flower pot, but I was secretly afraid. He wasn't in his car. I wondered if he'd gotten into the house somehow.

"Maren, I'll stay," Jake said.

"No, that will just make him more upset. I'll be okay."

"If he doesn't have a key to the house, where is he?" Jake asked, echoing my fears.

"I don't know. Maybe he got in through the garage."

"I'm coming in with you," Jake announced decidedly, unfastening his seat belt.

I put a hand on his arm. "No, Jake. Please. If I walk in with you, he'll freak out. I'll just go in there and calmly tell him to leave. It will be much easier without you."

"Are you sure?"

"I'm positive."

"Will he leave?"

"If I ask him to, yes," I said, trying to convince myself as much as him.

"Maren—"

"Really, Jake. It will make my life much easier if you just go."

"All right," he conceded. "Take care of yourself. Call me if you need me."

"I will."

Jake watched me pull the key out of the terra-cotta pot and hold it up before he backed away. I found Ted looking through the kitchen cupboards. He looked up in surprise when I walked in. "Hi, honey. Geez, what happened to you?"

"It's a long story. What are you doing here, Ted?"

"What do you mean 'what am I doing here?' This is my house. I miss the kids. I miss you . . . Where are the kids?"

I sank onto a barstool. I was torn between hugging him and beating him over the head with the nearby frying pan. "They're staying with my parents for a couple of days."

"Oh, so that's where you've been. I'm cooking some eggs. Want some?" he asked.

"Ted, you can't just come over here whenever you want to. You left four months ago. This is not going to work. We are *divorced*, Ted."

He leaned over the counter in his charming way, sandy hair falling into his eyes. "Come on, baby. I deserve a second chance. I love you." He leaned closer to me. My heart was pounding, my brain was swirling. I wanted to kiss him and have everything just go back to normal. I couldn't though. I just couldn't. At least not until he was getting some help for his problems. Then I realized that it was too late for things to go back to normal anyway. The divorce was final.

I turned my head at the last second and his lips brushed my hair. He stood up, pretending not to notice. Then he said with a gentleness that surprised me, "You look tired, Maren. Why don't you get some rest before the kids come home?"

"Ted, we are no longer married. Do you understand that? How did you get in anyway?"

He shrugged. "Be nice to me, baby. I need you."

"Ted, it's too late. The divorce is final. Please, get some help. Get well. Do it for yourself, Ted." He watched me quietly for a minute and I looked around, realizing that everything was clean. I could hear the dishwasher and the washing machine running. I wondered how long he'd been there. I was sure it was his own laundry that he was doing. And it must have been dishes that he'd dirtied. I'd left them all clean. Still, he'd done something. *Maybe he really would make an effort if I let him come around, if I tried to start over,* I thought. *But what about the lies and the drinking and the never being there for me?*

"I need you to help me, Maren," Ted pleaded. "I can't do this without you. Please." The words tugged at my heart. I wanted to help him. I did. He tried to kiss me again, and I stood up.

"Ted, please. You have to leave."

"I can't leave. I love you, baby. You're my wife."

"No, Ted. I am *not*. I'm not your wife anymore." It hurt to say it, but there was some relief in the words, as well.

"Maren, please," he begged. "I'll never get better without you. Just give me another chance. I deserve that."

"Ted! You've had four months to do something, and you haven't! And before that, you had ten years! It's too late. It's over. Whatever you do now, you do yourself. I hope you decide to get better, but if you don't, you have only yourself to blame."

"Maren, you are my *wife.*"

"No, *I'm not!* Get it through your head, Ted! Our marriage is over, dead, gone! Now, *please* leave."

I saw anger flash in his eyes again as he came around the counter. He leaned close to say, "Legal document or not, you *belong* to me, Maren. Nothing you can ever do will change that. We're still sealed, aren't we?"

"Technically, I suppose we are, but I think your choices voided that commitment years ago, Ted."

"Even if you kick me out, Maren, how do you know I won't come back?" So much for being nice. This was Ted. The part of Ted I hated, the part I could not live with.

"Ted, please . . . I'm so tired of these games." I sat down on the back of the overstuffed chair, my hand pushing against the pain in my chest. I felt suddenly weak. I just didn't have the strength to cope with this after my recent ordeal.

"This is not a game, Maren, remember? If I want to get in, I will. No lock is going to keep me out."

I felt ice creeping up my spine. He'd seemed normal at first, but now that he was so close to my face, I could detect at least a trace of alcohol on his breath. "How did you get in, Ted?" I asked.

"Through the broken window in the basement," he sneered.

"What broken window? . . ." I let my voice trail off as the awareness seeped in. "You *broke* a window, Ted? How could you do that?"

He grabbed my shoulders and hissed, "No, Maren, how could *you* do that? How could you leave me? How could you take my kids and my house and everything that I've worked for? *How could you?*"

"You left me no choice."

"Oh, *please.* Don't push your crap onto me." He shoved me away as he said it, but I caught the chair to steady myself. "You will never get rid of me, Maren. Do you hear me? *Never.*"

"Ted, I'll get a restraining order this time," I said, wishing that I already had. "Please don't make this get ugly."

"Oh, it's too late for that, baby. It already *is* ugly." His voice dripped with hate as he bared his teeth to grin.

I was finished with him. I wasn't going to put up with this anymore. I went for the phone, but Ted picked it up and hurled it at the wall. It broke. My stomach twisted into knots. At least I was grateful that the children weren't there. "Don't you *ever* call the cops on me again!" Ted shouted. "You got it, Maren? You ever do that to me again, and you'll be sorry! That's a *promise.*"

I just leaned against the back of the chair, struggling to breathe in spite of my aching lungs and racing heart. Ted looked around, apparently searching for something to throw. Finding nothing handy, he pushed over the glass-top table in the foyer instead. It clattered onto the tile, smashing the glass. Ted looked up innocently and said with a cold voice, *"Look* at what you made me do."

I couldn't take it. "Stop it!" I screamed. "I've never *made* you do anything, Ted! *You* keep getting drunk, *you* keep getting violent, *you* keep screwing up your own life!"

"Because you keep telling me what to do!"

"I'm not telling you what to do anymore, Ted," I said more quietly. "You're never going to get better until you take responsibility for your own actions. I am taking responsibility for mine. I'm getting out of this. Your life is your business, but that doesn't mean you can keep threatening mine. *Leave me alone.*"

He lunged at me and grabbed my arms, hollering in my face, "I will NOT leave you alone, Maren! I will NEVER leave you alone! You are going to live every moment for the rest of your life in FEAR!"

I covered my mouth with my hand trying to hold back the sobs, but I couldn't stop the coughs that raked over my chest, making it throb.

Ted ignored the coughing and stepped closer to me, forcing me to lean over the back of the chair. "Too bad there's no phone, Maren," he laughed. "Nobody to hear you scream, nobody to care. No one is going to save you this time, baby."

"You're wrong about that, Ted." Ted released his grip on me to whirl around and see Jake standing in the doorway. I stood up, but then sank down on the back of the chair. I felt too dizzy and weak to keep standing. I thanked the Lord that I had not locked the door, thinking that I might have to run back out if Ted was inside. I thanked Him again that Jake had come back and apparently heard the fighting. The momentary relief quickly turned to worry though.

There was total silence as apparent recognition seeped in. "What the—" Ted's words trailed off.

"I believe she asked you to leave, Ted," Jake said calmly, but I saw his jaw muscle twitch.

Ted just stared at him. "You can't be serious. This can't be . . . *Jake? What* are you doing at my house?"

"I heard you from down the block, so I came to investigate."

"From down the block? What are you even doing in this neighborhood? In this state, for that matter? I thought you lived back east somewhere," Ted challenged.

"I did," Jake acknowledged. "And then I came back, but that is really all quite irrelevant. The point is that Maren would like you to vacate the premises. Permanently."

"How do you even know where she lives?" Ted demanded. "What is this?"

"I happened to move into the neighborhood a couple of months ago."

Ted's voice went up a notch as he moved toward the door. "So now you're making the moves on my wife? This is *my* wife, *my* property. *Get . . . out.*"

Jake folded his arms on his chest and said, "You're wrong on all counts, Ted. I'm not making moves on anyone, she is not your wife, and she's nobody's property. *You* get out."

"Have you just been watching the house waiting for me to leave for a few days or what?" Ted spat. "I cannot *believe* this!"

"Ted, calm down," I said, moving toward him. "You don't understand." I touched his arm. He threw me off and shot me a venomous look.

He called me an awful name and demanded, "Did you kick me out just so you could fool around? You like your old pansy boyfriend better than me? Why don't you get him to pay your bills? Why don't you get him to put up with your crap? It won't be long before he gets sick of you too, Maren!"

"Ted, just listen to me. You don't even know what's going on."

"No, but I think I can guess!" he yelled as he slammed his fist into the wall. He turned around and lunged toward me again, but Jake stepped in front of me.

"Get out of my way, jerk," Ted warned. "This is none of your business."

"I'm making it my business," Jake said. "I'm not going to stand here and let you hurt her."

"You got a thing for my wife?" He narrowed his eyes at Jake.

"I wouldn't stand by and watch any man knock a woman around, Ted. I do have a great deal of respect and admiration for Maren, yes. And to repeat, for the record, she is no longer your wife."

Ted's eyes went wide. Then the corners of his mouth turned up and he laughed coldly. "It's easy to admire her when you've never had to live with her, Jantzen. Maybe you should try it. Maybe you should listen to her nagging and whining and complaining about all the things you don't live up to for a while. It's enough to drive a man to drink . . ."

I was furious. I tried to move around Jake, but he put his arm out to push me back behind him. He was taller than Ted, and slightly more muscular, but I doubted that he had a drop of violence in his blood. I didn't want to see him get pummeled by fists of drunken fury because of me.

"Move over, Jake," Ted demanded.

"I'd prefer to end this peacefully," Jake said. "But if you are going to insist on knocking someone around, I am going to insist that it be someone your own size. It's up to you, Ted."

Ted raised his fists, but Jake didn't even flinch. He just stayed where he was. To my surprise, Ted backed down. "Fine," he said to Jake, but then he sneered at me, "Someday you won't be so lucky."

"That sounded like a threat to me, Ted. I'd be careful if I were you," Jake said smoothly. "A judge might not show you the same mercy that I have. There are a lot of people in this neighborhood who are watching out for Maren these days. You'll get yourself into a lot of trouble if you keep this up."

Ted just glared at Jake before he slammed the door shut behind him.

I took a moment to breathe and waited to hear Ted's car drive away before I dared to speak. "Thank you for coming back, Jake."

"I should have come with you the first time," he muttered, turning to look at me. He was quiet for a minute before asking, "Is he always this bad, Mar?"

"Pretty much," I answered dryly. I was too ashamed to look at him. I turned and moved toward the hallway, not wanting him to see me bawling again, especially after what he'd just witnessed. He caught my arm and pulled me back. "For heaven's sake, Maren," he said, tilting my chin up to face him. "Don't go slinking away like you did something wrong. This is *not* your fault. Don't hide anymore. It's just me. Go ahead and cry if you want to. You don't have anything to be ashamed of."

"But I do. I've lost all my strength. I'm just an insecure mess." I felt the tears threatening and I pulled my face from his grasp to look away.

"Maren," Jake said again. "That's not true. You were strong enough to stay and try to make your marriage work, and you were strong enough to leave when you realized it wasn't going to. It's not you. It's him. *It is him.*"

My thoughts were churning and I turned to pull away, but Jake kept his hold on me. "It's *not* your fault, Mar," he insisted. "And it *is* all right to ask for help."

I didn't say anything.

"Why didn't you just let me come in with you in the first place?" he prodded gently.

"Because this isn't your problem!" I shot out. "I got myself into it. I can get myself out."

"How? He's a lot bigger than you . . . What would you have done, Maren, if I hadn't come back?"

I felt angry, and yanked my arm from his grasp. "The same thing I've been doing for ten years, Jake! You weren't here *then!*"

I was surprised to see a look of pain wash over his face as he answered quietly, "That's not my fault, Maren."

His words stunned me, and sent more than ten years of pain rushing to the surface. I turned away quickly, but he put an arm around my shoulders to turn me back around. "I'm sorry," he told me. "I shouldn't have said that."

I struggled against the dam of emotions, and tried to move down the hall once more, but Jake caught my arm again. "It won't do any good to bottle up all the feelings," he insisted. "You're in mourning. I understand, believe me. You can cry. You *need* to cry, in fact."

"Let me go!" I screamed at him.

He let go of my arm and said, "Okay, Maren, but you need someone right now."

"No, I don't! I don't need anyone anymore! I've had enough of dependence. If I can't make it on my own, I don't want to make it at all! You can't just breeze back into my life and fix everything, Jake! It's hopeless!" My voice cracked. "You can't fix it. It's just a hopeless . . . mess."

"I never meant to imply that I could fix anything. I just want to be your friend. Everyone needs a friend, Mar, especially during a divorce. It's all right to need someone. Let me be your friend, at least."

I looked up at him, at the sincere concern in his eyes. I felt everything rushing up from my heart and knew that he was right. I did need more friends. I needed him. I couldn't handle it all by myself. The tears began to spill with the realization.

"It's never hopeless, Maren," Jake said tenderly. "There's always hope." He opened his arms to me, and I only hesitated a moment before I fell into them. I leaned against his solid chest and sobbed.

"There you go," he whispered, wrapping his arms around me and kissing my head. "You be angry. You cry it all out. I'm here. You're safe."

"I hate him, Jake!" I sobbed. "I hate him for doing this to me! I want him to just be . . . gone."

"I know you do, Mar. I know."

"He hurt me all the time," I cried fiercely. "He bullied me, and treated me like garbage, and told me I was worthless."

"But you're not, Maren. He was so, so wrong."

"He was never there for me, never, not even once. Through school, and three pregnancies, and losing Ashlyn, and the babies, and the diapers, and the house, and the whole ten years of hell . . . I was all alone. And he wanted me to believe that it was all my fault—everything."

"And how did you feel?" Jake asked quietly, still holding me to him tightly.

"I felt mad, sad, lonely, lost . . . and I *felt* worthless. I felt like it *was* all my fault. But I tried everything, Jake, and nothing ever worked."

"Yes, you did, love. It's not your fault," he soothed. "None of this is your fault."

I cried for several more minutes, thinking of everything Ted had ever done that had hurt me or made me angry or made me feel ashamed. I cried thinking of everything I had dreamed of and lost. I cried with regret over my own decisions and wished that I had stood up for myself long ago. When my emotion was finally spent, I whispered, "Thank you, Jake. I do need a friend."

"I know that, Mar," he chuckled softly.

When I pulled away from him to wipe at my eyes, he asked, "Are you okay?"

I nodded.

"All right then, where's your phone book?"

"Why? Isn't it about time you went home?"

"Not yet. I need to make a couple of phone calls first. Do you mind?"

I nodded toward the heap of broken parts and said, "There's the phone. If you can get it to work, be my guest."

He sighed. "Are Ann and Tyler home yet?"

I looked at the kitchen clock and shook my head. "Not for at least a couple of hours."

"Okay, I'm going to run home, but I'll be back in a few minutes."

"You don't need to come back, Jake. I'm fine."

"I know you are. I'll see you in a bit."

A grateful lump rose in my throat and I could only nod.

"Give me your key." Jake held out his hand.

"What?"

"Your house key. Give it to me."

"Why?"

"Because I think you should go take a long hot bath, and I am going to let myself back in to clean up this mess." He tilted his head toward the pile of glass in the entryway.

"Oh, no you're not. I'm going to do that right now."

Jake touched my arm and said, "Maren, don't fight me. We've both had enough of that for one day, don't you think?"

I didn't say anything, so he prodded, "Your cough does not sound good, Mar. You need to rest. You're feeling pretty weak, aren't you?"

I still didn't say anything until he tilted my chin up to meet his gaze and said again, *"Aren't you?"*

"Yes," I reluctantly admitted and started coughing again, cursing the timing.

Jake held out his hand once more and wiggled his fingers.

I pointed to the single key that I'd set down on the foyer table when I entered the house. It was on the floor, swimming in a sea of broken glass.

He bent to carefully pick it up and said, "Go take care of yourself. I'll see you in a few minutes." He paused at the door and turned back, saying, "How did Ted get in?"

"He broke a window in the basement."

Jake shook his head and locked the door before he pulled it closed behind him.

I decided to take his advice and soak in a hot bath for a few glorious minutes. I couldn't recall ever being so grateful for a curling iron and makeup. When I finally looked and felt like I was back in the world of the living, I walked out to the great room to find Jake sitting on the couch. The iron frame of the foyer table was standing where it had been, the tile was swept clean, and the carpet was vacuumed. Jake had obviously taken a shower at home and changed clothes. His hair was still damp.

"Thank you," I said.

"You're welcome."

I sat down in the chair across from him and asked, "Are Jeff and Lizzy all right?"

He nodded. "They're not even home. Greg and Julie left a note and said they were taking them to a movie. They won't be back for a while."

"Did you get your phone calls made?"

"Yes. I called someone to come and fix your window, and someone to put in a security system. The security guy's on his way over, but the window guy can't come for a couple of hours."

"Jake!" I felt flustered. "You can't do that! I can't af—" I stopped myself. I didn't want to tell him that I couldn't afford a security system. I guessed that I would have to take money for the window out of savings, but I could live without a burglar alarm.

"I know you can't afford it, Maren," he said. "But I can."

"Oh, no! No, no, no. I have been humiliated enough. There is *no way* that I am going to let you pay for something I don't even need, Jake."

"You do need it, Maren. I heard Ted. He said that he would never leave you alone, that you were going to live in fear for the rest of your life."

"Idle drunken threats," I mumbled.

"His threats don't seem to be so idle, Mar."

I stood up and glared at him. "Jacob Jantzen, I will *not* take charity from you! You've done a lot more than you needed to, and I am grateful, but I'm not taking your money!"

"Maren, you watch my children every day—"

"And you pay me more than you need to for that, too."

"But, Maren—"

I stamped my foot. "I mean it. Do you hear me, Jake? I am tired of being bossed around, and I won't take it anymore! This is not your decision to make!"

"Maren, you need it. Your children need it."

He was right. I was going to be terrified twenty-four hours a day if I didn't do something. I flopped back down in the chair as I started to cough again. Jake finally got up and went to get me a drink of water, which I took gratefully. "I don't want to upset you," he told me. "I just want you to be safe."

"I know," I said quietly. "You're right. I do need it. But I'm going to pay for it."

"With what?"

"I have a little money in savings."

"Maren, just let me help you."

"No! This is my problem, not yours."

"Maren, why do you think the Lord led us to each other again?"

"What do you mean?" I tried to ignore the slight flutter in my heart again.

"I don't believe it was a coincidence," he said quietly. "Do you?"

I thought about it for a minute. The way that everything had worked out was just . . . too uncanny to be an accident. "No."

"Maybe God is using each of us to bless the other's life. Did you ever think about that?"

I only nodded quietly, and he continued, "You've certainly been a blessing to me over the past three months, and to my children."

"You've been a blessing to me too, Jake."

"Did it occur to you that God knows I have the means to help you, Maren?"

"Right now, I have the means to help myself. I'm very grateful to you, Jake, but I need to take care of myself. Please understand that."

"All right." He gave in. He considered me for a minute, tapping his fingers on the arm of the couch before he finally said, "I think you should file a police report and get a restraining order."

I just looked at him, not saying anything.

He took it as an invitation to prove his point. "It's a good time, Mar. The kids are gone, so it won't upset them. They could look at the window in the basement. You certainly have cause to keep him away from you. Maybe that would scare him into keeping his distance."

"You're right again," I conceded. "Will you call them for me?"

He smiled and pulled out his cell phone. "I'd be happy to."

I was thankful that the alarm installer was late. That gave me time to go through the awful police report nightmare again without any other observers. I was embarrassed enough to have Jake there. The officers took pictures of the basement window and told me that I could get a temporary restraining order to get me through the weekend. Then I would have to go to court for a permanent one.

They said they'd notify Ted that if he came within fifty feet of me or the children, he would be arrested.

Jake didn't leave until the window was replaced, the alarm system was installed, and I knew how to use it. "Do you want to stay in my guest room tonight?" he offered.

"No," I laughed.

"Do you want me to bring the kids over here and camp out with them on your living room floor?"

"And what would I do tomorrow night? And the next night? No, Jake, I'm fine."

"You remember that I don't have to go back to work until Tuesday?"

"Yes, and you're working on Wednesday next week to make up for it. I remember."

"Good. So, I'll watch Rebecca and Trevor for you while you go get your restraining order."

I opened my mouth to protest, but then changed my mind. What else was I going to do? "Thank you."

"Bye, Mar."

"Bye."

I started coughing and walked back into the kitchen to get a drink. I stood leaning against the counter and thinking for several minutes before I noticed the new phone that was plugged into the wall. I shook my head and smiled.

By Sunday I was feeling a lot better. A good night's sleep had done wonders for me. I still had a little bit of a cough, but I went to church anyway. The girls were glad to see me. I stood with them to recite the Young Women's theme and thought deeply about the first part of it. "We are daughters of our Heavenly Father, who loves us, and we love Him. We will stand as witnesses of God at all times, and in all things, and in all places, as we strive to live the Young Women Values, which are: faith, divine nature, individual worth, knowledge, choice and accountability, good works, and integrity . . ."

The theme played over and over in my head, making me think about my life. I decided that I was making a fresh start. Ted was gone. I was going to start my life over for me. I vowed to make a better effort to live those values myself so that I could set a good example for my

Laurels. I wasn't going to do it just for them though. I was going to do it for myself. I closed my eyes and tried to convince myself that I *was* a daughter of God, a woman of divine nature with inherent individual worth. I had let myself forget all that over the past ten years.

I decided that I would go to the library the next day and check out some self-help books. My counselor had recommended some, but I'd never taken the time to look for them. The thought of signing up for self-defense classes also crossed my mind. I knew they taught them at the community center as I'd seen a flyer tacked to the bulletin board at the gym. I was determined to find myself again.

Chapter 14

I was thrilled to have my children back home with me on Sunday night. Mom and Dad offered to stay and help me, but I assured them that I was fine. I knew they needed to get back to the farm. Though still weak, I opted to at least accompany Ann to the gym on Monday morning. While there, I filled her in on the details of my trip and what had happened afterward. I'd given her a very brief synopsis over the phone the night before and she'd offered to help me with the restraining order. I also talked her into signing up to take self-defense classes with me two mornings a week instead of doing our regular workout. "It will be an adventure," I told her.

"You're getting a little too gutsy for your own good," she teased. "But I guess I can't blame you after your harrowing weekend . . . Jake really did all that for you?"

"Yes," I answered humbly.

"That man is a gem," she said.

"He's definitely been a blessing to me," I admitted.

"You're not going to let him get away again, are you?" she demanded.

"I can't let something 'get away' that I don't have in the first place, Annie girl."

"Stop it, stop it, stop it!" she objected, but she smiled.

"Sorry. To continue, Ms. Ann L. Adams, attorney at law—"

"That's better."

"—as I have explained to you several times, Dr. Jantzen and I are friends, nothing more."

"It sounds like it's getting to be a little more," she remarked.

"Well, it's not. We're both going through a lot of the same struggles right now, that's all. We seem to be able to help each other here and there, and it's nice to have someone who's been through the same thing—for both of us."

"Whatever you say."

"Let's change the subject," I suggested.

She surprised me by answering, "All right. Speaking of helpful friendships and how they come about, I'll fill you in on a little observation of mine. I've been thinking a lot lately about how nice our friendship is, how we're at opposing ends of the spectrum."

"How so?" I asked.

"I mean we're total opposites. I'm proud and selfish and self-absorbed. I'm totally driven at work. I need to have solid confirmation of my success. I want power. I need to develop more compassion for other people. I should be more sensitive. I should make a bigger effort to keep my house uncluttered and be a homemaker. I should give more of myself. On the upside, I have no problem standing up for myself or going after what I want. I'm confident of who I am.

"You, on the other hand, can't say no. Your whole life is serving other people. You need to learn to take better care of yourself. You need to develop some self-confidence and assert yourself. You have a beautiful house, though, which you somehow manage to keep clean most of the time. You're so good at all that domestic stuff. And you're so willing to give. Maybe we'll eventually help each other get to a more balanced place in the middle."

I laughed. "That's some observation. I have to agree with you though. All except the part about you being selfish, that is. It's strange that we're as contrasting as we are, isn't it?"

She looked at me thoughtfully for a minute before saying, "Yeah. Maybe we were brought together for a reason, to help each other grow."

I smiled. "I'm sure of that. I feel the same way about Jake."

"Well, if that's the case, I might start to feel threatened," she teased. "I guess the kids like him, but they *love* me. And the man does seem to have impeccable taste . . . but I still don't think he's as fashion conscious as I am. He couldn't be as fun to go shopping with. And he doesn't clean your house, does he?"

"No." I smiled.

"Good. Keep that in mind. Don't go replacing me with some guy."

"Ann, I could never replace you," I laughed.

My conversation with Ann reminded me to stop at the library before I picked up my children. I checked out books on recovering from abusive relationships, families of alcoholics, helping children deal with divorce, and how to set boundaries. *What a novel idea,* I thought to myself.

* * *

The judge granted my restraining order and took away Ted's visitation. He called the next day to scream and yell at me. I guessed that the restraining order had scared him enough to keep him from coming over. With that and my new alarm system, I felt a lot safer. After a string of obscenities, I hung up on him. He called back and I picked up the phone, saying, "Ted, I don't have to take this anymore. I won't. You've got to make some changes if you're going to get your life together and see your children."

"What about you, Maren? Why don't *you* make some changes?"

"I'm trying to. And one of those changes is that I'm going to stand up for myself."

"Oh, that's great, Maren. Congratulations. I'm so sick of hearing how wonderful you are, how you think I should treat you like a queen."

"I've never said anything like that, Ted. I never told you that I was wonderful. I certainly never asked to be treated like a queen. I do have some worth though, Ted. I'm not garbage. I am going to demand some respect."

He laughed cruelly. "If you were *half* as wonderful as you think you are, Maren . . ."

"Did you have something productive to say, Ted? I have things to do."

"I want to see my kids," he demanded.

"Then learn to control yourself. Get some help."

"Help for what?!" he shouted.

"Help for your problem."

"I don't have a problem, Maren!" he yelled louder, and then lowered his voice to hiss, *"You* do."

"Good luck, Ted," I said quietly, and hung up again.

When the phone rang the third time, I lost it. I picked it up and shouted, "Leave me alone, Ted! I'm done! I will *not* be treated this way. Don't call me again unless you can be civil and have something worthwhile to say!"

I waited through a long pause that surprised me, and finally asked in annoyance, "Are you there?"

"Yes. I'm just trying to think of something worthwhile to say. Give me a minute."

"Jake!" I gasped. I felt the color rise in my cheeks and was at least thankful that he couldn't see my face. "I'm sorry. I thought that was the third time in a row that Ted had called and . . ." My words trailed off.

"Well, I must say I'm glad to hear you standing up for yourself," he laughed.

"I'll bet you are. I really am sorry."

"Don't say you're sorry anymore, Maren. You say that all the time."

"Do I?"

"Yes, you do. I just wanted to make sure that you're still planning on the kids in the morning, since we don't usually come on Wednesday."

"Yes, I am."

"How are you doing?" he asked more quietly.

"Fine, Jake. How are you?"

"Fine," he laughed softly. "See you in the morning."

"See you then."

* * *

By August, I'd firmed up quite a bit. I didn't know if I'd lost any more weight because I quit getting on the scales. I decided not to play that game with myself. I did know that I looked and felt better. I had a lot more energy. I could even jog on the treadmill. "You are a miracle worker," I told Ann.

"Maren, give yourself some credit," she said, exasperated.

Rebecca and Jeffrey started kindergarten at the end of the month. It was a little hard to get used to, but they both gradually got the hang of it. We all settled into a pretty good routine. Ann and I still met at the gym every morning. Then I would go home to meet Jake and get Jeff and Lizzy. Sometimes the kids and I did art projects or preschool lessons in the morning, or sometimes the children just played. There was the occasional dispute, of course, but all things considered, the four of them got along very well.

I put Rebecca and Jeff on the kindergarten bus after lunch. Then Trevor and Elizabeth had quiet time. I usually took advantage of the free hour to clean, but occasionally I read or worked on scrapbooks. When Becca and Jeff came home, we had snack time and story time. Then they played until Jake came around six o'clock to pick them up. It was working out well for everyone.

I asked Rebecca if she wanted to start taking dance lessons that fall. "I started them when I was in kindergarten," I told her.

"What kind of dance lessons?" she asked me.

"Ballet is the foundation for everything else, so you should probably start with that. You could take tap and ballet lessons together if you want to."

"Do you want me to take dance lessons, Mom?" she asked me.

I smiled and said, "I think you might enjoy them, but it's up to you, sweetie. I do think you'd be good at it. You're built like me. You have a dancer's body."

Elizabeth's eyes went wide and she asked, "Are you a dancer, Maren?"

"I used to be."

"I want to be a dancer!" she exclaimed as she jumped up and twirled around. "Can I take dance lessons?"

"You might be a little young, sweetheart."

She puffed out her bottom lip and said, "I'm three and a half!"

I smiled. "Yes, and you're very grown up. We could probably find something for you. Why don't you ask your daddy if it's all right?"

"Can't you teach us how to dance, Mommy?" Rebecca asked.

"I could, but it's more fun to take a class with other little girls."

"What if I don't want to be a dancer?" she tested.

"Then you don't have to be. You can be whatever you want."

"Yeah!" Trevor agreed as he pretended to swing a bat through the air. "I'm going to be a baseball player . . . and an astronaut!" he announced as he climbed up on the couch to jump off.

"What can I be, Maren?" Jeffrey asked.

"You can be anything you want to be too, bud. What do you think you'd like to do?"

"I like to draw," he pointed out.

"Yes, you're quite an artist. You're good with your hands, just like your dad."

His eyes went wide. "Is my dad an artist?"

"Not like you are, but sort of. He's a surgeon. That's kind of an art."

"I could be a doctor like my dad. That's cool 'cause there's blood and guts!"

"Or you could be an army guy and shoot the bad guys!" Trevor offered, demonstrating with actions and sound effects.

"Yeah. Or a cowboy," Jeffrey said.

"My grandpa's a cowboy," Trevor stated proudly.

"He is?" Jeff asked in awe.

"Yep. He has lots of cows, and some horses, and sheep, and chickens. And sometimes he wears a cowboy hat."

"I never saw a real cowboy."

"You didn't? Mom, can Jeff come with us to Grandpa's sometime? Then he could see a real cowboy, and cows and stuff."

I smiled. "I don't know, buddy. Maybe sometime. We'll have to see."

"What else could I be, Maren?" Jeffrey asked me.

"Well, you could be a teacher. You're a good leader. You make up games for the other kids to play all the time. Or you could be a writer. You have a wonderful imagination, and lots of good ideas. Or you could design buildings. You like to build with blocks."

"Or I could fly an airplane!"

"Yeah!" Trevor agreed. "Then I could race you in my rocket ship!" He made a rocket ship noise and zoomed around the room.

"Can I be more than one thing?" Jeff wondered. "There are too many fun things to be."

I laughed. "Of course you can, bud."

"Mom, what other kind of dancing is there?" Rebecca reverted back to our original topic of conversation.

"Well, there's modern and jazz and ballroom . . ."

Her face brightened with an idea. "Can we look at your dance shoes?"

"We haven't done that for a long time, have we?"

She shook her head.

"All right. Let's go look. Does anyone else want to come?"

"I do!" Elizabeth said.

"Not me," answered Jeffrey. "Hey, Trevor, let's go outside and race rocket ships!"

"Okay!"

The boys ran out the back door, and the girls followed me down the hall. I sat on the floor and pulled dusty boxes from beneath my bed. Rebecca removed lids and pulled out shoes while Elizabeth watched with wide eyes. When she opened my ballet shoe box, Lizzy gasped, "Ballerina shoes!" She lifted them out in reverent awe and ran the worn satin ribbons through her little fingers. "Are you a ballerina, Maren?" she asked.

"Kind of. It wasn't what I was best at, but I did dance ballet."

"If I do ballet, can I wear shoes like this?" she asked in wonder.

I smiled. "You can when you're older. At first you'd wear shoes like these." I lifted out the pink leather slippers to show to her.

"I want to do this kind of dance!" Rebecca announced. "What are these shoes for, Mom?"

I laughed as she struggled to stand up in silver strap sandals with three-inch heels. "Those are ballroom shoes, baby. I'm afraid you'll have to wait a while to do that."

"What's your favorite kind of dance?" she asked me.

"Jazz, but ballroom was next. That was a lot of fun in college."

"What's this?" Elizabeth peered under the bed and pulled out a photo album.

"That's my dance scrapbook."

"Can I look at it?" she asked eagerly.

"You may look at it all you want to, Lizzy." I smiled at her. She and Rebecca pored through the book, asking me about pictures and programs and costumes from the time I was five clear up through college.

When Jake came, Elizabeth ran to the door, still holding my toe shoes. "Look, Daddy!" she said, twirling around with them and watching the ribbons fly out around her. "I'm going to be a ballerina like Maren! Can I take dance lessons with Rebecca?"

He laughed at her and answered, "I don't know if you're old enough, Lizzy." He looked at me in question.

"She could do it," I told him.

"See, Daddy? I could do it!"

"Yes, I'm sure you could. I'll talk to Maren about it and we'll see, okay?"

"Okay!" She ran down the hall as I went to the backyard to call for Jeffrey. Before he came in, Elizabeth was back with my scrapbook. "Look at Maren's dance pictures," she said to Jake.

I felt suddenly self-conscious and told her, "He doesn't have time to look at all those, Elizabeth, but you can look at them again tomorrow if you want to."

"Can I just show Daddy my favorite one?" she asked me.

I smiled at her childish excitement. "If he wants to see it."

Jake laughed again and replied, "Oh, I want to see it." He sat down on the floor and watched his daughter flip to the back of the book.

"That's my favorite one," she pointed. "Because Maren looks so pretty, and she's grown-up like she is now, and her dress is shiny."

Jake took the book in his hands and smiled, "Ah, yes. I have to agree with you, Elizabeth." He studied the picture quietly for a minute until I leaned over his shoulder to see which one it was. I was standing with my dance partner at BYU, wearing a shimmery silver dress. I had silver glitter in my hair and on my cheeks and eyelids. I could see how the costume would appeal to a little girl. "I came to watch you in this competition," Jake said, looking up at me.

"I remember."

He looked back down at the picture he held and observed quietly, "Was I ever jealous of that guy."

"What?" I asked in surprise. "You never got jealous!"

He chuckled and turned around to face me with the book in his hands. "I may never have voiced it, Mar, but that didn't mean I never felt it."

"Really?"

"Oh, come on, Maren. How could I not have been jealous when he got to hold you that way and dance with you all night like that? It made my blood boil . . . It was enough to make me wish that I could dance."

I just stared at him.

He shrugged. "I always envied those guys you danced with. And then there was Ted . . ."

I was shocked at the insight into his feelings all those years ago. "I never knew . . ." I said quietly.

"Never knew? Please, Ms. Griffin, you're a much more intelligent woman than that."

"No, Jake, I didn't know. You were always so calm . . ."

He raised his eyebrow. "Calm behavior is not necessarily indicative of a lack of passionate feeling, my dear. You choose the way you behave; you don't choose how you feel."

I found myself wondering what else I'd misread all those years ago.

Chapter 15

Rebecca and Elizabeth started a tap and ballet class together in September and Jake's birthday was on the seventh of that month. "Are you doing anything tonight?" I asked when he dropped the kids off in the morning, trying to be inconspicuous.

"No. Why?"

I shrugged. "No reason. I just wondered."

He gave me a strange look. "Okay, then. Have a good day."

"You too. Bye."

I invited Ann and Tyler over for pizza and birthday cake. I hung up balloons and made party hats with the kids. We were all waiting when Jake got there. The children were too excited to contain themselves. Jake was barely through the door when they all ran toward him, yelling, "Happy Birthday!"

He laughed and knelt down to hug all of them "That is the best birthday greeting I ever got," he said. They gave him the cards they'd made and even talked him into wearing a birthday hat. I took pictures and told him I was going to keep them for blackmailing purposes.

"What are you going to try to get out of me?" he asked teasingly. "If I have something you want, Maren, you could probably just ask." He winked at me, and Ann gave me a smug look. I ignored her.

After we ate, we turned on a movie for the kids and the adults played games around the kitchen table. Jake and Tyler were getting to be good friends by then, too. They were so funny together. It was wonderful. The kids had all dozed off in front of the TV by the time Ann dragged her husband to his feet and said, "Let's go. These two both have children to put to bed."

Tyler shook his fair head and looked wistfully at our four children sprawled out all over the couch and the floor. "I wish we did too," he said. I was surprised. Although Ann and I talked about it all the time, I'd never heard him voice the longing so openly.

Tyler must have thought that Jake looked confused because he clarified, "Hasn't Maren told you?"

"Told me what?" Jake asked.

"Oh, just about our childless plight," he said jokingly. It made my heart hurt for them, like it always did.

"No," Jake said softly. "She hasn't told me. But I am sorry. You two would be wonderful parents." Everyone was quiet for a minute until Jake said, "I don't mean to pry, but have you considered adopting? My ex-wife was adopted. Her parents seemed happy with the situation."

Ann and Tyler looked at each other, as though trying to decide who was going to tackle that one. "We've talked about that, actually," Tyler admitted finally. "Ann would like to try it, but I just don't think I could do it."

"Really?" Jake asked. "Why not?"

Ann was beginning to look upset. I knew that she and Tyler had argued over this before. Still, I'd never really heard Tyler's side of it. I thought maybe it would be good for him to tell someone else about it. He sat back down and glanced over at our sleeping children once more before looking from Jake to me and back again. Ann sat down next to him and folded her arms on the table.

"To be perfectly honest," Tyler said, "it's pretty difficult to see other people's children, you know? You guys both have great kids, and I don't want you to get the wrong idea. I mean, Rebecca and Trevor have been coming over to our house for more than two years. It's just that . . . I don't think I could ever love someone else's child like my own. I don't think I could look at a child that I knew wasn't really mine every day and feel like a father should feel."

"I still think you could do it, Tyler," Ann said. "I don't think you could take care of a baby every day and not learn to love it." I agreed with Ann, but I knew it wasn't my place to say so.

"Maybe I'll feel differently someday if it comes down to that being our only option," Tyler conceded, as if to avoid an argument. "But that's how I feel right now. Anyway, we have a couple of things left to try first. We'll see." He stood up again and said, "Tonight was a lot of fun. Happy Birthday, Jake."

"You know, Jake," Ann said, as she got to her feet, "Tyler and I watch Rebecca and Trevor here and there. I think we could probably handle four kids for one night if you and Maren wanted to do something." Tyler nodded in agreement.

I narrowed my eyes reproachfully at her and she gave me a bright smile. I looked up to see Jake watching me, and I felt embarrassed. I wondered if he'd seen the look I gave Ann.

"Sorry about that," I mumbled after they closed the door. I started to clean up, not wanting to look at Jake. "Ann feels this incessant need to fix my life for me," I felt compelled to explain. "She doesn't understand."

"She doesn't understand what?" Jake asked as he started picking up crepe paper and paper plates to throw away.

"She doesn't understand our friendship," I admitted. "She doesn't understand that it's not some big romance. I mean . . . not that I've told her that or anything . . . not that she has any reason to believe there's some big romance . . ." I felt overwhelmingly flustered and suddenly wished that I could escape. It unnerved me further to look up and see that Jake had stopped picking up garbage to fix that gaze of his on me. I couldn't look him in the eye. I knew that he could read me like a book. I tried to grasp his expression without facing him head-on, but I couldn't tell if it was confusion or amusement or hurt that I saw in his face.

I closed my eyes and let out a deep breath, trying to gather my wits. I reminded myself that it was Jake, that we'd been friends for years, and that I could tell him anything. I finally faced him and said, "She still believes in fairy tales—that's all, Jake."

"And what do you believe in?" he asked quietly.

"Survival." I couldn't take those electric eyes boring into me any longer. "I'll finish cleaning up, Dr. Jantzen. You take your children home."

"I'll help clean up, Mar."

I took the trash bag from him and smiled. "No, it's your birthday. You go home and go to bed."

"Maren—"

"I insist, Jake. It's only once a year. Now get out of here."

"That was very thoughtful, what you did for me tonight," he said. "The most fun I've had in quite a while, actually."

I smiled and said, "Happy Birthday." I gave him a quick hug and helped him carry the children to his car. I didn't look back to see him drive away.

* * *

October was a difficult month for me. The thought of the approaching winter and our financial situation for Christmas was hard, but the pain of Ashlyn's birthday was worse. The wound her absence left in my heart somehow always seemed more raw that month. I visited her grave more often than usual, taking little bunches of pink carnations or white daisies to brighten up the dull gray gloom of the cemetery. I cleared the fallen leaves from her tiny headstone and ran my fingers over her name, and every time it rained, I cried.

It was always a relief of sorts when Halloween came, and I knew the torturous month would be over. That year they had a ward carnival at the church house. I thought that it was a good idea to get the children off the streets early. We went trick-or-treating just before dusk and then went to join the festivities set up in the church gymnasium.

Rebecca and Trevor were delighted when Jeffrey and Elizabeth arrived. "Look at my fairy costume, Maren!" Elizabeth exclaimed, twirling around to show me the shimmery fabric.

"Ooh, that's pretty, Lizzy." I smiled at her.

"Hey, you guys," Jeff said to my children. "Do you want to come with us? We can take turns deciding what to do. I want to play that game where you get to throw darts at balloons."

Rebecca put her hands on her hips and said, "Why should you get to decide what we do first?"

He shrugged. "You can go first if you want to, Becca."

She softened after that and suggested, "Should we let the little kids go first?"

"Yeah, let's do that. We can go youngest to oldest."

Jake and I followed the children around, watching them playing games and collecting candy. All four of them finally sat down on the floor in a vacant corner, admiring their cache of treats and trying to consume it in record time. Jake went to get us cups full of hot apple cider and we sat close by the children, talking.

"You seem a little down tonight," Jake observed. "More quiet than usual."

"Do I?" I studied the swirls of cinnamon in the bottom of my cup.

"Is there anything you need, Maren?" Jake asked.

I met his earnest gaze and smiled softly. "No, I'm fine. Thanks for looking out for me, and for your support and friendship." I looked around at all the happy families that were there together, all the husbands and wives holding hands, and I felt very lonely. I thought of what my counselor had told me about divorce being as traumatic as a death, that you had to go through the same process of grieving and acceptance to get on with your life.

Jake followed my gaze and said, "It's kind of hard coming to these things, isn't it?"

"Yes, it is."

"Do you miss him, Maren?" he asked suddenly.

I glanced up at him, surprised at his question. "Yes. Do you miss her?"

He looked back toward the crowd and said softly, "Not as much as I used to."

We were both quiet for a minute until Jake asked, "Is Ted paying you enough for you to make it all right?"

"He sends me what he's supposed to. He's been more cooperative since the restraining order."

"But is it enough?"

I took a moment to consider my response. "Truthfully?"

"No," he answered sarcastically. "Tell me a lie. I could use another one."

"No, it's not enough. I've been using little bits of my savings account here and there, which isn't good. It could disappear in a hurry. I need to figure out something else."

"Let me help you, Mar."

I shook my head and said firmly, "No. I told you, Jake—I need to make it on my own."

"For Christmas then. Let me help you with that."

"No, Jacob. No." I turned away so he wouldn't see the moisture in my eyes.

"All done trick-or-treating already?" Tyler asked as he and Ann came to join us. I was grateful for the diversion.

"I don't know about the kids," Jake laughed, "but we are."

We sat talking for a little while, stopping every few minutes to greet one of our priests or Laurels, or to tell the children to settle down as they ran around the gym with all the other kids in the ward. Ann watched the children wistfully and finally remarked, "I don't know why we come to these things. It just gets more painful every time."

Tyler shook his head and agreed, "Yeah . . . These Church functions do tend to point out the glaring incompleteness of our family." His gray eyes looked sad as he put an arm around Ann's shoulders.

"Funny," Jake commented. "Maren and I were just making that same observation . . . but for different reasons."

"I guess we're just the misfit corner," I remarked, feeling suddenly bitter at the rosy pictures of perfect families hanging in the air at these things like taunting mirages.

Tyler looked thoughtful for a minute and pointed out, "We don't know what all those other people are struggling with though. Lots of people in the ward think we choose not to have children. Maybe their lives aren't all sunny either. Maybe we just don't know."

Jake nodded and said, "Good point."

Chapter 16

When Ann came over that Saturday, she asked, "Do you need help for Christmas?"

"I wish everyone would quit asking that," I said in annoyance. "Do I just look like a walking charity case, or what?"

"Who beat me to the punch?" she asked, grinning wickedly and flipping her sleek brown hair back.

"Who do you think?" I looked away from her to finish loading the dishwasher.

"Why don't you just give in and marry that man?" she asked, folding her arms across her stomach.

"Will you give it up?" I threw my hands in the air in exasperation. "For the millionth time, Jake and I are *just friends!*"

Ann leaned back against the counter and said matter-of-factly, "Are you blind, Maren? The man is hopelessly in love with you."

"No, the man is hopelessly shattered over his broken marriage. He's kind and good, that's all. He has a big heart."

"Yes, and the whole thing belongs to you."

"Do you know what he told me, Ann?" I asked, slamming the dishwasher door and looking up at her. "He told me that he's too terrified to ever get close to someone again, that he's had enough pain."

"Ah. That explains it."

"Explains what?" I leaned against the opposite counter to glare at her.

"That's probably why he doesn't pursue you more aggressively. He's afraid of getting hurt again."

"Well, his wife hurt him badly, that's for sure."

"I was thinking more along the lines of him being afraid that *you* would hurt him again."

"What? I didn't hurt him!"

"Didn't you tell me that you broke up with him to marry Ted?"

I was quiet for a minute before reluctantly admitting, "Yes."

"After dating him for a *year?*" she prodded.

"Yes! So?"

"So, you don't think that hurt?"

"All right," I conceded quietly. "I'm sure it hurt him, yes. But it was more than eleven years ago. Besides, he got over it in a hurry."

"Are you sure about that?" she challenged.

"Yes, I'm sure about that! He just went on a mission instead and came home and got married."

"That may be, Maren, but I think it still hurts."

"Well, you think *wrong!*"

"Did he love you?" she asked.

I glared at her.

"Well," she demanded. "Did he?"

I still didn't respond.

"Maybe you weren't sure," she suggested. "Is that it . . . ? Did you doubt his feelings . . . ? Well? Come on, Maren, either you can answer me, or I can ask him . . ."

"How dare you threaten me like that! You . . . lawyer!"

She tossed her head back and laughed. "You ought to know better than to argue with me by now. Come on, let's have it. I want the truth."

I closed my eyes, thinking back a million years to the girl I'd been. I was surprised at the tears that suddenly rushed up and trickled out. I had not thought that the memories would have such an impact on me. "Yes," I said quietly. "He loved me. It's hard for me to believe it now, but it's true . . . He loved me completely."

Ann chuckled and wiped at her own eyes. "Oh, now look at what you made me do," she mumbled. "I never cry."

"It serves you right." I laughed softly too.

"Do you love him?" she asked gently.

"I did," I told her. "But that was a long time ago."

After several quiet moments, Ann finally said, "If you change your mind about Christmas, let me know. And even if you don't, you know that you can't possibly stop Santa Claus from coming . . ."

"Don't you dare," I said as I hugged her. "But, thank you."

"Guess what?" she suddenly brightened.

"What?"

"We have an appointment with some prestigious fertility specialist up at the university in March. We're thinking of trying in vitro fertilization."

"Really? Oh, Ann, I hope it works. I want you to have a baby so badly."

"That makes two of us."

"Did you say March?" I asked.

"Yes," she scowled. "They're backed up four months, can you believe that?"

I shook my head. "I guess there are more people who struggle with that than you think."

"I guess. I wish I knew some of them. Maybe it would help. Sometimes I feel like I'm the only woman in the world who can't have children."

"You'll have them sooner or later," I said cheerfully. "You have to."

"You're certainly optimistic when it comes to other people's lives, aren't you?"

"And you will let me babysit, won't you?" I went on.

"Haven't you had enough of kids?" she joked.

"No. Trevor's going to be four in a few months. I'm so baby-hungry I can't stand it. And I won't be having any more, so *you'd* better figure something out."

* * *

A few days later Ann burst in just after Jake arrived to get his children. "Maren! Guess what?" she said excitedly.

"What?"

"Your problems are solved!"

"Really?" I smiled and threw my arms dramatically toward the ceiling. "That's *fantastic!*"

"Oh, stop it!" she said, smacking me on the arm. She threw herself down on the couch and commanded, "Sit down. You too, Jake. You should hear this too. I could use some help with persuasion."

"Oh yeah," I muttered sarcastically. "That's definitely your area of weakness, *persuasion.*"

She only smiled and shook her head before she announced, "My firm is redecorating their whole office! I told them I know a great interior designer. Would you like to submit a proposal?"

"Ann, I can't do that! I don't work for a company. I've never even really done this outside of school. I wouldn't know what I was doing."

"Come on, Maren! You have a degree. You can do this. I'll help you."

"How will you help me?"

"I don't know, but I will. And Tyler will. Jake will help too, won't you, Jake?"

He laughed. "You do seem to have a gift of persuasion, Ann. I guess you talked me into it. When do we start?"

"Will you two quit planning my life for me?" I protested.

"You're great at decorating," Ann encouraged. "Your house is beautiful. This is just on a bigger scale. Come on."

I gave her a disgusted look and turned to Jake for support. He just smiled and nodded toward Ann. "I'm on her side."

"And when would I do it?" I asked smugly. "I don't have time."

"You don't have Jake's kids on Wednesdays," Ann pointed out. "You could do it then."

"Did you forget that I have two children of my own?" I reminded her.

"Oh, yeah . . ."she tapped a finger to her head as if in thought. "It's too bad you don't know some kind, generous, handsome, single man who's incredibly good with children, and also happens to have Wednesdays off . . ."

Jake bought into her ploy completely. "Yes, that is too bad." He nodded sympathetically. Then he brightened and said, "But *I* have Wednesdays off. I could take Becca and Trevor that day."

"Oh, that's just what you need!" I said. "On top of all the other stressors in your life, you really need to have my kids on your day off."

"I would love to do that for you, Maren," Jake said sincerely.

"And I could help with the kids on the weekends if you need it," Ann offered. "This is the answer to your prayers, my friend."

"You're both crazy," I told them.

"Yeah, that's why you love us." Ann grinned. "I'll tell them you'll be in on Wednesday. Does that work for you, Jake?"

"Do I have a say in this?" I asked.

"It doesn't look like it." Jake flashed that endearing dimple in his right cheek. "So I'll see you on Wednesday, Mar." He stood up to go collect his children and leave.

I started to feel excited in an apprehensive sort of way. Maybe I could actually do it, and even make money at it. Maybe it really would work.

On Wednesday I skipped the gym. I was too stressed out. I dropped Rebecca and Trevor off at Jake's house. "Good luck, Maren," he encouraged. "You can do this."

I managed to pull off a professional appearance at the law firm. Then I took Ann up on her offer to help with the kids on Saturday so I could get furniture quotes, fabric swatches, price lists, and anything else I could think of. On Saturday afternoon I decided to do something spontaneous. I planted tulip bulbs all through the flower beds. Thinking about them blooming in the spring added to my sense of hope.

By Monday morning I had everything ready. I met Ann at lunchtime so she could sit in the car with the kids while I ran my proposal in.

They called the next day to tell me that I got it. I jumped in the air and cheered after I hung up. I couldn't afford to hire a crew of people, so Ann and Tyler and Jake volunteered to help me once again. So did my parents; they came down to spend the Thanksgiving holiday with us. Ann and Tyler, and Jake and his children came to my house too.

Mom and Dad greeted Tyler and Ann when they arrived. The four of them knew each other fairly well from previous visits. When Jake got there, Mom hugged him and said, "It is so good to see you again, Jake!"

He smiled and said, "It's good to see you too, Mrs. Griffin."

Her eyes went wide and she observed skeptically, "You sound awfully formal for a boy who once called me 'Mom.' If you can't do that, at least call me 'Andrea,' for heaven's sake."

He chuckled and said, "All right. Which do you prefer?"

She smiled and answered brightly, "'Mom,' if it's all the same to you. We always wanted more children, so we try to adopt anyone we can."

Dad emerged from the hallway just then to laugh and slap Jake on the back. "How are you, boy?" he asked heartily. "It's been a while, hasn't it, son?"

"Yes, sir, it has," Jake answered almost somberly.

"And these must be your beautiful children!" Mom gushed over Jeffrey and Elizabeth for a few minutes, introducing herself and asking them questions about themselves. When she introduced Dad to them, Jeffrey asked, "Are you a real cowboy?"

"Yes, he is!" Trevor insisted. "Go put on your cowboy hat and show him, Grandpa!"

By the end of the meal, everyone was comfortable and happy. After that, Mom and Dad watched my children and Jake's for the better part of two and a half days and nights. Thanks to them, we spent one long whirlwind weekend and got Ann's entire law office finished.

We stood admiring our hard work late Saturday night. "Wow," Jake said, spreading his arms out wide. "This place looks fabulous."

"That it does," Tyler agreed.

"See, Maren," Ann said brightly. "I knew you could do it."

"I can't believe it," I said softly. "I can do this. I can do something." I blinked back tears as I hugged all three of them and said, "Bless you all."

My design business took off after that, with one referral after another. I used most of the profit from the first job to purchase the equipment I would need and to open an account so that I could hire people to help with the next job. I didn't have a lot left, but at least Trevor and Rebecca would have Christmas, and it looked like I would be able to keep the house and pay my bills.

After the exhilaration of that first job was over and the Christmas season was upon us, I started to think about what it was going to mean to spend my first Christmas as a divorced woman, a single parent. I felt a sad, sinking despair at spending the season alone, without my husband. I wasn't looking forward to my sister's upcoming wedding either. I didn't want to pretend to celebrate a new union when I was still mourning the dissolution of mine.

Chapter 17

The morning of December fifteenth dawned cold and clear as we left very early for the Idaho Falls Temple and Natalie's wedding. There were Christmas lights twinkling on a few of the houses in the neighborhood. I was glad that Trevor and Becca slept most of the way there.

I tried to relax and feel the peace as I walked into the temple and out of the world, but I just felt a kind of anxious dread. I kissed my children in the waiting room and left them in the care of my brother's daughters, well supplied with stories and coloring books. Then I went to meet Mom and Natalie in the brides' dressing room. Natalie's dark hair was swept up, with a few straight pieces hanging down here and there, and tiny pearls scattered through it. She looked radiant in her crisp white dress. I went to hug her. "You're beautiful," I whispered. She smiled at me.

I watched her with a painful twinge of remembrance as Mom buttoned up the back of her dress and helped her with her veil. All around us there were glowing brides, brimming with anticipation. They were anxiously getting dressed to go meet their soon-to-be eternal companions and dive into a blissful future together. The thought made me shudder.

Natalie ran to hug me once more before she went to meet Douglas. "Wish me luck!" she demanded sweetly.

I gave her my best smile and honestly wished her good luck.

Mom was all smiles and glow, just like Natalie. She didn't even cry as we walked silently toward the sealing room.

We greeted family and friends in quiet whispers as they filed into the green velvet room. After what seemed like forever, Natalie and

Douglas arrived hand-in-hand. They sat together quietly to listen to the words of the sealer, and then knelt together at the altar.

As I sat in that corner of heaven during my little sister's wedding, I cried. Not because the ceremony was beautiful, although it was. But because all I could see were broken dreams. I prayed silently for the couple, *Please let them find happiness. Let the dream come true for her.*

Natalie's reception was exquisite. True to her word, she kept her original wedding date, so she spent a lot more time planning than I had. There were lighted Christmas trees all around the church. The tables were covered in shimmering white cloths and topped with red and silver candles. Trevor had a little black tuxedo and Rebecca wore a red satin dress like mine. Everything was so vibrant, like Natalie. Red was always too harsh for me.

I watched her and Douglas all night. They seemed so happy. I watched my older brother, Clayton, with his wife, Sue. They kept smiling at each other too. I remembered thinking that their wedding had been enchanting. I was a teenager then, young enough to be caught up in the fairy tale. Even Mom and Dad stood close to each other in line, seeming happy and content. I felt like the black sheep of the family. I saw the stars in the eyes of my twelve and fourteen-year-old nieces, and hoped that they would watch Natalie instead of me.

The hardest thing about the reception was having to explain to everyone where Ted was. "We're divorced," I repeated over and over again. There were raised eyebrows, pursed lips, sympathetic pats on the hand—I hated all of it. It was no one's business where Ted was. I felt like I might as well be wearing a scarlet "D." I wanted to just shout out, "Yes, I failed at marriage! I blew it! I admit it! My children might be scarred for life, and it's all my fault! Now, leave me alone." I felt like an outsider, looking in on a world that I had stepped out of and might never be part of again.

After the reception we stood outside, coats covering our elegant clothes. We threw the acceptable birdseed at the happy couple as they ran down the sidewalk. I watched my little sister drive away into the same winter mist that had seemed so magical eleven years ago, on my own wedding night. It was too cold to cry anymore.

* * *

Rebecca and Elizabeth had a dance recital the week before Christmas. "I'll make you a deal, Mar," Jake told me.

"I'm listening," I answered with mild amusement.

"Trevor's still going to play T-ball with Jeffrey in the spring, right?"

"Either that or go to space camp." I smiled.

He laughed and continued, "So, if you'll do Elizabeth's hair and fix her costume and put that sparkly stuff on her cheeks that seems to be so desperately important, then I will practice baseball with Trevor all spring."

"*All* spring?" I teased.

He put a hand over his heart and said, "I promise. You won't have to pitch a baseball the entire season."

"Are you saying you don't think I can pitch?" I challenged.

"Not at all." He grinned. "But I will readily admit that I'm pretty useless with a curling iron."

"All right." I smiled. "You have a deal."

We went to the recital together with the children. During the brief intermission, Jake turned to me and smiled. "You love this, don't you?" he asked.

"It certainly brings back memories," I answered wistfully.

"Do you still dance?" he asked me.

"I break loose in the kitchen occasionally, but it's not the same thing."

He laughed. "I'd like to see that."

"I'll bet you would." I grinned.

He glanced unobtrusively to my waistline and then watched me thoughtfully for a minute before confessing, "I must admit, I am astounded that you've managed to keep that lithe dancer's figure through eleven years and three children."

My eyes went wide at his apparent sincerity, but I laughed off the compliment. "I'm afraid that figure is gone for good, Dr. Jantzen. I haven't seen it in ten years."

He smiled and asked, "Has it been that long since you've looked in a mirror?"

"All right, Jake, you've got me," I laughed. "Do you want me to make you cookies? Tend your children all night? What?"

He gave me a look of mild disgust and answered me seriously, "What I want, Maren, is to give you a sincere compliment. It seems that you have forgotten how to accept one. It's very simple, really. All you have to do is say, 'thank you.'"

I studied him for a minute before saying softly, "Thank you."

"You're welcome. There now, that wasn't so hard, was it?"

"Much harder than it used to be, actually," I confessed.

"Why, Mar?" he asked with genuine interest.

I shrugged. "I guess I'm eleven years out of practice."

His brows furrowed. "I know things were tough in your marriage, Maren, but surely Ted gave you compliments occasionally . . . didn't he?"

I wasn't sure whether to laugh out loud or burst into tears. Instead, I only shook my head in the negative.

Jake looked genuinely surprised. "He never told you that you were beautiful and graceful and kind . . . ?" He stopped himself, and I answered quickly, "No, Jake. He didn't." I was touched by his compliments, but upset that he pushed the issue with Ted.

Jake shook his head and muttered, "So, was he blind, or just completely moronic?"

I just stared at him until he looked away. Could he really mean all that?

We went sledding with some friends in the ward a few days before Christmas. Jake and I both decided to just take our children along. We spent a wonderful day racing down the hill, running through the snow, and having snowball fights. Afterward, Rebecca, Trevor, and I went over to Jake's house for hot chocolate. The children went downstairs to play in the toy room and Jake and I talked for a few minutes on the couch. "I'll miss you while we're gone, Mar," Jake told me. He was taking Jeff and Lizzy to spend the holiday with his family in New York.

"I'll miss you too," I admitted.

"Will you?" he asked, watching me intently. It had been a magical day, and I heard a rush of blood in my ears as I thought of Ann asking me if I loved him. Did I? Did I love him still, after all these years?

I could only nod. I had lost my voice. I suddenly realized how close he was and I felt my knees grow weak. I was glad that I was sitting down.

Jake reached up to stroke my cheek and I closed my eyes for a moment, marveling at the gentleness of his touch, at how wonderful it felt. He slid his hand around the back of my neck and into my hair and searched my face, as if seeking permission. I looked into his eyes helplessly, unable to move or speak. Gently, he leaned over and kissed my lips. I momentarily forgot where I was, who I was, and all the pain that I'd endured. I was completely consumed in a kiss, the likes of which I'd never known, not even with him. Jake's kiss was warm and his arms came around me, pulling me closer to him. I instinctively wrapped my arms around his neck and kissed him back, with all the tenderness and passion that I'd been denied for years.

He kissed me so sweetly and beautifully that I thought I might dissolve into him, become a part of him . . . but then came a gradual awareness of how vulnerable I had become. My mind drifted back to the present. I remembered Jake's words, that he didn't think he could ever let himself be close to someone again. I felt overcome with emotion and confusion. As reality seeped in, I pulled my lips slowly away from his. I looked down and squeezed my eyes shut, trying in vain to stop the rush of tears.

Jake lifted my chin with gentle fingers and looked into my eyes. When I met his gaze, a look of pain washed over his face and he brushed his fingers over my cheeks. "Oh, Maren, I'm sorry," he whispered. "I'm so sorry, Mar. I never should have done that." He held me to him as I struggled to regain my composure.

"Jake," I tried to explain myself. "I just feel . . . confused. I don't know if I'm ready for this." I looked back up at him, searching for the right words. They came tumbling out faster than I wanted them to, almost against my will. "Jake, I love you, but—"

His hand shot up like a lightning bolt to stop me. "Don't say it, Maren."

I stopped, stunned. I wanted to go on, to explain to him that I thought we needed time. I wanted to tell him how afraid I was to trust, to get close to someone again. I wanted to ask how he felt. But he obviously didn't want to talk about it, any of it. How could he have kissed me like that if he didn't feel something for me? Was it so horrifying for him to hear that I loved him? I just stared at him, not understanding the wall of ice he'd suddenly thrown up between us.

"I'm sorry, Maren," he whispered. "I just can't hear this. I can't. I never should have kissed you like that. It was a mistake, I know." It was a mistake. He'd said so himself. He hadn't meant to kiss me after all. He'd been overcome with loneliness and pain and given in to the hunger for affection, just like me. That was all.

I lay awake far into the night, trying to convince myself of that, feeling overwhelmingly confused and increasingly angry.

* * *

I celebrated a small and quiet Christmas with my little children. My heart ached over the incompleteness of my family. In addition to the void of a missing child, I had lost my husband. To add to the emptiness, my closest friends went away. Not only was Jake gone, but Ann and Tyler also left. They'd gone to Arizona to spend the holiday with her mother.

I hung a stocking up every year for Ashlyn. I'd made it a tradition with Rebecca and Trevor that each year we thought of something we could do for another person as our gift to her. We would write it down and put it in her stocking since we couldn't give her material gifts. I knew that my other two children didn't feel Ashlyn's absence like I did, but they enjoyed the ritual. They asked to hang Ted's stocking up too, so we did.

Ted actually sent the kids presents, and called to talk to them on Christmas. He'd called a handful of times, but when I talked to him that day, it was the first time that he had sounded truly remorseful. "I miss you, Maren," he said with a calmness that defied his nature. "I miss you all."

"I miss you too, Ted," I answered quietly.

"I really want to see the kids," he told me. "What can I do?"

"Get help. I can't send them with you until I know they'll be safe."

"All right. I'm going to try," he said for the first time. I knew I'd believe it only when I saw it, but I didn't tell him that.

Chapter 18

Rebecca, Trevor, and I went to spend a couple of days in Idaho after Christmas. The time with my family was a pleasant distraction. I almost didn't want to go home. Ann and Tyler came back before Jake did. "How did sledding with Dr. Jantzen go?" Ann asked, throwing her long legs over the arm of the overstuffed chair.

"Do you mean Jake?" Rebecca asked.

Ann laughed and said, "Yes. Did you guys have fun?"

"It was so fun!" Trevor exclaimed. "We're gonna go again, huh, Mom?"

"Maybe." I smiled at my children. "Why don't you two go downstairs and build something with your new blocks? I think Ann would like to see that."

"Oh, I would," she gushed. "Would you guys do that for me?"

They eagerly raced downstairs to construct a work of art for her to admire.

"So, what happened that's so racy you can't discuss it in front of the children?" she asked, grinning wickedly.

"He kissed me," I admitted.

"Well, it's about time!"

"But then he said it was a mistake," I added. "I started to tell him that I loved him, and he cut me off completely."

She watched me quietly, waiting for me to expound.

"Oh, Ann!" I said despairingly. "I think I do love him. The way he kissed me was so . . . wonderful. I was sure that he must love me too . . . but then he was so horrified when I tried to tell him—"

"Oh, will you stop!" she said in disgust. "He's so in love with you he can't see straight. Even Tyler can see it, for heaven's sake, and that's saying something." She grinned.

"But then why did he act so appalled when I told him how I felt?"

Ann shrugged. "I don't know. He told you that he's scared to death. Why don't you just ask him?"

"You're right. I have to talk to him," I decided. "But he doesn't come home until tomorrow. I think I might have a nervous breakdown before then."

"You can do it." She smiled. "Go talk to him tomorrow night. I'll watch the kids for you."

"Thank you. I think I will. I mean . . . I have to. I need to at least see how he feels and . . ."

She reached over to pat my hand. "Don't look so worried. He'll probably be so relieved he'll propose on the spot."

"I wouldn't bet on that," I laughed.

I watched the clock all day, wringing my hands, trying to think of what I would say to Jake that night. I thought of calling him first, but decided it would be better if I just showed up. I walked to his porch and drew a deep breath. It took all the courage I could muster to knock on his front door. I was putting the words together in my mind, but lost them when the door opened.

For a moment I wondered if I'd been so nervous that I'd knocked on the wrong door, but a peek into the entryway told me I was at the right house. "Can I help you?" the woman standing in front of me asked. She had long hair that hung in thick, sleek panes of auburn, and her eyes had something of an Egyptian mystique to them. She was taller than I was, and just the sight of her intimidated me. She wore expensive jewelry and smelled like expensive perfume. There was no mistaking who she was. I saw a miniature version of this woman running through my house nearly every day. But I hadn't expected her to look like she'd just breezed from the pages of *Vogue* magazine, or stepped off a runway in Paris. Her features were so finely carved they could be called exquisite, but there was a hardness in her eyes, a coldness about her.

I wished that I could melt into a puddle on the front porch and slither away into the empty flower beds. How could I possibly have thought that Jake might love me? I felt like the nothing that Ted had told me I was beside this woman, a woman I found myself suddenly envying beyond belief. She was obviously annoyed with the amount of time it was taking me to find my voice. "Who are you?" she asked, narrowing her pretty eyes.

I was filled with a mixture of relief and horror when Jake appeared in the doorway behind her. "Hi, Mar," he said cheerfully. He looked happy, a fact that added to my grief.

"Hi." I searched desperately for a reason to justify my presence on his front porch. I couldn't use the children as an excuse; I'd left them with Ann. There was no reason in the world why I would need to be at his house right then except to talk to him.

"This is Maren," Jake introduced me, smiling. "Maren, this is Tess."

I forced a smile and tried to sound enthusiastic as I said, "It's a pleasure to meet you."

She blew me off with a careless, "Yes . . ." as she turned to smile up at Jake. He smiled back, but with obvious hesitance. I thought it was probably because he sensed the awkwardness of my feelings and didn't want to embarrass me further. It certainly explained why he hadn't wanted to hear about them. He must still care for Tess. But how could he have kissed me like that?

"Why don't you come in, Mar?" Jake offered, stepping in front of Tess to hold the door open for me.

"No, that's all right," I answered, trying my best to hide my distress and appear casual. "I just thought I'd stop and say hi to the kids, see how the trip went . . . you know. I can see that you're busy, though, so I'll talk to you later."

"You're welcome to come in, Maren," he said gently. It only made me feel worse to see him trying to spare my feelings.

"Maren?" I heard Jeffrey's voice from inside the house. "Is Maren here, Daddy?" He burst out of the front door to hug me, and I blinked back the tears. I'd missed Lizzy and him terribly through the week that they'd been gone.

"Oh, I missed you, buddy," I said, kneeling to squeeze him to me. "Did you have fun?"

"Yeah!" He chattered away about everything they'd seen and done with their grandparents, and then Lizzy appeared in the doorway as well.

"Hi, Maren!" she greeted me, throwing her sweet little arms around my neck.

"Hi, sweetie. I missed you."

"Are you gonna come in?" Lizzy asked hopefully.

I saw the reproachful look her mother was giving me and said, "No, honey. I just came to tell you hi. I'll see you in a couple of days, though."

"Can we go to Maren's now, Dad?" Jeff looked up to ask. "I want to show Trevor my stuff."

Jake gave him a sympathetic look and said, "Not right now, bud."

"Can we go tomorrow?" Elizabeth pleaded.

"Don't you want to stay here and see me?" Tess asked them too sweetly. I thought that all the syrup in her tone didn't disguise the selfishness underneath it, but I didn't say anything. I wondered what in the world was going on though. Had she come back to stay? Was Jake still in love with her? I didn't know if I could handle the agony if he married her again.

Lizzy gave her a blank stare and Jeffrey scowled and turned back to me, muttering, "We have to stay and see our mom, Maren."

"Well, that will be fun, won't it?" I said brightly.

"No," Jeff mumbled.

"Now, Jeffrey . . ." Tess bent to take his arm.

"Why don't you just go away again!" he yelled at her and ran inside the house.

She looked annoyed more than hurt, but Jake's eyes followed him with concern.

I ignored Tess and looked at Jake, hoping that he wouldn't be so blind as to let this woman hurt his children. "I'll let you go take care of him," I said. "I'll see you later."

"Bye, Maren!" Lizzy called after me.

"Bye, Elizabeth." I smiled at her and left, wishing that I hadn't dared to hope.

I drove back to Ann's house slowly, trying to sort through my thoughts. I was relieved to a certain degree that I didn't have to bare my feelings to Jake. But I felt more confused than ever.

"How did it go?" Ann asked enthusiastically.

"Well, I was fortunate enough to meet his wife, anyway," I said sarcastically.

"His *ex*-wife, you mean?"

"Whatever. What difference does it make?"

"It makes a very big difference, Maren. Are you daft?"

"I must have been. I don't know what I was thinking. I'd like to slap him though."

When Jake brought the kids on Monday morning, I just gave him a curt hello and good-bye. I didn't even want to talk to him. Lizzy didn't mention her mother, but Jeff grumbled about having to spend time with her when he wanted to play with his friends, and how he wanted her to go away again. I didn't ask them any questions. I didn't want to upset them anymore than they already were.

When Jake came to pick the kids up, he said, "Maren, I want to explain some things to you."

"You don't have to explain anything to me, Jake," I retorted, digging in the closet for his children's coats and Jeff's backpack.

"But I want to, Mar." He crouched down on the floor near me. "Look, Tess called my parents' house while we were in New York and asked to see the kids. Then she flew back with us to stay with her mother for a few days."

"That's nice," I said, secretly wondering about her motives. I wanted to ask him if he'd kissed her too, but I didn't. He'd been married to her for seven years; I didn't know why it mattered to me whether he'd kissed her in the last week or not.

"And now . . ." Jake paused to clear his throat. "I guess she's decided to move back here to be near the children." My heart fell.

"How do the children feel about that?" I asked, pulling my head out of the closet to sit down on the floor. I wanted to tell him that I thought he was a fool for exposing his children to the woman who'd been coldhearted enough to abandon them, but I restrained myself.

Jake sighed and ran his long graceful fingers through his thick hair. I watched the familiar gesture tenderly, wanting to run my own fingers through his silken wavy hair. I shook the thought from my mind.

"Elizabeth is indifferent, and Jeffrey is upset," he admitted.

I wanted to be indifferent myself, but when I looked at him I couldn't do it. "And how do you feel about it?" I asked quietly.

He watched me for a minute before answering me. "Torn. She's their mother, but . . ." He fixed that gaze on me again, looking into my heart. "Does this upset you?" he asked.

I wanted to laugh in his face and sock him in the chin. "A little," I said hesitantly, not wanting to open my heart to him just to have him break it. "Jeffrey's been upset today, and . . . I guess I feel a little jealous."

"Jealous?" he asked. He looked so surprised that I wanted to scream. I thought he must be horrified at the thought, so I covered my feelings with a lesser truth.

"Yes. Jeffrey and Elizabeth almost feel like my own children now, Jake. I . . ." *I want to be their mother, not her,* I thought, but I wasn't going to tell him that either. "I just don't want to see them get hurt, that's all. And . . . well, I guess I don't want them to stop loving me."

"Oh." He furrowed his brows, looking confused. Then his look changed to concern and he sat down to take my hand. I couldn't believe he had the audacity to hold my hand after all that had happened, but I couldn't bring myself to pull it away either. "Maren, they'll never stop loving you. You've been . . ." He looked down at my hand in his and squeezed it. When he looked back up, his eyes were glistening. "You've been like a mother to them these past months. You've filled a void for them, and I am very grateful." I could almost hear him saying, *but now that their real mother is back, we don't need you anymore.*

I couldn't look at him. I looked away, pretending to study a piece of lint on the carpet.

"Maren . . ." he started again. "I'm sorry I kissed you. I know I shouldn't have done that. I hope it didn't upset you too much."

I pulled my hand away and glared at him, feeling all the anger rising up. How dare he kiss me like that, like I had never been kissed before, and then tell me that he hoped the fact that I meant nothing to him didn't upset me; that he had only used me for some kind of temporary solace and it was a mistake.

A pained look came over his face at my show of fury and he said softly, "It did upset you, didn't it?"

I wasn't going to go easy on him just because he had that hurt look in his eyes, and such an expression of innocence on his face. "You'd better believe it," I said. I wasn't going to take it. I wasn't going to sit quietly by and be hurt by a man again, not even by Jake.

"Maren, I'm sorry—"

I stood up, furious. "How *dare* you, Jake? How dare you do that to me!"

He stood up too, biting his bottom lip. I recognized the sign of nervousness. "Maren, I said I'm sorry. What more do you want me to do?"

What more did I want him to do? I turned away from him, too angry even to speak. When I found my voice, I spun back around and said, "This is not just going to go away for me, Jake. Do you realize that?"

He looked stunned. "Maren, I know I shouldn't have done it, but . . ."

"But WHAT?!"

"Well . . ." He shoved his hands deep into the pockets of his slacks and just stared at me, apparently bewildered. "It's just . . . It's just that you . . . You kissed me back, Mar. So . . . was it really *that* awful?" he finally asked sheepishly.

"Oooh!" I wished that I could break something . . . like his heart instead of mine. "Yes, I kissed you back! I'm a fool! I admit it! All this time, Jake, I thought you were different. Do you know that? All these years . . . I thought that you were genuinely good and kind and sincere, that you had integrity. I *trusted* you! Even after all the pain I've been through, I *trusted* you, Jake. And do you know what?"

He just stared at me, completely dumbfounded.

"You are just like all the rest of them," I told him. "You're just another selfish man, out for your own gratification and nothing more."

"Maren! How can you say that?"

"How can I say that?! I can't believe that you could kiss me like that and . . ."

"And what, Maren?" he asked quietly.

"I just can't believe it, Jake! That's all. I can't believe that you would . . . hurt me like that."

His face fell and he took my shoulders in his hands. "Maren, I have never wanted to hurt you—"

I pulled away from him and turned my back on him. "Well, you did, Jake. You did."

He pulled me around to face him and said, "Maren, *I am sorry.* Please believe me. I won't let it happen again. It's just that—"

"That doesn't even matter, Jake, because *I* won't let it happen again!" I looked away and muttered, "I can't believe that I was so *stupid!*"

Jake just stared at me, looking anguished. I was glad. I hoped that he felt bad about what he'd done. He should feel bad for making me believe that he might love me when it was all just a bunch of rubbish.

"I'll go down and get the kids," I finally said. I turned back to ask, "Are you still going to be bringing them?"

His jaw dropped open and then closed again quickly. "Well . . . yes," he stammered. "Unless you don't want me to . . . Do you want me to take them somewhere else?"

"No. I just wasn't sure if their mother was going to want to have them or something. I just need to know what to expect."

"She won't take them during the day. She'll be working."

"All right."

"Maren, if you're too upset with me to watch Jeff and Lizzy, or if you don't want to . . . I can find someone else."

"Do you want to find someone else?" I asked.

"No."

"Good." I sighed, feeling the anger diffuse, and said more quietly, "Jake, I love your children. It would break my heart to lose them."

He looked relieved. "I'm glad, because it would break my heart to have them lose you . . . Will you still trust me with Becca and Trevor on Wednesdays? Even though you don't . . . trust me?" It seemed agonizing for him to say the words, but I figured it was his own fault.

"Of course, Jake. They love you to pieces. They'd never forgive me if I tried to take them somewhere else . . . I trust you with my children, Jake. I didn't mean I didn't trust you in that respect."

"Well, I'm glad to know I didn't completely shatter everything," he muttered grimly, running those fingers through that hair again.

I couldn't look at him anymore. I went to get Jeff and Lizzy.

* * *

After Christmas I tried to fill my days up with children and design. Things with Jake were a little strained. He rarely left Jeffrey and Elizabeth alone with Tess, as far as I knew. They never stayed over at her apartment. But all four of them started to do things fairly regularly on the weekends. Unfortunately, I had to hear about all of it as soon as Jeff and Lizzy arrived on Monday. They seemed to be getting used to having their mother around again, and even enjoying her company. I would have liked to believe that Jake was just trying to protect his children by going with them, but common sense told me that he obviously wanted to spend time with Tess, too. I hadn't realized just how much time the two of us had grown accustomed to spending together with the children until a lot of it was gone. I felt more lonely than I had in months.

With Jake watching Rebecca and Trevor on Wednesdays, and occasional help from Ann on the weekends, I was able to keep up with my design projects. I was overwhelmingly grateful not just for the money, but for the distraction as well. I needed to stay busy. I tried not to think about Jake, but I couldn't avoid him. I saw him nearly every day, and it hurt.

My calling with the Young Women took up a fair amount of time, too. We had activities at least twice a month. They were a lot of fun, and another welcome distraction. I wanted no free time to think. One of those activities every month was combined, so Jake was there with his priests, but it wasn't too bad. I kept going to counseling appointments once a month. I read my self-help books and my scriptures, wrote in my journal, kept exercising and working on being a good mother—all the things my counselor told me to do. It helped, though I still felt empty at times.

Ann called me in February to tell me that she'd gotten a notice from Ted's attorney. He was taking me to court in the hope of having his visitation rights restored. "Can he do that?" I asked her.

"Has he been bothering you lately?" she asked.

"No," I admitted. "There were a few threatening phone calls after the restraining order incident, but those gradually stopped. He hasn't tried to come around since then at all. When I have talked to him on the phone lately, he's actually been pretty decent. But I don't dare send the kids with him yet."

"According to this, he's been getting counseling and treatment the last couple of months," Ann told me. "Did you know about that?"

"He told me he was going to get some help, but I didn't really believe him."

"The judge might grant his request, Maren," she said. "They don't like to keep parents separated from their children except in extreme circumstances. I think our best bet is to push for supervised visits again. At least then you know the kids will be safe."

I sighed. "All right. But he'll have to prove that he's getting some kind of help, won't he?"

"Most likely. But it looks like he is."

"Good. Maybe he'll actually get better. He could probably be a great dad if he'd get over the drinking."

"I hope he does, Maren—for your sake, and for Rebecca's and Trevor's."

The judge ordered Ted to enroll in anger management classes, to continue going to counseling, and to keep attending the Church-sponsored substance abuse meetings that he'd been going to. He granted him two weekends a month again, to be supervised by his parents. All I could do was pray that he would stay in treatment and that the Lord would watch over my children.

Chapter 19

On the first Sunday without Rebecca and Trevor again, my Laurel lesson was on living the Word of Wisdom. I was grateful. That was something I could talk about. I didn't think I could handle another lesson on temple marriage.

"Look," said Abby, popping her gum, "Lots of kids smoke. I don't think it's really that big of a deal."

I considered her rebellious appearance, and wondered if she was speaking from firsthand experience. I hoped that she wasn't.

"I realize that lots of kids smoke," I answered. "That is very unfortunate. You girls are aware enough of the risks to make a more responsible decision than that. I think it's interesting that the Lord gave us the Word of Wisdom one hundred and fifty years ago, and only now has medical science finally discovered the dangers of smoking, and even drinking."

I was surprised to hear Christine say, "Is it really that bad to drink socially? I mean, sure, you don't want to end up in a gutter as an alcoholic, but a little bit here and there isn't really unhealthy . . . is it?"

A knot formed in my stomach. I wondered what had made me think I could handle this lesson. It wasn't on eternal marriage, but the subject was almost as painful.

"So, Christine, if you decide to drink socially, let's first take a look at all the possible immediate consequences: drunk driving accidents, rape, embarrassing yourself in front of other people, distorted judgment, uncontrollable rages, not remembering what you did the night before, and probably a hundred other things that I haven't thought of. I would hope that list would be long enough to convince you of the dangers. If for some reason it's not, how do you know you won't become an alcoholic?"

She gave a self-conscious shrug, "I don't know. I just wouldn't. I'm not that dumb."

"Listen, girls," I said, "I would not be doing you any favors if I told you it was no big deal. The bottom line is, drinking causes all kinds of short-term problems. Then there's the long-term. Once you take a drink, it might be very hard not to take another one. Some people are more prone to alcoholism than others. It can kill you quickly in a car accident, or slowly by eating away at your body. Even worse, it can destroy your family and hurt those you love, which really isn't fair. I've seen what drinking can do to people, and it's awful. When you drink, you are no longer in control of yourself. And if you're not, who is?

"Even if you don't become an alcoholic," I continued, "do you want to gamble your life for a drink? If you never enter into the battle, you can't lose. If you never take a drink, Satan can't get his clutches into you that way. And if any of you already have tried it—any of it, drinking, smoking, drugs, anything—please stop now. Talk to your parents or the bishop or a counselor if you need help and support, but don't let it affect your life any more than it already has. This is *so* important, girls. I've had enough problems to face in my life that I'm extremely grateful that I committed to live this commandment, and that I've been blessed for that decision." I prayed the Spirit would confirm the truth of my words—convince them.

Christine nodded thoughtfully and said, "I guess I didn't think about all of that."

I smiled, but said seriously, "Christine, you are a very bright young woman." I looked at the other girls and said, "You all are. Your lives are too valuable, too important to waste on something so harmful. I think you're all smart enough and courageous enough to make decisions that will bless your lives and give you the greatest chance for happiness. What do you think?"

They all looked at each other and some nodded, even Abby. There was a quiet stillness, and I continued to pray that it would sink in. If only Ted had never taken a drink . . .

In sacrament meeting they announced a single adult dance on Friday night. It suddenly hit me that I was single. I'd been single for several months, in fact. I'd had no real desire to socialize with others in my predicament before then, but I was getting awfully tired of being alone all the time. And I was tired of hurting over Jake while he was out cavorting around with his ex-wife. I could go dancing again. Maybe I would. I had to start living again somehow.

Late on Thursday afternoon Ann came banging in the kitchen door, which I had somehow forgotten to lock. "Gotcha!" she called into the laundry room.

I jumped. "Are you trying to give me a heart attack?"

"Nope, just trying to keep you on your toes." She grinned.

I hauled a laundry basket out to the great room and sat on the floor to fold. She sat in her favorite overstuffed chair and reached for a T-shirt from the pile.

I slapped her hand, but not too hard. "Just sit there and talk to me," I ordered. "You can't sit on the floor and fold laundry in a five-hundred-dollar suit. Why don't you ever go home and change first? I'd think you'd be dying to get out of those nylons by the time you get home every day."

"I can handle the nylons. It's these darn high heels that are killing me." She kicked off her stylish leather shoes and crossed her legs to lean back in the chair. "And just so you know, I don't even own a five-hundred-dollar suit."

I smiled and waved my hand over her apparel. "Oh, all right. We'll throw in the jewelry and the shoes to make it add up."

She smirked. "I have to keep up my image. Unfortunately, I have nothing better to spend my money on," she added sarcastically. "Are the kids playing downstairs?"

"Yes. I'll be glad when spring comes again, if it ever does."

She stretched her legs out. "Oh, it always gets here eventually. So, how did your appointment go yesterday?"

"Good, I think. I have two weeks to get my proposal drawn up. This is a big account. Their offices take up one whole floor."

She smiled. "And how is Dr. Jantzen? I haven't seen him for a few days."

"The same," I answered distastefully. "Always running around with that dreadful woman. She came to get the kids yesterday, in fact." I gave an exaggerated shudder.

"Really?" Ann's eyebrows went up. "Did they go with her of their own free will?"

"Yes," I admitted sadly. "They've gotten used to her now, I think. It's like they just crave her attention. The whole thing makes me angry though. She doesn't even act like a mother. She likes to dress them up in expensive clothes and show them off like just another possession. She pays patronizing attention to them when it seems to suit her purpose, and then dumps them off on Jake when she has better things to do. I don't even think she loves them, Ann. She doesn't deserve them."

Ann's eyes grew misty and she said, "It doesn't seem fair, does it?"

I just watched her, chastising myself in my head for making such a thoughtless comment. "I'm sorry," I said quietly. "That was a stupid thing for me to say to you. No, it doesn't seem fair."

She looked over my head, out the French doors, and seemed almost to be thinking out loud. "Why would God send children to a woman who doesn't even want them, to a woman who chooses to live the lifestyle she lives, and then deny them to me?"

"I don't know," I answered softly.

"I know I'm not perfect, Maren. I shouldn't be sitting here judging Tess . . . But it's hard not to. Every time I've encountered her she's just seemed so . . . cold. She acts so selfish and undeserving . . ." Her voice trailed off and she wiped a stray tear from her face.

"And yet Jake still seems to love her," I said quietly. "Even after all that she's put him through. I can't understand how he married someone like that in the first place, let alone how he can still want her now . . . Of course, I married Ted, so what can I say? I'm sure Jake didn't know what he was getting into either."

Ann nodded in understanding and then said thoughtfully, "Tess has both the things that you and I are missing . . . and she doesn't even seem to care." She wiped at her face again. I was surprised to see her so emotional. I had rarely seen my friend in tears. "Do you know what I saw today?" she asked.

"What?"

"I went to the mall at lunchtime. I was in the check-out line at Dillard's, and there was the cutest little baby behind me, just adorable . . . Her mother couldn't have been over sixteen years old." I stopped folding laundry to watch Ann. "I was so overcome with jealousy that I wanted to grab that sweet little baby and run. I was so *mad,* Maren. Here I am, thirty-two years old. I'm well beyond being financially stable. I have an education. I have a house. I have a husband. I've been trying to get pregnant for six years. I should have two or three kids downstairs playing with yours. But I don't. Every month that's gone by in the last six years—what is that? . . . Seventy-two months? Seventy-two times that I have failed. Every month I get slapped in the face with the reminder that I am still not pregnant.

"And that girl at the mall . . . She probably made one mistake. One stupid decision, and God throws a baby at her. What is she going to do with her, Maren? How is she going to feed her, let alone pay for her to go to college? That baby is probably nothing more than a toy to her, something she gets to dress up and play with every day . . . Or maybe that baby has ruined her life—stopped her from going to school, taken away her social life, robbed her of her own childhood . . . all because of one terrible mistake . . . Why? *Why? What* did I ever do to deserve this?"

"You didn't do anything to deserve this, Ann. That's not what this is about," I said quietly. I wasn't sure what to say to her. I didn't know how to comfort her. I had never had to face what she was going through. I was painfully aware of that, thinking of how no one knew what to say to me about Ashlyn. There were some things you just had to experience to understand.

As if she had read my mind, Ann looked back to me and said, "I'm sorry. That made you think about Ashlyn, didn't it? . . . You know, Maren, I even envy you that."

I shook my head. "No, you don't. No one would choose to go through losing a child, Ann. It's absolutely . . . terrible. You don't wish for that, I promise you."

She held her hands out in front of her, almost as if she was cradling an infant, and said earnestly, "But at least you have something to mourn, Maren, *someone* to mourn. There's a little face in your mind, a memory to go with the pain. You know she's there, that you'll get to see her again someday. You carried her for nine months. You got to feel her growing inside you. You gave her life. You got to hold her . . . For me, there's nothing. There's no one. There's just all this . . . emptiness—never-ending emptiness . . ."

She stopped talking and dug in her purse for a tissue. I went to hug her and we cried for a long time.

Ann finally mumbled, "Look at me, sitting here wallowing in self-pity." She wiped under her eyes with the tissue, trying to save her face. "I have mascara all over me, don't I?" she asked.

I laughed and nodded. "You might as well give up. It's hopeless."

She chuckled and said brightly, "Hey, I heard there's a single adult dance tomorrow night. Speaking of wallowing in self-pity, why don't you quit pining away over Jake and go? Tyler and I could come and stay with the kids."

I looked at her for a few seconds before deciding that she was right. "You know, Ann, I just might take you up on that. It feels weird to think about being social again, but maybe it's time." I cracked a smile and admitted, "All this wallowing is getting a little old."

She laughed. "Amen! Let's move on to something more cheerful. This could really be fun. What are you going to wear?" she asked.

"I don't know. I hadn't even thought about it. Do you want to help me look through my closet?"

"Do I?" She jumped up and ran down the hall, obviously eager for a diversion. She rummaged through my closet, pulling out skirts and blouses, dresses and pants. "My gosh, Maren! When was the last time you cleaned your closet out?"

"Hey," I said defensively, "I didn't give you permission to rip it apart! I keep holding onto things thinking I'll fit back into them someday."

"You could probably fit into anything in here now, my friend, but some of this stuff is ten years out of style!" She held up a short hot-pink dress with a ruffle around the waist. "Make that fifteen years." She wrinkled up her nose.

"Oh, thanks a lot! For your information, I used to be quite fashionable in my day. It's just that it was a long time ago."

"Look, Maren," she answered jovially, "We're done with all that self-pity stuff, remember? It's your day *today!* You deserve to look good and feel good now. Let's go through this stuff."

"Sure, why not? I've got all day if you do." We made a work pile, a dress pile, and a casual pile for things I was going to keep. Those piles were not really piles so much as small scatterings, mostly the things I had bought when I went shopping with Ann. We made a very large pile, a mountain really, to take to Deseret Industries. I protested over several items before they were thrown into the DI pile, but Ann kept saying things like, "Stonewashed jeans, Maren? . . . Give me a break . . . You're never going to wear this again . . . When was the last time you wore this? . . . We should send this to Madonna . . ." I did keep some of my old prom dresses, the dress I wore when we buried Ashlyn, and a very few other sentimental items.

Ann pulled a flowing taupe skirt and a white blouse from a hanger in the back of the closet. "Now this is a timeless outfit, Maren. You don't even need to update it with new accessories. This is so pretty. Why don't you ever wear it?"

I smiled at the sight of it. "It's kind of had sentimental value. I guess I probably could wear it again now."

She raised her finely-arched brows at me. "Did you want to expand on that?"

"You'll laugh."

"I won't laugh." She grinned.

I sighed. "That's the outfit I wore the last time I saw Jake, before I married Ted."

"Ah . . ." she answered. "Well, since you see him almost every day now, you could probably start using it again." She gave me that evil grin of hers and said, "It would serve him right."

I laughed. "Somehow, I don't think it'll have much impact on him either way, but I guess I could use it again. Leave it out. I'll get it cleaned so I can wear it tomorrow night."

She gave me a bright smile. "I think that's a wonderful idea. Now let's go load all this stuff into my car so I can run it to the DI before you change your mind."

The kids had come upstairs by then, and were eager to help us pile most of my wardrobe into the trunk of Ann's car. We were still loading when Jake arrived.

"What are you girls up to?" he asked, smiling. "Running away?"

"Yes," I said. "Have fun with the kids."

"Do you want me to help you pack?" he quipped. Then he leaned closer to both of us and said confidentially, "I heard that's what you're supposed to say in this situation."

"Actually," Ann confided, "I just convinced Maren to clean out her closet. She's been avoiding it for ten years."

"That bad, huh?" Jake chuckled, peering at the contents of the trunk. "Hey, are you sure it's only been ten years? I think I recognize some of this stuff from college." He pulled out a black dress that had been almost elegant once and held it up to me. "Didn't you wear this when we went to see *The Phantom of the Opera?*"

I snatched it away and stuffed it back in the trunk, muttering, "Impressive memory, Dr. Jantzen. Don't get me reminiscing over my wardrobe. I might be overcome with sentiment and drag it all back to my closet before Ann can get it out of here."

He flashed me a mischievous grin and pulled the dress out again. "Does the memory of that particular evening make you feel overcome with sentiment?" he asked lightly, but the azure gaze he fixed on me was intense.

I pulled the dress out of his grasp again and replied, "I'd never fit into that dress again, even if it did." Why did he have to play with my emotions? Did he want to see me suffer?

Jake yanked it away and challenged, "How much do you want to bet?"

"Oh, cut it out!" I tried to grab the dress back, but he held his arms up over his head so I couldn't reach it.

He kept the dress held high as he leaned toward me and asked, "How much, Maren?"

I put my hands on my hips and said, "You'd better be careful, Dr. Jantzen. You have a lot more to lose than I do."

His expression turned serious and he replied quietly, "I think I'm aware of that."

I just looked at him, trying to decipher his meaning. I wished that I could get inside his head and read his thoughts. "Okay, Jake, fifty bucks."

"What?"

"I'll bet you fifty dollars that I can't fit into that dress."

"Do you even have fifty dollars, Mar?" he asked, smiling again.

"No."

He laughed. "A little overconfident, are we?"

I couldn't keep the corners of my mouth from twitching up. "Maybe. If I lose, I guess I'll have to work it off. I could do your laundry."

I looked over to see Ann leaning against her car, watching us with amusement. The children were running around on the grass, laughing and chasing each other.

"I have a better idea," Jake said. "*The Phantom of the Opera* is here again. If you fit into this dress . . . ." He held it up and looked from it to me, eyeing me up and down. It unnerved me. "Then you have to wear it and come with me."

"Come with you *where?*" I asked to clarify.

"Reminiscing." He smiled. "To see *The Phantom* again."

"And what if I split out the seams?" I asked, trying to look tough and not smile.

He grinned and replied, "Well, I can't take you out in public like that, so . . . I guess I'll have to buy you a new dress and take you to the opera anyway."

I stared at him, making a conscious effort to keep my mouth from dropping open. I wondered what his motivations were, but then I decided I didn't care. I knew he'd sensed the strain between us over the past two months, and I guessed that he was probably just trying to smooth things over, to make me feel better. And in truth, he had.

"That sounds reasonable to me," Ann put in.

"Who asked you?" I retorted good-naturedly.

"I thought it was an implied understanding of our friendship that my opinion is always welcome."

I laughed. "Well, that certainly explains a lot."

She looked at Jake and said, "So, did you want to go through anything else in this time capsule before I do the world a favor by disposing of it?"

He chuckled and said, "No. I might end up hauling it all over to my closet . . . just for sentimental value." He winked and threw the dress at me. "There you go, Mar. It's time for your moment of truth." He nodded at Ann and instructed, "You go with her. I don't want any tampering of the evidence."

"My pleasure," she said, slamming the trunk. "You'll keep an eye on these four little monkeys then?"

"I think I can manage." He grinned. "Try to hurry."

To my shock, Ann zipped up the back of my dress for me with room to spare. She giggled and said, "I think you're in trouble."

"There's no way!" I protested, walking over to my bedroom mirror. "I can't possibly fit into this!"

She peered over my shoulder at my reflection and observed, "Then it looks like you've accomplished the impossible, my friend. Those morning visits to the gym have paid off." She stepped back to look at me and remarked, "My gosh, you look skinny in that thing. You've had three kids and you fit into a dress that tiny? I think you're even thinner than me now, and I've never been pregnant. How could you ever have thought you were fat, even before you started going to the gym, Maren?"

I shrugged. "Ted always told me I was fat."

"Yeah, well, Ted has a perception problem. Look at yourself."

I did look at myself, and I tried to be objective. I tried not to see myself through Ted's eyes. "I swear, Ann, I looked a lot better in college. I used to have a twenty-two inch waist."

"What do you think it is now, twenty-three? Ted's been gone for nearly a year, Maren."

"But his voice is still in my head."

"So tell it to shut up."

I laughed at her and then tilted my head, still looking at my reflection. "Maybe I don't look as bad as I thought," I admitted.

"You look wonderful, my friend. Have fun on your date!"

"It's not a date." I scowled at her.

She rolled her eyes. "Unless Tess is going along with you, I'm going to classify it as a date."

I groaned. "I didn't even think of that. What a horrible thought. Do you think she will?"

Ann laughed. "No. And I think you're wrong about the esteemed Dr. Jantzen. I don't think he's in love with her at all. I think we've misjudged him terribly," she said dramatically.

"Will you quit trying to get my hopes up again? I just decided to go to a dance and get on with my life, remember? I'm giving up on Brother what's-his-name."

"Whatever you say. I think you should still go to the dance, high hopes or not. Come on, I have to present the evidence to the other side." She grasped my arm and dragged me to the front door.

Jake was standing on the porch, watching the kids in the yard. "Here's your untainted proof," Ann announced to him.

He looked at me and his face broke into a broad smile. "Well, I must say . . . You look stunning, Maren."

"Very funny."

"I wasn't joking," he said. "That is a beautiful dress. It's too bad it's out of style." He shoved his hands in his pockets and grinned. "So, you admit defeat?"

I looked down at the dress and back up at him. "I guess I have no choice. But I must point out that it's a bittersweet victory for you, Doctor. This is going to date you too, you know. You're the one who's going to have to be seen with me in it."

He raised an eyebrow and stroked his jaw with his thumb. "You make a good point, Ms. Griffin . . . Well, it's not fair to punish the innocent along with the guilty, is it? I guess I'll have to buy you a new dress anyway, for my own sake."

"Oh, no you don't," I warned.

"Oh, yes I will," he said. He waved a hand over me and grimaced. "Please. Get that thing off and get it out of here. I've seen enough."

Ann laughed. I shot them both a dirty look and called over my shoulder as I marched back down the hall, "You'd better watch it, you two. I'll start wearing this stunning gown whenever I go somewhere with either one of you. You'll curse the day you ever started conspiring against me together."

"My knees are trembling!" Ann shouted after me.

I changed clothes and came back down the hall to find everyone in the great room. I went to open the coat closet to get Jeffrey's and Elizabeth's things. "Hey, I think I recognize this too," Jake observed. Ann had hung the outfit I was going to get dry-cleaned on the door-knob of the closet. Jake pulled it off and held it up. "You could still wear this, though."

"Yes, and she's going to," Ann offered. I gave her a warning look, but she only grinned and went on. "I convinced her to go to the single adult dance tomorrow. Hey, maybe you could go with her, Jake. You ought to get out and socialize once in a while too."

I felt angry with Ann for putting Jake on the spot like that. She was really pushing it. He'd already offered to take me to the play to make up for things; I certainly didn't want him to feel pressured to do more. I suddenly remembered an important point. "He doesn't want to go, Ann," I said, pulling my head out of the closet and tossing Jeffrey's and Elizabeth's things on the chair. "He hates to dance."

Ann turned to Jake wide-eyed and asked, "Is this true?"

Jake opened his mouth to respond, but I cut him off. "Look, Ann, he doesn't want to go, okay? Will you let it alone?"

"All right!" She threw her hands up. "I know when I'm not wanted. I'm out of here." She smiled and hugged me before she left, saying, "I'll see you later. I need to get rid of your stuff before you change your mind, and then get home to meet my husband."

I shook my head after my friend and watched Jake hang my outfit back up on the closet door. He considered me carefully for a minute before saying, "Would you rather not go with me to the opera? I wasn't trying to make you feel pressured or anything."

"I would love to go with you, Jake," I answered sincerely. I wasn't going to completely blow off his attempt to repair our friendship.

"Good." He smiled.

Chapter 20

When I looked in the mirror on Friday night I was surprised to see myself looking back. "It's me," I whispered. "I'm back." I looked like myself, like the old Maren. My hair was a lot shorter than it had been in college, but the new style was much more flattering. My makeup was a little more subdued than it used to be too, but I looked well put together, like I knew what I was doing and had some confidence again. Maybe there was hope for me after all.

I dropped the kids off at Ann's before I drove to the dance. She'd decided to have them over there for a while, and then take them to my house to put them to bed. "I hope they'll be all right for you," I told her.

"They'll be fine," she said. "You just have fun. You look gorgeous."

"Yeah, well, thanks for the help. I guess I can't go wrong with one of the five outfits I have left," I teased her.

She laughed.

Walking into the dimly-lit cultural hall was a little eerie. There was a table near the door with name tags and a marker. Name tags? I walked past them, and the punch and cookies, to stand close to the dance floor. There was a slow song playing that was before my time. As I looked around the room, I got a sinking feeling. There were women from my age to my mother's age—and maybe even my grandmother's age—lined up all along the walls. Most of the men that I could see were out on the dance floor. A few of them sat around eating cookies and talking to each other, or to women they were sitting with. A lot of the men looked older too.

Oh, Maren, I tried to talk myself out of being disappointed. *You just came here to have fun, to dance.* That was certainly true. I didn't know if I'd ever trust enough to want to get married again, but at least I wouldn't grow old quietly at home.

A fat balding man stopped in front of me. "D'ya wanna dance?" he said gruffly. I gave him a weak smile and tried to ignore the punch stain on his shirt as he led me to the dance floor.

"Name's Hector," he offered, pointing to his name tag as he put a massive arm around my waist.

"Nice to meet you." I tried to be polite. "I'm Maren."

"Maren?"

"Yes."

"Hmmm. Used to have a horse named Maren back on the farm when I was a boy." I must have given him a strange look, because he added helpfully, "She was a beauty, that horse. And fast too." He winked at me.

Another slow song began just as the last one ended, leaving me no time to get away. I'd forgotten how to do this with grace. I found myself feeling thankful for Hector's belly. At least it kept me at a safe distance from him.

Hector stepped squarely on my toe with his huge lead foot and I wanted to cry out. I bit my tongue to keep from whimpering. "Whoa!" he called. "Watch it there!" As if I had been the one to step on him! I was feeling increasingly annoyed with this guy. "I've always been a good dancer," he pointed out. "You ever think about takin' lessons?"

"Actually, I took lessons for fourteen years," I retorted.

He grunted. "Well, I guess some's got natural ability, and some don't."

I really didn't want to hurt his feelings. I had to feel a little bit sorry for him, being fat, bald, and near to sixty. He obviously didn't have a lot of social skills. Then I thought of all the times I hadn't stood up for myself. I was making a new start, and I wasn't going to be walked on anymore, literally or otherwise. "Excuse me, Hector, but it was *you* who stepped on *my* foot. You might think about being a little more polite."

He seemed a bit taken aback. "Oh," he mumbled. "Sorry."

"Thank you," I said, feeling better. The song ended and I excused myself.

I stood on the sidelines and watched as a fast song came on. Oh, I longed to get out there and dance! It made me think about Ted and how much fun we used to have dancing. There I was, eleven years later, back at square one. Coming had been a mistake, I realized. I suddenly felt old and tired, too old to play these games again. What if I fell for another Ted? I started walking across the gym to the door at the other end.

Someone touched my arm and said, "Surely you're not leaving already?"

I was relieved to see that there was no punch on the clean ironed shirt in front of me, and downright impressed that he even wore a suit jacket and tie. I looked up and gasped.

"I see you didn't go for the name tag thing, either," he commented. "You know, I believe you're the most ravishing woman I've seen all evening—and you're certainly the most graceful dancer. Would you care to dance? I'm afraid I didn't catch your name."

I tried to resist the smile that tugged at the corners of my mouth. Maybe I wasn't so old after all. "Maren," I said.

"It's a pleasure to meet you, Maren." He smiled. "I'm Jake."

I took the arm he offered and followed him to the dance floor. "So, tell me, Jake," I teased. "Can you dance?"

"That all depends on how you define the term, but I intend to give it a valiant effort." He put an arm around my waist to pull me close as a slow song from our generation came on, something I knew.

I was stunned by how smoothly he led me and couldn't help exclaiming after only a few moments, "You learned to dance!"

He smiled down at me and said, "Did I?"

"But you hate to dance!"

"'Used to hate,'" he corrected. "Or 'hated,' or however you say that correctly. Anyway, Tess made me take lessons and I actually quite enjoy it now."

"No kidding?"

"No kidding."

"I'm impressed, Dr. Jantzen."

"Really? Then I guess all those hours of practice were worth it." He grinned.

It felt wonderful to dance again. We danced a few numbers and then stopped for punch and cookies. "You really have improved," I commented to Jake again. "You must have some natural talent after all, to learn to move like that."

He laughed. "You don't have to sound so shocked, Mar."

"I should have let you answer Ann yesterday before I cut you off and assumed for you. I'm sorry."

He touched a finger to my lips and scolded, "Don't say that, remember? It was more fun this way anyhow."

Before I could respond, a woman came up and tapped him on the shoulder, asking him to dance. I was pretty surprised, and I thought Jake was too. He gave me a "What-do-I-do?" look. I shrugged and gave him an evil grin.

She pulled him out onto the dance floor before he even had time to answer. I watched him, amused, as another girl grabbed him before he could get back to me after the first dance. The thought suddenly occurred to me that he might start dating again someday. I wondered how I would deal with that.

Someone interrupted my thoughts by asking me to dance. Figuring I wasn't going to be seeing much of my buddy, Jake, I accepted. I caught glimpses of him here and there while I danced with several other people throughout the night. I was surprised at how many men asked for my phone number, and I actually gave it to a few of them. I hadn't really intended to start dating again. I had only gone to have fun, to break out of my lonely shell, to force myself to do something that I had enjoyed years earlier. But I decided that maybe the thought of socializing wasn't so bad, after all. Maybe it would be good for me.

Jake finally grabbed me toward the end of the evening. He was out of breath. "Save me, Maren!" he whispered. "These women are crazy!"

I laughed at him. "Are you asking me to dance?"

"Yes, yes, hurry up!" He pushed me into the crowd trying to find a place to dance as another slow song began. He put warm hands on my waist, and I slid my arms around his neck.

After dancing for a few silent moments, I asked lightly, "So, did you have fun tonight?"

"It was all right," he said nonchalantly. "I suppose I should get out and socialize more . . ." His voice trailed off as he looked into my eyes. He seemed to be thinking for a minute before he confessed, "I did dance with one incredible woman this evening, so I guess it was worth coming."

My chest began to pound as I tried to ask him casually, "Really? What's she like?"

"Well . . . She has these intriguing blue eyes . . . and her hair looks so soft that it makes me ache to touch it. It's like spun silk . . ."

I laughed softly, trying to cover the sound of my racing heart.

He smiled and leaned closer to my ear to whisper, "I love the way she laughs . . . It has this enchanting effect of bubbling over me like pink champagne, and leaving me tingly . . . She ought to laugh more often."

I pulled back a little to stare at him as he went on. "She's full of sunshine. She draws people to her. She's smart and sweet and funny . . . and she has the most beautiful mouth," he whispered, leaning closer to me again. "I want to kiss her so badly it's almost more than I can bear . . . but I'm afraid she might be angry with me again if I tried."

His words left me feeling weak with awe. I stopped dancing and leaned against him to look into his eyes and whisper back, "I don't think she'll be angry."

"You don't?"

I shook my head, mesmerized, as he bent to kiss me. I didn't even care if anyone saw me kissing him at a church dance. The feel of his lips against mine filled me up with longing and wonder, and I never wanted to let him go. When he pulled away, he smiled and whispered, "Are you mad?"

I could only shake my head as I tried to find the words to explain. "Jake, I was only mad last time because . . ."

I stopped talking when I realized that the song had ended and someone was standing right next to us. She had danced with Jake earlier, and was apparently waiting to snatch him up for the next song. Another slow song came on, and the upbeat energy I'd felt all night started to melt away into exhaustion. The woman, a pretty, perky, thirty-something touched Jake's arm. "Excuse me—would you like to dance again, Jake?"

He had a sympathetic look on his face as he said softly, "I'm sorry, Lydia, but I already am." He pulled me close and we moved slowly away from her in the sea of people.

I forgot about what I'd been trying to tell him as I rested my head on his shoulder. I was lost in the wonderful aromatic mixture of soap, and shaving cream, and a hint of musky cologne that smelled so familiar and soothing. Jake brushed his cheek against my hair and all the people around us blurred into nothing as we danced. "Your hair smells nice," he murmured.

I closed my eyes and thought I might die of pleasure. He did love me. He had to. But what about Tess? I decided I didn't care about Tess. I wasn't going to think about her. I wasn't going to let her ruin the most magical moment I'd had in years.

Jake held me tightly for a minute after the last song ended, and then took my hand. "Let's go," he said, pulling me through the huge crowds of people. As we made our way out, not just one, but several women came up to him and handed him their phone numbers, or even tried to slip them into his suit pockets. I could not believe my eyes.

He almost ran to the parking lot, pulling me behind him. Then he stopped to catch his breath. He had been too polite to refuse anyone to their face, but he pulled several little slips of paper from his pockets and threw them at the ground.

"What *is* this?" he asked me, exasperated.

"I don't know." I shook my head, a little bewildered myself. "I suppose you're an eligible bachelor. I guess going to a singles dance is like advertising it. You certainly stand out in the looks department."

"Half these women don't even know me!" he said, disgusted. "I can't believe it! Men get accused all the time of seeing women as objects. What do you call this? I'm just a doctor, someone with a good job, or even just a man who doesn't have a wife. Even holding your hand, they still came up to me! How disrespectful to you!" He shook his head, and then asked, "Are the men this bad?"

"I don't know. More of them asked for my phone number than I expected. It seems more aggressive when the women behave that way, but maybe that's just because it's not the norm. I guess people are in a hurry. Maybe they don't want to mess around at this stage of life. Maybe they're just tired of being alone."

"You'd think it would be the other way around, that people would be mature enough to be more cautious, to learn from their mistakes."

"I'm not going to pretend to know what all those women were thinking, Jake. I have no idea. I'm more on the 'scared to death' side of things myself."

He watched me for a minute before he took my hand again and said, "Come on. I'll walk you to your car."

I wanted him to kiss me again, but he only bit his bottom lip and hugged me. I decided maybe it was better that he didn't. I didn't know if I could handle another kiss like that.

Chapter 21

Ann came over the next week and announced, "I've made a decision."

"How unusual," I remarked. "And I'm guessing that this decision of yours is likely to have some kind of earth-shattering impact on my life?"

She grinned. "Maybe. I think we should take Tess out to lunch."

I paused for a minute before saying, "Oh, that's a good one, Ann. You almost had me going."

"I'm serious."

"You can't be."

"Really, Maren. There has to be more to her than meets the eye, don't you think? She's obviously a lost soul. Maybe we can help her."

"Help her? How? Do you have a heart donor in mind?"

"She can't be that awful. Jake wouldn't have married her if she didn't have some good in her."

"So maybe she changed."

"Maybe. I'd like to get inside her head and find out. Are you with me?"

"No."

"Oh, for heaven's sake! You know how Jake feels about you now. Surely you don't still feel threatened by her."

"I'm sure that Jake must care for me, yes; but we haven't officially talked about it. There's still some uncertainty there . . . Honestly, I think I do still feel threatened by Tess."

"Why do you feel so intimidated by her?" Ann asked candidly.

"Well . . . She's gorgeous, for one thing."

Ann rolled her eyes and said, "So are you."

I looked at her skeptically and she continued, "Tess looks like a fashion magazine model, Maren, but your kind of beauty is timeless.

You'll still be beautiful when fashion changes. You'll still be beautiful when you're sixty. You have stunning classic features, but you have poise and grace too. You're gentle and kind. Tess has at least as much cause to be intimidated by you . . . maybe more."

I couldn't believe the sincerity in her expression. "Are you serious?" I asked her.

"Of course I'm serious! You're gorgeous, girl! Ask Jake. He'll tell you. Ask a stranger on the street for that matter."

I just gaped at her.

She smiled and shook her head. "You know how Jake is so attractive, but part of what makes him that way is that he's so unaware of it?" she asked.

I nodded slowly.

"I mean, he's confident, but he doesn't seem to realize that he stands out. And when you get to know him, he has so much depth that you almost forget about his looks. He's kind and cheerful and intelligent, and he has . . . presence. He's genuine."

"Yes . . ." I agreed with her.

"And you're just like him," she said firmly. "You radiate beauty, inside and out. The two of you go together perfectly."

I felt my jaw hanging open and forced myself to close it. "Okay, I love you for life," I finally managed to say humbly. "I already did, you know . . . But I still don't want to go to lunch with Tess."

"I'm not trying to win you over, Maren. I'm not trying to manipulate you into doing something you don't want to do. I'm trying to open your eyes to how the rest of the world sees you. I'm trying to give you a compliment."

I smiled and said gratefully, "Thank you."

"And you're sure you don't want to make an effort to get to know Tess?"

"Positive. Even if I didn't feel intimidated by her, I wouldn't want to be friends with her, Ann. She's horrible."

"Maren!"

I held up my hand and said firmly, "Ann, you are my best friend, and you can usually talk me into anything. That's because you are a levelheaded woman and your ideas tend to make sense. This, however, does not make sense—not for me anyway. I do not care to enter into any kind of relationship, however casual, with another sick, mean, self-centered individual."

"It's not really fair for us to hate her until we hear her side of things," Ann argued.

"There you go again, talking like a lawyer," I muttered in annoyance. "You're on your own, my friend, and that's final."

She shrugged. "Suit yourself. Just so you know, though, I'm going to do it, with or without you."

"How can you turn on me like this?" I demanded. "How can you threaten to fraternize with the enemy and expect me to take it lying down?"

"Are you mad?" she asked seriously.

I glared at her and said, "I'm not sure. I'm definitely annoyed."

"I can sympathize with that. And this is where I choose to behave like an emotionally healthy adult and say that I'm going to do what I think is best, whether you like it or not. Don't take it personally. I still love you, and I know you'll get over it." She grinned.

I shook my head and said, "You're going to get yourself into a lot of trouble someday with this 'save the world' thing you have going, Annie girl. Heaven help you."

"Thanks," she said brightly.

* * *

Ann met Tess at one of the nicer restaurants uptown. Once seated, the first few moments passed with some light small talk. Then Tess said outright, "So, what's the point of all this?"

"The point of all what?" Ann asked.

"It's no big secret that you're not especially fond of me," Tess stated bluntly. "Why did you suddenly invite me out to lunch?"

Ann tried to cover her amazement and answer smoothly, "I do feel badly for not being nicer to you. I decided I ought to make an effort to get to know you."

Tess looked a little surprised, but then she said, "Actually, I think I might be able to relate to you, Ann. I could never relate to Maren, though."

"Why?"

Tess shrugged and said, "We're too different—absolutely different. She's everything I'd never want to be."

"Which is?" Ann pried, curious about her perceptions.

"She's just so content to be the stereotypical stay-at-home, frumpy housewife. The very thought makes me want to scream."

Ann laughed and said, "You can't be serious about that. You've seen Maren. She's not frumpy, Tess, not even close."

Tess almost looked angry. "Okay, so she goes for the fifties thing. She stays home and cooks and cleans and still thinks she has some reason to do her hair and dress decently, like some perfect husband is going to come through the door with a token kiss that somehow pays her for all her hard work."

Ann's eyes went wide with amusement. "Well, we both know that doesn't happen, don't we? On the contrary, she does it for herself, which I think is admirable. I think it would be pretty easy to just give up in her situation, to just throw on sweats every day, quit caring how you looked, maybe gain twenty pounds. But she doesn't. She gets up and reckons with herself every morning, Tess. She takes some pride in herself, even though no one else is ever going to know it. I think that's a good thing for the kids to see.

"Maren feels strongly about staying with her children, but she has other interests. She never just sits around. She's getting her life in better balance, too. She goes to the gym with me in the mornings, she does a lot of reading on things she wants to improve about herself, she's started an interior design business that she does part-time, she's even started going to the single adult activities and socializing again. Not everyone who's been through a divorce like hers could pull it together as well as Maren has.

"She works as hard as I ever thought about working just being home all day, but she could hold down a full-time career just fine if that was what she chose to do. In fact, I think that might be an easier way out. She probably thinks about it sometimes. She loves the kids, but it's not like she never has hard days with them. True, her self-esteem has suffered as a result of ten years in a bad marriage, but she's a lot stronger than you think."

Tess looked genuinely surprised and was quiet for a minute before saying, "I guess I never thought about it that way."

"It's easy to judge a person you don't know," Ann commented. "Which is why I decided I'd like to make an effort to get to know you better. So, what makes you think you could relate to me?"

Tess tilted her head and studied Ann for a minute before answering, "Truthfully, I envy you to some degree."

"Envy me? Why would you envy me?"

"Because you have the guts to do what you want to do, regardless of what other people think. You haven't screwed up your life trying to live up to other people's expectations."

Ann looked puzzled and asked, "What do you mean?"

Tess waved a hand over her as if it were obvious, "You got married, you have a house, you still manage to pull off the Church thing—that's probably because you believe in it. But you got your law degree, and you go to work and enjoy it instead of tying yourself down at home. You don't buy into that perfect family myth and let yourself feel pressured into having children you don't want, who will only keep you from doing what you want to do."

Ann felt momentarily stunned and then admitted, "I'm afraid you've misinterpreted me, Tess. I do believe in the Church, I do love my husband, and I do enjoy practicing law. I like the money and power thing, and I did choose that over starting a family for a couple of years after we were married. Truthfully, though, it's not my first choice anymore. It hasn't been for a long time. I don't have children because I can't have children. I would gladly trade all of this," she motioned to her attire and briefcase, "to stay home and be a mother."

Tess looked mildly distraught. "I'm sorry," she mumbled, in a rare act of apparent regret. "I didn't realize . . ."

"It's all right." Ann shrugged. "You didn't know."

Tess was quiet for a minute before saying, "So—you can't have children?"

Ann shook her head.

"What have you tried?"

"Nearly everything. We have one last hope. We're seeing another fertility specialist next month. We're going to try in vitro fertilization. If that doesn't work, we might try to adopt. I'd like to, but Tyler's still pretty hesitant. He says he doesn't think he can love a child that's not his."

Tess nodded slowly and said, "I was adopted."

"You were?" Ann asked. "Actually, I think Jake mentioned that once, but I'd forgotten. How do you feel about it, if you don't mind my asking?"

"I'm not sure." Tess looked thoughtful. "My parents were wonderful to me . . . too wonderful, in fact."

"What do you mean?"

"They struggled to have children for so long . . . I think they were just so thrilled to get a baby that they went a little overboard. They tried to adopt another child for years, but never could. I was an only child, and I'm afraid I was a little spoiled." She rested her chin on her fist for a minute and then confessed, "Oh, who am I trying to kid? I was spoiled rotten. I got everything I wanted. It wasn't good, I can say now. If I'm honest, I have to admit it's had lasting repercussions."

"How so?" Ann asked, hoping to soak up all the information she could, just in case she and Tyler pursued this course of action.

"I just can't bring myself to go without things, even now. I think I'm entitled to what I want. It's hard for me to put another person before myself."

"That's honest of you," Ann said in surprise.

"What's the point in lying?" Tess asked, looking Ann straight in the eye. "I spent years pretending to be what everyone wanted me to be, and I was just miserable. I don't do that anymore. Think what you want, take me or leave me. It doesn't matter. I am who I am."

Ann felt mildly impressed with her statement, but sad for her at the same time.

"I am sorry to have disappointed my parents after all they did for me," Tess volunteered. "I sometimes wonder if all their goodness didn't make a difference, if I'm just a product of my wayward teenage mother and I can't escape my nature. Your husband might be right in having misgivings about the whole thing."

"That's a cop-out, Tess," Ann said.

Tess raised her eyebrows and acknowledged, "Maybe it is. But if your husband feels strongly that he doesn't want to adopt, I wouldn't push it, Ann. It could end up making you both very unhappy. If he says he can't love a child that's not his, you ought to respect that. He's probably right. Different people have different limits. If you push him past his when he's warned you, you'll have only yourself to blame for the suffering that results."

Ann felt taken aback and mumbled, "I suppose I didn't look at it that way . . ." Then she voiced another thought as it came to her, "What do you think your parents would say about the whole adoption experience?"

Tess hesitated, but then admitted, "Truthfully, they always said it was the best thing they ever did. I'm sure they would say that the problems were either a result of poor parenting decisions earlier on, or of my own choices later in life. They would tell you that the circumstances of my birth and how I came into their family are irrelevant. I have never doubted that they loved me as much as any mother and father could. I'm sure they would do many things differently if they could go back, but I guess all parents say that, don't they? My mother could probably give you some sound advice, actually."

Ann smiled and said, "I'll keep that in mind . . . So, how did you disappoint your parents?"

"Oh . . . I'm not the doting mother who brings the grandkids over all the time. My dad's gone now, and my mother's lonely. She'd like to have the perfect mother-daughter-grandchildren scenario, which just isn't going to happen with me. The biggest disappointment for them is probably that I gave up on the Church thing. I tried it, you know. I always had a hard time with it, but I tried it. They wanted me to get married in the temple, have a family, all the nice traditional things.

"When this knight in shining armor came along, I hoped he would be enough to make it work. The best thing about Jake was that he was the first decent guy I met who didn't tell me I'd have to stay home barefoot and pregnant if I married him. He told me he didn't want more than two kids, and even one would be enough. He said we could wait a while for that one. They didn't seem to be a huge priority to him. He told me that he wanted me to be happy, that I could do what I wanted to do. He was gorgeous, he had money, he was good to me. I figured that was as good as it was going to get."

Ann just listened as Tess went on, amazed that she was pouring her soul out to her. She wondered if she'd just been lonely all this time, desperate to talk to someone, to explain herself.

"So, I married him," Tess said. "He tried, Ann. I say I hate him. I say he's to blame for everything. But the truth is, he really tried. He was in medical school, though, and busy and I just didn't know how to handle it. Looking back, I can admit that I was selfish. I wanted all of his attention. I wanted him to dote on me, spoil me, treat me the way that I was used to being treated. He loved me, I think. But he wanted me to grow up.

"He told me we'd be poor for a while, but I didn't believe him. I knew his family had money, and I thought he'd take it. He wouldn't. I got a decent job in New York, but I really couldn't handle being on a budget like he wanted to be. I decided to go for the ideal family thing, thinking somehow that it would make things better. I mean, of course you have to have kids, right? Heaven forbid some Mormon woman should admit that she doesn't want kids. I figured maybe there was something to it, maybe it would help."

Tess shook her head and tugged on a gold hoop earring. "Boy, did that backfire on me," she remarked. "I thought that once you had a baby, this mothering instinct just took over somehow. I thought I'd know what to do. Being pregnant was hell, losing my figure for nine months like that. But having a baby was worse. I never had any brothers or sisters. I'd never been around kids. I loved Jeffrey, but I just didn't know what to do with him. The diapers and the screaming and the bottles and the getting up all night . . . It was all way more than I could cope with. I had no idea what I was getting into.

"I thought that having a baby would make Jake . . . I don't know. I'm not sure what I wanted him to do. I wanted him to be home more. I wanted him to take money from his family . . . I wanted to be his whole world, I guess. Honestly, that wasn't fair, because I wasn't willing to make him the center of my world either. The baby certainly changed him, but not in the way that I'd expected. He just fell in love with him. Jeff was the most important thing in the world to him. Instead of taking money from his family, though, he was even more determined to make it on his own. He was still gone so much, and any time that he had at home, he spent taking care of the baby—feeding him, changing him, holding him, catching up on the laundry and washing bottles, and all the things I didn't care about and didn't do.

"When I went back to work, Jake nearly lost it. He just couldn't believe that I would leave our baby in the care of someone else. I told him I couldn't take it, that I wasn't cut out for full-time motherhood. He finally apologized and said we'd deal with it. I got pregnant with Elizabeth while I was on birth control pills, and I was just devastated. It got worse after I had her. Jake was more adamant that time about me staying home, because we had two little children, and Jeffrey was old enough to cry when we left him. I felt like I was suffocating," Tess admitted.

Ann watched her with fascination, trying to have empathy for what she'd felt. She couldn't imagine feeling that way, but then she'd never had children of her own. Maybe it was harder than she thought. "How so?" Ann prompted.

"I had these two little people who were totally dependent on me, sucking everything out of me all day long, whining and crying and needing this and wanting that. By the time Jake came home from a shift at the hospital, he was completely exhausted, but I didn't care. I had to get out of there. I left him alone with the kids as much as I could. I finally went back to work under plea of insanity, and we fought all the time. I was so mad at him because he'd turned on me. He promised me liberalism, and defected to conventionality. He said he couldn't help it, that he just hadn't known how it would be to have children. I said I hadn't known and couldn't help it either. It was worse than I ever imagined. He suddenly wanted me to be everything that he knew I wasn't, and I regretted ever attempting to be any of it."

Ann nodded, as a new perspective on this woman was coming to light. "That must have been very difficult."

"Extremely. I went back to work and found myself. That was where I wanted to be—where I could see the results of my efforts, where people appreciated me and respected me, where I didn't have impossible demands placed on me by totally dependent people. I started working longer, or going out with friends at night. I was home less and less, until leaving just seemed the natural thing to do . . . I suppose you know about the affair?"

"Yes," Ann admitted, seeing no point in denying it.

"Vance saw me as the woman I wanted to be—independent, strong. I was just Tess to him, not somebody's wife or somebody's mother. He told me I was gorgeous, he lavished me with attention and gifts. He spent money on me, he took me where I wanted to go. He had no children to put in front of me. That was what I wanted."

Ann felt acutely sorry for Tess, for the life she'd chosen, the eternal happiness that she was denying herself. She didn't know what to say.

"So, I left," Tess said simply. "Jake tried to save me, to convince me to pull my life together and come home. That surprised me. I think I almost hoped he'd tell me where to go when he found out so I wouldn't have to feel guilty and take all the responsibility. I never thought he'd try to work through something as big as that with me. It just wasn't the life I wanted though. It still isn't. I suppose I should feel sorry for hurting him, but I also feel like it was largely his fault. He didn't know what he wanted . . . Or maybe he did, and he denied it."

"What do you mean?" Ann wondered aloud.

Tess considered her for a minute and then shook her head, apparently thinking better of it. "Nothing. Anyway, I'm not a complete monster. I do love my kids. I just don't know how to be a mother. I try. I'm here for the moment, but it's difficult. I don't know if I can do this forever."

"But, Tess, you can't just come and go from their lives!" Ann protested.

"Why not?" Tess asked simply. "I'm their mother. I'm me. This is what they get. Something's better than nothing."

"Do you really believe that?"

"Yes."

Ann shook her head and said, "That is only going to bring pain to all of you. Stay or go, but make up your mind. You can't do both. You can't have it all."

Tess looked annoyed. "That's what Jake says. If I have to choose between living the life I want to, and pretending to be the mother I'm not, no one is going to like my choice."

"Are *you?*" Ann asked. "You're the one who's going to have to live with it."

Tess shook her head slowly. "I'm not sure. That's why I haven't made it yet."

Ann was glad to hear that she was at least taking the time to make such an important decision, but couldn't imagine how she felt. She was grateful, however, that she had taken the time to get to know Tess a little better. Many things made more sense now.

* * *

Ann came over a few days later, "Okay, do you want to hear the story?"

"What story?"

"I had lunch with Tess."

"Really? Who paid for it, you or Jake?"

"Me."

"That's nice. No, I don't want to hear the story."

"I'm going to tell you anyway."

"That's what I figured."

She flopped onto the couch and I reluctantly sat in the chair to hear her out, feigning a mild degree of interest.

Ann proceeded to give me every painful detail of their lunch together. I interrupted her once to say, "Are you telling me this verbatim, or are you embellishing?"

She rolled her eyes in disgust. "I am giving you the most accurate account that I possibly can."

I shrugged in self-defense. "I just wondered."

Against my better judgment, I found myself becoming fascinated with the conversation they'd had. It was somewhat of a relief to hear more about Tess's character and get an idea of where she was coming from. In some ways, she didn't seem like such a threat anymore, though I couldn't really put my finger on why.

"So that was about it," Ann told me when she finished her story.

"Wow," I mused. "Compelling tale. So, do you think she still loves Jake?"

"I don't know. But he's not what she wants, even if she does, and vice versa. I'm not sure she even knows how to love someone. I pity her. She's definitely lost."

"I'm glad you stood up for her kids. She needs to hear that."

"I think she does hear that—quite often, in fact. Maybe that's why she's at least making an effort."

I nodded in agreement.

Chapter 22

I went to *The Phantom of the Opera* with Jake a couple of weeks after the dance. He brought me a box the Tuesday before our date.

"What's this?" I asked him.

"Well, honestly, I couldn't figure out how to do this," he explained. "I really wanted to take you shopping and let you pick out your own dress, but I figured I'd spend the whole time arguing with you. You would have protested, and resisted, and looked at price tags, and refused to try on anything that was worthy of you."

I folded my arms across my stomach and raised my eyebrows at him.

"And I thought about buying you a gift certificate, but I didn't know which store you'd want to go to. So . . . I'm afraid that I had the audacity to pick out a dress for you. I wanted to bring it to you early, so that you'd have time to take it back before Friday if you don't like it."

"Jake, you didn't have to buy me a dress."

He grinned. "Oh, but I did. I have a reputation to think of, you know."

I shook my head and smiled. "I wouldn't really make you be seen with me in my fifteen-year-old gown, Jake. I'm sure I can find something that will work, and that won't completely humiliate you." I waved a hand toward the box he held and said, "Take that back."

He lifted his chin and replied, "You offend me—do you know that? You hurt my pride. I will do no such thing." He held the box out to me, and I took it.

I sucked in my breath when I opened it. "Oh, Jake!" I exclaimed as I held up the black silk dress. It had short sleeves and a wisp of an overskirt that swept across the front and tied in a delicate knot at the side. "You are amazing! How did you pick something so . . . perfect?" I looked at the label and added, "It's even the right size . . . I think." I saw the sparkle in his eyes and it caught my heart.

"Yes, apparently I'm a better judge of that than you are." He smiled. "I must confess, though, I sneaked a peek at the size in the old one."

"Ah," I said, grinning. "You cheated."

"I don't really think of it as cheating," he defended. "Especially since you fit into the old dress perfectly, despite what you thought. I give myself full credit for accurately judging what size you *look* like you wear. I'm just not good with the numbers."

I laughed and then wondered out loud, "Why are you so good to me?"

He shrugged. "Because I love you, Mar."

"You do?" I asked softly.

He only nodded.

"What would Tess say about this?" I asked on impulse, holding up the dress. I wanted to see his reaction.

He gave me a strange look. "I don't know." He shrugged again. "Probably something along the lines of, 'If you can afford to be buying things like that, you'd better be buying them for me. Hand over your credit card.'"

"Do you buy her things like this?" I asked, looking at the dress again and then silently rebuking myself for my brashness.

He raised his eyebrow at me and looked utterly bewildered. "Maren, why do you even ask that?" he said. He was obviously annoyed. I didn't blame him. Maybe he did buy her things. It was none of my business, anyway.

"I'm sorry," I told him. "I love it, Jake. It's beautiful."

I didn't even try on the dress until the night of the opera. I knew I wouldn't take it back. It fit perfectly, and was actually quite flattering to my figure. I couldn't have done any better if I'd gone shopping for myself. I put on a little more makeup than I usually wore and a deeper shade of lipstick. My hair had grown out enough that I could pin it up in an almost-elegant twist. Delicate rhinestone earrings, necklace, and bracelet completed the ensemble. Jake stood on the porch for a few silent moments when he came to pick me up, just staring at me in the doorway. His silent appraisal made me feel incredibly self-conscious until he whispered, "You are . . . simply breathtaking, Maren. You do that dress more justice than it deserves."

I ignored the pounding of my heart and smiled as I took the arm he offered. "You're actually quite striking yourself, Dr. Jantzen," I remarked of him in his dark suit with his black and silver tie.

He smiled back and I wanted to reach out and touch that sweet dimple of his.

We did have a good time at the opera. A hint of confusion still lingered from the night of the dance, but the tension between us had melted away. Jake held my hand during the entire performance, and it felt wonderful. I decided to just enjoy the evening for what it was, and try not to build any expectations. It was impossible not to think about my feelings for the man sitting next to me though. He looked so handsome in his black suit with his black hair and those deep blue eyes of his, that I could hardly stand to look at him at first. No one else seemed to have a problem looking at him though. I'd forgotten what it felt like to go somewhere with Jake, how so many women just stared at him. He was just as oblivious to it as he'd been in college, almost laughably so, but I wasn't nearly as confident as I'd been back then. I felt a little better when I recalled what Ann had said to me though, and Jake's generous compliments. I looked up at him, silently marveling.

As Ann had pointed out, there was so much more to Jake than good looks. He could have been cold and awful like Tess, and I wouldn't have wanted anything to do with him. But he emanated warmth. He was good, kind, successful, and funny. He had faults, I knew. In fact, I knew that better than I had in college. But the good in him outweighed the bad. As the night wore on, I thought less about his blatant attractiveness and more about who he was. The more we talked, the more comfortable I felt, and the easier it became to look him in the eye and listen to him. He was a good man. He was a wonderful friend. I kept thinking of what he'd said to me at the dance and earlier that evening, and thinking that he had to love me. Jake wouldn't say things like that if he didn't mean them.

When he took me home, he hugged me tightly and I let myself just relish his nearness for a few moments before I dared to look up at him. I saw something like fear in his eyes, and I wanted to dispel it. Maybe he was just as afraid as I was. Maybe Ann was right. I did love him. I couldn't deny it. I knew that he cared for me, though I wasn't sure of the depth of his feelings. He'd said that he didn't know if he'd ever want to get close to someone again, and I didn't want him to feel pressured. I wanted him to know that he would be forever dear to me, even if he didn't love me the way that I loved him. I hoped that if I opened the door, he might walk through it. "Jake," I whispered. "You know I'll always love you—"

He touched a hand to my lips to silence me. "Don't say it, Maren," he whispered urgently. "Please. You don't have to. I understand." He released his hold on me and walked away quickly, leaving me completely perplexed again.

* * *

Ann and Tyler went to their appointment with the hotshot fertility specialist, but Ann came home feeling a little discouraged. "It's almost like we're back at square one, Maren," she admitted. "We have a whole calendar filled with more tests, more procedures, more poking, more prodding, more counseling. It's like we're trying out for the Olympics. If we somehow manage to make it, we win the privilege of paying this guy an exorbitant amount of money for what amounts to a hand at poker. If we win, we win big—we get a baby. If we lose, we lose big—another failure, another dashed hope, another shattered dream . . ."

I hugged her and encouraged, "Then you'd better win."

"I guess so, because Tyler still says no way to adoption. How can he say that, Maren? If that's the only way we're ever going to get a baby, how can he say no?"

"I don't know, Ann. Maybe that's a harder thing for men to deal with. Maybe he'll change his mind if it comes down to that."

"Maybe. I can understand that it's hard for him to see other people's children. Heaven knows I go through that every day myself. Church is the worst. Everyone's either pregnant or has a baby. They all assume that I just choose to be a career woman, when I'm really begging to live the life they all take for granted. But if we adopted a baby, it *would* be our child, not someone else's. How could you not learn to love a child—any child—that you took into your home and cared for every day, Maren? I love your kids. Even though looking at them makes me ache for my own, I'd be a fool not to appreciate the joy your children bring into my life." She sighed and shook her head. "I'm so tired of fighting with Tyler over this."

"Do you fight over this a lot?"

She rolled her eyes and said, "Do we? We fight over it so much lately it's ridiculous. Maybe Tess is right. Maybe I should just give it up. Tyler and I have a good marriage. It's stupid to mess it up fighting over children we can't have."

"You're going to have them, Ann," I said with conviction. "One way or another. You just have to have faith."

"That's easy for you to say," she snapped, almost bitterly.

"You're right. I'm sorry. I shouldn't have said that. I wish I could do something for you."

"I know you do. I guess all the stress is just getting to me."

* * *

Jake and I both started going to some of the single adult activities. Sometimes we went together, and sometimes we went by ourselves. He seemed to have cooled off since the opera. I didn't know if my professions of love had scared him or horrified him. I decided to give him space and vowed not to say anything like that to him again. I figured that he would come and talk to me when he was ready, after he'd had a chance to sort through his emotions and deal with whatever it was that was holding him back. In the meantime, I tried to distract myself with other things.

I started dating again, just to get out and do something. I didn't have any interest in a serious relationship; I knew I loved Jake. I started to make quite a few friends at the single adult activities and worked on rebuilding my self-confidence, doing things I'd liked to do before I lost myself. Most of the people I met were sincere, good people, who had found themselves alone for varying reasons. Though the majority were honestly trying to live the gospel there were different commitment levels. A few were bitter. Seeing that in other people humbled me.

Rebecca and Trevor knew that I'd started dating again. They didn't seem too uncomfortable with it, but one day Trevor did ask, "Mom, are we gonna have to have a different dad someday?"

"No, sweetie," I told him. "You will always have the same dad, and he will always love you very much."

Rebecca chimed in, "But are you going to get married to someone else?"

I hesitated. "Well, I'm not sure, Becca Bug. I might like to get married again someday if I find the right person. But I'll never marry anyone without talking to you two first. No matter what happens, I'll always be here to take care of you."

That seemed to satisfy them, but I was a little unnerved when Rebecca commented, "If I have to have another dad, I'd want it to be Jake."

"Yeah, me too," Trevor agreed.

"Don't go getting any ideas, you two," I told them. "This is just not something we need to worry about right now." I prayed that they wouldn't volunteer their opinions to Jake. After the way he'd reacted to my expressions of affection, I figured anything more might make him turn and run.

My calling with the Young Women helped me to grow a lot. In some ways, I felt like I was back where they were, struggling to gain a firm identity of myself and what I wanted out of life. I worked so hard to instill a sense of divine worth in them that it started to rub off on me. My counseling appointments helped too. I did start to feel better about who I was, and accept the fact that people might actually enjoy my company.

Ann came over late on a Saturday afternoon in early March. The kids were with Ted. She looked at the hot rollers in my hair and said, "Are you going on another date tonight?"

"What do you care?" I teased.

"I don't. I suppose it's good for you. I just hope you don't go breaking a bunch of hearts when you're really in love with Jake."

"I'm not breaking hearts. I'm beginning to wonder if Jake's hopeless though. Maybe he doesn't love me, Ann."

"Oh, he does."

"I don't know . . . Ever since I told him that I loved him again, he hasn't wanted anything to do with me. I mean, he's friendly, but that's it. He's obviously careful not to get too close. He and the kids still go with Tess a lot on the weekends. Maybe he loves her . . . Or maybe he doesn't. He still goes to the singles activities . . ." I hesitated to voice another fear, but then did it anyway. "What if he starts dating too, Ann? What if he falls in love with someone else? There are certainly plenty of women who'd love to snatch him up. Maybe that's it. Maybe he does want to date other people, but he just hasn't gotten up the guts to do it yet."

"No, that's not it." Ann shook her head firmly.

"How can you be so sure?"

"He talks to Tyler quite a bit and I hear about some of it. They played racquetball at lunchtime yesterday. They've been doing that once a week or so."

"Have they? That's good."

"Yes, it is. It's good for both of them, I think. So, do you want to hear what he said?"

"You're going to gossip?" I smiled.

"Only if you pry it out of me."

"Okay, I'll pry . . . Hey, wait a minute! Does this work both ways? Do you go home and tell Tyler what I say, and then he tells Jake?"

She laughed. "No. I'm better at keeping my mouth shut on this end of things than I am on the other. Tyler doesn't think it's a big deal. I don't think men admit that they're divulging their innermost feelings and make each other promise not to tell like we do."

"All right. So, how do you know Jake isn't in love with some other woman in the singles ward?"

"Because they ask him out all the time and he always says no thanks."

"*What?*"

"Tyler finally inquired as to how many women have asked him out, and how often. I think he was mostly joking, but when Jake was obviously flustered at his question, he pushed the issue. It seems that Dr. Jantzen reluctantly admitted the numbers are staggering."

I just stared at her.

She laughed. "Are you so shocked, after what you told me about the dance, and the other activities you've seen him at? You said the women throw themselves at his feet. He's a good catch. I suppose if a woman was going to bring herself to drop at a man's feet, it might as well be his. Though I can't imagine bringing myself to do it, personally."

"Neither can I. Maybe I have better self-esteem than I thought."

"Maybe. Anyway, Jake told Tyler that he just isn't interested in dating anyone else, that there's no point. On the downside, he said that the woman he's in love with doesn't feel the same way, and he's wondering if he should give it time, or just give it up. He doesn't know if he can handle any more pain."

"But that's not me!" I said, feeling my stomach twisting into knots. "I've told him that I love him! If he loved me back, then we *would* feel the same way. Ann . . . he must love Tess . . . But then why did he say those things to me, and kiss me that way?"

"Look, my friend, I'm going to tell you the same thing that Tyler told Jake. Quit moaning, buck up, and go talk to him. You might as well find out for sure. I think he loves you. I pray he loves you. If it's Tess, he's in for a lot of heartache. She simply will not listen to reason."

"And when you say *reason,* you are referring to yourself?" I tried to say lightly and forget feeling sick over Jake. She was right. I needed to talk to him.

She smirked and said, "I'm trying to be her friend, but it's harder than I thought it would be. I mean, she's all right to talk to, and I have to admit that she's given me some good insights into myself, but . . . well, it's like I said. She won't listen to reason."

"What are you trying to reason with her over?"

"Straightening out her life, for one thing. Wickedness never was happiness, you know. It somehow seems to be for her though. She thinks she has no power over her carnal nature. She doesn't seem to *want* to overpower it. The worst thing about it is her kids. She thinks she can just come and go from their lives. She talks about going back to New York a lot. She says she hates it here. I keep trying to convince her to stay, to try to be a mother. But truthfully, I'm afraid she's just going to pack up and run one night. She could probably be a decent parent if she tried. She's entertaining, that's for sure, and smart. Maybe she'd get over some of her selfishness if she spent more time with her kids . . ."

"You can't change her, Ann. You can't change a person. You know that."

"I don't want to change her. I just wish she'd get her life in better focus."

"And see it through your eyes? Not everyone sees the world the way you do, my friend. Tess is an adult. She gets to make her own choices. It doesn't matter if you think they're rotten. They're her choices to make, regardless of the pain they might bring on herself or others."

She sighed. "I suppose you're right. It's just . . . sad to see it."

"I know it is. That's why I don't want to try to befriend her. I think she's self-centered and mean, and she doesn't care who she hurts as long as she gets what she wants. It's not like she's in denial, Ann. She knows what her problems are. She knows exactly what she's doing. She's making her decisions with open eyes."

"Yes, she is," Ann admitted sadly. "I can sympathize with her in some ways though. She has some valid points."

I felt a spark of anger and leaned across the table to say, "There is *no excuse* for bringing pain on innocent children, Ann. None. She needs to take responsibility for her life."

"In many ways, she does, Maren. Maybe she genuinely can't live up to the expectations of motherhood. Maybe she simply lacks the capacity."

I shook my head and muttered, "I just can't understand that."

"I know you can't," Ann sympathized, "anymore than Tess can understand how you sacrifice so much to stay home with your own children, and still have it in you to take care of hers too."

I raised my eyebrows in surprise, but then defended, "Look, Ann, all mothers feel pressure and stress. I suppose I can understand how some women would prefer to go to work and leave their children in daycare. I'm sure there's a much more tangible form of gratification in it, and different people have different needs. There might even be some good in it for the children. Maybe they develop better social skills or more independence. Personally, I don't think that's the ideal situation if you can avoid it, but I wouldn't judge someone else for disagreeing with me. I'm on the opposite end of the spectrum, I realize. I should probably take more time for myself and let my children learn to do more things on their own.

"But wanting to have a career, or needing space to be yourself are not the same as simply dropping your responsibilities all together. You can't just pop in to see your kids when it's convenient for you and forget about them when it's not. Parents don't get extended vacations. It's not in the job description."

"Point taken," she said.

I shook my head. "I can only imagine how frustrating it must have been for Jake to feel strongly that his children should have a mother at home, and be married to a woman who simply couldn't do it. I guess he couldn't change Tess anymore than I could change Ted."

"I guess not." Ann smirked.

I gave her a wry smile and remarked, "I'm glad you find the irony so amusing."

She laughed.

I made up my mind to talk to Jake then, but I wanted to take a few days to get my thoughts and feelings together.

Chapter 23

It was only a couple of days later, a Tuesday, when Ann banged on the kitchen door. Trevor and Lizzy were outside playing while the older kids were still at school.

"What are you doing home already?" I asked. "And wearing jeans? Are you slacking off at work?"

"No. I had a doctor's appointment, so I left early. I'm not in the mood to go back."

"Fertility stuff?" I asked sympathetically.

She stared into the house and answered absently, "Sort of."

"Is everything okay?" I asked nonchalantly.

There was the briefest pause, and something about the look on her face jolted me. "Ann?"

"I'm sure everything's fine," she said.

I stepped out onto the side porch and pulled the door shut behind me. "Sit down, old friend," I told her as I sat and patted the concrete beside me.

I was glad the comment made her laugh. She looked over at me, her eyes sparkling. "I don't know about the 'old' part there, Maren."

"Sorry," I giggled. "That's just an old Idaho expression I picked up from my grandpa. So, tell me what's going on. You look like you need to talk."

She sighed. "Actually, I guess I really do." She picked an early tulip from the flower bed and started pulling petals off as she explained. "You know we've been going through all these tests."

"Yes."

"Well, the doctor found a lump in my breast at my first visit."

"Ann! Why didn't you tell me?"

She shrugged. "I hoped that it was nothing, just another roadblock in the way of me having a baby. I didn't want to think about it."

"So what are they doing?" I asked.

"I went in for a mammogram two weeks ago, and they found a tumor. Today, they did a biopsy."

"What did they say?" I asked, as a feeling of foreboding crept into my chest.

"They won't have the results back for a couple of days," she answered.

"I'm sure it's nothing," I said firmly. Nothing like that could happen to Ann.

"Probably not," she answered. Then she looked over at me and I thought I saw some doubt in her expression for the first time. "But I'm scared, Maren. I've been ignoring it, pretending everything's fine, but I'm going to have to face it in a couple of days. I'm nervous."

"What does Tyler say?" I asked.

"He doesn't know," she replied.

"What?! You've been going through this for nearly a month, and not only have you kept it from me, your best friend, but you haven't even told your husband?"

"Nope."

"What are you, some kind of masochist?"

"He's been through enough, Maren," she said simply. "This whole fertility thing . . . it's been hard on him, harder than he'll admit. I know he feels guilty about not wanting to adopt. He knows it's hard for me, but I guess he can't change the way he feels. I just didn't want to give him another thing to worry about, not until I know for sure if there's anything to it. I'll tell him when I get the biopsy results back."

"But, Ann! How are you going to hide a biopsy from him? Aren't you sore?"

"Not too much," she answered. "It's no worse than a cut under my arm. It hurts a little, but I can pull it off for a day or two."

"You're awfully young to worry about breast cancer, aren't you?" I asked.

"I should be. But I do have some of the risk factors."

"What risk factors?" I wondered.

She sighed and threw the bare tulip stem back into the dirt. "I have dark hair and eyes, I'm over thirty and I haven't had a baby yet, and there's my dad . . . I told you he died when I was twelve."

"But he had lymphatic cancer. That's different. No one in your family's had breast cancer, right?"

"My aunt had it—my dad's sister."

"But she's okay now?" I assumed, by her use of the past tense.

"No, she died."

I was silent for a moment. "What can I do to help?" I asked.

"Just pray for me."

I put my arm around her shoulders and hugged her. "You're going to be fine, Ann. You are," I insisted.

She leaned her head against mine. "You know you're the sister I never had," she said.

"Yes, and you're my guardian angel."

I prayed every time I thought of her during the following two days, but I didn't really worry too much. She was too tough to get cancer.

On Thursday she knocked on the kitchen door, early and wearing jeans again. "I went to meet with the doctor," she said. "They got my results back."

I couldn't make myself ask. I could tell from the look on her face, and I didn't want to know. She started to cry. I hugged her and then pulled her inside. "Come in and sit down," I invited. "The kids are playing in the backyard."

She sat down on the couch, and I sat next to her. "Do you want to tell me what they said?"

"I met with the surgeon and the oncologist. They were all there. They want to operate next week. I have to have a mastectomy on my left side, and begin chemotherapy as soon as possible. They won't know for sure how bad it is until they operate."

I was stunned. "Oh, Ann!" I said.

"I can't believe it, Maren. I just can't believe it. One day I'm going along, thinking everything is fine, trying to get pregnant, planning for this miracle baby I keep hoping I'm going to have, making dinner, going to work . . . Then, suddenly, I have cancer. I'm losing a part of my body, I have to go through nightmare treatments, and I might die."

"No!" I shook my head emphatically. "You are NOT going to die, Ann. Don't even *think* of that."

"I have to, Maren. I have to face the facts." She shook her head and said, "Poor Tyler. My poor sweet husband. Here he's thrown away ten years of his life on a barren woman, and now, after all this, not only is he faced with the possibility of never having children, but he might lose me too. At least I'm glad we've been saving money. Even as expensive as all this fertility stuff has been, we've still been able to save. We've been very blessed that way. At least this won't be such a huge financial burden on him."

"Ann, don't even talk like that! Tyler loves you beyond belief, children or not. Don't start sounding like me," I joked, swallowing a sob. "And you've never been a burden to anyone, least of all your husband."

She smiled and sniffed. "That did sound like you, didn't it? Maybe this will be an adventure. Maybe we'll get to trade places for a while."

"Maybe this will be an opportunity for me to repay a small portion of what you've done for me," I said honestly.

She sat quietly, watching the children playing outside, tears running down her cheeks. I wanted to scream. Why did she have to go through something so horrendous?

"Ann, there is no way God is going to take you," I tried to reassure her. "Too many people need you. You're one of the best people I know. You can't go anywhere."

"I hope you're right, my friend. I hope you're right." She wiped her eyes and stood up. "I have to go. I called and asked Tyler to come home early and meet me. I have to go tell him." I watched numbly as she choked back a second flood of tears.

"You know I'll be here for you," I said with conviction, "Whatever you need."

"I'm so grateful for you, Maren."

I smiled. "This, from my guardian angel."

She stood up and walked toward the front door. I watched her go and looked at the blue, blue sky. She had to be all right. I couldn't lose anyone else, and Tyler certainly didn't need any more grief. No one deserved to live more than Ann.

Jake took one look at me when he came to pick up his children and asked, "What happened, Mar?"

"I wish you couldn't read me like a book," I mumbled.

He ignored the comment and said, "Let's have it."

I had to talk to someone. The fear was tearing me up inside. For once I couldn't talk to Ann about it. "Ann has cancer," I whispered, hearing the terror in my voice.

He looked shocked. "No . . ." he mumbled. "She can't."

I pressed a hand over my mouth and nodded.

Jake pulled me into his familiar comforting embrace. I squeezed my eyes shut and leaned against him. "I can't lose her, Jake. She's the best friend I've ever had. She's like my sister."

"I know it, love. She'll be all right. She has to be."

He asked me for the details, and I told him everything that Ann had told me.

"How could God do this to her?" I asked, clenching a fist against Jake's chest. "First she can't have children, and then just when she's getting some hope again, He smacks her with this. Why? I don't understand why."

"I don't understand either, Mar," he whispered, squeezing me tight. "I just don't."

When I pulled away and looked up at him, I observed, "You look as terrified as I feel."

He smiled softly and told me, "She's my co-conspirator. I need her. I could never handle you by myself."

"Oh, you!" I hit him on the chest, but the thought made my heart ache.

"More importantly," he said seriously, "she's a wonderful woman. Even if I didn't know her, I'd have to love her just for what she's done for you. But she and Tyler have done plenty for me too. Jeff and Lizzy love them."

"I know," I said. "All the kids love them. They should get children of their own. It's just not fair."

"Life's not fair, Maren. But she'll get well. We'll just have to pray."

* * *

Ted came to get the kids the following evening with his father. "So, the kids tell me you're dating already," he said right off. *Already?* I thought. *He moved out over a year ago, and we've been divorced for eight months.*

"Ted, that is really none of your business now," I said simply. Dating was the last thing on my mind at that moment. I hadn't even thought of having a serious discussion with Jake any more. I felt like my life had been suddenly paused, that the only picture in focus was Ann. Ted seemed surprised at my boldness. I still worried a little bit about sending Rebecca and Trevor with him, but there wasn't much that I could do about it, except to pray and call to check on them. I did both every time they went with him. So far things had gone well. The children liked to go with him and their grandparents. I kissed them. "I'll see you tomorrow night, guys. Have fun with Daddy!" I shut the door as soon as they were out, before he could say anything else to me.

I had design projects that I couldn't put off working on that weekend, but I thought about Ann constantly. She had to get better. She just had to.

Chapter 24

The day of the surgery, I prayed all day. Tyler called late in the afternoon. "How is she?" I asked with concern.

"The surgery went fairly well. It took quite a while because they also removed seventeen cancerous lymph nodes." I tried not to gasp. "She's not feeling very well, and—" His voice cracked. "Just pray for us, Maren. She's not well enough to talk to you. I'm sorry."

"Tell her I'm praying, and I love her," I said.

"I will. I'll let you know how she's doing later."

"All right."

Jake called me before he left work and said, "I just talked to Tyler. Would you mind keeping the kids a little longer? I'd like to stop at the hospital and help him give Ann a blessing."

"They can stay as long as they need to," I assured him. "Maybe you should go eat dinner with Tyler. He could probably use some company if Ann's still out of it."

"Thanks. I'll see how it goes."

"Don't worry about Lizzy and Jeff. I'll just see you when you get here."

I fed the children dinner and played a game with them, trying to distract myself as much as anything. When the phone rang again I answered it eagerly, hoping for information about Ann.

"Hello . . ." the voice on the other end drawled. "This is Tess." That was just like her, to not even acknowledge my name.

"Hi," I said, a little annoyed.

"Is Jake over there?" she asked. I detected something in her voice, anger or irritation.

"No, he's not."

"Do you have Jeffrey and Elizabeth?"

I wanted to answer in the negative, but I didn't. "Yes, they're here."

"Oh, that man is *irresponsible,*" she complained. "I suppose I'll have to come and get them myself." I couldn't believe she had the nerve to call Jake irresponsible. I had to bite my tongue to keep from telling her who I thought the irresponsible one was.

"You don't need to come and get them. They're fine. Jake should be here soon, anyway," I told her.

"I'm sure he will be. Bye!"

I hung up without even bidding her farewell. My blood was boiling. I wished that I could talk to Ann . . . Ann. The thought of her made me sick with worry again.

The doorbell rang a few minutes later. I hoped that it was Jake, but it was Tess. "I came for the kids," she said, obviously put out. "I can't wait all night."

"Are you taking them somewhere?" I asked.

"By myself?" Her heavily-lined eyes flew open wide. "You must be joking. I couldn't handle those two alone in public." I felt overwhelmingly irritated, thinking of all the times I'd taken all four children somewhere with me. It wasn't a picnic, but it was certainly doable. It wasn't hard to believe that this woman had never taken her two children anywhere alone, though.

She rambled on and said, "I should just take them to Jake's. Do you have a key to his house, by chance?"

I was surprised that she didn't have her own key. Maybe she did. Maybe she'd just forgotten it.

"No," I lied. "I don't." Jake had given me a spare, but I wasn't going to tell her that.

Her voice held a hint of sarcasm. "I'm sure you don't. I suppose I'll just have to take them to my mother's house."

"Tess, Jeffrey and Elizabeth are welcome to stay. Jake is planning on picking them up here."

"Won't he be surprised then?"

I thought, suddenly, that she would be so much prettier if her personality wasn't so selfish. "I'll get the children," I said. I left her in the doorway and went to call down the stairs to them.

Jeff and Lizzy ran upstairs, but they both seemed a little apprehensive when they saw Tess. She'd come to pick them up a handful of times before, and they'd been all right. I thought maybe they sensed the uneasiness hovering in the air that day because of worry over Ann. "Is Daddy with you?" Jeffrey asked her.

"No, sugar, just me." I hated the way she spoke in that honey-glazed voice to her children, as though they were too unintelligent to see past it. I didn't want to send them with her.

"Where's Daddy?" Elizabeth asked.

"I don't know." Tess shrugged her shoulders carelessly. "I can't believe he forgot you. Come and give Mommy a hug."

"He didn't forget you, guys," I cut in, as Elizabeth softened and obediently went to throw her arms around her mother's neck. I couldn't let them think that their father would forget them. They had enough to be insecure about with their mother. "He called and said he'd be a little late. He was stopping at the hospital to see Ann."

"Is Ann okay?" Jeffrey asked me.

"She's sick, buddy, but I'm sure she'll feel better soon." I crouched down to talk to him. The children all loved Ann. They knew she was ill, but they didn't understand. They were concerned for her regardless.

Tess surprised me by asking, "How is Ann?" I still couldn't picture Tess being overly concerned about anyone besides herself.

I wasn't sure how to answer her, especially with the children listening. "The surgery was pretty major," I finally said. "She has a long road ahead of her."

Tess almost looked sad. "That is too bad," she commented.

"Can we wait for Daddy?" Jeff asked his mother.

"No," she snapped. "We're going."

"Where are we going?" Lizzy asked. "Are you going to take us somewhere, Mommy?"

"Yes. I'm taking you to see your grandmother."

"Are you going to stay there with us, Mom?" Jeff asked hopefully.

His little face fell when she replied, "I don't know. We'll see, sugar. Mommy's very busy you know." She opened the front door and instructed, "You two run and get in the car."

I told the children good-bye and watched them walk toward their mother's car.

"Keep your feet off the seats!" she called after them.

"Should I tell Jake that the children will be with your mother, then?" I asked Tess.

She gave me a sly grin and said, "You can tell him whatever you want, honey."

I was feeling increasingly annoyed. "He'll want to know where they are, Tess. It's been a stressful day for everyone."

She almost looked amused, a fact that upset me immensely. "Oh, he'll manage to track me down," she said, and then added quietly, "He always does." I wondered what that was supposed to mean, but I didn't give her the satisfaction of asking. She seemed determined to agitate me as she asked innocently, "Didn't he tell you how he hunted me down this time?"

I furrowed my brow, not sure what she was getting at.

"How he dragged me out here from New York?" she continued.

I felt my heart dropping down to my stomach as I slowly shook my head.

"Really?" she asked innocently. "It's quite a story. You should ask him about it sometime."

I wondered if she could possibly be telling the truth. Jake had seemed so sincere when he told me about her coming back to Utah . . . Had he lied to me? Had I been so foolish as to believe another man's lies?

Tess looked suddenly worried and said, "You look upset. I hope I didn't upset you."

I shook my head again, not trusting my voice.

A look of enlightenment came over her face as she asked, "Has he been leading you on?" She rolled her eyes and said, "That man . . . I guess that explains what he's said about you . . . Did you actually believe him, honey?"

I blinked back tears, struggling to hold onto my composure. What did Jake say about me? Had he really just been leading me on? Had he honestly begged Tess to come out here with him? Did he love her? Jake wouldn't say things to me that he didn't mean . . . would he? I knew him better than that . . . didn't I? Then again, I had thought that I knew Ted well too. How could I have let myself trust a man again? I had been a fool.

Tess leaned closer speaking conspiratorially, "Let me give you some advice, Maren—men are men. I learned a long time ago to use that to my advantage rather than try to fight it. Maybe you'll figure that out for yourself sometime instead of knocking your head against a brick wall over and over again. Forget about Jake. His taste is a little more . . . extravagant." She waved a careless hand at me. "But you're not completely hopeless, honey. You could be pretty . . . in a simple sort of way. If you tried."

I had never wanted to hit someone so badly in my life. I would have liked to just sock her pretty jaw and smudge her lipstick. Oh, the thought was scrumptious.

Tess turned her back and closed the door before I could even think of anything to say to her. I caught a glimpse of Jake's car pulling into the driveway before I leaned against the door and clenched my hands into fists, refusing to let myself cry. Tess seemed to have the same ability that Ted had to make me feel terrible, to twist everything around and rip away any shreds of self-esteem that might be left clinging to my ravaged self. I was so angry with myself for letting her get to me, for allowing myself to feel so intimidated by her, but I couldn't deny the huge seed of doubt that she had planted in my heart. Maybe Jake was still in love with Tess. Maybe he was just another selfish man. Maybe he couldn't have cared less about me. Maybe I didn't even know Jake at all.

His voice on the front porch cut into my thoughts. I knew I shouldn't do it, but I pressed my ear to the door, listening. I heard Jeffrey and Elizabeth calling to him, and him telling them to wait in the car for a minute.

"What are you doing here, Tess?" he asked.

"What does it look like I'm doing? I have better things to do than sit around waiting for you all day. The least you could do is give me a key to your house. Then I'd have somewhere to wait."

"I don't trust you," he said flatly. "What have you been waiting for? We didn't have any plans tonight."

"I thought we should have plans," she cooed. "I thought you ought to take the kids and me to dinner."

"Were you going to take them by yourself since I didn't show up when you thought I should have?"

She gave that haughty laugh and answered, "You know I can't handle them by myself, darling."

"So, why did you bother to come and get them? Maren was going to keep them. She was fine with them."

Tess's voice turned bitter as she said, "I don't think you should leave them any longer with that woman than you have to." I bit my tongue to keep from screaming. How could she say something like that when I'd been taking care of her children for an entire year, while she had better things to do?

Jake sounded angry. *"That woman* loves them, Tess. Do you even comprehend that? She *loves* them. And they love her. You should be thankful." I felt immensely grateful for his defense of that at least. At least he knew that I loved his children.

"Oh, *please,"* Tess drawled, reminding me again of Ted. "She doesn't watch them for my sake. And I don't believe it's because she loves them, either—although she is pretty good at putting up that sappy front, just like you."

"Yes, she also needs the money. You're right, Tess. But that's only because she doesn't want to leave her own children either. If she was willing to put them in daycare, she could make it just fine by herself. She runs a very successful business." I was surprised again.

"Why don't you just admit it, darling?" Tess said in that syrupy voice. "You're an arrogant fool. You know that poor little simpering girl is so smitten by you she can hardly stand it, and it gives you a thrill to string her along. You know they drop like flies after you, don't you, sugar?"

"Give it up, Tess."

Tess's voice turned icy. "Does she know, Jake?" she asked. "Does she know how you really feel about her?"

"That's not your concern."

"She doesn't, does she? You don't have the guts to tell her the truth."

"You don't know what you're talking about."

"Give me some credit, darling. Don't play stupid—it's so unattractive. You've been living with this ghost in your closet for years, and you still don't have the guts to face it."

"What in heaven's name are you talking about?"

"I know what's going on, Jake. It's quite amusing for me actually."

"You're dreaming, Tess. You have no idea what's going on. You're completely wrong about this whole thing."

"Am I? Well, if Maren's not completely smitten by you, then *something* must be wrong with her. She's certainly upset."

"Upset over what?" he asked slowly.

"I don't know, darling . . . Oooh. I hope it wasn't something I said."

"What did you say?" he questioned. I could hear anger in his voice again.

There was silence for a moment, and then Jake asked again, "What did you tell her, Tess?"

"Nothing she didn't already know," she answered. "I'd like to take the credit for enlightening her, but I can't imagine that even your little protégé is that naive."

"Enlightening her on *what?*" Jake hissed at her.

"Don't worry, sugar. I'm sure she already knew. I just confirmed it for her so she can stop languishing over you and get a life. I did her a favor, really."

"You don't even know what you're talking about!" Jake hollered.

"Really, darling. The poor thing can't help but be infatuated with you. I can't stand living with you, but even I never denied how incredibly attractive you are."

"Tess . . ." He lowered his voice so I could barely hear it through the door, but I could still detect the fury behind it. *What did you tell Maren?*

She hissed back at him. "Why don't you figure it out? . . . *Don't* touch me, Jacob!" she raised her voice to warn. "Don't you *ever* touch me!" I wished that I could see what was going on.

"Tess, if you hurt her, I swear—"

"Oh, no you don't, Jakey. You're too perfect for that."

"I'm not joking, Tess. You leave Maren *alone.*"

"Or what, darling? You'll cut off my allowance? You won't share your kids? You'll deprive me of your charming company? What *exactly* will you do, Jacob? There is *nothing* you can do to hurt me that a judge won't remedy in a hurry. But there's an awful lot that I could do to hurt you."

"Like what?" Jake challenged.

"Maybe I could permanently mess up your life the way you've permanently messed up mine!" she shot out.

"I didn't mess up your life, Tess. You did a nice job of that all by yourself."

"Did I? Well, maybe I could mess it up a little more by fighting for custody of your children then. This would certainly be a good state to go to battle with you in. They always favor the mothers in this unenlightened provincial place."

"You wouldn't dare."

"Wouldn't I?"

"What do you want, Tess?"

"I want what you took. I want what you can't give me. It's too late for what I want."

"Tess, I don't know what game you're trying to play, but I'm not buying. You know darn well that you don't want the kids. You can't handle the responsibility. But if you would actually sink so low as to fight for them to further whatever your sick hidden agenda is, then I will fight back with everything I have. If you have something to say, spare me your threats and say it. Leave the kids alone. Leave Maren alone. And leave me alone. I mean it."

"You don't scare me," Tess nearly laughed. "You've amused me. You've disgusted me. You've annoyed me. You've even made me furious. But you've never scared me, sugar. You don't have the guts."

"If you keep pushing it, Tess, you might find out that I do."

She laughed again and lowered her voice to warn, "Don't tempt me, darling. That might be something I'd like to see."

"Give me the kids and go home, Tess," Jake ordered. "And don't show up here again."

"Why? Are you afraid your precious Maren might find out how you really feel?"

"Just shut up, Tess. For once in your life, shut up." I was surprised to hear Jake talking like that to someone, even Tess.

I heard him walking back down the sidewalk as Tess called after him, "Aren't you going to kiss me good-bye, sugar?"

I hoped that he would really take the children with him. I wanted to ask him about Ann, but I couldn't bring myself to open the door and go out. I didn't want to see him. I felt like a fool for believing that he'd cared about me, for letting him string me along. He certainly didn't sound like he was helplessly in love with Tess, but then he did sound like he felt threatened. The relationship obviously wasn't healthy, but that didn't mean he didn't love her. I understood that all too well.

I heard car doors and a vehicle driving away. It surprised me to hear a knock on the door a few seconds afterward. I wondered if Tess had been unable to resist the temptation to pour salt in my wounds. I took a deep breath and tried to muster some degree of poise. I certainly didn't want her to think she'd gotten to me. It wasn't her though. It was Jake. I was relieved to see Jeffrey and Elizabeth with him.

"Hi, Mar. Do you mind if the kids go downstairs with Becca and Trevor for a few more minutes?"

I smiled at them and said, "Of course not. Go ahead, you two." They ran back downstairs.

"Do you want to sit down?" I asked Jake.

He sat in the chair and I sat on the couch across from him. He looked intently at me and asked, "What did she say to you, Maren?"

"Who?" I feigned innocence, trying to buy myself time to think of a response.

He angrily loosened his tie and undid the top button of his shirt, as though he felt trapped and needed to breathe easier. "My gracious ex-wife, that's who. What did she say to you?"

"Nothing I didn't already know," I answered flatly. Or at least nothing I *shouldn't* have already known. I didn't even want to have this discussion with him.

He raised a skeptical eyebrow and said, *"Nothing?"*

"What are you worried about, Jake?" I asked, feeling suddenly angry. "Do you have something to hide?"

"What?!"

"Nothing. Never mind. It just doesn't matter."

"What doesn't matter?" he pried.

"Oh, Jake, I know I've just been stupid, and it's obvious. Whatever you've said, or whatever is between you and Tess is . . . I just don't care. I just don't even want to know, okay?"

"Maren, there *is* nothing between Tess and me. And what do you mean, 'whatever I've said'?"

I just looked at him, searching his face, wishing that I could trust my own judgment.

"Maren, whatever she said . . . it's not true," he told me quietly.

When I still said nothing, he leaned forward on his knees and looked at me, those electrical currents trying to read my heart again.

As though he'd found what he was looking for, Jake sat up and said simply, "You don't believe me, do you." He wasn't asking me.

"No," I whispered. "I don't."

"But you'd listen to her?" He sighed and looked away. When he looked back at me he asked softly, "Why don't you believe me, Mar?"

"It's just safer that way, Jake. I don't believe anyone. I don't trust anyone. I don't even trust myself."

That look of pain washed over him again and he leaned toward me. "Maren, please. I don't know what Tess said to you, but please use your own good judgment. Listen to your heart. Don't let anything she said get to you. She weaves a pretty tale."

"You sound like you're afraid of something she might have told me," I observed.

"I am!" He sat up and smashed his fingers through his hair. "I know her, Maren. I know her well. She has a gift for causing pain. She seems to especially enjoy causing *me* pain, and . . . she knows that I care for you. She knows that she can hurt me by hurting you. Just . . . be wary. Ignore anything cruel that she said, Mar. You're worth more than that."

I looked into his eyes and I did believe that he cared about me. But I was still afraid.

"You've known me for years, Maren," he reminded me.

"I know."

"And have you ever known me to lie to you?"

"I've never *known* you to, no," I had to admit. "But experience has made me wary, Jake, that's all there is to it."

He scooted to the edge of his seat and reached out to take my hand. "Maren," he said quietly. "If she said something that concerns you . . . If you want to know something . . . please just ask me. I'll tell you the truth, I promise—about anything."

His face was so sincere. It made me feel terrible. "I'm sorry, Jake. You don't have to tell me anything or justify yourself to me—"

"Maren, please just stop it. I know that having Tess around makes things difficult . . . but if my children can have even some semblance of a mother . . ." He let go of my hand and laid back against the chair to study me for a minute. "Look, I know you . . . I know that you and I do not feel the same way about our relationship right now . . ."

I was shocked and I felt the embarrassment rise to my cheeks with the hurt. There it was, plain and simple. He didn't love me.

"But you're still my best friend, Maren, and I would much rather have you come and ask me something point-blank, than have you wondering or worrying. I know I don't *have* to tell you anything, but I would *want* to." He leaned forward again, looking earnestly into my eyes, and said, "I mean it, Mar."

"I know you do. And I do believe you, Jake. I'm sorry for saying that I didn't. You're my best friend too . . ." I stopped to swallow the lump in my throat and looked away. I still didn't understand how he could have kissed me like that if he didn't love me. I remembered Ann telling me to buck up and just ask him, to take control of my own life. I took a breath and plunged in. "Jake . . . if you knew that we didn't feel the same way . . . why did you kiss me? Why did you say the things you said to me? It's made things very . . . difficult for me."

He bit his bottom lip and said, "I guess . . . because I didn't know until after that, Mar. I wasn't sure until after we went to the opera, actually. I'm sorry. I didn't mean to make things difficult for you. I guess I thought that because we were so close once, it might not be so hard to rekindle those feelings . . . I was wrong."

I nodded and blinked back tears. It made sense that he'd tried to revive the old feelings when he realized how I felt, but that they just weren't there for him anymore. Maybe he hadn't intentionally led me on, or meant to hurt me . . .

"How is Ann?" I asked as I suddenly forgot about myself and remembered where he'd been all evening.

He sighed and looked at me with drooping eyes. "They had to take out seventeen lymph nodes. They said the surgery went well. They want her to start chemo as soon as she can, preferably in a week or two. They would like her to hold off on reconstructive surgery until after she gets through six months of treatments. Tyler said they're hopeful." His voice was monotone.

"I know all that. I talked to Tyler on the phone. But what does all that mean, Jake?" I prodded.

He studied me as if trying to decide what to tell me. He finally opted for honesty. "I'm not a cancer specialist, Mar, but I am a doctor. I'm not impressed with all the smiles and medical jargon they dish out to the families. The fact that the cancer had already spread to so many lymph nodes is a bad sign. It could be in other places, too. The prognosis is not good considering her family history. The surgery was pretty major, and she'll likely have a difficult recovery. The doctors want to start chemotherapy within the next week or two, but it's doubtful she'll be ready. I don't know, Maren. I just don't know . . . All we can do is pray."

I looked at him blankly for a minute before asking, "You got to talk to Tyler then?"

"Yes. Ann was completely knocked out. He didn't want to leave her, but he just looked exhausted. I did manage to drag him down to the cafeteria to eat something, and we talked for a few minutes. I didn't tell him what I just told you."

I nodded. "He needs encouragement right now, anyway."

Chapter 25

Ann began chemotherapy on the same day that it snowed for the last time that year. Every two weeks she went in for a treatment. She would be so sick the first couple of days that she couldn't really be alone. Her mother came up from Arizona to help as much as she could, but she wasn't able to stay as long as she wanted to. She always had to get back to work. Tyler stayed with her as often as his job schedule could possibly allow. Sometimes he couldn't leave work though, so I took the children over and stayed with her whenever possible.

Ann needed a lot more help than I had thought she would. I felt like my life had been thrown into turmoil. I felt sick with worry over her. I felt overwhelmingly upset over things with Jake too, but I just didn't have time to think about that. He did make an effort to be my friend and to be a support to me. I just tried to be grateful for that and forget about being angry with him for the time being. I needed him. I quit dating and quit going to the single adult activities. I cut back everything I could in order to be there for Ann. I didn't miss anything that I gave up. There wasn't a whole lot that seemed very important in light of what my friend was facing. I took care of my children and Jake's, and worked as much as I had to in order to pay the bills. I still went to an occasional counseling appointment. I figured everything else could wait.

Ann slowly got used to the chemotherapy schedule. She started feeling better by the fifth day after a treatment. Then she'd have a pretty good week before she had to go in for the next one. She was tired and weak and had to be very careful about being exposed to any germs, since the chemotherapy destroyed her immune system. I was grateful that winter was over since it meant the kids didn't have colds all the time.

I spent a lot of time with Ann. Sometimes she came over to my house, but lots of days the kids and I just went to hers. Because she couldn't really go out a lot, I tried to bring her things to keep her busy. I checked out books from the library for her, and rented movies for her to watch. I started teaching her how to do flower arrangements, and she often helped me when I had to do them for one of my jobs. Tyler bought a video camera and started filming everything. I tried to pass it off as an obsessive hobby, rather then a panicked effort to record their lives. Ann ignored it, or at least she pretended to.

I got very familiar with her house. When the children weren't in school, they played together in Ann's basement, or in the backyard when it was warm enough. Ann and Tyler had a fabulous backyard. The kids could stay out there for hours on a nice day. I cleaned and did laundry and kept Ann's sunny bedroom full of flowers from my garden. Sometimes I helped her with paperwork or looked things up for her. She wanted to keep up with things at work.

"Why do you clean my house, Maren?" she asked. "I don't even do that. Stop it."

I laughed. "It makes me feel useful. I have to do something. Besides, revenge is sweet."

One day when Ann was just starting to feel better after a treatment, I sat on her bed with her, holding a mirror while she tried on wigs. Her beautiful shimmering hair had fallen out in thick dead clumps until she was almost bald. She had lost a lot of weight and moaned about not being able to go to the gym and lacking the strength to exercise.

"How do I look?" she asked, turning her head back and forth in a curly auburn wig.

"Like your mother," I said, and we both started laughing.

She tried on a short stylish wig that looked very much like her own hair and she smiled at herself in the mirror. She stuck out her tongue. "Look at me, Maren. I look like a lizard." I thought that losing her eyebrows and eyelashes had been more traumatic for her than losing her hair. She did look pale and skinny and foreign, her pretty features sunken. Only her sparkling eyes hadn't changed. She wiggled her tongue and laughed at herself. Then, without warning, she started to cry. She grabbed the mirror out of my hand and threw it across the room. Luckily, it landed on the cushioned window seat and didn't smash. She stood up in her pajamas and threw a pillow. "I hate this! I HATE it, Maren! Why did this have to happen to me?" She jumped up and down in a fit of rage.

"I don't feel like myself. I don't even look like myself! I can't do anything I want to do. I can't go anywhere," she ranted on, pacing around the room. I was glad the kids were outside. "And do you know what the worst thing is?" she yelled.

I shook my head when she looked at me expectantly.

"I have to pretend that I'm FINE! They all see me looking sick and awful. Every time Tyler, or one of our family members, or someone from the Relief Society comes into the room, I can see the horror in their faces. I can never yell. I can never say I feel awful or I hate God. I can never cry. I'm the one who's sick, Maren, *me!* Why do I have to be tough for everyone else? I can't even *cry!*" She fell down on the bed, sobbing, her small burst of energy spent.

I patted her back. "You can cry, Ann. I can handle it. Tyler can handle it too."

"Oh, Tyler! He won't yell, he won't cry. He's just always sweet and calm and jamming that stupid video camera in my face! He thinks I'm going to die!"

"No, he doesn't!"

"Why does he have to record every second left in my life, then? I don't want people to remember me looking like this! My family will have so many horrible images of me on tape, they won't even remember what I really looked like!"

"Ann," I said calmly. "No one has forgotten what you look like, least of all your family. You're beautiful. You're not going anywhere anyway. And you don't need to be tough for everyone else. Everyone has a different way of coping. Yell if you want to. Cry if you want to. In fact, send people away if you want to. They'll just have to understand. You're the one who's going through this."

* * *

In June, Jake and I went together to watch Rebecca and Elizabeth perform in their closing dance recital. We also went to see Jeffrey's and Trevor's last T-ball game of the season. Ann was halfway through her chemotherapy treatments, and went in for a midway check-up. When I went over to her house the next day she was in a more contemplative mood than usual.

"What's up with you, Annie girl?" I asked.

"Hmm?" she said, gazing out the window. We were sitting in the family room working on my children's scrapbooks. She enjoyed helping me with them, and I appreciated the help. The early summer sun was streaming in, and we could hear the children's screams of delight as they ran through the sprinklers in the yard behind us.

"You're too quiet," I told her. "I just called you 'Annie girl,' and you didn't even protest."

She smiled and said, "You'll remember me that way, won't you?"

"What?" I asked, wondering if I'd heard her right.

"As 'Annie girl'? I always did like it. You'll remember it?"

"Remember it? How can I forget it when I see you every day?" I answered teasingly, but a formless dread began to swell in my chest.

She kept working on a page with blue baseballs and Trevor in his T-ball uniform as she answered quietly, "I want you to have something that's just yours and mine, something that you'll remember me by. We've had some wonderful times together, you and I."

"Of course we have. And we'll have many more."

She shook her head, as a tear dropped onto the paper she held. "No, we won't. A few more maybe, but not many."

I swallowed the knot in my throat. "Ann, you're halfway done with chemo. You're going to get better. You're going to be fine in a few more months," I tried to convince her.

She looked up at me and her voice was clear. "There's cancer in my ovaries."

"There is?" I was shocked.

"There is. They think that's where it started, in fact. That's probably part of the reason I haven't been able to get pregnant."

"But you can have them taken out. And you can adopt children." I felt what was coming.

She didn't flinch. "I'm never going to have children, Maren. It's in other lymph nodes."

"But they can take those out, too."

"It's all through me," she whispered.

I stared at her in disbelief. "What?"

"There's nothing they can do. I'm stopping chemotherapy. I want to feel as well as I can for as long as I can. I'm quitting my job. I need to spend time with my husband, my family, my friends . . ." We sat looking at each other for a minute, saying nothing. "So, will you remember my name?" she whispered.

I nodded as the tears came running. *No*, I thought. *No, God, no. Take me. Let her stay. Leave her alone.* I went over to hug her and we sat crying together for a long time, watching the children outside, running and laughing, just being alive.

When someone you love tells you they're going to die, you're suddenly smacked in the face with mortality. There's no going over it. There's no going under it. There's no going around it. The only way out is through it. You know you're entering this unknown wilderness with them, and that when you come out the other side you'll be without them, but there's nothing else you can do. You can't send someone you love through that alone.

So you go, trying to soak up every second you can with them. You try to remember every detail, every look, every smile, every laugh, every word, hoping that you can store away enough to fill up the hole that's going to be left in your heart when they're gone. You try to hold on as tightly as you can, never resting, never looking away, always on alert—lest they slip away in a flickering moment of unawareness. And always, you're praying. Praying with gratitude in your heart for every second more that you're allowed with your loved one, praying for strength, praying for peace, praying for a miracle . . .

Chapter 26

I left the children playing downstairs for a minute on a Friday afternoon while I went across the street with some hot rolls for Ann, and some flowers from my garden. Tyler answered the door and said, "Hi, Maren. Oh . . . thanks." He took the rolls and the flowers, but he seemed distracted.

"I can't stay, but could I just tell her hi really quickly?" I asked him.

"I'm sorry, Maren. Ann's really in a lot of pain. I'm just getting ready to take her over to the hospital."

"Oh, no! What can I do?"

He shook his head and wiped at tears that suddenly spilled down his cheeks. "Can you save her?" he whispered, and then chuckled dryly.

The harshness of the reality seemed unbearable. I touched his arm and said softly, "I'd do anything if I could, Tyler."

He patted my hand and said, "I know you would. So would I. I guess God wants her, though." He cracked a smile and wiped at his face again, saying jokingly, "I wonder why that is?" But then he covered his mouth to bury a sob.

I hugged him and said brokenly, "I'm sorry, Tyler. I'm just so sorry." I didn't know what else to say. I felt like I was dying inside myself.

"She's in so much pain," he said, standing up straight and mopping his face with the back of his hand. "I don't want to see her suffer anymore . . . but I can't let her go. I just can't let her go yet."

I stood looking at him, wishing that I could rip out my heart and give it to Ann to save her.

After several emotional moments, Tyler pulled himself together and asked, "Do I look presentable enough to go get her?"

I chuckled and said, "I think you'll do."

"Why don't you stay here a minute?" he offered. "You can tell her good-bye before we leave. She'd want to see you."

I nodded and tried to hide the signs of my own distress before Ann came downstairs.

Tyler went up for her and helped her slowly down the stairs. She had a peach silk scarf tied around her head. Her face was drawn and pale. I held back a shudder, watching how slowly and painfully she walked, the left side of her chest sunken. It must be the worst thing in the world, cancer. There is no more real nightmare than watching the silent black death creeping through the body of someone you love, slowly drawing them away from you. There's nothing you can do to stop it. You are completely powerless.

I smiled at her, kissed her on the cheek, and picked up her bag to help them out to the car. She smiled back at me. "Don't look so worried, Maren. A little morphine, and I'll be as good as new." She put on that cheery voice of hers, but it was strained. I could hear the fear behind it.

When Jake came to pick up Elizabeth and Jeffrey, he asked, "How's Ann?" like he did every day.

I swallowed the fear in my throat to answer, "Tyler took her to the hospital this afternoon. She's in a lot of pain . . . She looks awful, Jake."

He shook his head and muttered, "I wish I could do something. It's terrible to have to watch our friends go through this, and not be able to do anything for them."

"You do a lot for them, Jake. You've helped Tyler give Ann blessings several times, and you're a great friend to him . . . to both of them. You've been a big support to Tyler."

"I just wish that I could do something more. I'm a doctor, Mar. You'd think that I could do something."

"Jake, even her doctors can't do anything. God wants her back . . ." My voice broke and I fought back the tears before continuing, "For whatever reason. I wish He didn't . . . but He does."

"I know," he answered softly.

"She's going to die, Jake . . ." I whispered. "She's really going to die . . . isn't she?" I looked up at him with terrified eyes. I already knew, but I somehow needed someone to voice it for me.

He touched a hand to my cheek and whispered, "Yes, love. I'm afraid she is."

I squeezed my eyes shut and brushed my cheek against his hand. Jake put his other arm around my waist to pull me close to him and rested his head on mine. I silently prayed for Ann to have peace. I wanted her pain to be taken away. But I didn't want *her* to be taken away, not yet. I felt so helpless. Ann was going to die. She'd told me herself. I had known, but I had accepted it numbly until then. I suddenly felt all the feelings rushing up that I had tried to ignore.

I felt horrified at the thought of losing my best friend. I felt sick that God would require her to leave her husband so soon, when she was still so young. I was anguished that she had no posterity to leave behind. I hung onto Jake, hoping that it might somehow keep me from being sucked into the rapidly growing black hole inside me.

I was alone the next morning. Trevor and Rebecca had gone with Ted. I took a shower and got dressed, the bare minimum. I shoved my hair up in a clip to get it out of my face. I didn't bother to put on makeup or make my bed. What was the point? Those things seemed so trivial in light of what I knew then. I couldn't even bring myself to eat anything. I went straight to the hospital. I knocked on the door and Tyler softly called, "Come in."

"Hi," I whispered. Ann was asleep in the bed, so I asked, "How is she?"

"Better. She finally got over the worst of the pain. She's been sleeping for quite a while."

"Have you had any breakfast?" I asked him.

He shook his head.

"Why don't you go get yourself some?" I offered. "Go home and take a shower if you want, or rest. I'll stay with her until you get back."

"You don't need to do that, Maren. I'm fine."

"I know. I want to do it. I want to be with her." I stopped to clear my throat. "Please let me stay, Tyler. Please?"

He smiled. "Okay. I'll see you in a little bit. I won't be gone long."

I looked around me at the dark and sterile room. I put the brightly colored flowers I'd brought on the bedside table and watched my friend sleeping for a moment before I kissed her forehead. I was surprised to hear her voice. "Hmmm . . . the smell of fresh flowers,

Downy fabric softener, and Beautiful perfume . . . Must be my best friend, Maren." She smiled and opened her eyes.

"You faker," I teased.

"Well, if they'd ever open the blinds around this place, a person might know when it was morning and wake up."

I laughed and opened the blinds. The morning sun streamed into the room, filling it with warmth.

"Oh, that's better," she sighed contentedly.

"I hope this won't be a big disappointment, but you get me for a bit instead of your husband," I said. "I made him leave."

Her eyes were sad, but she quipped, "Are you kidding? I could use some girl talk. Tyler's not so good at applying makeup either, so your presence is a welcome surprise."

Later in the morning, she asked how things were going with Jake. "I can't even deal with that right now, Ann. I don't know. I told you what he said about not feeling the same way that I do. Maybe I don't really love him either. Maybe I just got carried away because I was lonely and mistook our growing friendship for romance." She smiled and shook her head before drifting back into medicated sleep.

Chapter 27

July was a difficult month. The hot sunny days defied the bitter coldness that I felt inside. Ann's absence was profound. She was too sick to leave the hospital. It seemed worse, somehow, for her to be locked away in that horrible place during the long midsummer days. I talked to her on the phone a lot, and once in a while, if she was feeling up to it, I took the children over during the day. I put off designing temporarily and spent a lot of Wednesdays at the hospital. Jake didn't mind watching Rebecca and Trevor while I went, and I was grateful for the time with Ann. Sometimes I watched the children while he went over for a while. I thought that Tyler was probably grateful for his company. I knew that Jake would drag him out of that dreary hospital room for a few minutes here and there, and remind him to keep living. I prayed for Ann to feel well enough to go home soon. It seemed like she'd been in that awful hospital forever.

Near the end of the month, I went to spend the day at the hospital with Ann while Tyler caught up on some things at work. My children were with Ted's family again that day. It was another bright and sunny morning, a fact that made me angry. How could the sun shine like that without Ann? I tried to act cheery as I walked into the room.

"So, how are things with Jake?" Ann asked me almost before I sat down.

"You don't waste any time, do you?"

"I don't have much time to waste," she muttered dryly. "So . . . are you going to answer me or not?"

"I'm thinking," I told her. "Be patient."

She shot right back without even moving, "I've been a patient for far too long."

"Oh, Ann!" I started to cry at just the wrong moment. "How can you think so fast? You're such a bright light in a dark world." A world that would be so much darker when her light went out.

She sat up and gave me a tender smile. "You're so sentimental, Maren. I'm sorry. What's going on with Jake?"

"I don't know. He's a wonderful friend. He helps with the kids so I can be here. He's still with Tess a lot, but I can't figure out if that's because he loves her or not. It's been so long since he kissed me and said those wonderful things to me that I'm beginning to wonder if I just dreamed all that up."

"How do you feel about things?" she asked.

I stared out the window and said, "I just don't care anymore."

"Come on, Maren, the truth now," she prodded.

I couldn't believe that my best friend lay dying, and I found myself pouring out my simple troubles to her again. She was the ever-patient listener. "I feel lost," I confessed. "I feel afraid."

"Maybe he does too," she pointed out.

"Maybe. I don't know if I love him or if I'm just lonely, Ann. I'm afraid I'll be alone forever. It's getting old, you know? Ted's been gone for over a year." I winced at the word "gone" after I'd said it. "I guess I just keep hoping that things will change, that Jake will figure out what he wants, that he'll forget about Tess and somehow fall desperately in love with me again and come after me . . . I'm dreaming, aren't I? Here I am, wishing for some fairy tale, even after all that I've been through. I swore I'd never do this again. I guess it's time I face reality and get on with my life."

Ann chuckled softly, as if she could see something behind her closed lids that I couldn't. "Silly Maren," she said.

"What do you mean?" I asked her.

"I'm not going to point it out again for you, sweet friend. I've certainly told you more than once already."

"Point out what?" I asked.

She continued as if she hadn't heard me. "But I certainly hope that you and Jake figure it out eventually. I wish I could be here to see that . . . On the bright side of things, maybe I'll be able to have an impact from up there somehow. Maybe I can hit you both over the head with something."

I couldn't help but laugh, though softly. "Oh, that's a lovely image, Annie girl. Every time I get hit on the head with something now, I'll think of you."

She laughed.

"Maybe you could hit Tess over the head instead," I suggested. "Hard."

She clicked her tongue and scolded, "Maren, Maren. You've got to be kinder to that poor lost soul. Hating her doesn't do you any good, you know . . . She must be so lonely."

"Lonely? She's not lonely!"

"Oh, but she is. She had a family who loved her and she left. She has to be lonely."

I just watched her quietly.

"She's been here to see me a few times," Ann told me. "I've enjoyed the visits."

"Really?" I asked in surprise. "Maybe she's not completely heartless after all."

"I don't think she is. She just has her priorities mixed up in a big way. I know I can't change her, but I keep praying for her. And I do feel sorry for her."

"I don't. Jake still loves her, Ann. He must. It's hopeless."

"No, he doesn't. He loves you, silly."

"I think you've had a little too much morphine today," I told her.

She shook her head. "It's not that, Maren. It's that the more I fade away from here, the more I can see over there . . . It's all so clear when you look at it. Think of the way he came back into your life after all these years. Do you think that was by accident?"

I felt tears stinging my eyes, but I only stared at her, feeling confused.

"You know it wasn't, Maren. The Lord is watching out for you. Don't be stupid."

I laughed again. "Thanks for the encouragement."

She looked at me and smiled. "You've got to tell him, my friend. You've got to tell him that you love him and straighten things out with him."

"I have told him, Ann! He doesn't want to hear it. He freaks out every time. He doesn't feel the same way. How can I tell him again?" I argued.

"You just look into his eyes and say, 'Jake, I love you.' What have you got to lose?"

"What have I got to lose? Are you crazy? I could lose *him!* I could push him over the edge this time. I could ruin our whole friendship. At least now I have that."

"You know what, Maren?" Ann asked quietly as she struggled to sit up.

I propped pillows behind her back to assist her. "What?" I asked quietly.

"Life is too short. We spend all this time worrying about things that just don't matter. We don't want to screw up or make fools of ourselves or be embarrassed. We worry about what we wear and what our houses look like and who has the nicest yard . . . There are a million things, and you know what? None of them matter. I've been lying in this room for a month, looking back on this life, and getting glimpses of the next one. I miss my house, I admit. Even though the doctors want me here, I'd rather be wasting away at home. Or better yet, at your house . . ." She smiled and I smiled back, wiping at the tears that refused to stop.

"But when I think about what I'm leaving and where I'm going, there is only one thing that matters—the people I love. Every wonderful memory of this life, every tender moment, every joyful occasion . . . it all boils down to who I loved here, and who loved me back. I won't miss my clothes, Maren. I won't miss practicing law. I won't miss pizza or chocolate cake. I don't even think I'll miss the mall . . ." We both laughed and I grabbed the box of tissues from the table to put on the bed between us.

"But I'll miss you, my friend." She stopped to cry, and then to get control of herself. "I'll miss Tyler. Oh, I'll miss him! I'll miss your beautiful children, and Jake's beautiful children. And Jake, of course. I hope he can manage you without me."

We both laughed and cried for several minutes again before she went on.

"And I'll miss my family. My only real regrets or heartaches from this life revolve around people too, you know? There are people who I wish I'd been kinder to, people who I wish I'd reached out to more . . . And I still can't help wishing that I'd been blessed with children."

I didn't think I'd ever be able to stop crying.

"I suppose it's for the best that I'm not leaving little motherless children behind . . ." she said quietly, "But in some ways, I wish that I was. I wish that Tyler had children to take care of, to keep him busy and comfort him . . . But we'll have them in the next life, I'm sure."

"I'm sure too," I agreed.

She smiled at me and squeezed my hand. "You know, Maren, even the gospel is about people. The whole idea is to create eternal families. That's the whole premise of the truth that we're blessed to know. That's also what I'm looking forward to in the next life—the people. I can't wait to see the people I love again—my dad, my grandparents, everyone that's gone before me. And I want to meet your sweet little Ashlyn." She sighed. "I know she might not still be little there, but maybe I can borrow her until Tyler and I have our own family someday, do you think?"

"Nothing would make me happier." I smiled through the tears. "You find her for me. She'll love you."

"I'll do that, my friend. I promise . . . I just wish I didn't have to leave anyone behind, you know? I wish you could all come with me."

"Ann, don't talk this way," I finally pleaded.

"I have to talk about it, Maren. Don't you see? I don't have much time left. I need to say what I want to say to the people I love so that I don't leave here wishing that I had."

"Ann, you don't know how much time you have. It could still be months. Maybe you'll get better . . ." I rambled.

She held my hand, smiled through her tears, and shook her head slowly. "Maren, please. Just listen to me."

"Okay." I gulped.

"What I'm trying to tell you is that you have to take a chance. You could end up wasting your whole life, Maren, being lonely and afraid, when you could have been sharing it fully with the man you love."

"But maybe I don't love him," I cried. "Maybe I'm just too attached to him because he's good to me . . ."

"I know you're confused and scared," she said sympathetically. "But it's time to get your feelings straightened out and take charge of your life. Take a risk. I think you do love Jake, Maren. I think you love him so much it terrifies you. And when you finally come to terms with that, just tell him. The worst that could happen is that he won't love you back, which is what you keep thinking anyway."

"But he told me that he doesn't already, Ann."

"Maybe you misunderstood him somehow. Or maybe he's still scared too. This is your life we're talking about here. Try again. Make sure you've done everything you can to make it what you want it to be."

"You're right," I whispered.

She started coughing—deep, racking coughs. I held a glass of water to her lips. "You need to lay back down, Ann," I prodded gently.

She shook her head. She looked so small and pale and fragile. It frightened me.

"You're the dearest friend I've ever known, Maren," she said softly. "I love you like my sister. I will miss you so much. I want to know that you'll be happy. Just remember to enjoy every moment, to live life to the fullest, to go after what you want. Do it for me. I won't be here to do it anymore." She chuckled softly and added, "And I won't be here to boss you around."

"I know," I admitted tearfully. "What am I going to do without you? You're my guardian angel."

She smiled her beautiful smile and looked at me with her sparkling eyes. "I guess God must think you're tough enough to make it on your own now," she said, squeezing my hand again. "And I'll still be your guardian angel."

"Promise?" I asked her.

"I promise," she laughed. Then she added, "You need to know, Maren, how much you've done for me too. This has never been a one-sided friendship. You have shared your children with me, your heart with me. You've served both Tyler and me so much, especially through these last months, and you've made my life richer than it ever could have been without you."

I held tissues to my mouth and sobbed.

"My sweet husband . . ." she went on. "You and Jake will watch out for him, won't you?"

I smiled and promised, "You know we will."

"He's been more wonderful than I ever could have asked for,"

Ann said, smiling too. "I have been so blessed."

"We've all been blessed to know you, Ann," I said truthfully. "It's not hard to see why the Lord needs you. You'll be a fireball up there in heaven, saving all those lost souls . . ."

She laughed and hugged me. We cried together for several long minutes.

Ann finally squeezed my hand again and lay back down. Then she asked quietly, "What do you think it's like there, Maren?"

I was silent for a minute before I finally whispered, "It has to be beautiful, Ann. I'm sure it's peaceful and full of light and joy. Everyone you love will be there to meet you, don't you think? I'm so grateful for the gospel. It's a comfort to me to know you'll be in such a good place . . ." I was crying too hard to talk anymore.

"I'm sure you're right," she said.

I was terrified of leaving her that night, but I finally tore myself away to leave her with her husband. I went back to the hospital early the next morning though.

"Maren!" Ann smiled when I knocked on the door and walked in. I was shocked to see her. She had taken a shower, gotten dressed, and put on makeup.

"Ann! My gosh, you look wonderful!"

"I feel wonderful!" she said.

"Where's Tyler?" I asked.

"Oh, I sent him home to change and eat breakfast so I could take a shower in peace. That's the first time he's been able to leave me without looking terrified."

"I'm glad." I smiled.

"I have to get out of this place, Maren," she confided earnestly. "They won't let me walk out of here, but they'll let me go in a wheelchair. Will you take me outside?"

"I guess you talked me into it." How could I refuse that? I wrapped a light blanket around her frail legs, and pushed her out into the warm July sun. I listened to her chattering happily all morning. Her sudden exuberance washed over my ravaged soul like a soothing balm.

I went to buy her some fresh fruit for lunch. "I feel like eating for once. I don't want to waste that appetite on hospital food," she joked. When I came back Tyler was there, and so was Jake, with his children and mine.

"Hi, guys!" I ran to hug Rebecca and Trevor. "How did they get here?" I asked Jake. He was smiling. Tyler was smiling. Ann was smiling. The kids were all smiling and climbing all over her. She was kissing all four of them, tickling them, asking about what they'd been doing.

"Tyler called me and asked me to bring them all over since Ann was feeling so well. She wanted to see everyone. I hope you don't mind. I called Ted and he let me have your kids."

I stared at him in disbelief. "He did? Of course I don't mind!"

After spending another wonderful hour with Ann, we decided we ought to leave her with her family. Her mother, and some other close family members had arrived during the hour that we'd been there. She hugged and kissed Trevor and Rebecca, and Lizzy and Jeff. "I love you guys so much!" she said as she squeezed them all and laughed at their little giggles.

"Love you too, Ann!" they called, blowing kisses as they walked out the door.

I gave her a hug. She smiled and said, "Good-bye, my friend. You know I love you."

"I love you too, Annie girl." I smiled and she laughed.

Jake and I took our children to McDonald's to buy them lunch and let them play. "She looked wonderful, didn't she?" I said to Jake.

He smiled. "Yes, she did, love. It was good to see her feeling so well."

"Oh, it was!" I said brightly, feeling more hope than I'd felt in weeks.

Elizabeth ran over to me from the slides and held out a tiny gold chain with a heart pendant. "Will you put my necklace back on, Maren?" she asked. "It came off."

"I'd be happy to, sweetheart. What a pretty necklace."

She turned around to say proudly, "Grandma and Grandpa Jantzen sent it to me!"

"Did they?" I smiled at her.

"Yep. Open it. There's a picture of them inside."

I obediently reached out to open the little locket and observe, "So there is."

Elizabeth touched the picture and said, "Grandma Jantzen has a necklace just like it, with me and Jeff inside."

"What a sweet idea." I smiled at Jake. He smiled back and

nodded in agreement.

"And tonight," Lizzy continued, "We get to go stay at Grandma Brulett's house."

"All night?"

"Yeah, all night! Huh, Daddy?"

"Yes, sweetheart." Jake smiled at her. "That will be fun, won't it?"

"Yes! Grandma said we can make cookies!"

He laughed at her as she flitted off to play again.

"So, you get a whole night to yourself, huh?" I smiled at him.

"Yes, I'm kind of looking forward to it."

"I'm sure you are. What are you going to do?"

He hesitated before saying, "Actually, I was thinking of asking a certain lady to dinner . . . but I haven't had a chance yet."

"Ah . . ." I looked away from him, not wanting to hear about another woman, or even to think about who it might be.

"Do you have any plans tonight?" he asked.

"To tell you the truth, I hadn't thought about it. I have some laundry to catch up on . . . and I've been meaning to clean out the fridge . . ."

"Sounds exciting." He grinned.

"Maybe I'll be really irresponsible and just curl up with a good book all night," I mused out loud.

"I could give you another option," he offered tentatively.

I furrowed my brows at him.

"I'm not sure how it would compare to the book, but I do think you might prefer it over cleaning out the fridge."

"I'm afraid you've lost me," I told him simply.

He smiled. "Let me clarify myself . . . I wondered if you might care to join me for dinner this evening?"

"Me?" I squeaked out.

"Yes, *you*, Mar. I think we could both use a brief reprieve from our troubles. If you think the book would be more effective though, I understand . . ."

I smiled and answered resolutely, "I think dinner sounds wonderful."

I took Rebecca and Trevor back down to Ted's parents' house before going home to get ready. I took a moment to kneel and say a grateful prayer, "Father, I am so thankful that Ann is feeling so much better. Help her to continue to feel well and happy," I said. "And thank you for the hope we saw today. Please make her well. Please." I hadn't even asked that for a long time. At least she might make it through Christmas, I hoped.

Chapter 28

I had a hard time trying to decide what to wear. I wanted to look casual, but still dress up a little. I finally decided on a long khaki-colored skirt, and a form-fitting white blouse with little pin-tucks at the waist-line. I pulled my hair back on the sides and put on straw sandals with heels and ankle straps. Jake came to the door in light slacks and dark shoes. "New shirt?" I asked.

"Yes, actually." He smiled.

"I love that pale green color," I commented.

"You always did like pastels . . . And you look very pretty."

"Thank you."

He grinned and remarked, "You're getting better at that."

I laughed.

Dinner with Jake was like a breath of fresh air. He was so fun to be with. I took notice of the way his eyes sparkled when he looked at me, and began to wonder if Ann could possibly be right, if he might somehow still care for me. When we left the restaurant, Jake put his arm around my shoulders and said, "I don't want to go home yet, Mar. Let's go see a movie."

"A marvelous idea," I agreed happily.

It was nearly midnight when Jake finally walked me to my door. I was still laughing at a joke he'd just told me as I turned my key in the lock. I looked back at him to say, "Tonight was the first time in so long that I've just . . . had fun, without worrying about Ann or the kids or . . . anything."

"Me too." He smiled. "It's so good to see you laugh, Mar . . . You look just like you did in college tonight."

"Do I?" I asked in surprise.

"Yes . . ." he answered gently, as he reached up to brush a strand of hair behind my ear. "Only you're even more beautiful . . ."

I thought of Ann's words and felt a glimmer of hope. Had Tess just been trying to upset me? Had I misunderstood Jake? Could he possibly love me? I searched his face as he moved closer to me. Those eyes. Those incredible blue pools of mystery. All I wanted in the world was for him to love me. My hands seemed to travel up his arms by their own will to rest on his biceps. I let his magnetic gaze pull me up to my tiptoes, and when he hesitated, I couldn't resist. I closed my eyes and pressed my lips to his, wondering what had possessed me to be so brazen.

I was briefly afraid of what Jake's reaction would be, and then tremendously relieved when he kissed me back. He kissed me softly, almost timidly at first. But then he pulled me into a firm embrace and kissed me more and more deeply until I thought I would drown in the moment. I didn't know if I could ever make myself stop, but Jake finally broke away and moved his lips to my forehead. "Maren . . ." he whispered.

I rested my head against his chest as he squeezed me to him tightly and buried his face in my hair. "I love you, Mar," he whispered. "Oh, I love you . . ."

In the security of his arms, time stood still for a moment as I marveled at his confession. Ann had been right. I wondered briefly about what Tess had said weeks earlier, and about Jake telling me that we didn't feel the same way. "Jake . . ." I looked up to ask him about it, but he kissed me again before I could say anything.

The sound of the phone ringing inside the house startled me away from him. "Rebecca and Trevor!" I gasped as I hurriedly pushed the door open. They were the only reason I could think of that I would get a phone call so late at night.

Jake followed me into the house and closed the door as I ran for the phone. I sighed with relief when I heard Tyler's voice. "Hi, Maren," he said quietly.

"Hi! How's Ann?" I'd thought of calling to talk to her again before I left that night, but I'd decided against it with all the family that was there. I figured maybe they'd finally all left and she still felt like talking. I mouthed the word, "Tyler," to Jake, and he looked relieved too.

Tyler cleared his throat and said, "She's, um . . . She's gone, Maren."

"What?" I asked, trying to shake the sudden fog from my mind.

"She passed away a couple of hours ago." His voice cracked. He took a few seconds to find it again and added, "I thought you'd want to know as soon as possible."

I wanted to protest, to scream, to cry, to ask a thousand questions . . . but it was his wife. I couldn't intrude on his grief like that. "Are you all right?" I asked softly. "Jake's here. Would you like us to come over there for you?"

"No," he whispered. "Both of our families are here. I'm okay. Thank you." His voice broke again and he made no effort to hide the sobs. "She loved you so much, Maren. You were the best friend in the world to her."

"It was the other way around, Tyler," I said reverently. "I'll never have another friend like her . . . And she was so blessed to have such a wonderful husband. The two of you went through a lot together."

"Yes . . ."

"What can I do for you?" I asked, trying to think logically about what he might need.

"Nothing right now. Just give her eulogy like she asked you to. The funeral's going to be on Wednesday I think, but I'll let you know. Will you tell Jake for me?"

"Yes. Call if you need anything, anything at all."

"I will."

I placed the phone back on the receiver and just stared numbly at it. I was in shock. I couldn't feel, I couldn't move, I couldn't comprehend the reality of what Tyler had just told me.

"What is it, Mar?" Jake asked me quietly. I'd almost forgotten he was there.

I turned blank eyes to him and said in a bewildered voice, "Ann's . . . gone."

"What?" He furrowed his brows in confusion.

I forced myself to say the words. "She died . . . I think he said a couple of hours ago."

"Oh, no. Is Tyler all right?" Jake asked slowly.

"How could he be? . . . But he said both of their families are there, so he doesn't need us to come over."

CANDIE CHECKETTS

Jake nodded, but his eyes looked tortured.

I stood frozen for a long time before I finally found the words to ask him, "How could this happen after today, Jake? You saw her today. She was feeling so much better! How could she . . . die?"

He shook his head, as though trying to rid his mind of the confusion before he answered me quietly, "It's the flicker before the flame goes out, Maren. You see it all the time in terminally ill patients. They get this last burst of energy and enthusiasm right before they die. Medically speaking, it's the body's way of getting ready to shut down I guess. For those of us who believe, it's one last little gift from God. It's an opportunity for families to say good-bye to each other and remember their loved one happy and alive instead of lying there half dead." He shook his head again and muttered, "I didn't even recognize it."

"First Ashlyn, and then Ted, and now Ann . . ." I whispered. "I can't cope with another loss. I can't . . . I'm just . . . empty. There's nothing left."

I watched Jake's eyes fill with moisture as he came toward me. "Maren . . . you'll get through this."

"How . . . ? " I whispered in stunned confusion. "What am I going to do without her?"

He stroked my cheek and whispered, "The same thing you always do. You're going to survive. You're going to keep on living. You're going to remember how blessed you were to know her, and someday you'll feel happy again when you think of her."

I looked up at him, awed by the wisdom of his words. I felt the pain pressing in to soak up the numbness and I bit my knuckles, fighting against it. Jake put an arm around me to pull me close, but I resisted. I didn't want to feel it. I didn't want to feel anything. I watched as the tears in his eyes spilled over and ran down his cheeks, and I sank my teeth further into my fist. Jake leaned down to look into my eyes and say gently, "Maren . . . honey, you have to cry. I know it hurts, but you have to cry. You can't suppress it."

I forced away a sob to answer, "But that's all I ever do, Jake. All I ever do is cry. If I let myself start crying again . . ." I whispered, "I'm afraid I'll never be able to stop."

"This past year has been pretty tough for you, I know," he said with empathy. "But it won't be like this forever. It will get better.

Someday you're not going to want to cry any more, love." I hoped that he was right, but I couldn't imagine it.

He tried to pull me into his arms, but I resisted again. He kept one arm around me and wiped at his eyes with the shirt sleeve of his other arm. "Let me hold you, Mar," he pleaded. "Please . . . just let me hold you, if not for you then for me."

He looked so sad. He loved Ann, just like I did. He loved Tyler. He was hurting too, I realized. I pushed my arms around his waist and leaned against him and let the tears come. I pressed my hands to his back and sobbed. Ann was gone. Another piece of my heart torn away . . . But Jake loved me. It was such a comfort to be back in his arms, to feel his strength, to breathe in his clean soothing scent. It helped to make the pain almost bearable.

It was a long time before Jake finally kissed the top of my head and whispered, "I'm too worn out to keep holding us both up, Mar."

"Don't leave me," I begged, clinging to him tightly. "Please don't leave me." I didn't think I could survive the rest of that dark night alone in my empty house.

"I won't leave, love. But we have to sit down." I let him lead me to the couch. He laid back against the cushions and drew me into his arms, urging my head to his shoulder. He held me while I cried myself to sleep.

Chapter 29

The funeral was difficult. Rebecca and Trevor sang "Families Can Be Together Forever" with Jeffrey and Elizabeth and Ann's nieces and nephews. Ann's brother spoke. Bishop Rowley gave a very comforting talk, and I did manage to get through her eulogy without bawling. I told the story of Ann's life as she'd told it to me, with some added insights from her mother. I tried to find the words to sum up the kind of life she'd led, the kind of person she was, and how large a hole her absence would leave in the fabric of the lives of all those she had touched. Jake and I sat together during the rest of the meeting. He kept a comforting arm firmly around my shoulders, for which I was overwhelmingly grateful. Our children huddled near us, and we all cried. My parents came down for the funeral and sat near us too. Once I turned around, and was surprised to see Tess sitting in the back of the chapel. Ted was there also, but that wasn't such a shock. He'd lived across the street from Ann and Tyler for two years.

Life settled back into a routine within a matter of days. I thought it was strange how mankind could suffer a blow like losing Ann, and yet the world didn't stop. Those of us who were left behind still had to go on living. It was the same feeling I'd had when I lost Ashlyn, only not quite as horrible. For a long time after I lost my baby, I'd only wanted to lie down and die too. This time I had other children to take care of. I had the thought of Ann's words to me about how I had to keep living, because she couldn't. I had Jake. Those things inspired me to keep breathing.

I was immensely relieved after Jake told me that he loved me. He made a big effort to offer me comfort and support. He invited

Rebecca, Trevor, and me to go places with him and his children, and tried to keep us busy. He did still take Jeff and Lizzy to do things with Tess sometimes, but I didn't have the strength to begrudge it. I just appreciated his nearness, and put off discussing our relationship until I'd had some time to get over my grief.

I still went to the gym in the mornings. I'd been going alone for the past months while Ann was too ill to go with me, but her absence was more profound then. Some days I worked myself into exhaustion, just trying to force away the anger and the pain. Late afternoons were the worst, and the long lonely Saturdays when we didn't go somewhere with Jake. I would watch the kitchen door, longing for Ann to come bursting in and flop down on a chair to talk to me. I missed her enthusiasm. I missed her guidance. I missed her support.

Tyler came over one evening to tell me that he was moving. "Did Jake pick the kids up already?" he asked.

"Yes. He was early today. They were going to have dinner with Tess."

"Oh. I'd hoped to tell you together. Well, anyway, I'm leaving. I'm taking an engineering position in St. George. Maybe the sunshine will do me some good."

"Are you sure you have to go, Tyler? We'll miss you so much." I knew he'd been thinking about it, but I hadn't expected him to leave so soon.

He swallowed and nodded, trying to keep the moisture out of his kind gray eyes. "It's just so empty without her, Maren. I can't stand the emptiness. Maybe we should have adopted a baby years ago. Maybe if we'd had children . . ."

I touched his arm and said, "Don't do that to yourself, Tyler. I am sorry about everything. I wish you'd had children too."

He patted my hand and said, "Well, we can't have everything, I guess. It's hard to feel gypped over that when I got to spend ten years with an incredible woman who . . ." He cleared his throat and wiped away a couple of tears that managed to escape. "Who was the love of my life," he finished. Then his look brightened and he smiled at me. "And I know that I'll get to be with her again someday, Maren. I know she'll be waiting for me, that I'm sealed to her. I'm so grateful for that . . . Oh, geez, look at me. I'm a wreck. I've got to get away from this place. Maybe I'll be able to stop bawling then." He sniffled and wiped at his eyes, and I wiped at mine.

"Anyway . . ." He smiled again. "We'll have children in the next life."

"I'm sure you will, Tyler. And maybe you'll still have them here. Maybe you'll get married again someday."

"Oh, I don't know about that," he said softly. "I'll pick up my life and move on eventually. Ann wouldn't want me to give up and die, too. But . . . I just can't imagine ever loving someone else like I love her."

"You've been through a lot," I acknowledged. "I don't know what to say. You and Ann were always so good to me, from the day I moved in. I wish that I could do something for you."

"Maren, you've been a wonderful friend to both of us. You've done plenty. You brought Ann so much comfort. It was good for her to be able to talk to you about the infertility, and to have you there through these last few months of her illness . . . Thank you."

"It just doesn't seem fair, Tyler. You and Ann are both so good. You deserve to be happy."

"We were happy . . . and we will be again. It's hard to keep focused, but I know how much I have to be grateful for. I certainly see a lot more of the eternal perspective than I did before, and I'm a fortunate man. I've been greatly blessed."

"You're an amazing man, Tyler. I wish you all the best." I hugged him and watched him go. I noticed the FOR SALE sign in front of his and Ann's house with a twinge of pain as he walked back across the street. I couldn't help thinking about what he'd said. He and Ann had been denied children in this life, and he'd just lost his wife. And yet, he was telling me how much he had to be grateful for. I started to look at my own life in a new light. If Tyler could see the blessings and the good in his life, then I could certainly acknowledge the good in mine.

* * *

I had two graves to visit at the cemetery then, and I went often. Rebecca and Trevor would chase each other across the lawn while I visited Ashlyn's small grave, and then while I sat talking to my dear friend.

I still tended Elizabeth and Jeffrey four days a week, and I started watching them two nights a month while Jake took his turn at the night clinic. It was easier on them than staying with a babysitter. Ann wasn't there to take a turn with them anymore, and getting a teenager to babysit on a busy Friday night was becoming increasingly difficult for Jake. Jeff and Lizzy usually just slept over on those nights. I sometimes caught myself wondering why their mother didn't take them, but then decided I should just be grateful that she didn't. At least when they were with me, I knew they were loved and safe.

I was glad that it was summer and that the children were home all day to keep me busy. I threw myself into my design business with a passion, trying to fill up any empty hours. Jake still watched my kids on Wednesdays so that I could keep up with it all. With that, the child support from Ted, and what Jake paid me to babysit, I could pay the bills. I even started to save a little bit for Christmas.

My counselor reminded me about the grief process. As if I needed reminding. "If there's one thing I'm familiar with, it's the grief process," I snapped at him. "Maybe you could tell me something I don't know." I thought about telling him that I was still in the "anger" stage, but I guessed he'd probably figured that out for himself.

I spent more time planning lessons and activities for my Laurels during those last few weeks of summer. The girls were so full of life. They brought me a lot of consolation. I didn't go to the week-long girl's camp as I had planned to, but I did go up to spend one whole day and night with them there while Ted and his parents kept the kids.

I looked at those beautiful young girls with a new perspective and thought of all the wonderful things they had to look forward to in this life. I knew they were all going to hurt sometimes . . . but I hoped they would all have a friend like Ann . . . or Jake, and children, and moments of wonder and joy and contentment. I hoped they would make choices that would bring them happiness. I hoped that they would never give up, even when things were difficult.

It was funny; I'd been so worried about Abby all that time, and yet she seemed to be coming around. Her hair was back to its natural shade, she had more color in her face than she used to, and she was starting to look almost happy when she came to church. I watched her laughing with the other girls and wondered if all that rebelliousness had simply been for show, to cover up teenage insecurities. The thought suddenly struck me that Abby had been coming to church that whole time. I smiled at her, thinking that she was a lot stronger than I'd given her credit for. If she hadn't been making good choices, she wouldn't be as happy as she was then. I was grateful that she was finally gaining the confidence to let her true self show through.

When Ann had been gone for a few weeks, I started to think about talking to Jake. We hadn't discussed our relationship since the night Ann had passed away, and I had never expressed my feelings to him. He hadn't kissed me again either. I was sure that he respected my need to grieve. I decided that it was time we clarified things and began to get on with our lives. When he picked up his children one night, I followed them out to the car.

After Jake closed the side door on the van, I put my arms around him and hugged him. "I want to thank you for being here for me through all of this, Jake," I told him. "Your friendship and your support have made it so much easier to get through." I pulled away to look at him. I knew it wasn't the time for an in-depth conversation, but I wanted to give him the general idea. I searched for the words to sum up my feelings. "Jake . . . you know how I feel, how I've felt all this time. You've always had a place in my heart, but—" I was going to finish by telling him how my love for him had been rekindled after all these years and that it had grown a thousand fold, but he didn't give me time.

His eyes flew open wide with horror, and he quickly placed a hand over my mouth to silence me. He squeezed his eyes shut and scrunched up his face in apparent disgust. *"Maren!"* he hissed as he forced himself to look at me. *"Don't* say those words to me again! Just *don't!"*

I was completely shocked. I took a step back and stared at him. "Jake, I don't understand . . ."

"You don't understand what?!" He threw his hands in the air. "That I've heard enough of this? That I can't take it anymore? Just stop torturing me, okay? I can't handle it, Maren! I can't handle any of it!"

"But, Jake, you said that you loved me—"

"Thanks for reminding me, Maren!"

"And you kissed me . . ."

"Did I? Or did *you* kiss *me?* You can't blame me for responding! *What* were you thinking?"

"What? Jake—"

He held his hands up and said, "Look, let's just drop this whole thing, okay? We'll just pretend it never happened."

Pretend it never happened? I could only stare at him in anguish and bewilderment.

He pressed a thumb and forefinger to the bridge of his nose and closed his eyes for a moment. Then he took a deep breath and opened them to say quietly. "I'm sorry, Mar . . . I shouldn't have gotten so upset. You can't help the way that you feel . . . I'm still planning on watching Rebecca and Trevor tomorrow. I'll see you in the morning." I watched him drive away and sat down on the porch in stunned confusion.

I tried to figure out what was going on. I didn't understand how I could have misinterpreted him telling me that he loved me. Had he only been trying to comfort me because of all that I'd been going through with Ann's illness? Had it only been an expression of friendship, of all that we'd seen each other through? Why did he have to keep kissing me like that if he felt nothing for me? Maybe it was like he said. Maybe it was my own fault for starting it. I felt dark despair creeping into my soul, slowly strangling all the budding hope that had finally begun to grow there.

When I dropped my children off the next morning, Jake said, "Maren, I'm sorry for being so harsh last night." Silent tears pushed past my willpower and raced angrily down my cheeks. He drew me into his arms helplessly, as though he had no choice, and said, "Don't cry, Mar. Please don't cry anymore. I can't stand it . . . It's all right. We'll always be friends."

His words should have been a comfort to me, but they tore through my heart like barbed wire. I pulled away from him, unable to take his embrace any longer. My torture was complete when Trevor ran into the room to throw his arms around Jake's leg and proclaim, "I love you, Jake!" Darn him for making my son love him.

Chapter 30

I worked fast and furiously all day, trying to get past the anger and the hurt and forget about Jacob Jantzen. By that evening, I decided that I could live without him. I was stronger than I'd ever been, and I was going to make it, one way or another. But I thought of all the kind and generous things that he'd done for me, and I couldn't make myself hate him. I vowed that I would be civil, that I wouldn't let him see me cry anymore, and that I would be grateful for what I had. On the way to pick up my children I prayed that I would somehow be able to get over the pain, and just appreciate the friendship I shared with Jake and the fact that he had blessed my life repeatedly.

Jake answered the door and said, "Come in, Mar. I just have to get the phone." He ran to the kitchen to answer the ringing telephone, so I closed the door behind me.

I couldn't help overhearing Jake's end of the conversation in the kitchen. "You *what?!*" he nearly shouted. "When? . . . How can you do this? *How can you do this?* . . . *You?* What about your *children?* . . . Yes, I know that . . . No, it's not easy, Tess. It's not easy for any of us . . . No, I will *not* tell them! The least you can do is come over here and tell them yourself. You're supposed to be here right now to take them anyway. You promised . . . No, they won't Tess. They're children. They will not understand. They do *not* understand! Even *I* don't understand, and I'm an adult!"

I wondered what she could possibly be telling Jake that had him so agitated. I got the gist of the idea that she was backing out of plans with the children that night, but there had to be more to it than that for Jake to be so upset.

"Yes, I know that! I know all about that!" he was saying heatedly. "Have you ever taken a moment of your life to think about someone else? . . . I don't know, either! I must have been completely insane! . . . Fine. If you're going to do this again though, Tess, this is the end. I want you to sign those papers. They're mine, and you're out of their lives. They don't need this . . . Yes, it was a mistake. This whole thing was a mistake, but adding another mistake on top of it is not going to help." Jake was quiet for a few moments, listening I supposed.

"Fine . . ." he finally said quietly. He sounded defeated. "Yes, I'll tell them. What choice do I have? But I mean it. You sign those papers and send them before you get on that plane . . . Okay, then . . . No, I'm not . . . No, I don't . . . Maybe you're right. Maybe I never did . . . Whether she is or isn't has nothing to do with you. She's a better mother to your children than you ever even thought about being!" Was he talking about me? "Yes, they do . . . Yes . . . No, you won't, not ever. Just send the papers and forget us, Tess. It will be easier for everyone."

I heard the click of the telephone being placed back on the receiver, and waited a few moments before walking hesitantly into the kitchen. "Are the kids downstairs?" I asked Jake.

He nodded and said distantly, "I told them to clean up the toy room." He was leaning on the counter, one hand shoved deep into the pocket of his slacks, the other tangled in his hair. He just stared into space, looking distraught.

"Are you all right?" I asked softly.

He chuckled and looked up at me, his eyes brimming with anguish. "No, Maren. I am *not* all right." I guessed from what I'd heard that Tess must be leaving again. He must be heartbroken. He must still love her. That had to be it. It was the only thing I could think of that would explain all of his strange behavior.

"Do you want to talk about it?"

"Talk about it?" he chuckled again. "Why?"

I shrugged. "I don't know—to make you feel better? You always pry everything out of me."

Jake folded his arms across his chest and said, "She's leaving again . . . going back to New York. It seems her old lover can't live without her, but her children can. She doesn't even have the decency to come and tell them herself . . ."

"I'm sorry, Jake."

"Sorry? You're *sorry?* What is *wrong* with me, Maren?" he asked fervently, holding his hands out in front of him.

"Nothing! What do you mean?"

"My wife left me for some pompous moron who's so full of himself he can't see anything else. She even left her children."

"That's not your fault, Jake. Tess . . . has some problems. That's pretty obvious. She chose to violate her temple covenants and break a very serious commandment. You didn't make her do that." I paused to search inside myself and find my strength for him. "You're one of the kindest, most generous people I know, Jake," I managed to say without bawling. "You're sweet, you're good—"

He cut me off, narrowing his eyes and shooting electrical daggers at me. "Then why did *you* leave?" he demanded.

"What?" I was stunned. Was that what this was all about . . . vengeance? Could he still be angry with me over that, even after so many years? That seemed impossible. It was too unlike him.

"You left me too, Maren," he shot out. "If I am so wonderful, why did you leave me to marry a drunk abuser?"

I gasped and searched for words. "Jake, I didn't know he was going to be that way! I married him in the temple! I had no idea—"

"You had *no* idea?" he asked cynically. "For months, Maren, I listened while you bawled to me about Ted. I tried to love you and support you and trust you. I encouraged you to search your heart and fast and pray and make the best decision for *you* . . . What did Ted do?"

I just stared at him, too shocked to speak.

"You don't want to answer me?" he asked sarcastically. "Fine. I'll tell you what I know. From what I saw and from what you told me, Ted never thought about anyone but himself. He told you what to do, how wonderful he was, how right he was for you. He put me down and tried to convince you of my deficiencies. He gave you an ultimatum. Did you ever talk to Ted about how you felt, Maren? Did you ever tell him how confused you were? Did he ever tell you to do what was best for you? Did he ever hold you while you cried over me?"

I put a hand over my mouth, trying to hold back the sob that threatened to erupt.

Jake took a step toward me, and leaned down to look into my eyes. "He didn't, Maren, did he." It wasn't a question.

I looked away. I couldn't believe Jake was bringing all this up, especially after the pain he'd recently caused me. But then, what could I say? I supposed I had it coming.

Jake pushed my chin up with his finger so I had to face him again, and said coldly, "So . . . here we are, my love. Look at us. We're both divorced—you with a long trail of bruises and police reports and broken windows, me with credit card bills and Church courts and motherless children."

"What are you saying, Jake?" I demanded, finding my voice.

"I'm saying, 'thank you,' Maren." I'd never seen him look so cold. He'd never been unkind to me in all the years I'd known him.

"For what . . . ? " I asked hesitantly, wondering what he was getting at.

He dropped my chin abruptly and said calmly, "For ruining my life."

"What?!" I gasped. "This is *not* my fault, Jake!"

"Isn't it?" He was still standing right in front of me, and he was a lot bigger than me. If I looked straight ahead I couldn't see over his shoulder. I thought that perhaps I should feel terrified, like I did with Ted. But I didn't. I only felt angry.

"You told me that you were going to fast and pray like you never had when you were trying to decide what to do, Maren," Jake reminded me.

"I know, and I did!"

"And what happened?" he asked.

"What?"

"What happened when you fasted and prayed, Maren? When you decided to marry Ted?"

I felt a sick knot forming in my stomach.

"I want an answer, Maren Griffin. You at least owe me that."

I felt my bottom lip quivering and bit it to hide the emotion. "Nothing . . ." I whispered.

Jake pushed his handsome face closer to mine. His eyes bored into my soul. *"What?"* he asked with quiet vehemence.

"Nothing, Jake. Nothing happened. I felt nothing."

His eyes went wide with horror as he said, "You felt *nothing* when you decided to marry Ted?"

"That's right," I answered quietly, looking him straight in the eye.

He stood up again and asked, "How did you feel when you were with me?"

"I don't know. It was too different to even make a comparison." I closed my eyes for a moment, trying to think. "I was so confused at the time, Jake. Things just seemed so . . . calm with you, almost too calm. Looking back now, I guess maybe it was peace that I felt, but I didn't recognize it."

He chuckled dryly and shook his head, staring at me as though I were on fire.

"What?!" I threw my hands in the air.

He quoted scripture to me through gritted teeth, with barely concealed fury, ". . . if your decision is right, your bosom shall burn and you shall feel that it is right . . . and if it is not right, you shall have no such feelings, but you shall have a stupor of thought . . ."

I just stared at him. I felt like he'd just struck me across the face. "Are you telling me," I asked slowly, "that you think God told me not to marry Ted by not answering me, and that I am somehow responsible for all of this . . . mess because I didn't recognize it?" I was furious.

"That is exactly what I'm telling you," he replied coolly.

"How can you say that to me, Jake?!" I hollered at him. "I was still a teenager, for heaven's sake! Yes, there were red flags I should have seen! I was a fool! I made a stupid decision as a young girl that has impacted the rest of my life, the rest of my eternity! Do you think I don't live with that every day? But I refuse to believe that all this is just a punishment because I ignored God. The Lord does not want us to suffer like this!" I took a breath and tried to calm down before saying, "We have our agency, Jake. We get to make our own decisions, and God left *that* decision to me!" I thought of the dream I'd had so many months ago on the river run and knew that I was right.

"And where did that leave me?" he asked.

"Jake, I didn't tell you to marry Tess! I was long gone! That was your own decision. At least I didn't marry you for your money! I didn't charge up your credit cards. I would never violate my temple covenants. I would never cheat on my husband. And I would *never* leave my children, Jacob Jantzen! For that matter, I would never even leave *your* children! I *love* them, Jake."

His eyes turned liquid, and he looked away from me.

I said with quiet fervency, "Jake, I'm sorry for any pain that I caused you twelve years ago. And I am sorry for the trials and the hurt that you've been through since then. But there is *no way* that I am going to stand here and take all this on. I live with the consequences of my decisions, and you live with the consequences of yours. We've both had some pretty awful things happen to us as a result of other people's choices. Your wife turning out to be a . . . whatever she is, is no more my fault than Ted's alcoholism, Jake."

"But I knew, Maren. I *knew* that we were meant to be together," he insisted, clenching his hands into fists at his sides.

"Well, maybe you should have said something back then, Jake, because it's obviously too late now!" I couldn't go back and change things even if I'd wanted to.

"I did say something back then, Maren! I tried to stay calm. I tried to support you. I told you that I loved you, and I tried to prove it to you. None of it did any good. *You ripped out my heart,*" he accused. "You left me standing there—absolutely alone, completely empty. You took *everything* with you, Maren, and you never gave it back."

I stared at him, stunned, as he went on, "It just wasn't enough, was it? I gave you *everything* I had . . . and it still wasn't enough. You wanted me to 'get mad.' You wanted me to 'fight for you.' Guess what, Maren? You finally got it! *I am mad!* In fact, I am *furious!* Are you happy? Who do you want me to fight? If I went over and punched Ted's lights out right now would that impress you? Is that what you wanted back then? Would it have made a difference? *What* did you want me to do?"

"Why didn't you tell me how you felt, Jake?" I hollered. "Why didn't you tell me that you thought we were supposed to be together? Why didn't you run after me? You could have done anything back then, Jake. *Anything.* Do you have any idea how confused I was? But you did nothing. That was the biggest confirmation I received, the fact that you did nothing."

"You have your agency, Maren, remember? I wasn't going to try to force you to marry me against your will! You made your choice, and you got *exactly* what you wanted! You married an angry man who fought with you for ten years! And you chose to stay there. You chose to stay every day that he was getting drunk and knocking you around."

I felt blinded by anger. "You're right, Jake, okay? You're right! I married Ted, and I should have seen what I was walking into. I have no one to blame but myself! But what about you, Dr. Jantzen?" I shouted. "Why don't you be a man and take responsibility for your own choices? You're not so perfect yourself!"

"I know!" he shouted back at me. "So tell me what's wrong with me!"

"All right, fine! You just sit there and let people walk all over you. You let people take advantage of you. You hope that things will work out the way you want them to, but you don't do anything to ensure that they do. Didn't you see any red flags with Tess, Jake? Did you pray about that? Why don't you fight for what you want? Why don't you stand up for yourself? Why don't you set some boundaries to protect yourself and your children so your ex-wife can't continue to trample all over you? Why don't you say no?"

Jake just watched me for a long moment. Angry currents zipped through the air as we sat glaring at each other. I saw the pain in his eyes and the anguish in his expression, and my anger melted away. I felt only empathy. And then I felt awareness. I sighed and pushed my hair back, looking away and saying quietly, "I know why. Because you're too much like me. That's what's wrong with you."

His face finally relaxed, and after a few more silent moments he chuckled softly.

"You know what's wrong with us, Jake?" I asked. "We've both been living our lives as though we had no say in them. We act like we're just victims of other people's whims. Ted hurt me a lot, and he did some awful things. That wasn't my fault. But you're right. I chose to stay there for ten years and let him hurt me. I let him push me around for five years before I even called the police on him. I let myself suffer. It felt a whole lot better to stand up for myself, to ask him to leave, to get a restraining order. I think it's even been good for him.

"But I've let myself continue to suffer. And you know what? I'm done. I'm going to live my life," I said with conviction, thinking again of Ann's admonishment. "In fact, I'm going to enjoy it. Survival isn't enough anymore. I want joy and passion back in my life . . . You could do the same thing, if you wanted to."

Jake didn't have time to answer me before Rebecca marched into the room and said, "Hi, Mom. Let's go."

"Did you finish cleaning up like Jake asked you to?"

She folded her arms on her chest and said, "Jake told me I have to help clean up and that's not fair. Trevor and Lizzy threw the Legos all over, not me."

"Rebecca, you have to mind Jake," I said wearily.

She put her hands on her hips and glared at Jake. "Why do I have to clean up stuff that the other kids got out?" she demanded.

Jake answered her calmly, "You know the rule, Becca. Everyone who plays in the toy room has to help clean up the toys."

"But that's not fair!" she protested. "I cleaned up the stuff I played with, and I told those guys I wouldn't help them if they didn't help me. They're still messing around, and I'm not gonna clean up while they're playing!"

Jake raised an eyebrow and considered her for a minute before saying, "That does sound reasonable, Rebecca. I can see your point. Would you rather play in the toy room when it's clean, or when it's messy?"

She shrugged. "When it's clean, I guess. It's easier to find things."

"I'd rather have it clean too," he said. "So, I'll make a deal with you."

"What deal?" she asked skeptically.

"Since I want the toy room to stay clean, I'm willing to come down and help straighten up even though I didn't play in it. If I come down to help all of you, will you help too?"

She considered his offer thoughtfully for a minute and then said, "I guess so."

"Good. You go back downstairs and tell the other kids. I'm going to finish talking to your mom, and I'll be down in just a minute."

"Mommy!" Trevor called from the stairway as he burst into the room.

"What, buddy?" I asked him.

"Who's yelling?"

"Nobody's yelling, Trev. Will you please go downstairs with Rebecca and help clean up? Jake and I will be down to help you in a minute."

He furrowed his little brows at me, but then said, "Okay. Come on, Rebecca."

"Okay," she agreed and turned to go, but then she turned back and asked hesitantly, "Are you guys . . . fighting?"

I saw the fear in her eyes and it made me feel sick. My first instinct was to lie to her, but I knew she was smarter than that. "We were having a disagreement, Rebecca, yes," I told her honestly. "But everything's fine now." I wanted to explain to her that it wasn't like the fights that Ted and I had, but I didn't know how.

"See! You *were* yelling!" Trevor pointed out.

"Yes, but we're not now, buddy," I defended.

They both studied me quietly for a minute. Rebecca glanced warily at Jake, before looking back at me. "Are you okay, Mommy?" she whispered.

I knew she loved Jake. I knew she trusted him. I knew she felt more secure with him than she'd ever felt with her father. Hearing us fighting seemed to have unnerved her though, shaken her feeling of security with Jake. I felt terrible. I went to kneel in front of her and said, "I'm fine, honey. You don't have to worry about me. I can take care of myself, and I will."

"But . . ." She glanced down and then looked up at me again. "I heard you guys fighting. I don't want you to be sad anymore. Jake yelled at you, and . . . I don't want anyone to hurt you."

Trevor's eyes flew open and he darted over to pound a little fist at Jake. "Don't hurt my mom!" he hollered tearfully.

I wondered how I could have been so thoughtless as to lose my temper with Jake within possible earshot of my children. I didn't think they could have heard us from the toy room, but maybe they'd been on their way upstairs. I chastised myself for not maintaining better control, for not thinking of the trauma they'd been through, for not realizing that it might terrify them if they heard us arguing. Still, I had to admit that I was a little surprised to see them so affected by it, especially since Ted had moved out nearly a year and a half ago.

I tried to think of the appropriate response, but Jake beat me to it. He caught my little son's arm before he could strike him again, and said quietly, "Trevor . . ." Then he dropped to his knees and put an arm around him, reaching out to pull Rebecca to him too. He looked into their little faces with urgency as he spoke in his usual gentle voice. "Sometimes grown-ups get angry or disagree, just like children do," he explained. "I felt angry and upset over something that happened, and I yelled instead of talking about it like I should have. I made a mistake and

I'm sorry. I shouldn't have lost my temper like that. But I would *never* hurt your mom, you two. Not ever. I would never hurt you either, Trevor, or you, Rebecca. I promise. I love all of you and I want you to feel safe."

I stood and turned quietly away to blink back the moisture that rose in my eyes.

"I'm going to apologize to your mom now too," Jake told them. Then he turned to look up at me and say, "I *am* sorry, Mar."

I wanted to say I was sorry too, but I didn't trust myself to speak. I just nodded and looked down, trying to swallow the knot in my throat. Jake hugged both of my children to him tightly, and they hugged him back. "Do you feel better now?" he asked them.

They looked into his eyes and nodded.

"You know," he told them. "Your mom's pretty tough. I think you can trust her to take care of herself. And you know she'll always keep both of you safe too, don't you?"

"Yes," Rebecca answered quietly, and Trevor nodded.

"And I would do anything to keep you both safe too," he promised.

Trevor considered him quietly for a minute before challenging, "Would you ever drink beer?"

He glanced toward me, and I could see that he felt as sick as I did. "No Trev," he answered firmly. "Never."

"Why not?" Trevor asked skeptically.

"Because Heavenly Father has asked us not to do that, for one thing," Jake said. "Also, because I know that it's not good for my body. And even if I wasn't worried about the other things, I would never drink because I don't want to hurt people that I care about."

Rebecca threw her arms around Jake's neck and said, "I love you, Jake."

"And I love you, sweetheart," he responded. Then he hugged Trevor and added, "You too, buddy."

When they released him, he stood up and said, "Okay, you two run downstairs now and ask Jeff and Lizzy to help clean up. I'll be down in just a minute."

When they'd gone, Jake looked at me and said with more than a hint of self-reproach, "I am so sorry. After all that you and your children have been through . . . for me to behave that way was just . . . inexcusable. I never meant to upset Rebecca or Trevor, or to treat you the way that Ted did—"

"You didn't, Jake. Not even close . . . Besides, I guess I had it coming."

"No, Maren, you didn't. I'm sorry."

"Me too," I whispered, looking away.

After a few moments in silence he chuckled softly and said, "That's quite a feisty little girl you have. She certainly knows how to stand up for herself and get what she wants."

I shook my head and wondered aloud, "I don't know where she gets it."

Jake's eyes went wide and then he laughed. "I do. She gets it from her mother."

"What?"

"Oh, yes," he mused. "I knew her very well once. She thought she could do anything she set her mind to. She was driven, intelligent, outgoing, full of life and vision. She had a gift for drawing people out of their shells, getting them to open up. She could convince anyone to try anything. She knew who she was and where she was going. She thought she could conquer the world. She was an amazing woman, that little girl's mother . . ." He looked pointedly at me and added, "She still is."

I just stared at him in disbelief, until he winked at me and went downstairs. My brain was going a hundred miles an hour as I tried to figure out what kind of game he was playing with me. I did believe that he was genuinely hurt by me all those years ago, but I was beginning to think that Tess was telling the truth when she said that he got a thrill out of leading women on and breaking their hearts. Maybe I'd even had a hand in that by what I did to him all those years ago.

Chapter 31

I spent several days thinking. A million different thoughts churned in my mind. I thought about what Tess had said to me, and what I'd heard her say to Jake. I wondered what she'd meant, how much truth there was to her words. I could not figure out what was going on with her, or Jake. I briefly entertained the idea of confronting Tess. Maybe I could get somewhere with her. Every time I tried to talk to Jake I ended up feeling more confused than I had before. I thought that if I was going to do it, I'd better do it soon. I didn't know when she was moving back to New York, but I figured that she probably wouldn't be sticking around for long. I didn't know how I could face her though. As much as I hated to admit it, I still felt incredibly intimidated by her. Finally, in desperation, I decided that I would fast and go to the temple when Ted took the children that weekend.

It surprised me to see Ted when I opened the door on Friday night. He had on nice slacks and a polo shirt, his haircut was new, and he looked . . . almost happy. I felt a brief twinge of regret and longing for the man I'd thought I married when he smiled and said, "Hi, Maren."

"Hello, Ted."

"You look nice," he commented on my work clothes.

"Thank you. So do you. How are things?"

"Things are improving," he answered. "These meetings I'm going to for people with . . . addictions and things . . . I think they're actually doing some good."

"Really?" I asked in surprise.

He nodded. "I haven't had a drink in over four months, Maren. It's rough, but so far I'm making it."

I wasn't sure if I felt gratitude, relief, or remorse. "I'm glad Ted," I answered quietly. "I hope this will be a good thing for you, and for the kids."

His eyes lingered on me for a minute. Feeling uncomfortable, I broke the silence by calling down the hall, "Becca and Trevor, get your things to take to Daddy's, okay?"

"Okay!" They both called from Rebecca's room.

"Do you want to come in for a minute?" I invited him. The air felt a little chilly, like a summer storm might be blowing in.

"Thanks." He stepped inside. After a brief silence he asked quietly, "Maren?"

"What?"

"I want you to know that I regret everything, all the pain I caused you. I'm sorry." I was shocked. I studied him for a minute. He was handsome when he was sober, and still a little charming when he wanted to be.

"Yeah, well, I wasn't perfect either," I answered honestly. "But thank you, Ted. I appreciate that."

"I just . . . got lost, Maren, you know? I felt so much pressure to be what everyone thought I should be. After we got married, I was overwhelmed with the thought of living up to what I'd promised you. I guess . . . I guess I was afraid that if I disappointed you in any way, you wouldn't love me."

I just stared at him, completely baffled that he was even having these insights into himself at all, let alone that he was admitting them to me.

"Then I set myself up to fail by drinking to cover up the worries. I had to *keep* drinking to bury the guilt for all the pain I brought on myself, and you, and the kids. The worst thing was watching you lose the strength and the vibrancy that had attracted me to you in the first place. It killed me to see that. It made me hate myself. When I hated you, Maren . . . I really hated myself.

"I wanted to undo the damage I'd done to you, but I didn't know how. I just kept causing more damage, more destruction, filling myself up with more rage . . . I know I tied myself up in a thousand knots, and I was spiraling completely out of control . . ." He sighed deeply and flipped back that lock of sandy hair that perpetually hung over his forehead. "It was a nightmare. You know that. You got the worst of it. I am sorry, Maren. I know you stayed longer than most women would have."

I was stunned. For Ted to be so aware of himself, for him to humble himself enough to apologize to me . . . he must genuinely be in recovery. I couldn't believe it. "That is the first time in all those years that you've ever truly apologized to me," I told him quietly. "You always said that everything was my fault."

He looked away from me and took another deep breath. "It wasn't," he admitted softly.

"You were never there for me, Ted. I needed you so much . . . but you were never there."

He swallowed hard and shuffled the toe of his shoe across the tile floor. "I know that. I'm sorry."

I just stared at him for a few moments before I finally drew the courage to ask him something I'd wanted to ask him for years, but never dared. "I never understood, Ted . . . why you started drinking in the first place. Why did you turn to that after going on a mission and getting married in the temple? Why would you suddenly decide to try something so dangerous at that stage of life?"

He looked at me for a long time before he nervously cleared his throat and admitted, "That's the problem, Maren. I didn't just decide to try it at that stage of life."

I gave him a confused look and said, "I don't understand."

He looked heavenward, as though seeking fortitude, and then met my gaze again. "I started drinking in high school, Maren, the same time all my friends started drinking, for the same stupid reason—because I didn't have the guts not to."

I made a conscious effort not to gasp as I listened to him.

"I didn't think it was going to be that big of a deal. I told myself I could stop whenever I wanted to, but it was a lot harder than I thought it was going to be. I learned to cope with all of my problems by drowning them in alcohol. After high school, I decided I just had to pull myself together. I wanted to go on a mission, to marry the kind of girl that would want me to take her to the temple. It was *so* hard, Maren. It took everything in me to confess my mistakes to my bishop, but it was

the right thing to do. He helped me turn myself around. It wasn't difficult to stay sober on my mission. I was constantly praying, reading my
scriptures, trying to do what the Lord wanted me to do with diligence. I
know I was very blessed for that. After I came home, I kept up the same
routine to avoid the temptation. When we got married, I'd been sober
for three years, I'd made it to the temple . . . I thought I was home free."

He sighed and shoved his hands in his pockets. "That was my big
mistake, I guess. I thought it would be easy after that. I let my
defenses down. Marriage was a big adjustment, a huge responsibility,
harder than I had expected. There was work, and school, and you . . .
and then you got pregnant . . . When things got difficult, I didn't
know how to deal with them. I didn't know how to talk to you. I
knew that I was hurting you and shutting you out . . . but I didn't
know how to let you in . . . That made it even worse. I turned back to
alcohol to help me deal with the stress a couple of times, and I was
hooked again. I couldn't get away . . . I tried. I tried so many times to
give it up, Maren, but it was like I was just . . . powerless."

"Ted, why didn't you tell me? Why didn't you ever tell me any
of this?"

He sighed. "Before we got married, I told myself that it didn't
matter, that it was in the past. Honestly . . . I guess I was afraid that
you wouldn't marry me if I told you the truth about my history."

"I might have, Ted. If you had been honest with me, we might
have worked through it together. It might even have helped you avoid
going back to it."

"Maybe," he admitted.

"What did your parents do?" I asked him. "Didn't they try to help
you? Why didn't they warn me, or try to help us when they saw the
problem resurface in our marriage?"

Ted chuckled dryly and shook his head. "You know my family,
Maren. We're not the best at . . . communicating. And there's this
unspoken law that you can't have anything wrong with you. To admit
that you might need counseling? That you could be powerless over an
addiction? It's unthinkable. It just wasn't an option in my house. I'm
sure my parents thought they were doing the right thing, but they
were incredibly rigid. Their philosophy is that their prayers and faith
can fix anything—despite other people's actions. They don't realize

that while those things help, sometimes they're just not enough. They don't think we should need therapy, or AA programs, or outside help of any sort. That's part of the reason I got rebellious and started drinking in the first place, just to prove that I could—that I was in charge of myself.

"I thought I was fooling them, all those years. But looking back, I don't know how they could not have known that I was drinking. I think they just didn't know how to deal with it, so they ignored it and hoped that it was a phase, that I'd outgrow it. And I suppose they thought I had when I got it together and went on a mission . . ."

I was surprised that I actually felt empathy for him, a whole lot of empathy, in fact. All of his destructive behavior suddenly made a lot more sense to me. It didn't excuse it, but it made things easier to understand. "Ted, even if you'd been willing to be honest with me after we were married, if you hadn't told so many lies, if you had just admitted that you had a problem . . . maybe we could have worked through it together."

His eyes sparked for a second, but then he confessed sadly, "Do you think I haven't told myself that a thousand times, Maren?"

I watched him silently for a long time before I finally said, "Well, at least I've found my strength again. I can take care of myself."

He nodded. "I've seen that . . . Maybe this has been good for me, too. I've had to start relying on myself since you left me . . . to make my own life work, deal with my own problems. No one else is there to do it anymore . . ." He paused and seemed to be drawing courage to ask, "Do you think there's any chance we could work things out someday?"

I was absolutely floored. I'd wanted to hear those words so badly a year ago, but then? . . . I wondered for a minute if it could work. He was improving. I did miss him. What if he got better, got his testimony back, became the man I thought I'd married all those years ago?

No. The Lord had given me the assurance that I was doing the right thing when I divorced him. I thought of the increasing peace I'd felt in my decision, and all the help that I'd received since. I had to admit that Ted seemed to be making progress; but I knew the chances of him truly changing were remote at that point, especially if I went back to him. Besides, my heart really belonged to Jake, and no one else. There was nothing I could do to change it. I couldn't go back to where I'd been. I looked at him and said softly, "No, Ted. Just keep getting better . . . for yourself."

"Do you think you could . . . pray about it?" he asked hesitantly.

I was shocked that he would suggest such a course of action after all the years of bitterness at God. The words got to me for a moment, but then I caught myself. "I did pray about it, Ted. I prayed about it twelve years ago. I had all the facts I thought I needed, and God left the decision to me. I absolutely believe that the Lord offers us guidance and assistance when we need it. But the Lord also knows that I am a competent, intelligent woman—much more so now than I ever was before. Our divorce is a profound loss for me, Ted, but too much damage has been done. I cannot go back. I will always care for you. I wish you all the best in your recovery and in your life. You're making progress, and I hope you'll continue to. I believe that you can change. But I cannot go back, Ted. I can't."

He nodded and said gruffly, "I just had to ask."

I touched his arm. I did feel concern for him. "You'll be all right, won't you?" I asked.

He sighed and shook his head. "I hope so. I'm trying to get back on the right path, but it's difficult. I knew you'd say no. I know it's not supposed to be that way."

I was surprised to hear him say it like that. "You're improving, Ted," I told him.

"Thanks. Actually, I'm better than I've been in twelve years."

I impulsively hugged him. The kids appeared with their arms loaded and I kissed them good-bye. "Have a fun weekend with Daddy," I said.

As they walked into the breezy night, I heard Trevor ask, "Daddy, what makes wind?"

I laughed to myself and closed the door. I leaned against it, amazed at what I'd found inside myself. I was going to make it. I was going to be all right. And maybe Ted was too.

* * *

I told my counselor about my conversation with Ted at my appointment the next morning. "It sounds like you're getting healthier," he told me. "Learning to trust your own judgment again."

"Yes . . . to a certain degree," I admitted. "But not completely. How do you ever know if you can trust someone? If they are who they say they are?"

"Trust is something that's built over time, Maren. But there is never an absolute guarantee that you won't get hurt. If that's what you're looking for, you won't find it."

"So, how do I avoid another bad relationship? How do I know if someone's lying to me?"

"Do you still believe that you would only be attracted to an addict? Or an abuser? Or a liar? Someone who would hurt you?"

"Maybe."

"We've talked about your family of origin. You come from a fairly healthy family with good communication skills and attitudes."

I nodded.

"And you've had many good friends and relationships throughout your life."

"That's true."

"In fact, the only relationship you've been in that was really unhealthy was your marriage."

"Yes."

"And looking back, you can see that there were some possible warning signs, but at the time you thought you were marrying a good man in the temple. He was successful and stable and living the commandments when you made the decision to marry him."

I nodded again.

"Your husband made some poor choices that brought on some unfortunate results, but you really couldn't have predicted that beforehand, Maren. You can't blame yourself for that. You've learned from your mistakes—you're learning how to set boundaries and respect yourself. You know how to choose good friends and relationships."

"I guess so," I admitted thoughtfully.

"So, when it comes to men, like anything else, you trust yourself to make responsible decisions. You're going to have to be willing to open up and take some risks though, if you hope to have another close relationship someday. If you do find someone you love, and if you choose to enter into a committed relationship again, you do it with a positive outlook, you let yourself trust, you expect it to work.

And if, for some reason, you find yourself involved with someone who begins to make poor choices again, or even if you marry someone who does that again, you're smarter now. You'll know how to assert yourself, how to protect yourself and your children. You'll know what your expectations of him are if you're going to continue to work on the relationship. You'll know what your bottom line is, and what you will not tolerate. You know you could leave and take care of yourself and your children if it came down to that again."

"I guess you're right," I told him, feeling suddenly better about things.

I went straight from my appointment to the temple, still fasting and praying for direction, for comprehension. I was trying to decide whether I should talk to Tess to see if it would help me understand what was going on with Jake. I was surprised at how quickly the answer came, at how simple it was. I'd told myself repeatedly that talking to Tess would be too difficult. She was too intimidating, too mean, too terrifying. I looked around me at everyone dressed in white. We all dressed the same in the temple, we were all on the same level there, all equal in God's eyes. No one thought they were better than another person, no one felt threatened or intimidated by anyone else. Tess was a fellow human being, an ordinary woman, just like me. Why on earth couldn't I go and talk to her?

After I changed back into my street clothes, I looked in the dressing room mirror and thought about what Jake had said to me a few days earlier, all the good qualities he'd told me that Rebecca had inherited from me. "Pull yourself together, Maren," I whispered to myself. "You can do this." I told myself that I was perfectly capable of having a mature conversation with Tess, and there was no reason why I shouldn't. It seemed a logical place to start for some clarification.

I said a prayer of thanks, and also prayed for guidance to speak to Tess as I drove from the temple to her apartment. To my disappointment she wasn't there. I went home and called her. Her answering machine said that she was out of town for Labor Day weekend, that she would be back on Monday. I resigned myself to waiting.

I was more nervous by the time Monday arrived, but so anxious to get it over with that I could hardly stand it. It was Jake's turn to work the holiday afternoon and night clinic. I'd agreed to watch Jeff and Lizzy even though Ted still had our children because of the long weekend.

"Are you sure?" Jake had asked. "If you have other plans or even if you just need a break, I could probably get a girl from the ward to watch them."

"No, Jake. They're comfortable here, with this routine. Let's not do anything to shake them up right now. It's been hard enough on them finding out that Tess is leaving again."

"Thank you." He sounded relieved. "I'll come and get them when I finish. I should be done around ten o'clock."

"You don't need to. They can stay overnight."

"I don't want to take advantage of your generous heart any more than I already have. I'll come for them as soon as I can."

I thought about his words as I drove over to Tess's apartment late in the morning, before the children came. She still wasn't home.

Chapter 32

The afternoon proved difficult for Jake's children. They fought incessantly. By dinnertime I was ready to scream. I hoped that things would settle down a little bit that evening, but they didn't. Jeff and Lizzy fought more than they ever had in a single day. Jeffrey kept teasing his sister, and she kept screaming and crying. I inwardly cursed their mother and wished that she could see what she was putting them through. I hoped that once she left she would never come back. They were obviously feeling the stress of having her leave again, even though she hadn't acted like much of a mother when she'd been there.

Near bedtime Jeff tried to take Elizabeth's blanket away. She screamed and bit him on the hand. He pushed her down and tackled her. "Jeffrey!" I said, pulling him away from her. "You need to calm down and leave your sister alone."

I sat him down on a chair in the living room. He kicked me in the shin so hard that I had to fight the urge to swat his little backside. I didn't believe in spanking, but at that moment I was sorely tempted. "Stay right there," I instructed firmly, as I went to run a bath for Lizzy. I left the bathroom door open so that I could hear her while I talked to Jeffrey. He sat with his arms folded across his chest and a defiant look on his little face. My heart softened when I thought of all the trauma he'd been through over the past weeks.

I crouched down in front of him and said, "Do you want to talk, Jeff?"

He shook his head.

"Okay, you don't have to. I love you, bud, but I can't let you hurt Lizzy. I want you to stop teasing her, and I think you need to settle down a little bit."

"You can't tell me what to do!" he shouted. I was surprised at his behavior. He had his moments, like any six-year-old, but he'd never been so blatantly obstinate with me.

"Jeff, you have choices, but you may not choose to do something that hurts someone else. When I am watching you, I *can* tell you what to do if you break a rule. That's the way it is at your house too, Jeff. Your dad doesn't let you hurt Lizzy, and he expects you to obey him, just like I expect you to obey me at my house."

"No, you *can't* tell me what to do!" he yelled.

I tried to take his arm, but he yanked it away and hit me on the chest. He pounded his little fists at me and screamed, "You are *not* my mom!"

I was tempted to just give in and let him do whatever he wanted to. How horribly unfair for a young child to be abandoned by his mother—not once, but twice. I knew that wouldn't be the right thing to do though. He needed to know that the boundaries were still the same, that his life still had structure, that someone would be there for him. I grabbed his wrists and said firmly, "I know I'm not your mom, buddy. I love you though, Jeffrey. I love Elizabeth too, and I won't let you hurt her, just like I wouldn't let anyone hurt you."

"I want my mom!" He jumped out of the chair to run away, but I didn't let him. I picked him up from behind to avoid his flailing fists and feet and sat down in the rocking chair, holding him. I prayed for strength to deal with this. The fact was, I'd been so stressed all day that I felt like screaming and hitting something myself.

"I know you do, Jeffrey. I know you miss her, honey."

He struggled with me for a minute before he broke into sobs. I rocked him and kissed his head. "It's okay to cry, bud. You can cry." I wanted to cry with him, but I was too worn out.

Jeff let me hold him for a long time, until the sobs turned into sniffles. I listened to Elizabeth splashing in the bathtub, and wondered if Jeffrey had fallen asleep, until he quietly asked, "Can I take a bath now?"

I kissed his dark little head again and said, "Of course you can."

While Jeffrey got into the bathtub, Lizzy put on her pajamas and brushed her teeth. I read her a story and tucked her into Rebecca's bed. She asked to sleep with Becca's soft pink teddy bear and rubbed it against her cheek after I handed it to her. "When's Daddy coming?" she wanted to know after she threw her little arms around my neck and squeezed me.

"He'll be here in a little while, sweetie, after you fall asleep. He'll take you home, and you'll wake up in your own bed in the morning, okay?"

"Okay." She closed her eyes and was quiet for a minute before she asked, "Mommy's not coming, huh?" Her sweet little statement pained me. I was sure that she'd heard Jeff. I wanted to leave that question for Jake to answer, but I was the only one there.

"No, Lizzy. Mommy's not coming."

"Is she ever coming, Maren?" she asked innocently.

My heart just ached, but I didn't want to lie to her. "No, honey. She isn't."

"Maren, why doesn't Mommy love us?" she asked.

I thought my heart might break in two. "Oh, Lizzy, she does love you, honey." I struggled to find words of comfort for her. "No one could know you and not love you. And she loves Jeffrey. She just . . . has a hard time being a mom, I guess. It's not because of you, sweetheart."

"How come she doesn't love Daddy, then?" she wanted to know.

I forced away the knot in my throat to say, "Elizabeth, sometimes moms and dads just can't live together anymore. Maybe your daddy can explain more about that to you. I don't understand why your mom does some of the things that she does, but I do know that your mommy and daddy both love you and Jeffrey. And I love you too."

She watched me quietly and finally asked, "Would you ever leave Trevor and Becca?"

I blinked back the moisture in my eyes and said, "No, Elizabeth. And I would never leave you or Jeffrey either."

"And Daddy won't leave, huh?"

"No, sweetheart, your daddy won't ever leave . . . Would you like to say your prayer now?"

She nodded and knelt down to pray for blessings for her family, even her mommy. Her innocent words jolted me. That was the last straw. I couldn't take anymore. Not only did I want to talk to Tess for me, I wanted to tell her what I thought of her packing up to leave her children again. She needed to know what she was putting them through. I was furious. I found Jeffrey already in his pajamas, brushing his teeth. "Put your shoes on, you two," I told them. "We're going for a little ride."

"You have toothpaste on your shirt," Jeffrey pointed out to me after he got a drink. I glanced down at the clothes I'd been working in all day. They looked awful. I decided to change while the children were getting their shoes on, and searched my closet for something quick and comfortable. I pulled a cool white linen dress over my head that hung almost to my ankles and hurriedly slipped on sandals while I ran a brush through my hair. "Let's go!" I said to Jeff and Lizzy.

They obeyed, apparently anxious to get out of the house too. It was nearly dark when we left, and they both fell asleep on the way to Tess's apartment. I prayed that I could get a close parking place, and maybe watch them from her window while I talked to her, so that I wouldn't have to wake them up. I thought it would be better for them if they didn't see her. Her apartment was on the ground floor, I knew, so it was a realistic possibility.

I said a silent prayer of thanks for a vacant parking spot on the front row. There were only a few yards of sod between my car and Tess's living room window. I turned off the engine and rolled down my window to get some air. I sat silently for a few moments, trying to gather my thoughts. The light was on in Tess's apartment, and her curtains fluttered a little in the breeze. I was grateful for cover of dark, so she couldn't look out and see my car before I decided for certain what I was going to say. I felt apprehensive, and found myself pausing to wonder how she would react when she saw me. I was just about to get out of the car when I heard laughter drifting from her open window into mine.

There were two separate laughs, one of which was definitely not hers. The other sound was softer, harder to pick up, but it was distinctly masculine. My heart sank when I realized that she was not alone, and I wondered whether I should still pursue talking to her. I saw Tess move to gaze out at the Indian summer night. She looked almost directly at me. I prayed that she wouldn't be able to see me in the dark. I decided it would be better to come back another time and put my key in the ignition.

The sound of Tess's laughter drew my eyes up again, just in time to see a masculine figure step in front of her and take her in his arms. His back was to the window, clad in a familiar dark blue shirt. He was several feet away from me, but I was close enough to tell that he was tall and lean with black hair, and that he was completely absorbed with holding Tess and all but devouring her with kisses. I watched him bend to kiss her throat as she held her head up and giggled, and then fell away from the window.

I wanted to throw up. I wanted to scream and yell and hurl something through the glass. I wanted to march in there and slap Jake across the face so hard that the force of it would send him reeling. Instead, I started the car and drove away, struggling to see the road through my tears. I had to stop a few blocks later and let myself cry. Gratefully Jeffrey and Elizabeth slept on in the backseat while my heart was breaking in the front. I couldn't believe that Jake had the nerve to leave his children with me to go . . . carouse with his ex-wife, who was supposedly departing the state. She'd looked plenty happy to me. Maybe she wouldn't be leaving, after all. I figured that it didn't matter either way.

It's your own fault, Maren, I told myself. *You should have married him the first time around, when you had the chance.* Then I stopped to think about that. The tapestry of my life was complex. If I hadn't married Ted, I might not be the person that I was today. And if Ted had admitted to his problem and sought help earlier, maybe we would have grown together and things would have worked out fine. And maybe Jake had gone through more growth without me than he ever would have with me. It was impossible to pick the threads apart and say that certain strands were just mistakes. They were all part of the picture.

I finally pulled myself together, telling myself that I should have known about Jake and Tess all along. Hadn't it been right there in front of me the whole time? As I pulled back onto the road and drove home, I whispered over and over again, "You can survive this, Maren. You will survive."

I carried Jake's sleeping children into the house and tucked them into Rebecca's and Trevor's beds. I kissed their little heads and then trudged back down the hall to the great room. I looked with dismay at the disaster that had struck that afternoon. I still hadn't had time to clean up the dinner mess. The children had left toys all over the floor. I just couldn't deal with it. I was too tired. I was emotionally spent. I lay down on the couch, but I couldn't sleep.

When Jake finally knocked on the door, he looked as tired as I felt. I guessed that he'd spent all his energy smooching with Tess. He stepped into the room and looked around. He was there nearly every day. He knew that my house was usually clean. "Rough night?" he asked seriously.

"That's an understatement," I muttered. I wanted to just let him have it, but I was trying to think about how to go about it. What was I going to say? *Hey, Jake, I dragged your sleeping children over to your ex-wife's apartment to interrogate her, but then I ended up spying on you and I didn't like what I saw?* I wished Ann was there. She'd know what to do.

While I was still thinking, he sighed and said, "I'm sorry, Mar." He took off his jacket before he bent down to pick toys up off the floor, revealing his dark blue shirt.

"You don't need to do that, Jake," I said curtly.

"Oh, okay. Why don't I just leave this disaster that my children made for you? Wouldn't it be great to know you had this waiting for you tomorrow morning?"

He started downstairs with an armload of toys, so I scooped up a pile of storybooks and followed him to the family room, determined to find a way to confront this whole nightmare. But then I wondered if he was solely to blame. He'd told me that he didn't want to hear about my feelings for him . . . but then he'd led me on by pretending to care about me . . . hadn't he? He'd told me that he loved me, and his kisses had certainly seemed to mean something. He'd never even kissed me like that in college. Of course, he hadn't seemed to have a problem kissing Tess, either.

I put the books on the shelf, and Jake deposited his cargo in the toy box. "I usually have the children clean up, you know," I felt compelled to say. "It just . . . didn't work out that way tonight. It wasn't worth the effort."

He smiled sympathetically. "Some nights are like that." I wondered if he was just trying to be nice, to cover up his guilt for lying to me about where he'd been.

After another trip to the basement the great room was sufficiently back in order. Jake rolled up his shirt sleeves and started to rinse dirty dishes to put in the dishwasher.

"Okay, Dr. Jantzen, you've done enough," I insisted, feeling embarrassed and angry and flustered. I was starting to wish that he would just leave. I couldn't think of anything to say to him that wouldn't make me look like the poor simpering fool that Tess had accused me of being. When he didn't stop I said, "Please don't do my dishes, Jake."

He gave me a mechanical grin and said with a tone of authority, "Request acknowledged, and denied."

I tried to resist it, but I had to laugh.

"So, are you going to stand there and watch me, or are you going to make yourself useful?" he teased.

I shook my head and started to wipe off the counters and put things away, not knowing what else to do. Ten minutes later the kitchen was clean. I stood looking at Jake, wondering how he could seem to be so good and kind to me, so sincere. Was I completely blind? Totally lacking in judgment? I stared at him for so long that he finally raised his eyebrow at me in question. "I'm guessing that you neglected to eat dinner again tonight?" I blurted out, to cover my anxiety.

"What makes you think that?" he asked.

I shrugged. "I've noticed that you're not too great at taking care of yourself lately."

"Have you?"

"Yes. Let me feed you. It's the least I can do now that you've found the kitchen table for me."

"I'm fine, Mar."

"Yeah, well, I insist." I decided that it was an effective way to stall for time and fixed him a plate. I sat down across the table from him while I sorted through my thoughts, still trying to decide how to approach this. I had to talk to him. I couldn't stand the turmoil going on inside of me.

"So, what happened tonight?" Jake asked.

I gave him a brief synopsis, mildly annoyed with the distraction, but thinking that he ought to know how his beloved Tess was hurting his little children. He rested his chin on his hands and shook his head sadly. "I'm sorry you had to deal with that, very sorry."

He seemed so genuine . . . I sighed and said, "Actually, I'm amazed at how well your children have coped with all of this over the past couple of weeks . . . They haven't seen Tess since they found out that she's leaving, have they?"

He shook his head. "No. I've been surprised at how well they've done myself. It's been a blessing."

"Have *you* seen Tess lately?" I asked, trying to appear casual. I hoped that maybe he would at least redeem himself to some degree by admitting the truth.

He raised an eyebrow and answered, "No." I noticed that he looked suddenly despondent. He pushed his plate to the side and chewed on his bottom lip.

"Is something wrong?" I asked.

"Why do you ask that?" he wondered.

I shrugged, but watched intently for his reaction. "You just seem nervous . . . dejected . . . Is it because Tess is leaving?"

He twisted up his face to give me a very strange look and answered, "No."

"So, what's bothering you?" I prodded. "How do you feel?"

"About what?" He narrowed his eyes skeptically.

"I don't know," I tried to say lightly. "About anything."

He studied me carefully through a lengthy pause before conceding, "I don't even know what I feel anymore, Maren."

I watched him expectantly, waiting for him to say more.

He stared at some distant point above my shoulder and said, "I've done a lot of thinking lately. I guess the best way to get a man to his knees is to knock his feet out from under him."

"What do you mean?" I wondered.

"I mean that I've certainly been humbled."

"You were always humble, weren't you?" I asked to move the conversation along to his point. I couldn't help noting that I had always believed that before, but now . . . ?

He chuckled dryly and shook his head, fixing an earnest gaze on me. "Forgive me, Maren," he whispered after a few seconds of silence. "Please forgive me . . . for all the horrible things I said to you that night. I didn't mean it. None of this is your fault. It's my own stupid fault for being so completely . . . arrogant."

I was shocked at the moisture that rose in his eyes. How could he be so two-faced? I'd known him for twelve years, and this just wasn't like him. Could I somehow have been mistaken about what I'd seen at Tess's apartment? "Arrogant?" I finally asked him. "When were you ever arrogant?"

"When was I ever not?" He looked down, but then shifted his gaze back to my face. "Don't you remember how proud I was in college, Mar?"

I shook my head.

"You must. You have to."

"No, Jake. I never thought you were too proud. I certainly didn't think you were arrogant," I answered honestly.

He gave me a curious look. "Remember when you asked about all the things that concerned you? When you pointed out all my flaws?"

"No." I didn't know what he meant.

"You told me that I was materialistic, you asked why I let my parents support me, you wondered why I hadn't thought of going on a mission."

I nodded slowly. "But that wasn't really pointing out your flaws."

"Yes it was, Maren. And I didn't even acknowledge any of them. I explained them all away. I was so presumptuous that I even assumed you'd want to live in New York, just because I did."

"Jake—" I interrupted. Why was he going off on this tangent? What was he getting at?

He ignored me and continued, "And when you told me that you had feelings for Ted and that you had to choose between us, I was so darn arrogant."

"Arrogant? No, you weren't. You were so understanding that it was unbelievable. Remember how good you were to me? You pointed all that out yourself a few nights ago," I reminded him, getting suddenly caught up in the conversation at hand.

"Yes, I did, and I'm sorry. That was just another example of my overactive ego. I wasn't so understanding back then, Mar. I told you that I trusted you to make the right decision."

"Yes! You did."

"Because I was so certain that you would choose me."

I furrowed my brows at him.

He looked at me and smiled wistfully, shaking his head. "I know, it's laughable now. It's like I told you the other night, I was so confident that we were meant to be together, that you were supposed to be mine, that I was the better man. I just knew that you would choose me." He looked over my shoulder again, wandering back in his thoughts. "I was sure of it until the day you came to tell me that you were going to marry Ted. I couldn't believe it when I saw it in your face. I still couldn't believe it when I watched you walk away. I couldn't believe it for a couple of days after that either, and then it suddenly hit me all at once. The grief was terrible. It was enough to bring me to my knees. Only then did I realize that all those things you pointed out to me had been true."

"But, Jake—" I tried to interrupt him again.

He looked back at me. "Oh, it's all right, Mar. I needed to hear them. I just had to be humbled enough to face them. I heard some familiar words soon afterward too, 'Every worthy young man should serve a mission.' I'd heard them before, but I thought they meant every worthy young man—except me. I told myself that I was too old. I let myself believe that I was entitled to enjoy the blessings of the gospel without paying the price."

I watched him with amazement. This couldn't be a ploy. This was Jake, the way he'd always been. Was I losing my mind?

"You will never know how grateful I am to you for pointing that out to me, Maren. I can't imagine what I would have given up if I hadn't served a mission. I think of all the people I taught . . . people like me, waiting for someone to bring them the truth. I can't believe the growth that I went through during those two years. Do you know what the single most important blessing that I received from serving my mission is?"

I shook my head.

He laughed softly again. "It's the very thing that you said it would be."

"What's that?" I asked, confused.

"It's that I can look Jeffrey in the eye and tell him that I did it. When we moved here and I opened a savings account for his mission, I was so grateful for that. I thought of you asking me how you could tell your sons to serve missions when their own father didn't go, and I couldn't imagine having to face my son with that."

I felt tears burning behind my eyes as I listened to Jake. I forgot about Tess, and became absorbed in his words.

"That all humbled me for a while, but not enough," he went on. "I worked hard to get through medical school, Maren. I worked very hard. I worked to build a good reputation for myself throughout my residency and after we moved back here. I'm good at what I do. I'm a good doctor. I'm a good surgeon. I made it, though I must acknowledge that it was only by the grace of God. But what good has it done me? Sure, I'm a doctor now. I fulfilled my dream. I make a lot of money, and it's mine—not my father's or my grandfather's. I'm able to help other people, to help children. That's something, I suppose . . . but my family fell apart in the process."

He paused to shake his head again and said, "What a humbling experience for me to watch my wife walk away, for me to see my marriage disintegrate in front of my eyes. I watched my children suffer, and I couldn't do anything about it. And I was so stupid that I let her come back into their lives, only to watch her walk away again. I go to work every day to heal other people's children, but I am powerless to stop the pain of my own. In fact, it's my fault that they're going through it again . . . And because of my own stupidity, I've lost what I love most . . . forever, this time, I'm afraid. What a harsh reminder of all that I am not. I'm powerless. Maybe this lesson in pride and humility will be sufficient."

"She's still leaving then?" I asked him quietly.

He only nodded. So, he hadn't convinced her to stay, after all. He did love Tess. He was admitting it. Looking at his pained expression though, I couldn't hate him. I knew how it felt to love an emotionally unhealthy person, to feel desperate to hold onto them. I'd lived it for ten years. How could I fault him for feeling the same way? Maybe he'd tried to forget her by loving me, but it just hadn't worked. Maybe he'd mistaken our deepening friendship for romance, like I once had. That would explain a lot of things. I finally placed a hand over his and said, "Jake, you couldn't have changed everything if you were more humble—other people made mistakes and choices too."

He looked up at me again. "I know that, to some extent, Maren. I know that God doesn't seek vengeance on us for our flaws. I know that He didn't make Tess leave to punish me. It was her decision. It's better that she's gone, anyway. And I know this whole mess . . . all the heartache . . . that's not His fault either. I do know, though, that my life's experiences have made me more aware of my weaknesses. I have been a fool, an arrogant fool."

I just watched him, not sure what to say. I withdrew my hand, feeling uncomfortable. He was obviously in a lot of pain as a result of Tess's plan to leave again, and I was in a lot of pain myself.

"Life is just . . . brutal sometimes. That's just the way it is. We have pain, we have trials, we have disappointments . . ." He looked into my eyes again and I looked back. "I had this vision of my life, Mar, when I was young and egotistical and foolish. I had it all planned, this neat little course that it would follow. It just didn't work out that way, any of it."

"Lots of things worked out, Jake. You're a doctor. You have two beautiful children. I know your marriage brought you a lot of heartache, but there are good things in your life."

He tilted his head just a little, studying me. "Yes, I suppose there are, but I can't help wanting more sometimes. Isn't that terrible? I'm not even grateful for what I have. I have two great kids, I love my job, I have good friends . . . and yet I still mourn for what I don't have."

"And what is that, Jake?" I asked quietly.

"I want a wife. I want to be married to a woman that I love more than life . . . and I want her to feel the same way . . . There, I admitted it. After all these months in denial, that's the truth of it."

I raised my eyebrows in surprise, but then I squeezed his hand again. "I think we all want that, Jake. That's the big dream, isn't it?"

"Yes . . . the dream. You know what else, Mar?"

"What?"

"I even want more children. *Me.* Can you believe that?" He withdrew his hand to smash it through his hair. "Oh, I was just so *stupid!*"

"Jake, you weren't stupid. You weren't arrogant."

"But I was, Maren. I was." He looked at me intently and said, "Because of my blasted pride, I lost the woman I loved more than anything else on earth . . . twice. I watched her walk away the first time and I couldn't make her stay. And then when I was blessed enough to have her back in my life, and I thought there might be some hope of her loving me again someday . . . I ruined it. I ruined it by jumping into things too quickly, by violating her trust, by hurting her . . . by being a stupid overconfident fool. I never should have let myself believe that I could possibly deserve her."

I was stunned at his admission. I felt sick to hear that his feelings for Tess still ran so deep, even after all the hurt and destruction that she had caused. I couldn't believe that he still thought he was to blame for their failed relationship. Jacob Jantzen was never going to love me again. It was hopeless. He loved Tess. I hadn't dreamed it. The nightmare was real.

I squeezed my eyes shut, searching deep inside myself for some kind of emotional anesthesia to numb the pain. Then I looked back at Jake, at the agony etched in his handsome face, and my only concern was for him. "Jake, this isn't your fault. It's not. You have to believe that." I tried to comfort him, but the moisture spilled from his eyes and trickled down his cheeks. He looked away, embarrassed. I couldn't restrain myself. I touched his face, brushing my fingers over the day's growth of roughness and wishing desperately for his masculine presence in my life. The agony of knowing that he was forever gone to me, the admission of how deeply his feelings for another woman still ran—on top of losing Ann and everything else I'd seen and struggled with that day—was simply too much.

I tried to stop the feelings that I'd been avoiding, but they came rushing up to hit me with full force. I laid my head on my arms and sobbed. "What did I say, Mar?" Jake asked me. "I didn't mean to upset you. I'm sorry for telling you all of this. I should have known that it would be too much." He put a hand on my arm and let me cry for a minute before saying, "Maren?"

I couldn't answer him. He helplessly stroked my hair in an effort to comfort me. When I finally took a breath and looked up, his face held a pained expression. "I'm so sorry that I upset you. I don't know what's wrong with me. The last thing I want to do is cause you more pain."

I looked at his sweet, sincere face and wept. He didn't mean to hurt me. He'd tried to love me, but he couldn't. He still loved the woman he'd married, a fact that kept bringing him pain. I knew that feeling.

"Maren, I didn't mean to make you cry. I'm sorry, love."

"Jake," I pleaded, sniffling and wiping at tears, "Don't call me that. Please. I can't stand it."

"What?" He looked confused.

"Don't call me 'love' like that," I begged again. "I can't handle it, not when I feel the way I do. You know I love you, but—"

"Maren, *stop it!*" he demanded fiercely.

Once again, I was stunned at his behavior. "Stop *what?*" After what he'd done that night, how could he possibly be angry with me for anything?

He leaned forward to say vehemently, "Your little speech, Maren. I know the whole thing, believe me. It's permanently etched in my mind, and forever seared into my heart. And every time I try to express how I feel to you, you throw it in my face again. Will you *stop?!*"

"*What little speech?!*" I demanded, feeling overcome with anger and frustration.

His face was white and almost contorted with pain as he clenched a fist on the table. "The 'I love you, *but . . .*' speech, Maren! I know that, okay? It's the same speech you gave me twelve years ago! I remember it all too well. You love me, but not that way, or not enough, or not as much as you love another guy. You'll always love me, I know. I'll always have a place in your heart. I know all that! What I want to know is *where* in your heart, *exactly,* is that place?"

"Jake, that is NOT what I've been saying!"

"I have one question. You owe me that," he insisted before I could say anything else.

"What's your question?" I tried to ask calmly.

"Would it have made a difference, Maren? If I'd run after you, begged you, yelled at you, anything. Would it have made a difference when you decided to marry Ted?"

I was quiet for a minute, trying to calm down and think. "Honestly, Jake, I don't know. In retrospect I can say I think it would have. I was so confused, and I did take your silent acceptance to mean that you agreed with my decision on some level. But I can't go back, so I'll never know for sure."

"And what about now?"

"What about it?"

"If I fell on my knees and begged you now, would it make a difference? If I told you that I need you desperately, that I love you with all my heart, could you possibly ever love me again, Maren?"

I stared at him for a few horrific seconds before something exploded in me. I stood up and leaned over the table toward him.

"How can you do this to me?!" I shouted. "What kind of heartless monster are you? Are you trying to *kill* me, Jacob?"

He looked absolutely stunned. "What on earth are you talking about, Maren?"

"How can you pretend to love me when I mean nothing to you?" I demanded. "Does it give you some kind of thrill? Do you just feel sorry for me? Do you think my weak heart can't take it, and I'll be shattered if you tell me the truth? What is it, Jake? Why do you play games with my heart like this? *Why?!*"

Jake rushed around the table to take my arms in his hands. "Maren, what are you talking about?"

"You don't love me!" I shouted at him. "I don't mean *anything* to you!" I hid my face in my hands as agonizing, heartwrenching sobs overtook me. I was too shocked to resist when Jake engulfed me in an iron embrace and pressed his face into my hair, holding me to him desperately while I cried. He trailed kisses across the top of my head and down my cheek. "Maren," he whispered in my ear. "Listen to me. Please, love. You have to listen to me."

I could feel his warm breath in my hair and the feel of his heart racing under his shirt. I forced myself to quiet down and listen.

He brushed his lips over my cheek and whispered urgently in my ear again, "I don't know what I've done to make you think otherwise, Maren, but you are *everything* to me. I do love you. I *do* . . . I love you completely. I love you absolutely. I love you with everything in me and around me and through me . . . I love you so much it hurts. I would do anything for you, Maren. *Anything.*"

I clenched fists against his chest and cried, "But what about Tess, Jake?"

"Tess? What do you mean?" He pulled back to look at me.

"Do you love us both?"

"*What?* No! I love *you*, Maren, *only you!* I told you, Mar . . . you took everything with you. You have my heart. You always have . . . What did she say to you that day . . . last spring? You were different after that." He searched my face.

I felt the tears creeping up to claim me again and it made me angry that her words could still be painful for me. "She said that you wanted her, that you dragged her back here from New York. She implied that you said mean things about me. She said you were leading me on and didn't really care about me. She pretty much said that I was too plain and simple for a man as gorgeous as you."

Jake's mouth fell open and then closed again. "How could she be so *horrible?*" he hissed, clenching fists at his sides. "Tell me you didn't let that get to you, Maren. You know that's an absolute bunch of nonsense."

I looked down and wiped at my face, saying nothing.

After a long pause, Jake put his fingers under my chin to tilt my face up. He looked deeply at me for several moments before he stated firmly, "You, Maren Griffin, are the most beautiful woman ever to walk the earth. Anyone who tells you otherwise is either insanely jealous, or completely blind. You're even more beautiful now than you were in college, Mar. The years have only served you well."

He was persuasive, but I still couldn't bring myself to speak.

"None of those things Tess said are true," he told me softly.

"Why did she say them then?" I shot out, feeling angry and hurt again.

He shook his head and looked bewildered. "I don't know."

I took a deep breath and gave him one last chance to redeem himself. "Where were you tonight?" I asked him.

"What?" He furrowed his brows at me. "You know where I was. I've been at the night clinic all night."

"Anywhere else?"

"No. I drove straight there and straight back . . . What are you getting at? This isn't like you."

"You don't want to tell me the truth then?"

He took my arms in his hands again and insisted, "I *am* telling you the truth!"

I shoved him away with all the strength that I could muster. "I saw you, Jake! *I saw you!* I am *not* going to let my heart be shattered by another man! I am *not* going to believe any more lies! I won't listen to you justifying and explaining and denying, and twisting things around to make it seem like it's all in my head!"

He leaned toward me again and pounded a fist against his chest. "Look at me, Maren!" he implored fiercely. "This is me. It's *me.* I am *not* Ted! I have *never* lied to you!"

I was furious. "I know you're not Ted!" I shouted. "But I'm not stupid. *I saw you, Jake!*"

"You saw me *where?* You saw me do *what?*"

"I saw you at Tess's apartment! I saw you laughing with her, holding her, kissing her!"

"Are you *insane?* I haven't so much as touched that woman in years! The whole thing was a huge mistake, a nightmare! You were right when you said that I chose it. I did, and I tried to make it work, but it was a hopeless cause." He shoved his hands in his pockets and softened his voice to say, "When I walked up to your doorstep a year ago and saw you there, Mar, it was like . . . a miracle. I couldn't believe it. And then when you got divorced and you were free . . . I realized that I loved you just as much as I had the day you left me—more, in fact. I thought you needed time to grieve, to get over your divorce and find your own strength. I tried to be your friend, to help you, to offer support. I thanked God for a second chance, Maren. All these months, I hoped that there might be a possibility of you loving me again someday, of you and I being together.

"I've been scared, I admit. After the agony of losing you the first time, I didn't know if I could survive being rejected by you again. I've held back. I've been overly cautious. I'm beginning to see that I may have misinterpreted your expressions of affection as rejection. I'm realizing that I've probably sent you mixed messages and confused you . . .

"Even if Tess turned her life completely around today, Maren, I would never want her back. I hope the best for her. I wish that she could enjoy being a mother to her children. I'd like to see her get back on the right path. But I love *you*, Mar. I want *you*. If you don't love me, I'll try to be content with just being your friend forever if you'll let me. But I will never even try to love anyone else again. I could never love anyone else like I love you."

I felt completely exhausted. I wanted so desperately to believe that he was sincere, but I knew what I'd seen. I couldn't let him make a complete fool out of me. Tess was right; men were men. I didn't have the energy to scream at him again, but I did find the words to insist quietly, "Jake, I *saw* you, earlier tonight. You were even wearing the same shirt." I waved my hand over him weakly.

He just stood there and watched me for a minute, looking tormented.

"Just go, Jake. Please. Just go."

He finally moved away. I didn't even help him carry his children out to the van. I let him do it all himself. He pulled the front door shut after him and I managed to drag myself to the couch before I collapsed.

Chapter 33

I didn't know how long it had been when the doorbell rang. I hesitated to answer it. "Maren!" Jake called through the door. "I know you're in there. Please open the door."

I pulled it open and fought the urge to weep again at the sight of him, praying that maybe he'd at least come back to tell me the truth. He stood with his hands shoved deep into his pockets and his jaw muscle twitched. "Will you please just answer one thing for me?" he asked quietly.

"You already asked your one question, Jake. You've reached your quota." I considered the question he'd posed earlier. Could he have done anything to make me change my mind when I decided to marry Ted? I'd told him that I thought he could have. What difference did it make now, though? It was irrelevant; it was too late to go back.

"It's a very simple question, Mar. Please?"

"If I answer it, will you leave?" I just wanted him gone, so I could cry and get it over with, and move on with my life.

"Yes, but I want you to promise me that you'll answer honestly."

I leaned against the door frame and said, "All right. I promise."

"Do you love me?"

I blinked back the moisture that rose to my eyes. I had not anticipated that his simple question could be so thoroughly difficult. Why did he insist on torturing me?

"I want the truth, Mar. You promised . . . Do you love me?"

"Yes . . . Now, go."

His shoulders dropped and he sighed with apparent relief. He held out his hand and said, "Come with me."

"You said that if I answered your question, you would leave, Jake."

"I will, but I'm taking you with me."

I wanted so badly to take the hand he offered and go, but I could not deny what I had seen. I stepped back into the house and moved to close the door, but Jake caught it and pushed it back open. "Maren, please . . ." he insisted as he stepped into the house.

"Jake, go. Just go."

"I won't go, Maren, not without you."

I felt angry and upset. I wasn't afraid of him, but I felt an extreme need to escape him, to run away from the confusion and the hurt. I fled down the hall, thinking that I could lock myself in my bedroom until he left. To my shock, he ran after me and caught me around the waist. "What are you doing?" I demanded, pushing against him.

"I'm running after you," he said fervently as he pulled me to him tightly. "I'm begging you not to go. I'm telling you that I know we should be together, that you're wrong. I'm doing *something.*"

I quit fighting him and stared up at him as he stated firmly, "I will not stand quietly by and watch you walk out of my life again, Maren Griffin. If you love me too, then I will fight whatever it is that's coming between us to my last breath. If my life does not turn out the way that I want it to this time, at least I'll know that I did everything in my power to make it otherwise."

I was overcome by the sincerity in his eyes, the urgency in his words, the resolve in his embrace. I was defeated. I couldn't fight him. I loved him with everything in me. I had to at least give him a chance. I nodded and slipped my hand into his. He squeezed it and led me to his car. "Where are we going?" I asked.

"We are going to Tess's place to straighten out this whole mess once and for all." The thought made me mildly nauseous, wondering what I was going to find.

I glanced in the back of the van and asked, "Where are the children?"

"I took them to their grandmother's house. She agreed to keep them overnight."

We rode across town in silence. Jake took my hand firmly in his when he pulled me from the car and held it tighter still when he knocked on Tess's door. I was glad that her lights were still on. I didn't want to think that we were waking her up.

Tess looked very surprised when she answered the door and saw Jake. "Can we talk to you?" he asked her. When she narrowed her eyes suspiciously, he added, "Please?"

She glanced to me and back to him again. I prayed that there was an explanation . . . but how could there be? I'd seen them together. I looked away from both of them, but Jake wouldn't release his hold on my hand when I tried to pull it from his grasp.

Tess stepped away from the door and motioned us inside. I glanced around at the expensive furnishings as she waved her hand toward the couch. "Do you want to sit down?" she asked tentatively, almost as though she hoped we would decline.

"Thanks." Jake sat and pulled me down with him.

Tess sat down on the leather love seat across from us and folded her gold-bangled arms. "What do you want, Jake?" she asked bluntly.

"Clarification."

She raised her eyebrows, and then furrowed them, saying nothing.

"You're still leaving, right?" he asked. I wondered again if he'd been there earlier to try and talk her out of it. Maybe things had just gotten out of control. Maybe he'd been overcome with emotion and regretted it now.

"I told you I was. And I believe it was on that note that we agreed not to see each other again."

"I'm aware of our agreement, Tess."

"Then what are you doing here?"

"I want to straighten some things out, for my own peace of mind. Before you go, I'd like to ask you to undo some of the damage you've done."

"Excuse me? If you simply came over to insult me, Jacob, I have better things to do with my time."

"Tess, I'm trying to put my life back together here, but you can't seem to restrain yourself from attempting to sabotage it. You're getting exactly what you want, free and clear, and leaving me with all the baggage. Do you have to see me completely miserable in order for you to be happy? You're riding off into your sunset to live the life you've always wanted—can't you at least leave mine intact?"

Tess leaned forward to rest her slender elbows on her knees. The lamplight glinted off all those golden bracelets on her arms and reflected amber sparks in her dark eyes. "Take a reality pill, Jacob," she hissed. "Sunsets? Who are you kidding? I gave up *ever* having exactly what I wanted the day that I bought into your tale of valor. I was stupid enough to think you were sincere. Let's talk about who ruined whose life, Jacob, shall we?"

Jake studied her silently for a minute before he leaned back on the couch and crossed his right ankle over his left knee. "Clarify yourself, please," he said simply. "I'm afraid you've lost me."

"You told me that I could do whatever I wanted to, Jake. You were real. You were the first decent Mormon guy I met who wasn't all caught up in the 'perfect wife and houseful of kids' fantasy. You treated me as an equal, as an intelligent human being who could decide what I wanted to do with my own life. It was hard at first, after we were married, because you didn't pay enough attention to me . . ."

Jake shook his head and answered her quietly, "Tess, I tried to make you happy, but there was no way that I ever could have lavished you with the amount of attention you demanded. It just wasn't possible. I had to have some space to be me you know."

I was surprised when Tess admitted seriously, "Yes, I know. I might have forgiven you for that. It was having Jeffrey that drove us beyond the point of no return."

"You were the one who started pushing to have a baby. I wanted to wait until I was further along in my residency. I admit, I didn't know how difficult it was going to be, but I was a lot more concerned about it than you were. I gave in and let you have your way, just like I always did."

"I know that too," she snapped. "I thought if I had a baby that someone would be with me all the time. I was lonely. I thought I'd have this doting little person who loved me unconditionally. I had this vision of a child making our family complete, making you want to tear yourself away from that horrible hospital and come home once in a while. I thought if you saw me in a new light, as the mother of your child, maybe you'd finally love me the way I wanted you to."

I was enthralled, watching the two of them talking like this, seeing insights into a relationship I'd wondered about for months.

Tess sighed and leaned back. "All that baby did was put another person in front of me, place another unfeasible requirement on me. And he changed you completely, Jake."

"He didn't change me completely," Jake defended himself. "He shed new light on what was important, he made me reevaluate my priorities, he taught me a new level of love, he made me want to become better. But it wasn't like none of those things were in me at all before, Tess. I was never some careless, coldhearted business tycoon with no thought but self-gratification. I was never driven by money and power. It was more that Jeffrey put me in better tune with myself, not that he changed who I was."

"But you did change, Jake," she insisted. "You turned on me. You tried to get over it after Jeffrey, but you never really did. You resented me inwardly for not changing along with you. After Elizabeth though, you resented me outwardly. That was not fair, Jake. It just wasn't fair. You suddenly wanted me to be everything that you knew I could never be."

Jake was silent for a minute before he said quietly, "I just wanted you to get your priorities lined up too, Tess. I didn't want you to be someone you were not."

"That is *exactly* what you wanted me to be, Jacob—someone I was not. That was an impossible demand. The whole thing was impossible. I left, but I will *never* have the life I want. I want to be *free*. I want to live life for me, with no thought of tomorrow. That is unattainable now.

"Everywhere I go I'm haunted by the faces of two children that I brought into the world under false pretenses. I'm torn over them every day. I'm faced with the glaring reality of hypocrisy, pretending to be something I'm not. I can make a show of loving them the way that I should, trying to take an interest in their daily comings and goings, pretending that I don't resent them for preventing me from living my own life, trying to ignore my incompetence as a mother. Or I can admit what I am and leave, but then I'm faced with the guilt of abandoning my own children. What kind of mother abandons her own children? Only my kind. I'm no kind of mother.

"I was foolish enough to think that I could make it work somehow. Either way now, I'm a failure. I lied to myself just like you did, Jacob. The only difference is that there's still hope for you to redeem yourself, to get what you really wanted all along. I can never have that. It's too late for me."

"What are you talking about, Tess?" Jake said. "I didn't lie to myself. Maybe you have more insight into yourself than you did before, but I didn't tell you to be someone you weren't."

"Do you think I don't know, Jake? I sensed it when we were married, I think, though I could never quite put my finger on it. But it's all too clear now. I knew you were terrified that I was going to leave you, but I didn't realize where that came from. That's why you let me have my way with everything until it came down to something so important you just couldn't do it. And you lost me over it all right. Of course, I think that's a relief for you now just as much as it is for me. But I still have a right to be angry. You tried to make an impossible situation work, when that was never what you wanted in the first place. You ruined my life and I resent it. Why did you deny it to yourself all those years?"

"Deny *what?*"

"I suppose I can't fault you for it, Jacob. You couldn't help it any more than I could, but you should have been more honest with yourself before you married me."

"Honest about *what?*"

"About what you wanted me to be."

Jake sighed and admitted, "Tess, I didn't know you. You were not who I thought you were."

"You knew exactly who I was, Jake. You just never dealt with who I *wasn't.* You've been running from it for years. Are you still running, when it's right in front of you?"

"When what's right in front of me?"

Tess laughed bitterly and shook her head, lifting her long legs to curl them up on the seat beside her. She waved an angry hand at me and said, "Her, Jake. You wanted me to be *her.* "

I stared at her, and then looked at Jake. He finally let go of my hand to run his fingers through his hair.

When he made no comment, Tess went on, "What did you do, Jake—search the world over for the woman least like her, hoping that would make you forget?"

Jake glanced over at me before turning back to Tess and saying, "I told you about Maren before I ever married you, Tess. I was honest. I told you I didn't know if I'd ever completely stop loving her. What do you think I should have done, laid down and died? I tried to live my life. I did love you, Tess. I tried to make our marriage work. I wasn't the one who ran away with someone else. Even after you left, I tried. I gave it every effort that I could . . . I can't say I'm sorry that it's over, though. We both realized it wasn't what we wanted and got out. That's all we could do. We both have repercussions to deal with and lives to rebuild . . ."

Jake leaned forward to rest his forearms on his thighs and continued, "I'm sorry, Tess. I can't blame you for being angry with me. But it's not Maren's fault. Don't take it out on her." He looked back at me again and said, "I guess I've helped to muddle up both of your lives. Part of the reason Maren left was because I told her I didn't want the things that I eventually realized I did . . . the opposite problem that you and I had, Tess." He sat back up and chuckled humorlessly. "What a fine mess . . . I am sorry. I'm saying that to both of you."

I could only look at him in astonishment. Had I really affected his life so deeply? Did he love me so ardently? Jake returned my gaze and I was surprised at the vulnerability I saw in his eyes. It was as though he was finally opening himself up to me completely, risking everything . . .

I thought of him kissing Tess and looked away from him.

Tess stared at the empty fireplace for several long quiet moments. We all sat in uncomfortable silence. I tried to process all the new bits of information and sort through them in my mind.

Tess finally looked at me, and I was surprised at how human her expression seemed. "I've made enough mistakes," she admitted thoughtfully. "I suppose if I can do something to redeem myself before I leave, I should . . ." She inhaled deeply and forced herself to say, "I apologize, Maren. I lied. Jake wasn't leading you on. He didn't drag me back from New York. It was my own guilty conscience that brought me here. Jake is far from perfect . . . but he is good—too good in fact. He would not have done that.

"I shouldn't have said that you were too simple for him. I'm sure you know you're beautiful, though not in the way that I'd want to be. And you're exactly what Jake wants, what he's always wanted . . . It's not that I envy you, Maren. I wouldn't want to be you, any more than I think you'd want to be me. It's not even that I love Jake. I don't. He's not what I need. I wanted him to hurt, I guess. I wanted to interfere with his life, like I felt he'd interfered with mine, give him a taste of never being able to get what he really wants.

"When I moved back here and started to put the pieces together, I began to see what role you had played in Jake's life and, consequently, in mine. I just admitted that I'm angry, that I regret the irrevocable decisions that Jake and I both made. I was enraged when I first started to see it all. I suppose I took it out on you. It's not your fault . . . It's not really even Jake's fault. He's right. He tried to make things work between us. I'm at least as much to blame for the catastrophic failure as he is . . .

"The only thing I might envy you, Maren, is that you seem able to love my children in a way that I never could. I suppose I did want them to love me more than you . . . But they don't, and that's my own fault."

I spoke for the first time. "You're wrong, Tess. They do love you. The past few days have been extremely difficult for them since they found out that you're leaving again."

"Really?" She seemed floored.

"Yes," I told her quietly, looking her straight in the eye. "I wish you could see what they're going through. It's very painful for them."

Her eyes filled with moisture, something I'd never seen or even imagined possible. The evidence of feeling in her softened my callused heart. I felt twinges of regret. "I'm sorry for being less than kind to you too, Tess. It wasn't fair of me to judge you. Ann tried to tell me that . . . Although you and I are very different, I can relate to certain aspects of your situation. I definitely understand disillusionment."

Tess nodded and then seemed thoughtful again for a few moments. She actually wiped away a couple of stray tears—a sight that shocked me. "Just a minute," she said as she got to her feet.

I leaned back against the couch as relief began to flow through me at all that I had learned. Jake did love me, not her. But the thought of what had started all this suddenly shocked me back to awareness. "Jake?" I touched his arm, breaking him out of his own quiet reverie.

"Hmm?" He turned to look at me and take my hand again.

"Please be honest with me, okay?"

He nodded.

"Why did you kiss Tess earlier tonight?"

"Maren, I didn't! Do you still doubt me after listening to all of this?"

I didn't have a chance to answer before Tess came back into the room. She soberly handed Jake a manila envelope. "There are your papers," she said. "They're signed . . . They're yours. I may not be able to be the mother that my children deserve, but at least I can do this for them. I can spare them any more pain. I'm sure I'll be tempted to breeze back into their lives after another year or two away . . . but I suppose that's not fair to them. You're right. Ann was right." She nodded toward the envelope that Jake held as she sat back down and said, "This will keep me from doing that. At least they'll be protected from me."

"Are you sure about this, Tess?" Jake asked quietly.

She nodded and brushed away a few more tears. "Maybe someday they'll understand to a certain degree . . . that's the best that I can do for them. They deserve more, I know. They're lucky to have you, Jake." She hesitated a moment before adding, "And you, Maren."

I was astonished.

"Before we go," Jake said, "Could you remind me when I last saw you?"

Tess gave him a strange look. I still felt uneasy, wondering if he could be trying to send her some unspoken message. "I don't know . . ." she finally answered. "Probably the last time we did something with the kids . . . Maybe three weeks ago? Why?"

He shrugged. "I was just trying to recall . . ."

We all turned at the sound of a key in the lock, something that surprised me. I was quite sure that Tess lived alone. She looked momentarily uneasy as she glanced toward Jake, but her face eased into a smile as the door opened and a man stepped into the room. "Hi, gorgeous," he said to her before he glanced at Jake and me. He was tall and lean with black hair, but his skin tone was more olive than Jake's and his eyes were dark. He had an overly-confident stance, and I detected an aura of mild conceit as he cocked his head when he saw us. Still, the sight of Jake seemed to unnerve him a little.

I saw Jake's jaw muscle tense for a minute, and his grip tightened on my hand, but then the corners of his mouth twitched upward, almost as if in amusement. He stood and pulled me to my feet beside him. He tilted his chin to acknowledge the man facing him and said calmly, "Vance."

The man nodded back. "Jake."

Jake looked from him to Tess and said, "Best of luck to you both." On our way out he winked at me just before he slapped Vance on the shoulder and remarked, "Nice shirt. Blue's my favorite color too."

Chapter 34

As we walked back across the grass toward the dark parking lot, Jake gave me a smug look of triumph. I felt so relieved, so giddy, that I couldn't resist falling on the grass at his feet. "All right, I'm sorry!" I cried dramatically. "I misjudged you. I never should have doubted you. Can you ever find it in your heart to forgive me?"

"Oh, get up here, woman!" he muttered in mock annoyance. He bent to pull me to my feet, but then thought better of it, and dropped to the grass beside me to tickle me.

I squirmed over the lawn, laughing and screaming. He didn't give up until I remembered my white linen attire and warned, "Stop it, Jake! You'll ruin my dress!"

He finally leaned over to kiss me and said, "Now *that* would be a shame. You look like an angel in that dress." I tangled my fingers in his hair and returned his kiss with everything in me.

When we stood up, he brushed grass from my hair and said, "Look at you. You're a mess. You look like a wild little girl."

I smiled and reached up playfully to ruffle his hair. "I feel like one. I haven't felt this carefree in years. By the way . . ." I looked down and pointed to his knees. "You have grass stains on your perfectly ironed pants, Dr. Jantzen. I never thought I'd live to see the day . . ."

He laughed and pulled me close to kiss me again.

"I love you, Jake," I told him resolutely when he pulled his lips from mine.

"That's a relief." He grinned. "Come on, I want to take you somewhere."

"Take me somewhere? Look at me! I'm a mess, remember?" I brushed grass from my dress and tried to comb my hair back with my fingers.

Jake laughed. "Here," he offered, "Let me help you with that." He slid his fingers slowly through my hair and pushed it over my shoulders. "It *is* as soft as spun silk," he murmured as he ran his hands down my arms and back up again. I shivered at the gesture.

Jake clasped my upper arms in his hands and looked into my eyes to say, "I've never seen you look more beautiful, Maren. And you smell wonderful . . . the way your shampoo and your perfume mixes so enticingly with the scent of that freshly cut grass . . ." He kissed my neck and I giggled, pulling away and running across the parking lot.

I turned around to see him standing in the same place, watching me with his hands on his hips. "Well?" I called out to him.

"Well what?" he called back.

I moved a few steps closer to him and asked coyly, "Aren't you going to run after me?"

He stood still for a minute and then suddenly lunged at me with no warning. I screamed and ran again, but it didn't take him long to catch up with me. He seized me by the waist and twirled me around with him as he laughed. When he finally set me down he kissed me once more and said softly, "I'll always run after you, love."

I smiled. "I probably won't make you do that again."

He grinned and took my hand. "Come on, Mar. We have an appointment."

"Appointment?" I asked, following him to his van. "At this hour?"

He held his watch up to read it in the moonlight and furrowed his brows. "Yes . . . and we're twelve years late. Let's get moving."

I stared at him wondrously, my heart beating loudly in my ears, as I followed him to his car.

"So, what's in the envelope?" I asked Jake when he tossed it on the floor of the van between the front seats.

He started the engine and pulled out of the parking lot as he answered me. "Tess and I talked about a new agreement when she decided to leave again. I guess she signed it."

"What's your new agreement?" I asked bluntly. I wanted to know.

He glanced at me and replied, "She gave up her parental rights. I'm not paying her any more alimony because I'm supporting the children fully—"

"Weren't you doing that before?" I interrupted.

"Yes, but this time I did agree to take over her credit card bills."

"Why did you do that?" I asked.

"Technically, I can still be held liable for them because my name was on them. She's gone back to her maiden name so she's harder to track down. All the debt and the late payments have been adversely affecting my credit. I figured I'd end up paying them off eventually anyway, so I decided to use it to my advantage."

"And how did you do that, again?" I asked, confused.

"I agreed to pay them off if she would give up her alimony and the children, permanently. She gets to keep what matters to her, I get to keep what matters to me, and we never have to see each other again. That's about the best that I could hope for."

I nodded slowly. "So, that's what she was talking about . . . Well, it's too bad, but I suppose it's probably for the best."

"Yes, Mar, it is."

"Good for you," I told him.

"Thanks." A slow smile spread across his face. "Does that qualify as standing up for myself and setting boundaries to protect myself and my children?"

I laughed and said, "I think that qualifies. I'm sorry for saying those things to you though."

"Don't be. Once again, I needed to hear them. It's a relief to know I won't be trampled on anymore." He grinned and winked at me.

"In that case, I'm glad I could help." I smiled back at him.

Jake got on the freeway and headed south. I suspected that he might be going to BYU, but I didn't care if he'd suddenly taken it into his head to go to Disneyland. I would have followed him anywhere. I kept glancing over at him as he drove, just to make sure that I wasn't dreaming. He held my hand the whole time, occasionally turning to smile at me. We rode mostly in comfortable silence, exchanging a few words here and there. Soft, romantic music was playing on the radio and I basked in the sentimentality of it all—and remembered how much Ann teased me about my romantic side, and how pleased she'd be. As I mused to myself, Jake drove past Lehi, American Fork, and Orem.

Finally, he took the Provo exit and drove toward the city. Driving through the streets of our college town with him sent my heart racing again. I shifted in my seat to study his profile, something I hadn't done closely for years. The laugh lines were a little deeper, but he still had the same wavy black hair, chiseled chin, smooth mouth. I noticed that his biceps were tensed under the dark blue of his cotton shirt. His jaw muscle twitched slightly, like he was biting down hard. I reached over and stroked his hair, brushing out a few stray blades of grass. "Are you nervous being with me tonight?" I asked him.

He turned to look at me, surprise showing on his face. When he looked back to the road, he admitted, "Just a little."

I continued to watch him with fascination, marveling at the day's turn of events. When I finally looked up, we had driven past campus, and my heart began pounding as we rounded the crest of the hill that led to the temple. There was the familiar golden spire, beckoning us back to that long-forgotten place. I had never been to that temple. I always went to Jordan River or Salt Lake. I'd been to Idaho Falls, Manti, Logan, Ogden, even Los Angeles, but never that one. I could never do it.

Jake pulled into the quiet parking lot. He shoved a nervous fist into his pocket after he got out of the van before he came around to open my door. He grabbed my hand with his free one and held it tightly to pull me from the car and up the grassy hill into the stars. I dared not say a word, but I made certain that he couldn't let go of my hand even if he wanted to.

The temple was lit up like a piece of heaven. The night, fall breeze brushed against my skin, and I wasn't sure if it caused the goose bumps, or if it was the butterflies flitting around inside me.

There it was at the top of the hill, our tree. That day twelve years ago seemed galaxies away, when we were young and thought we knew so much about life and love. That was a day before children, divorce, or death had visited us. It was before loss, pain, growth, and trial. It was before responsibility, agony, or loneliness.

I was a woman now, following this man up the hill, but I could hear whispers of the girl that I had been. So many thoughts ran through my mind as I looked back on all the pain and trials of the past twelve years. What did I want to say to that girl? What would I change if I could go back? What growth would I give up? Would I risk not having my children? Would I want to never discover the sisterhood of a dear friend who would teach me so much both through her life and through her death, just to avoid the loss? Would I give up knowing how completely Jake loved me, even after so many years apart? Would I sacrifice the refinement we'd both been through as a result of all the pain? I saw the whole picture coming together with a clarity so dazzling I could never have dreamed it.

I felt overwhelmed at the love God had for me. He hadn't deserted me as I'd sometimes thought. I thanked the Lord for the chance to be back there once again with this man that I'd been tied to for so long. I was too overcome to speak, so I sank to the ground under the tree.

Jake sat in front of me, cross-legged, just like before. Behind those eyes was that twenty-four-year-old boy, but he was so much stronger. He'd served a mission, become a father, a doctor, gone through a difficult marriage and divorce, suffered through heartache, faced his fears, learned to stand on his own.

Jake took my hands in his and smiled. "So . . . here we are again, love," he said.

"Jake," I whispered.

He touched a finger to my lips. "Shh. I have to say this before I lose my nerve. Please, just let me get it out."

"Okay," I agreed as a lump formed in my throat.

"Maren, I don't know if I wish we could go back and change it or not. We've both been through so much pain . . . but we've both been through some serious growth too. I only love you more because of it, Mar."

I could only nod in understanding.

"I don't think I've ever felt as alive and full of hope as I do tonight," he continued. "I've been through such a struggle these past months, wanting to express my feelings to you, but afraid that you didn't love me. It's been difficult, but I've grown to appreciate you even more and to love you more deeply than I ever imagined, especially because of all the waiting and the bonds of friendship we've built again over the last year and a half."

I watched him with amazement, relishing the feel of my hands in his, overwhelmed with gratitude. I was so relieved to be there with him, to hear his sweet words.

I just squeezed his hands and let him continue.

"I've been praying so hard these last few weeks, begging for courage and strength, asking for direction, seeking hope. I've spent a lot of time in prayer tonight too, Mar, and I'm filled with peace and love and joy. I am so grateful to God for giving me another chance at the life I've always wanted."

I nodded in absolute agreement.

"I know you've asked why I didn't get angry or fight for you the first time, Maren," he acknowledged. "Maybe I should have. All I know is that I will never let you go again. Never."

"Jake, I'm sorry I didn't believe you earlier tonight," I told him. "I should have known better."

"It's all right," he said. "We've both been hurt badly. But we're going to forget about all that now and start over. Right?" He interrupted his speech to smile down at me. "We're going to make a pact to be completely honest with each other so neither of us has to doubt anymore . . . I will never lie to you, Maren. I will never intentionally do anything to cause you pain. You can trust me, always."

I threw my arms around him to hug him and said, "I know. I always did. I just . . . forgot. I won't lie to you either, Jake, not ever."

He pulled back to raise that eyebrow and asked, "Never?"

I shook my head resolutely.

"Good, because I have something to ask you, and I'd like you to be very honest with me."

"*Another question?*" I smiled. "You promised no more questions . . . Did you lie?"

He chuckled softly and shook his head. "Oh, now that is not fair, Maren."

"A promise is a promise," I insisted sternly.

He shrugged. "I suppose you're right. I guess I'll put off the question and go on with my speech then." He clasped my hands in his own again and said, "I know it's not going to be easy—"

"What's not going to be easy?" I interjected.

"Oh, so you can ask questions, but I can't?" he teased. He watched me comically for a moment and then observed, "I believe you've made me completely lose my train of thought."

"You love me," I reminded him.

He laughed and leaned forward to cup my face in his hands. "Yes, I do," he said seriously. "I've always loved you, Maren, and I always will. I know this is pretty sudden, but it's been thirteen years. After the torture of these last months, I don't want to risk losing you again. I'm going to ask you . . . something . . . tomorrow, but there's no pressure. If you say no, I'll follow you around until you change your mind."

I felt like my heart might pound clear out of my chest. "What are you going to ask me?" I said softly.

Jake grinned. "I'll tell you tomorrow."

I leaned close to him to whisper, "I could answer one more question today . . . if you ask me nicely."

He considered me for a moment with such a serious expression that I finally protested, *"Jake!"*

He laughed and kissed me as he conceded, "All right, if you insist." He stood up and pulled me to my feet. Then he got down on one knee, took my hand, and kissed it. "Maren Griffin, would you do me the honor of accompanying me to this beautiful temple you see here behind me, and becoming my wife? I promise to love you and cherish you forever."

I couldn't believe it was finally happening. Jacob Adam Jantzen— my Jake—was asking me to marry him . . . after all this time, after all the confusion and all the pain, after all the years alone. I was filled with love for him. It was more than I ever could have hoped for. I was so full of happiness I thought I would burst. I stared down at him in awe.

"You don't have to answer me right now, Maren. You can take some time to think. Pray about it."

I dropped to my knees to look into his eyes and smile. "Take some time? I think I've had plenty of that, Jake. There is nothing I want more in this world than to be your wife."

"Is that a yes?"

I threw my arms around his neck and shouted at the starlit sky, "Yes, yes, yes!" Then I kissed him on the lips, the forehead, the nose, the cheeks, the eyelids. "You wonderful, darling man!" That girl of nineteen was back.

He laughed and looked wondrously at me. "You're sure about this, right?"

"I've never been as sure of any decision in my life."

"Good," he answered firmly. Then he stood and pulled me up to stand beside him, shoving his left hand into his pocket again. "I have something for you." He grinned. "I've been saving it since . . ." His eyes grew misty and his voice turned husky with memory as he finished. "Since the last time we stood here."

I stared at him wide-eyed.

He shook his head and chuckled softly. "You can't imagine how many times I almost talked myself into getting rid of it . . . but I just couldn't do it. And now, I must admit, I'm grateful that I didn't."

I watched as he pulled his hand out of his pocket, wrapped protectively around something. He slowly uncurled his fingers to reveal a purple velvet box in the palm of his hand. I looked up at him in wonder.

"Well," he teased, "aren't you going to open it?"

I lifted the lid and felt the tears rush into my eyes. It was the most beautiful ring I'd ever seen. The delicate circle of platinum met at a marquis diamond in the middle, and then swirled off in two different directions with a tiny diamond on each side. The pure silver color sparkled in the moonlight. I must have been speechless for too long, because Jake finally asked hesitantly, "Do you like it?"

I looked up at him and smiled. "I *love* it. I've never seen anything like it."

"I looked for it for months," he told me. "I wanted to find something perfect, something that looked like you. When I found this one, I knew . . ." He took it out of the box and tilted it for me to read the inscription in the glow of the outdoor lights. *I'll love you forever . . . . Jake.*

As the shock wore off, I began to perceive the reality. "You mean . . ." I looked up at him in question. "You had this with you the day that I came to tell you good-bye?"

He nodded quietly. I didn't miss the tears in his eyes.

"You were going to ask me to marry you then?" I asked slowly.

He only nodded again.

"Oh, Jake . . ." I whispered.

He reached for my left hand and slipped the ring on my finger as he kissed me tenderly. "Just marry me now," he whispered back.

"It fits perfectly," I observed in wonder.

He chuckled and said, "Size five and a half . . . I had Jana steal your class ring for me so I could measure it."

"My roommate Jana?"

"Yes."

"I can't believe she did that for you!"

"I was a little surprised myself," he laughed.

"She never even told me!"

"I'm grateful to her for that." He smiled. "It made the surprise much more effective."

"It's beautiful, Jake."

"Yes, but it pales in comparison to you, love."

I smiled up at him, put my arms around him and said, "I love you, Jake." Then I laughed softly. "Are you going to scrunch up your face or hold up your hand to stop me, or do you want me to say it again?"

He grinned. "Say it again."

"I love you."

"Those are the most wonderful words I've ever heard." He flashed that sweet dimple in his right cheek. "I love you too, Maren, more than I can possibly express. I'll love you forever." He brushed away the warm tears on my face and asked tenderly, "Are you crying again?"

I looked into his deep blue eyes and knew that I could see forever. I laughed softly as I touched his cheek and whispered, "Only because I'm so happy. It's all been worth it to get to this moment, Jake. I've never been so happy."

He wrapped me in his arms to hold me close and said, "Neither have I, love."

I leaned against him and closed my eyes to absorb it all for a moment. Then I mused, "So, I guess Ann's pretty pleased with herself." I smiled at the thought.

Jake pulled back to look at me, questioning, amusement dancing in his eyes. "How do you figure?" he asked.

I shrugged. "She told me that you loved me and that I should get things straightened out."

He smiled. "She said something similar to me."

"Really? I guess when we still didn't get it, she reverted to Plan B. Did she also tell you the part about hitting us both over the head with something?"

He laughed. "No, but it's not hard to imagine."

"So . . . maybe she had a hand in things tonight." I considered the thought fondly.

"Which part do you suppose she had a hand in?" he asked while squeezing me closer. "The part where I kissed Tess, or the part where I proposed to you?"

I smiled and answered, "Maybe a little of both."

"Well, I am certainly glad she came through." Jake leaned in for a brief kiss.

"Me too," I agreed before kissing him back.

Walking back down the hill, I marveled at the scene in front of me. The moon and stars stood out against a perfect curtain of black-velvet sky. The overhead lights cast a soft glow over the deserted parking lot. "What a magical night," I breathed. "It looks like a giant stage . . ." I paused at the edge of the grass to soak it all in.

Jake put an arm around my waist to pull me close. "Ah, yes . . ." he agreed contentedly. "And I believe it's been set just for us. Perhaps we can thank Ann for that too."

I smiled up at him.

Jake sighed loudly and shook his head. "It's too bad that I can't dance," he said remorsefully.

I didn't even have time to refute his claim before he spun me out to the asphalt with a flick of his wrist and caught my hand with impressive skill. I gasped as he pulled me back into his arms. "You've been holding out on me!" I teased.

He gave me a mischievous smile and led me into a complicated dance step. "What does that scripture in Ether say?" he teased back. "If men humble themselves . . . I will make weak things become strong?"

I laughed. "Then you must have been right when you said you'd certainly been humbled. I guess you're not hopeless after all."

"There's always hope, Mar." He grinned and kissed me. Then he waltzed with me all the way across the parking lot.

© Scott Breen

About the Author

Candie Checketts has been writing for as long as she can remember and usually has multiple works in progress. Feeling driven to surpass mere personal enjoyment in her writing, Candie hopes to offer a new perspective on some important LDS issues. *Another Chance* is her first novel in this venture.

Candie holds degrees in elementary and early childhood education, and enjoys working with children. She currently serves as a Primary teacher in her ward. Candie and her family live in Riverton, Utah.